# SCREAMING SNOWFLAKES

# AMBER TESIA

A CIP catalogue record for this book is available from the British Library.

ISBN: 978-0-9573402-0-6

To The Gohil Family – Mom, Nim, Shush, Gohil & Ush:
words cannot describe how much I love you.
To Anj & Sanj, my twin pillars of fortitude and wisdom:
I am nothing without you. Thank you for keeping me grounded.
To Deepak, you rock my world and light up my life:
thank you for being you.


I would like to thank from the bottom of my heart, each and every one of you who have bought my book. To bring Raphael and Eleanor to life has been an absolute pleasure and I would love to hear from you! Sending you all tonnes of love, peace and virtual cupcakes (or French Martinis – whatever floats your boat),
Amber. X


www.ambertesia.com

# CONTENTS

Excerpt from Screaming Snowflakes: The Sequel

# ACKNOWLEDGMENTS

Merci beaucoup to all who have supported me in my journey from crazy contractor to newbie writer, I wouldn't be here if it wasn't for you. To Ba, Bapa and Pupa, I will always love you. I have met some fabulous people along the way and I apologise sincerely if I have missed anyone out. To Mom for your unfailing support – I owe you. Big time. To Shani and Christina for being beautiful, genuine people – I am lucky to know you. To Anj, Heeren and Chetan – I am richer for having your astute and awesome selves in my life; thank you. A special shout out to Sanj, soul-mate and ab-fab cupcake maker – we can be in different places, but that's just geography baby (I love you and always will). Continue to shine, you bright, gorgeous thing. To Av – thank you from the bottom of heart, for being my biggest cheerleader and never tiring of it. I heart you more than James Bond. (Really.) To superstar Carlo Cortes for his terrific illustration that graces this book – you're a genius and it has been a privilege working with you. To James Sharples for being wise beyond your years – I will NEVER forget that conversation in Costa; you rock dude! To Steven Hartshorne et al (you know who you are) who provided brilliant, constructive advice in the early days – I am eternally grateful. Thank you to those cool bods at Rhode Island who sated my caffeine cravings so efficiently and didn't mind as I took over their coffee shop whilst writing this book (Rosi makes the perfect Americano!). I owe a quick mention to the legendary Yash Chopra, for his wonderful vision that inspired the pivotal first chapter in the book and who made me believe that rain dances can be très cool – RIP to a total genius and true rock star.

# PROLOGUE

*'And the Lord said, "I will destroy man whom I have created. It repenteth me that I have made them. I will destroy them with the Earth"...'*
*Genesis 6:7 – 6:13*

Eleanor stifled a chuckle to say, 'What do you mean, like the X Files? I don't expect aliens to descend to Earth and *"Phone Home"* or anything!'

She was silenced by his sombre stare. He wasn't impressed. She answered lightly, 'Well, I *do* think there's life out there, not sure exactly what though. I did believe in UFOs like a decade ago. I was eight and had rubbed my eyes too hard when I thought I was seeing spinning discs in a kaleidoscope of crazy colours.'

His grave look was in stark contrast to her cheeky grin. His thoughtful eyes continued to rake over her face as he pressed on. 'What if someone handed you an elixir which guaranteed eternal life. Would you drink it?' Raphael's resolute voice amplified the unusual question.

Eleanor tried to be serious. 'With eternal life, I assume you'd never be ill? That would be sort of cool. Hey did you ever see Mork and Mindy? Robin Williams was out of this world!'

She was teasing him and he knew it. A sense of urgency crept into Raphael's determined voice. 'I'm serious Eleanor.' He waited for her to respond, his eyes never leaving her face.

Twirling a few strands of hair, Eleanor pondered Raphael's question. 'Nope, I wouldn't drink it. What's the point of a life with no friends or family? I can imagine it to be a thoroughly lonely time. You?'

His eyes flashed up at her. He said flatly, 'I'm no fan of eternal life.' He continued glaring through the dull window. 'What if you didn't have a choice in the matter? What if it was something you were born with?' He exhaled deeply before saying, 'And you're right, it *is* a lonely place to be.'

Her chatter came to an abrupt standstill. Those few moments of self-realisation seemed to take forever to pass, yet weirdly flew by with lightning speed. The confession afforded lucidity as she suddenly realised Raphael was immortal.

# 1 RAIN DANCE

Eleanor Hudson glanced around the room and tried to take in her new surroundings. Cardboard boxes lay stacked ceiling to floor in the spacious lounge. The towering taupe blocks like smooth walls of sand snaked through the lounge, into the hallway and beyond. She would be staying in her great great grandmother's Richmond house. This would be her home for the next three years. Having had her belongings carted all the way from Manchester, she felt a sudden twinge of guilt.

This was the first time Eleanor had lived away from home and she wondered how her mum was getting on. Tiredness through lack of sleep and muscular aches in her shoulders swiftly overcame the fleeting moment of guilt. Awash with weariness, she wanted nothing more than to curl up in bed. But it was only 2:30pm and she had all weekend to sleep.

Unpacking the colossal cargo would take ages. It was easier to stare at the sand-like cardboard walls. Eleanor suddenly found herself wondering what it would be like to live in a sandcastle, before the sudden buzzing of her phone pulled her out of her daydream. Peering at her mobile, she laughed out loud whilst reading the flashing caller ID: *Lucille – BEST MUM EVER*. Ignoring her nagging exhaustion Eleanor answered the phone smiling, ready for the inevitable deluge of questions.

'Hey Elle! Take it you reached there in one piece? How was the drive? Just touching base to see if all is OK there..?' Lucille's voice trailed off, contemplative with just a hint of concern.

'Hey Mum. I got here, like ten minutes ago and-'

Lucille cut Eleanor of mid-sentence, her speech accelerated with the realisation that Eleanor had officially left home. Lucille twittered, 'It's not every day your only kid goes off to uni! You'll know what it's like when you're a mum one day! About the house – I know you were preoccupied when we saw it last time. So what do you think of it now? Very-'

'Judi Dench?'

'Striking, grand and ever so slightly intimidating? Definitely.' Lucille couldn't help but laugh.

'The house is fine Mum. It's just been empty for a while.'

'A century is a long time! A Munsters' style mansion wouldn't have been my first choice but hey, you'll have plenty of space to throw a wild party or two. On the plus side, the area's quiet and safe. PS just kidding about the wild parties.'

'Not in the mood for parties Mum...'

Lucille said regretfully, 'I really wish I had been there to help you unpack, but work is keeping me super busy, I'm practically chained to my laptop! Listen, I'll try to pop down to see how you're getting on.'

'Come visit soon! And I've only just noticed, but when did you change your name on my phone?'

Lucille's tinkling laughter brought another smile to her daughter's face. 'Knew you'd find that funny! Oh Elle, you're going to be *so* busy at uni, I couldn't have you forgetting the very obvious, could I?'

'You're not bad as far as mums go...'

'Not bad?!' Lucille exclaimed in mock horror before they burst into renewed laughter.

As Eleanor's gaze fell on the boxes she said listlessly, 'Honestly Mum, I didn't realise I had so much stuff. I know Liberty's doesn't need the extra competition but I could easily set up my own department store. Think I'll start unpacking, at least I can relax once everything is out of the way.'

'First day by yourself, *without* adult supervision and that's the first thing on your hit-list?' Lucille's astonishment evaporated as she said calmly, 'See, *that's* why I'm not overtly worried about you being by yourself. Most teenagers would simply run amok in the absence of adults, getting drunk and- I'm not giving you *any* more ideas. You, my one and only gorgeous daughter... You, want to unpack.'

They both just about managed to stifle another giggle for a few seconds before collapsing into laughter again. What sort of teenager needed encouragement from an adult to get out and about? Eleanor. Her mother caught her breath before restarting her positivity crusade. 'Come on, why don't you go and explore your new home-town? The weather is beautiful here up north so it must be positively tropical down there!'

Mulling over the sound advice Eleanor shifted from one foot to another. 'I'd just feel a whole lot better if everything was away in its place. The clutter's annoying and I think-'

'Elle. Don't think, just do. Listen honey, I've got to prep for a breakfast meet tomorrow. A few things before I forget. I asked the removal company to put the labelled boxes in their corresponding rooms – should save you lugging them around the house. Oh and I borrowed your silver bracelet the other day – did you know the clasp was loose? I *think* that's it, although I'm sure I had something else to tell you... Try and get the bracelet fixed. Love you lots, miss you more!'

Then click, she was gone. Eleanor's mother was getting busier by the day. As publicist extraordinaire to a gaggle of celebrities, Lucille was in demand. The recent economic downturn had paradoxically been a busy time for her. When desperately despondent bank chiefs were viewed as the unsavoury catalyst that kick-started the global recession, they had sought crisis management advice from the best and Lucille's workload had unexpectedly increased ten-fold ever since the recession.

Growing up with Lucille had been fantastic. Since her parents' divorce just before she was born, it had been Eleanor and her mother all the way. Dad hadn't been in touch, and Eleanor didn't really miss him. How could you miss something you never had? Eleanor and her mother had always been close and Eleanor hadn't found it necessary to rebel. If she wanted to do something (within reason of course, no-one had it *that* easy), Eleanor would simply ask. Chances were, Lucille would have already thought about it and pre-empted Eleanor's thoughts.

They shared more than just an intuitive bond; Eleanor had inherited her mother's raven hair and honey coloured eyes too. They were frequently confused with being siblings, much to Eleanor's amusement and Lucille's delight. Sifting through the pile of junk mail on the bulky teak cabinet, Eleanor thought about how she had come to live in Richmond.

After the death of Lucille's great grandmother (formidable matriarch and last survivor of the Winter clan) last year, Lucille had found herself the unexpected owner of the Richmond house. Mrs Winter, a battle-axe traditionalist had disowned Lucille for her divorce which she considered a flagrantly unforgivable act. Eighteen years had passed, along with any chance of reconciliation and death had brought closure to the old quarrel. A stoic Lucille had put the house up for sale soon after. As the recession had staved off interest from potential buyers, the sprawling property lay languishing on the unsold list for a year before Eleanor's snap decision to become the new tenant.

Eleanor saw the house as something of a mixed blessing. Craving a new scene after a heart-breaking few months, the Richmond house had emerged as a practical alternative. Eleanor wondered how different her life would have been if–

She stopped herself from pursuing that forbidden train of thought. The key was to remain positive, avoid thinking about her immediate past and focus on a different kind of history instead.

Eleanor had always known she would study Ancient History. She loved studying historical literature to gain a greater understanding of a bygone era. It was by sheer luck that King's College University had ticked all the right boxes. It offered the Ancient History degree she had originally wanted to study and was in the opposite direction to her ex-boyfriend. Eager to avoid living in chaotic congested London, it made sense to use the currently empty Richmond house which was a mere thirty minute train commute to university.

Somehow, it had all worked out for the best. Lucille had also bought her a second-hand run-around that was small, functional and perfect for Eleanor. Not relishing the cramped parking spaces in the Capital, Eleanor had dismissed Lucille's protestations for a larger car, putting her foot down and being doubly insistent on the three-door Peugeot that now graced the drive-way.

She glanced around the generously furnished room flanked by large windows. Steel trellis work ran through the thick sheets of window glass giving the room a bleak and draughty look. The antiquated furniture which seemed too grand to touch only reminded Eleanor that she was the sole occupant of the vast house. Continuing her exploratory journey in her new abode, Eleanor hurried to the next room.

The large polished six-ring Aga took prime position in the wide kitchen. This was Lucille's touch and the keen cook in Eleanor couldn't help but grin appreciatively at the welcome anachronism. A cavernous fridge stood empty in the far corner and suddenly her stomach let out a repressed rumble of hunger. Making a mental note to pick up some food from the local grocery store, she decided to quickly scan the rest of the house and sprinted up the solid oak stairs. The heavy doors hung open for all five expansive bedrooms. Only one door remained closed.

The room at the far side of the house seemed different. Eleanor couldn't help but be drawn to it. The tarnished brass handle stubbornly refused to move. Trying to catch a glimpse through the key-hole was futile. The door was locked.

She hadn't noticed this room before. Then again, she hadn't really been paying attention to anything then. She had floated through the summer and her first Richmond trip in a blurry haze of inertia. On the day of her visit, some sort of repair work was underway on a floorboard segment just outside the secluded room. Casting her mind back, she vaguely recalled the upstairs section near the banister had been out of bounds. The gigantic solid door like a burly bodyguard refused entry and a mildly curious Eleanor made another mental note to ask her mum about the locked room.

She chose the room facing east to be her new bedroom. A keen Feng Shui acolyte, Eleanor loved its simple rules of life enhancement. Her mother knew her only too well and had lovingly accommodated by organising Eleanor's belongings to be placed in that room.

The past few difficult weeks had seen Eleanor lose her spark. Gone was the spontaneous, loquacious personality that friends knew and loved.

Nowadays her subdued and measured approach to life had prompted concerned friends to advocate the pros of *not* having a plan. That was one of the joys of being a teen and one that was apparently lost on the new, serious Eleanor.

Now accustomed to the various "You only have organised fun!" quips, Eleanor decided this would be a turning point. This was her fresh start. Richmond would be a clean slate where she could really focus on positive transformation. She *could* be spontaneous if she wanted. And whoever heard of a teenager having controlled fun? Here was her opportunity to prove otherwise.

Ripping open a box marked *FANCY FROCKS*, she decided to wear the first item of clothing she touched. Reaching into the cool box, her hand was quickly filled with gossamer material which felt like a fluffy cloud in her hand. Pulling out a white chiffon frock, she discovered the spaghetti strapped ethereal number was her eighteenth birthday party frock.

By wearing the eye-catching evening dress in a quiet, sleepy street in Richmond, Eleanor knew she would stand out like a single boat stranded at sea. Spurred on by newfound spontaneity, she plucked off the plastic covering of the dress which came away easily in her hand, like a sweet wrapper willingly volunteering its contents. Stripping off her comfortable jumper and jeans before she could change her mind, she stepped into her new outfit.

The dress complemented her sun-kissed complexion and fit like a second skin. Suddenly Eleanor felt wide awake. Darting downstairs in her tan gladiator sandals, she snatched the house keys from the mantelpiece. Pausing a moment at the door in preparation of her first trip in her new town, she exhaled and stepped onto the porch.

Walking towards the tree-lined avenue leading to the main road, Eleanor cast a backward glance at the house. It towered over her, throwing an oppressive shadow as she stared at the arresting carved masonry and windows like expressionless eyes. With an involuntary shudder, she quickly stepped away into the warmth of the sun. The house would take some getting used to. She just had to stick with it. The heady scent of lavender hung sweetly in the air as she started to slowly appreciate her first proper day in Richmond.

Her delicate dress floated weightlessly in the warm breeze and she was glad she hadn't worn a jacket. Feeling calm and free, she was finally starting to relax. People sometimes took life for granted and focused on the negative. Eleanor didn't want to wind up bitter. She found herself thinking more positively about the small, simple things in life, like Mother Nature at her best on this gorgeous September afternoon. The sun shone brightly with just the right amount of heat on her skin. There wasn't a single cloud in the clear blue canvas overhead.

An unexpected rumble sounded from the sky. Her stomach too growled with hunger, yet being simply high on life, she had forgotten her hunger pangs. Eleanor only reached the corner when the low rumble became distinctly louder.

It happened so quickly. The sky suddenly turned an intimidating shade of anthracite. Rapidly moving clouds appeared out of nowhere. Fat woollen rainclouds shrouded the sky as Eleanor realised a downpour was imminent. Quickening her pace she naively hoped to make the grocery store in time which was still a few hundred yards away.

The heavens suddenly opened and the few drops which Eleanor felt on her neck gained weight with each passing second. She felt as if she was being pummelled by a power shower. Only a minute ago, Eleanor had mentally extolled the virtues of Mother Nature and she noted the irony with wry amusement. The rain confronted her from all directions as she stood rooted to the spot. Suddenly thinking how unpredictably entertaining life could be, a smile stole across her face and she couldn't help but laugh aloud.

The rain seemed to have a magical purifying notion, each drop cleansing her mind to gently wash away her problems. As the raindrops kissed her awake, an invigorated Eleanor spread out her arms as she slowly twirled around. She soaked up the relief like a thirsty plant, the rain energising her whilst filling her with a renewed passion for life. A sudden gust of wind tempered with further rain seemed to secretly whisper that everything was going to be alright.

It had been a long time since she had felt completely at peace. For those few minutes, she didn't care about anything. As her eyelashes caught the now softly falling raindrops, she looked up at the sky in euphoria. With her arms still outstretched and palms facing upwards, she leapt up a few times and kicked some water on the pavement.

It was a liberating feeling not having a care in the world. Laughing and twirling in the downpour, Eleanor couldn't have been happier. If someone saw her antics in the rain, she wouldn't blame them for thinking she was an escapee from a mental asylum. Now, joy spilled over from her heart and she had little control over it.

Looking to the sky, Eleanor remembered her maternal grandparents. They had passed away nearly five years ago but she sometimes felt their watchful presence from afar, like guardian angels looking over her. Eleanor felt she was being watched now.

She suddenly felt supremely loved. She continued twirling and laughing in the rain for a few more minutes. Her dress wasn't designed to handle inclement weather and with the chiffon plastered to her skin, Eleanor darted into the local grocery store.

Manoeuvring her way through the cramped aisles, she deftly balanced milk, bread, butter and cheese in her arms before heading to the till. Suddenly very self-conscious, she decided to leave the extensive shopping list till tomorrow and concentrated on a speedy exit. From doing a lonesome mini rain dance to now feeling six pairs of eyes on her, a flustered Eleanor tried to appear composed. It was now glaringly obvious that she was new in town.

Eleanor could feel the judgment being passed from those strangers' eyes, mildly mocking her unwise choice of clothing and northern accent too. Her now ravenous stomach couldn't handle this either, growling encouragement with each step as she sprinted back home in her now squelching gladiator sandals. She might have been soaked, judged by complete strangers and risked near death by pneumonia. But at least she had been spontaneous.

# 2 ACCIDENT PRONE

Eleanor spent her first few nights in Richmond in a state of muted happiness as she tried to adjust to her new surroundings. Checking to see how her daughter was settling in, Lucille rang Eleanor on the Sunday afternoon. As always, Lucille's sunny disposition lifted Eleanor's spirits. 'How are you honey? Spoken to the neighbours yet?'

Already smiling Eleanor said, 'I'm fine Mum, not really had much of a chance to mingle with the locals. Wouldn't mind Corrie's Norris as a neighbour, he'd definitely liven things up! Hey, you missing me yet?' Eleanor suddenly leaned over to mute the TV. Narrowing her eyes to watch the silent news coverage for a few seconds, she exclaimed incredulously, 'Is that your client on the news..? *Did he really say that?!*

'Don't believe everything you hear. I've got 24 hours to spin this before it really hits the fan. Enough about me, have you settled in OK?'

'It's going alright, I just need to get used to the house. Hey Mum, what's with the locked room upstairs?'

'*That's* what I had to tell you last time, except I forgot. Every room has a key except that particular one. I assume your great great grandmother used the room for storage. It's been locked ever since I can remember. The estate agent specifically said there was no key for that room and as I thought the house wouldn't be in my possession for much longer, I didn't bother to investigate or have a key made. It's probably filled with a tonne of pointless junk.'

'But Mum, don't you want to find out what's in it..?'

Lucille's measured tone reflected her respectful indifference. 'No, I don't. Your great great grandmother was a complicated character. We parted on unrepentantly bad terms. We hadn't spoken in years and news of her bequest was more of a surprise than her actual death. I didn't think she would leave me anything, let alone her only worldly possession. Just goes to show that I didn't really know her. I don't see the point of getting to know her now. Just let the room be. Pretend it's not there.'

She was silent for a few more seconds, optimism filtering back into her voice as she said, 'I'm thinking the Manchester house is due a revamp. My fabric swatches may have been packed with your belongings. Could you do me a favour and just keep an eye out for them?'

'Course Mum, I'm pretty sure I saw them in my craft box. Will find and post out this week.'

After wishing her daughter all the best for her first day at university, Lucille rang off. Eleanor clutched her silent phone for a few seconds. She was starting to realise how much she missed Lucille, a best-friend and mum rolled into one. Shaking off her impending gloom and wanting to keep herself busy, she headed upstairs to locate the fabric swatches.

The craft box looked like a pirate's treasure chest and was something Eleanor had started in secondary school. Eleanor knew she was no Picasso and was in awe of anyone who could draw. Acutely aware of what she saw to be limited artistic talent, she militantly classified her work as strictly private. Only her tutor saw her work and that too, with extreme reluctance on Eleanor's embarrassed part.

Eleanor rifled through the box, extracting the misplaced fabric swatch bundle before leafing through hundreds of drawings and sketch pads. She spread out numerous charcoal etchings on the table, instinctively feeling fiercely protective about her artwork, yet quietly satisfied. There was something gratifying in seeing her progress and steady improvement in the pictures before her. If only she was a naturally talented painter, she thought to herself. Living vicariously, she placed herself for a few moments in the paint-splattered shoes of Titian. She imagined the ecstasy when creating beautiful prints, yet mentally cringed at the prospect of her work being exhibited for public viewing.

With a deprecating smile she firstly consoled herself that she was never going to be a world-famous painter. Secondly, it would be a cold day in hell before she let anyone see her artwork. Being an artist was simply not her vocation in life. She would leave that to the Vettriano's of the world.

Her Heaton Park sketch caught her eye. Eleanor vividly remembered the moment when inspiration had struck one fine evening in June. She had been blown away by the simplicity of the supple weeping willow trees in their exquisitely simple surroundings. Painting imbued her with a sense of contentment and Eleanor suddenly wondered why she had stopped.

It was at that moment that Eleanor decided to take up art again. For motivation, she would carry around one of her paintings as a reminder. She instinctively chose the weeping willow drawing and placing it in a loose opaque plastic wallet, set it next to the fabric swatches. She needed to reconnect with her art and in the quaint town of Richmond, Eleanor was sure she would find huge inspiration. She silently thanked her mum for mislaying the swatches. A new place packed with possibilities was just what Eleanor needed. This was going to be her time.

Eleanor awoke feeling positive yet slightly nervous on the morning of her first day at university. She wondered how different it would be from college whilst sipping her double shot coffee. As the dark caffeine-rich fluid worked its magic to dissipate clouds of sleep, a contemplative Eleanor thought about her weekend that had flown by.

In between unpacking, stocking up on food and exploring Richmond, Monday had arrived sooner than expected. She felt the familiar butterflies in her stomach as she remembered for the umpteenth time that she didn't know a living soul here. She tried not to think too much about the people whom she had left behind. In particular, Michael. Her ex. He was her first boyfriend at college and it had been a year long, serious relationship. The happy couple had even applied to the same universities so they could be together.

Which is why it was a complete shock when he had broken up with her. A week before the A-Level results were due. On her birthday. Being dumped in a rowdy restaurant was just the icing on the cake and a humiliating end to a painful evening. He said the relationship wasn't going anywhere and decided that going away to university was a great time to have a clean break. He said they were too different. Eleanor remembered chalk and cheese being mentioned. Crushed by Michael's appallingly ill-timed disclosure, the shock break-up was a triple-blow for Eleanor who suffered the break-up blues, exam result stress and anxiety about attending the same university as Michael. During that anguished fortnight her friends had rallied around and her mum had been fantastic. She swore then that no-one would ever make her feel vulnerable and utterly helpless again.

She didn't want to be anywhere near Michael. Getting as far away from him had been her priority. With Edinburgh being his first choice, Eleanor quickly accepted an alternative university place in the southern locale. She still missed him. He had been part of her life for so long and now they didn't even talk. Had it not meant as much to him as it had to her? Had she done something wrong? These questions, familiar ground to those seasoned in the rituals of a break-up, were new and raw to Eleanor. They came back to haunt her sporadically. Like reluctantly riding an emotional rollercoaster, Eleanor went through periods of being totally fine before lapsing into thought of what Michael would be doing at that particular moment in time.

Once a single thought of Michael had crept into her subconscious, it was only a matter of time that the flood-gates would open. Eleanor had gone a full seventy-two hours without thinking about him. She knew she was on the right track. She would focus on her study and not be distracted by trivial matters, especially boys. She had a life to start living.

A thirty minute train journey and short walk later, Eleanor found herself in the university grounds being ushered inside by a flock of second year students. Keen to impart their knowledge, these self-assured seniors were in stark contrast to the first years, the majority of whom wore uneasy yet inquisitive expressions. She wondered if she too would assist the new intake of students next year and if she would be as happy as they seemed to be. Clutching her new semester timetable and Recommended Reading Lists, she hastened towards the NUS Card photo queue.

The line wasn't very long. The girl in front glanced in Eleanor's direction whilst waiting. She was tall and lissom, perfect curls of strawberry blonde hair resting on her slender shoulders. The pretty creature turned to Eleanor and said lightly, 'I *hate* having my photo taken. I'm not very photogenic.'

Eleanor gave a small smile. What she wanted to say was, 'Don't be daft. You look like a flipping model.' Instead she resorted to saying the much safer, 'You're perfectly pretty.' Eleanor added as an afterthought, 'Although I totally get the whole photogenic thing. I find cameras unnerving. It's like you're being watched. Well, you *are* being watched, but you know what I mean.'

The model lookalike turned round with a huge smile and stuck out her hand. 'Hey, I'm Astrid. What are you studying? I'm doing Philosophy.'

'I'm Elle. Ancient History's my thing.'

'Nice to meet you Elle. Thank God someone understands the whole photo thing. Although I really can't understand you not liking photos. You're probably one of the most photogenic people I've met.'

Eleanor chuckled. 'Ditto! I didn't want to sound sarcastic! Nice to meet you Astrid!'

Both girls laughed out loud and immediately bonded. 'Are you based here Elle? I do hope you are. I *know* we're going to be good friends, I can just tell. Hey, where are you lodging?'

'Richmond.' Eleanor shrugged to say, 'Commute's OK, location's cool too. You?'

Before Astrid could answer, a bespectacled official popped her head around the stand and shouted, 'Next please!'

Astrid mouthed, 'Be right back' and disappeared into the booth, emerging a few minutes later whilst rapidly waving her NUS card to and fro like a mini fan to make the picture dry quicker. She muttered, 'They just catch you unawares. You've been warned. Count of five my eye. Damn it, mine looks like a Hugh Grant mug-shot...' More cheerily she said, 'Listen, I've come here with my dad, he'll be really pleased to meet you. You know what parents are like, wanting the low-down on new friends! Wanna tag along with us?'

'Wish I could, but I've gotta dash to sort out my parking permit. How long are you around for?'

'Drat, maybe see you later? There's a tonne of stuff going on. Freshers' fairs, nights at the SU. I'll be staying at Princess Alice Court. Tell you what, take my mobile number and give me a bell later. We can catch up and maybe check out the talent later? Unless you have a boyfriend. Or girlfriend, whatever floats your boat, in which case, you can still "window-shop"..?'

Eleanor hesitated. She would have to get used to saying she was single again. Acknowledging there was no better time to start like the present, she flashed a confident smile to say, 'Here take my number instead.' Astrid punched in the digits whilst Eleanor recited her number. She added quietly, 'And um Astrid..? There is no boyfriend. I'm really not looking anyway.'

Astrid grinned to say, 'Sorry to go all cliché on you babe, but there's plenty of fish in this wide blue sea! I'll bell you later. And *don't* forget you'll be papped on the count of two not five.'

Then she was gone. A thoughtful Eleanor entered the booth. Smiling almost immediately to catch the quick camera flash whilst mulling over Astrid's comments, Eleanor decided she would most definitely not get side-tracked with another boy.

In a whirlwind of lectures and meeting what seemed like hundreds of people, Eleanor's first few days at university flew by. Each lecturer for the seven different modules seemed to have the same mind-set; get the student involved as early as possible and with it, the completion of prerequisite essays. Too busy to eat on her first day, she munched on a take-away sandwich from the canteen en route to lecture.

Eleanor ventured into the canteen feeling calmer on the third day as she contemplated lunch. She was slowly adapting to her new routine and felt further relaxed with the news that her Latin Epigraphy lecture had been cancelled due to the tutor being off sick. Having a full ninety minutes at her disposal, Eleanor decided to have a leisurely lunch and be productive by studying.

She glanced around the refectory which buzzed with the movement and chatter of a few hundred students. Lined throughout with wooden benches in a typical canteen style, Eleanor headed for the salad bar towards the far end. Picking up a chicken caesar and fruit juice with a Wispa bar as an afterthought, she scanned the large room for a potential place to sit.

She clocked the cliques in a few seconds and noted the group formations with quiet amusement. Sporty jocks sat with badminton rackets and other sporting paraphernalia at the foot of their table. Gloomy Goths were bunched together with their trademark black garb, features accentuated by heavy eyeliner and bed-head hair. The fashionistas didn't disappoint either, sitting swathed in the latest trendy gear. Balmain-inspired jackets teamed with Victoria Beckham skinny jeans seemed to be the prevalent look at their table.

Eleanor was about to settle at a corner table for a lone study lunch session when she heard someone shout her name. Looking up she noticed a girl from one of her lectures sitting with a group of three others. They seemed like a pleasant group with a happy vibe and Eleanor made her way over to their table without further hesitation.

'Hiya, I'm Christina, we're in Classical Antiquity. Come on over and sit with us if you like..?' The dark-haired beauty with a pleasing smile motioned to the empty seat next to her. Smiling she continued, 'Come on guys, scooch round so there's more space. This is Eleanor, we're in Classical Antiquity together.'

'Yeah yeah, we heard the first time round.'

Eleanor looked up at a mischievous blonde haired lad who waved from across the table. He had a friendly open smile. 'Hey, I'm Jack. I've seen you around actually. We bumped into each other at the entrance yesterday, remember..?'

Eleanor had no recollection and politely explained she had been somewhat preoccupied with lectures and reading lists. Jack continued in a playful tone, 'Actually, you probably don't remember. You looked like you were a million miles away. The reason *I* remember is because you were holding your sandwich in one hand and Theodosian Codes book in another. It was obvious you were dying to get stuck into study and I remember thinking how abnormally conscientious you were. No offence, it's actually a compliment. Hey if you're like this now, what are you gonna be like a week before exams?'

Suddenly self conscious she clutched her books to her chest whilst trying to sum him up. His teasing attitude suggested he meant no harm and a huge grin spread across his face within seconds. Eleanor was on the verge of responding when Christina cut in.

'Eleanor, he's only pulling your leg. Seriously Jack, don't be mean. At least wait to get to know someone before you start ribbing them. Bullies do that.'

Jack said in mock disappointment, 'What?! She knows I'm joking, right Eleanor? Most students here seem to have Friday afternoon off. Are you going to do voluntary study then too?'

He flashed a cheeky dimpled grin at Eleanor and she couldn't help but smile back. Christina shook her head as she gestured around the table. 'Eleanor, you've already met *Jack*. There's Serena and Katherine. Jack and Katherine know each other from home. The rest of us met only yesterday.'

With a shy wave Eleanor said, 'Hey! Most people call me Elle, but I answer to Eleanor too!' The friendly party smiled back. With introductions out of the way the following ninety minutes flew by as the conversation came thick and fast. Eleanor was pleased with how easily they bonded in a short space of time. Katherine seemed to be the quietest of the bunch, whilst Serena was more of a witty chatterbox. Eleanor was content she had found a cheery bunch of people to hang out with and when she was invited to the new fair in town, she jumped at the chance to get to know them better.

Later that evening Eleanor and her friends boarded the Jubilee Line to Hyde Park. She was soon caught up with her new friends and almost didn't mind the overcrowded carriage and uncomfortably warm tube journey. Thirty minutes later they arrived outside Hyde Park.

It seemed as if the whole of London had descended onto the fair that evening. It was a busy park packed with children, adults and masses of students. The cool September air was the perfect antidote to the warm density of the crowds. Eleanor loved the hubbub and distinct aroma of the fair. The smell of caramelised toffee apples, bittersweet charred onions and perfumed candy-floss floated together to create a heady, cloying concoction. Momentarily lost in a cloud of contentment, she was quickly pulled out of her daydream and into the crowds by Serena to the nearest coconut shy stand.

After polishing off a hearty hot-dog and buying fair-ride tokens, they milled around the noisy crowded stalls. Large rides jutted out, their flashing fluorescent lights like unnatural stars in the dark autumnal sky. Pausing at the shooting stall to see Jack hit the moving target on his fourth attempt, Eleanor laughed as she watched a smugly satisfied Katherine beat him in two tries.

Their friendly chatter imbued Eleanor with sudden gratitude as she realised she was slowly building a new life for herself. It was going to be difficult, but she knew she would be OK. Stepping back to survey her new life with a contented smile, she accidentally bumped into a sturdy body behind her. Quickly spinning around she made to apologise, yet the hooded figure quickly disappeared into the dense crowd.

Her attention was distracted as Christina shouted, 'C'mon Elle!! We're headed to the *Furious Octopus* now! The queue's mental, come on!'

Glancing behind one last time Eleanor sprinted towards her friends as they headed towards the ride. Having already been on the *Helter Skelter*, *Dodgems* and *Crazy Shake*, the final stop was at the largest and most popular of the rides. The boasting billboard promised to deliver "The Biggest Ride Of Your Life". Its reputation preceded it, the structure standing as tall as the length of the queue which snaked twice around the enclosure and towards the tarot card tent for half a mile. Twenty-five minutes and a few bags of candyfloss later, Eleanor and her friends found themselves at the front of the jostling queue.

Searching for the ride token in her jacket pocket, Eleanor found only her purse and keys. She was so sure she had placed it in her right-hand pocket. Katherine, Jack, Christina and Serena had already handed their tokens to the fairground operator who in turn fixed Eleanor with a stern stare.

'C'mon, I haven't got all day.' He spoke gruffly, growing impatience evident on his dour face as he continued to scan the seemingly never-ending queue behind her. Eleanor looked at the operator and then at her friends in a state of panicked confusion.

'I'm so sorry. Wait, I'm sure I had it on me just now. Hang on-'

She continued her frantic futile hunt, like repeatedly scouring an obviously near empty cupboard for that elusive treat. Despite knowing the token was definitely not in her bag which had remained closed since buying the food, she unzipped it regardless for a quick cursory check. Someone heckled behind her to get a move on and all Eleanor could do was stare in dismay whilst rifling through other various pockets. The token was nowhere to be found.

Jack shouted humorously, 'I know you're scared of the huge ride, but do you *really* have to pretend to lose your token?'

'I... I can't find it anywhere, seriously!' She faltered and tried to explain her predicament with limited success. 'It was in my pocket a few minutes ago and-' She turned her attention to the glowering fairground operator who looked dangerously close to losing his patience. She said apologetically, 'Look, I'm *sooo* very sorry. I promise-'

The operator growled, 'Do you think I enjoy standing out here for hours on end? Get a move on. I've seen enough kids pull a fast one, you're no different. No token, no ride. End of.'

Now openly embarrassed for causing a scene she tried one last time to cajole the unyielding gate-keeper. She pulled out the first note from her purse and thrust it under the beady eyes of her tormentor. 'Look, what if I just *give* you the money? Here's a tenner-'

He eyed the note suspiciously. 'That's nearly double the price of admission.' Squinting his eyes he said, 'Listen kid, I don't need the hassle of counterfeit money. Now move *away* from the queue.'

Eleanor pleaded with the grumpy gate-keeper again. 'I'll run and buy another token, I'll Usain Bolt it. I can see the token booth from here. Please can you hang on for a *teeny tiny* bit?'

Katherine shouted over the turnstile, 'We'll hold your place in the queue and wait for you!'

The huffing operator rolled his eyes and said sharply, 'Go on. Be quick. You three wait here.' To the crowd he bellowed, 'Next four move up now! C'mon, I haven't got all day!'

A grateful Eleanor ran headlong towards the token booth, willing the attendant to work faster and not be distracted by his pretty co-worker. She checked her pockets again and conceded that the token must have fallen out at some point during the evening. Having finally bought the all-important token she clutched it like an expensive gold coin and dodging the crowds, ran back to her friends. Nearing the ride she stopped a few metres away, slightly out of breath. It was a few seconds before she realised something was wrong.

She instinctively looked to the sky and at the ride that was now mid-journey. The waving tentacles of the mechanic octopus looked curiously menacing. Flashing bulbs lit up the pod-like carriages against the dark sky. Joyous revellers screamed as the adrenaline of the rapid downward descent coursed through their veins. Amongst the screams of delight came a sudden grinding, loud and unmistakeably incongruent. The fairground operator looked up. Confusion clouded his craggy face as his eyes searched the machine's whirling tentacles in the now black sky.

The sudden noise of a cable breaking was like the harsh sound of whiplash magnified a thousand fold. The abrupt ear-splitting grating of metal drew hundreds of pairs of eyes to the sky as Eleanor remained rooted to the spot.

The riders' shrieks of delight changed like quicksilver into screams of terror. Eleanor caught her breath and continued to stare as two carriages flew off the main body and crashed to the floor. From ground level, the detached spinning carriages looked like heavy, oversized buttons haphazardly thrown by a reckless giant. It was a surreal sight seeing the lofty fall from grace of these once splendid carriages, as they hurtled to the ground in sickening, thunderous collisions.

The falling carriages were unable to hold the revellers, who plummeted to the ground like mini matchstick men. Eleanor gulped, unable to look away from the horrific sight unfolding in front of her. A further three carriages smashed to the ground as screams of terror increased to an ear-splitting level. She was soon enveloped by a gathering crowd, some people who were hysterical, some who simply wanted to catch a glimpse of the action.

Eleanor felt as if everything was being played in slow motion. She was unsure how long she was standing there for. It was a few minutes before she realised that the distant police sirens were getting progressively louder. The sirens punctuated her stunned state of mind and she quickly scanned the crowds for her friends. Jack was the first to find her. Still gawking at the ride he said, 'Did you see that! Those people certainly got the ride of their life!'

They continued staring at the sky in disbelief before being herded to one side by uniformed paramedics who poured out from three nearby ambulances. The panicked voice of the fairground manager blasted through the tannoy as he addressed the anxious crowd in shrill tones. 'Can everyone from the fairground please step away from the *Furious Octopus*! All rides are now suspended! I repeat, all rides are suspended! Please evacuate the grounds NOW!'

The mass exodus saw Eleanor and her friends leave the park in a dazed state of horror. Walking to St. James's tube station amongst the bewildered and oddly cautious crowd, Eleanor said, 'I can't believe it. I hope those people... I hope they're going to be OK.'

Serena said quietly, 'To think, that could have been us.' Everyone was quiet as the disturbing thought took hold.

Jack shook his head and ever the optimist said lightly, 'Elle, thank God you lost your token. The injured guys are in hospital now, they'll be OK.'

With the group now shocked and complacent, no-one felt like staying out and headed home separately. Later that night in bed, Eleanor shuddered in the realisation that people may have died.

She finally fell asleep in the early hours of the morning and was awakened by her trilling mobile. Catching a glimpse of the screen she answered groggily, '*Mum*? *You OK*? What's up?'

Lucille sounded relieved and said quickly, 'Oh thank God you're OK! I've only just seen the news about this terrible fairground accident. Do you know anything about it? Apparently there were a tonne of students there.'

Eleanor was immediately lucid. She contemplated telling her mum the truth. How she had been inches away from boarding the ride. It was pointless mentioning that now. She sighed, 'I'm fine Mum, *chill*. We were at the fair but didn't stop for long. Besides, scary rides aren't really my thing. You should know that.'

'Glad you're in one piece! Uh oh, I woke you didn't I? Go back to sleep hon. And Elle, take care!'

Eleanor lay in bed for a few more minutes. Fleeting guilt of having lied to Lucille put her more on edge, yet she knew she had done the right thing. Succumbing to a craving for hot coffee, Eleanor soon found herself downstairs watching the local BBC news over breakfast. Staring at the footage of the accident, she turned up the volume when she saw a fairground employee being interviewed. The tired spokesman who seemed like he too had endured a sleepless night spoke emphatically regardless. 'I *can't* understand it. The *Furious Octopus* has a clean record. This is a freak accident and the first one in its four decade history. A full inquiry is underway. Good news is that there were no fatalities. The *Furious Octopus* is closed until further notice.'

Eleanor switched off the TV, unsettled by the chilling footage captured on a mobile phone by an intrepidly curious passerby. The accident kept her preoccupied as she walked into university, where it continued to be the talk of the campus. Having stood a mere few metres from the scene of the accident qualified Jack to give a blow-by-blow account. His flippant manner and the fortunate fact of there being no casualties put Eleanor at ease and she quickly put the accident to the back of her mind to concentrate on her lectures.

Having done a little background reading on Bartolommeo Borghesi earlier that week, Eleanor was well prepared and enthusiastic as she set out for university on the Friday morning. Giving her bag the prerequisite last check for keys, purse, phone and make-up bag, she also packed her mum's fabric swatches which were ready to post in an envelope.

Her motivational charcoal painting lay in her bag too. She glanced at the silver bracelet on her wrist. Her mother had reminded her twice so far to get the lock fixed, but as it seemed to be locking sufficiently for now, she decided to wear it just this once and get it fixed at the weekend.

Eleanor walked into her final lecture of the week. Noticing Christina, Jack and Serena already seated in the far left corner of the full room, Eleanor started making her way over.

Whilst walking towards them, her slightly loose bracelet came away and fell to the floor. Eleanor was momentarily thankful that it had fallen in view. Reaching down to pick up the bracelet, she inadvertently kicked it forward another two metres. In a simultaneously clumsy movement she accidentally dropped her bag to the floor whilst her painting, keys and phone tumbled to the ground.

In a room full of strangers standing with the contents of her bag spilled onto the floor, Eleanor felt the colour rise to her cheeks and flush a darker shade of crimson. She heard Jack guffaw from the corner and when he spied her shy face full of embarrassment, she saw him quickly get up to help her.

Her painting lay in full public view. She desperately tried not to focus on this unnerving fact as she scooped up her belongings from the floor like a hungry hobo scrabbling for food. She suddenly realised there were another pair of hands helping her.

'Nice painting.'

In a blind panic she snatched the offending painting and launched into a diatribe at the owner of the pair of hands who she assumed belonged to Jack. 'HEY THAT'S PRIVATE?! *What the frick!!* How *dare* you Ja-'

The low voice that growled back was curt and icy. And not Jack's. 'You looked like you needed a hand. Forgive me. And nothing is *private* when thrown in full view of a packed lecture theatre.'

In a state of panic Eleanor had assumed it was Jack who had attempted to help her. She suddenly looked up to acknowledge the owner of the voice.

The first thing Eleanor noticed about him was his glowering coal-black eyes flecked with hints of slate grey. They glittered with disdain as she blinked, slowly digesting the vision in front of her.

She wasn't sure if he was good looking. But there was something about him that made her stare as if he was the only person in the room. Slightly tanned skin. Thick, dark brown hair offsetting his angular jaw-line. And a piercing look that could kill.

She continued gaping at him as he knelt beside her and noted he was considerably taller than her. His broad shoulders filled out his crisp ivory shirt and she immediately felt unnerved. His long eyelashes only accentuated his unblinking stare, which unwittingly increased Eleanor's annoyance. She was surprised to find herself more irritated and not quite knowing why, felt her anger increase with the time those potent eyes rested on her.

She pulled her eyes away from him and was struck by his singularly odd attire. It was an unseasonably chilly September morning and the whole classroom was swathed in jumpers. Yet he remained unaffected by the ice cold temperature, opting instead for a lightweight shirt.

Before she had a chance to respond to his barbed remark, the owner of the curiously mesmerizing eyes got up in one deft movement and moved away to his seat. Just then, the lecturer entered the room and called the class to attention. Having finally managed to cram her belongings back into her bag she hastily took a seat next to Serena.

Jack as usual was the first to comment despite receiving a warning elbow in the ribs from Serena. That didn't stop him as he said, 'You OK Elle? Wow, I thought I was clumsy,' whilst mouthing to Serena, 'oww, that hurt!'

Eleanor had a few moments to calm down, whilst Jack's easy grin diluted her anger furthermore. Managing a small smile Eleanor sheepishly replied, 'And that guys, is how to look like a complete moron. I make Charlie Chaplin look positively graceful.'

Serena piped up, 'What did Raphael say? He looked like he was going to bite your head off.'

Eleanor was still a little flustered by the idea that her private painting had been seen in public. She whispered, 'Who's Raphael?'

A smiling Serena said, 'The guy who was helping you. Or tried to help you. You should take it as a compliment. He doesn't say much. Very standoff-ish. Very dreamy.'

Jack grimaced and looked questioningly at a flushed Eleanor who pulled out a hair-tie to quickly scrape her hair back into a tight ponytail. She answered quickly, 'I don't even know the guy. How can I think he's dreamy when I barely noticed him?'

Eleanor listened to her fawning friends in silent curiosity, her scattered attention like hundreds of dispersed dandelion spores caught in a warm summer breeze. Serena sighed, 'He could be a walking L'Oreal advert with his perfect, bed-head hair. He's *sooo* worth it...'

With her eyes fixed on Raphael's back, Christina said somewhat robotically, 'That's one hell of a swimmers physique. His body's a temple. I'm sure he'd bleed Evian. Hey Serena, your advert would have to be a silent one though. He's in all my classes but barely says two words to anyone. He always knows his stuff when the tutor is doing his rounds though.'

Serena covertly whispered, 'He seems a little odd. Special even...'

Eleanor's brow furrowed in confusion as she said, 'One flew over the cuckoo's nest special?'

Serena muttered, 'Noooo. He's got that loner James Dean thing down to a tee. You just *know* he's bad.'

Eleanor shook her head gently. Lifting her chin defiantly she said with a soft yet sardonic smile, 'Great. As if there weren't enough bad boy clichés in books and movies, they have to infiltrate real life too. I'm tired of boys full stop. *Bad* boys can just go to hell.'

Christina was still staring at Raphael's back as she said distractedly, 'Seriously Elle you'd be in a minority not to notice him. Every other girl is Lady Gaga over him.'

'Pretty much like you are, right?' Jack's comment earned him a playful smack from Christina and the two started mock punching. It took Eleanor a short while to totally focus and eventually the lecturer started to make sense. She still felt on edge about the way she had unwittingly exposed her private painting and by default, her innermost thoughts to the full lecture theatre.

Post lecture she headed straight for the on-campus post office. Remembering the image of her artwork lying on the floor for all to see, she conceded that carrying around a private memento was a bad idea. Hot humiliation spurred Eleanor into action. She had to get rid of the painting. Conceding that destroying it would be one step too far, she decided on the next best thing. Stuffing the painting in the same envelope as the fabric swatches, she hastily re-sealed it. She felt a wave of sweet relief wash over her as the envelope plunked into the belly of the post-box.

Walking back to the Student Union bar, Eleanor summarised her painting trauma in a text to her mum, asking her to put the painting back in her old room. Shaking her head free of the image of captivating coal black eyes, Eleanor entered the bar with the intention of forgetting about the painting. Her friends however, had other ideas.

Leaning on the bar a smiling Katherine said, 'So, you gave Raphael a piece of your mind?'

Eleanor frowned and said imploringly, 'Not you as well? He was looking at my personal paint-'

She was cut short by Serena's indignant yet playful tone. 'He was *trying* to help you until you bit his head off!'

Christina backed up Serena. 'She's right Elle. He was only trying to help, you seemed to be in such a panic. This guy barely talks to anyone. Which reminds me, what exactly did he say to you?'

Eleanor remembered his voice clearly. With smoky undertones at first, then icy cold with derision after her rebuke. She cleared her throat and said somewhat sheepishly, 'Um, something about how it was a nice painting.'

Serena and Christina broke into simultaneous peals of laughter which quickly quietened down after a subdued look from Eleanor. Jack simply looked on whilst Katherine, normally the quietest of the group said lightly, 'Let me get this straight. This guy – Raphael, tried to help you. He then complimented your art. You not only rejected his offer of help, but then proceeded to shout at him? That too, in full view of the class?'

In the harsh fluorescent light of the Student Union bar, Katherine made sense. Eleanor's shyness for her artwork did not give her the right to be indiscriminately rude. Eleanor eagerly tried to justify her behaviour, which was a half-hearted attempt to convince both herself and her friends. 'Do you guys know how private my paintings are to me? It feels as if someone's read my diary. It's intrusive and frankly, I feel almost violated.'

Christina joked, 'I'd love to be violated by Ra-' She stopped, swallowing her words after catching a glimpse of Eleanor's downcast face.

Jack was unable to contain himself much longer and offered his input albeit begrudgingly. 'I'm no fan of Raphael, but he didn't *know* you were going to get like that over your painting.' Nudging a small smile out of Eleanor he said, 'Enough about Raphael, look at what I've ordered.' Everyone glanced up to see an approaching bar-tender carrying a wooden yardstick laden with alcoholic shots. 'This is to celebrate our first week at uni. We survived – just about!'

Everyone cheered collectively. Downing her peach flavoured vodka shot, Eleanor knew her friends were right. She owed Raphael an apology. That could wait till Monday.

# 3 APOLOGY

Eleanor rarely drank alcohol and thought hangovers to be pointless acts of self-inflicted debilitation. Friday night however had turned out to be an all-nighter and she had returned home just before 5:00am. She didn't plan on drunken intoxication every weekend but enjoyed her new lifestyle and embraced it wholeheartedly. The busier she was, the less likely she would be thinking about Michael.

During her first week, Eleanor frequently wondered what had happened to Astrid. With an ever expanding social circle, Eleanor visited the main bars in town and knew many students on different courses. Yet no-one had seen or heard of Astrid. It was the following Monday when Astrid finally made contact.

Reading Astrid's text, Eleanor was initially glad to hear from her, yet disheartened to learn that Astrid was back in Ireland after dropping out of university. Citing family problems, she wished Eleanor all the best and promised to look her up if she was ever back down south.

Eleanor read the text with dismay. She tried calling Astrid, but it went straight to voice-mail. Quickly texting an understanding reply, she promised to keep in touch, because despite their relatively short meeting, Eleanor had felt they had somehow bonded.

The following week at university was busier than the first, yet she found herself wishing to fast forward to Friday. Although Latin Epigraphy was her favourite subject, Eleanor suspected she was looking forward to it for an entirely different reason. Ashamed of her behaviour towards Raphael and keen to redeem herself through apology, Eleanor anticipated expressing her regret at the earliest opportunity.

Eleanor didn't have to wait till Friday. She spied Raphael the following day in the library. Poring over a pile of books, he was oblivious to her hovering by the door. Not wanting to disturb him, Eleanor nearly turned away before begrudgingly acknowledging her mini-outburst was rude and uncalled for. She walked steadily towards him. Lowering herself into the vacant seat next to Raphael, she gently placed her bag on the table.

Sunlight streamed through large hexagonal windows in the near empty library, highlighting floating dust motes in the warm room. All was quiet, except the low hum of the computer and the hushed telephone conversation of the librarian seated at reception near the entrance.

Eleanor whispered to Raphael, 'Hey.'

Raphael placed his hand on the page where he had paused.

Eleanor tried to speak but no words came out. She was hit by a wave of abrupt ambivalence as her instinct told her that something was amiss. She remembered being unsettled when Raphael had tried to help her during their first meeting. But being preoccupied with painting trauma, Eleanor had disregarded that feeling almost instantaneously.

Focusing on the matter at hand she whispered earnestly, 'Look, *it is* Raphael, isn't it? My behaviour the other day – it was just so out of character. Call it a Christian Bale moment, not one of my finest. I may seem a *little* unhinged at the mo but I promise you, I'm not. Rude outbursts are *sooo* not my thing, honest. My friends said I should apologise and-'

Raphael cut her short. Swivelling his head in her direction he said quietly, 'Your friends say you should apologise. Do you?' Raising his unblinking eyes to finally make eye contact with Eleanor, he patiently awaited an answer.

'Well, I *was* going to say that so do I, before you interrupted me.' A hint of reproach crept into Eleanor's voice. Her friends back home had always teased her about being transparent. If she disliked someone they would very quickly know about it. Fearing her annoyance would be obvious by a give-away frown or severe stare, she decided to expediently wrap up the conversation.

She continued adroitly, 'As I was saying, I'm sorry. My paintings are very personal and to have them exhibited like that, just made me flip out. It wasn't your fault and I'm sorry. Truly sorry.'

The sun was now in his eyes. In all its harsh blinding glory, Raphael blinked only once. He continued to stare at her. Eleanor on the other hand was feeling increasingly awkward and on edge. Her uneasiness, initially a slight nagging feeling, had now grown to a full-blown yanking tug, her inner voice telling her to finish the conversation and walk away before causing further offence.

She murmured, 'Anyway, must dash. I was going to apologise to you on Friday but I'm glad I've seen you now, I feel so much better already and-'

'You apologised to make yourself feel better?'

She was thrown off guard by his cavalier response. Eleanor pictured an emotional barometer. Measuring pure annoyance, it seemingly increased with the amount of contact she had with Raphael. Only a few minutes had passed since she had walked into the library and already, the imaginary mercury had risen to a dangerous level. She whispered vehemently, 'No – Yes – I mean NO!'

She took a deep breath and tried to stay in control. No longer whispering she said somewhat loudly, 'I apologised because it was the right thing to do. Have you never reacted in the heat of the moment? Of course you have, you're human. Like John Prescott packing a punch when he was egged a few years ago, which might I add, was a *totally* provoked attack. Not to say that you provoked me. Well, you technically *did*, but-'

Eleanor was cut short by the librarian who had stalked over. Not fitting the stereotypical elderly librarian, she was not a day over thirty. Her blonde hair slicked back in a tightly wound bun indicated she meant business. Her pencil skirt teamed with the fitted black silk shirt gave her an authoritative air; this was not someone to be taken lightly.

The irate librarian sneered, 'Can't you read the signs – all *seven* of them around this library? No talking, definitely no shouting. Carry on this conversation outside if you have to, but you,' she said, jabbing a perfectly manicured finger accusingly at Eleanor, 'YOU have to leave. Now.'

A contrite Eleanor tried to explain earnestly, 'Look, I really didn't *mean* to shout. If it's any consolation, the library's virtually empty anyway. I'm sorr-'

'Get out. NOW.' The librarian's word was final, leaving a gobsmacked Eleanor mortified and rooted to the spot. Mentally cursing herself for not being the most tactful apologiser, she cringed with embarrassment, trying to ignore her burning cheeks that were now flushed with fiery frustration. Avoiding Raphael's stare she grabbed her bag in her clammy hands and half-ran towards the exit.

Suddenly hearing hushed conversation she looked over her shoulder in surprise. The librarian had struck up a surreptitious dialogue with Raphael, leaning over him and pointing to his books whilst making obvious small talk. The dragon diva had now mutated into a charming coquette, bestowing flirtatious smiles and coy glances on Raphael.

Quickening her pace Eleanor burst out of the library. She inhaled the cool air, a welcome change to the stifling oppression of the humid library. Eleanor had never been forcibly removed from any building, which in combination with her badly executed apologies increased her growing anger.

What surprisingly bothered her more was Raphael's reaction. He was nothing to her. Yet the thought of him thinking negatively about her, bugged Eleanor. She decided if Raphael was too stubborn to accept her well-meant apology, then that was his problem. Running to her next lecture, an image randomly surfaced in her mind; that of the fawning blonde glancing playfully at Raphael as he fixed the librarian with coal-black eyes. Eleanor didn't know why but she didn't like it.

In her second week at university, Manchester life seemed but a distant memory. She had little to complain about. The house was as daunting as ever yet she was rarely indoors to be significantly affected by it. She didn't even have time to think about Michael. She had built up a solid social circle and enjoyed studying and spending time with her new friends.

Eleanor was in a positive mood as she walked into her Friday lecture. Watching Eleanor pull out her books, Christina chirped, 'Hey, did you manage to speak to Raphael? He looked up when you came in.'

Answering as nonchalantly as she possibly could Eleanor mumbled, 'Yeah, I apologised earlier this week, unsure if he-'

She was interrupted by Mr Berlis who arrived a few minutes later than planned and was keen to start his lecture with an enthusiastic smile. Like the majority of lecturers, he had set an assignment the previous week. Studying the interpretation of the oldest Latin inscription from Praeneste fascinated Eleanor and she thought questioning the date may be an interesting facet to explore in the essay.

Waiting till the lecture had ended, Eleanor told the others she would catch up with them after a quick word with Mr Berlis. Jack whispered to her mischievously, 'Ms Swot strikes again..! Most of us are headed to the SU bar, see you there? I'll have a nice cold beer waiting with your name all over it.'

Jack hurried off with the crowd of students ready to start the weekend early. For a split second Eleanor wondered if she really was too studious. It was a Friday afternoon and instead of propping up the bar, she was waiting to discuss work that wasn't due in for another fortnight. Pacifying herself that proactivity was a positive trait, she waited to catch her lecturer's attention whose back was to her.

'Mr Berlis..? Hey, it's Eleanor Hudson. Great lecture by the way! I started the assignment at the weekend and have a quick question about approach. Could you spare a few minutes?'

Mr Berlis talked whilst packing up his briefcase. 'Of course, Eleanor. You'll have to be quick as I have another student waiting and I have to dash off to a debate across town.'

Eleanor was sure she had seen the class empty. Wondering who else was waiting, she turned around. Raphael was leaning on the adjacent work-bench reviewing her quietly.

Since the day in the library Eleanor had made a conscious effort to avoid looking in Raphael's direction. Now he was standing behind her and she hadn't even realised.

Suddenly hyper-conscious of his presence a few metres away, she cleared her throat and continued adroitly. 'For the assignment I just wondered if I could also include a short piece on why I think the Praeneste inscription's a forgery? It could be a really cool debate why I think the date is falsified. If you're too busy now, I can pop by to see you tomorrow?'

Mr Berlis appeared to be mulling it over. 'Hmm... What can I do for you Raphael?'

Raphael hesitated a micro-second before answering, 'My question was about approach too. I would like to include a précis on restoration techniques followed by an in-depth analysis of two of my favoured methods.' He paused another second before saying, 'And for the record, I think the Praeneste inscription is authentic.'

Mr Berlis looked first at Raphael then Eleanor. 'Deadline's not for another fortnight, I'm impressed.' Putting on his overcoat whilst talking he said, 'Interesting takes on the assignment, would be great if you could work together and present separate projects. I'm always encouraging healthy debates and you guys have wonderfully opposing views. Consult with each other to get the ball rolling and we can touch base next week to see how you're doing. Really sorry, have to dash!'

Mr Berlis bid a hasty goodbye and disappeared before Eleanor could protest. She had her back to Raphael and knew she had to turn around sometime to face him, yet not wanting to move or even look in his direction, she remained rooted to the spot.

She wondered how long she could stand there without seeming rude or stupid. Shifting her gaze to the window near the exit, Eleanor was momentarily side-tracked with the sudden change in weather. Minutes ago it had been light and sunny. Now rainclouds heavy with rain and discontent gathered on the horizon of a rapidly greying sky.

Eleanor was painfully aware that she was alone with Raphael. The room suddenly felt distended, brimming with expectation and tension. She stared through the window, trying to prolong an impending conversation with Raphael whilst wondering what had happened just now.

She decided that trying to be a responsible individual had its drawbacks; first with her awry apology, now this. In trying to be efficiently studious she had inadvertently managed to acquire a study partner whom she disliked and who no doubt felt the same way about her. Unsure of her next move, she chewed her lip in uptight concentration and defensively clutched her books closer to her chest.

From his indecorous behaviour towards her in the library, Eleanor was positive of Raphael's extreme reluctance to work with her. Even now his stony silence was sufficient proof that he wasn't keen on her company. Maybe they could both agree not to work together but tell Mr Berlis they had. A quick five minutes together on the day of the assignment submission would be enough and Mr Berlis would be none the wiser. Keen to avoid another argument she whipped round to face Raphael. 'Look. I think we can both agree that this is-'

'An interesting idea. Just like Mr Berlis said. The deadline's a fortnight away. That gives us plenty of time to get a handle on it. You free this weekend?'

*He actually wanted to work with her.* In Eleanor's limited experience of dealing with closed off, difficult characters, she was unsure what her next course of action would be. James Joyce's Ulysses was easier to read than Raphael.

Eleanor stammered, 'Seriously – what..? Mr Berlis asked us to work together, but we don't really have to. I work best on my own anyway, so it's really no big deal.' Eleanor knew she was making excuses and sorely wished they weren't glaringly obvious.

Tilting his head so his eyes were level with hers, Raphael said in his smoky voice, 'Do you not want to work with me, Eleanor?' He was quietly challenging her and she knew it.

His black eyes were like two hot chunks of coal, searing into her consciousness and holding fast onto her gaze with little intention of letting her go. Eleanor felt the pull, a strong magnetic force grounding her and rendering her almost speechless.

Her brain was sending signals to her mouth to piece conciliatory words together yet Eleanor remained quiet. She tried to look away from him, but found herself unable to do so. She briefly contemplated denial but couldn't stop the truth rushing out. She said firmly, 'Considering our last conversation, I just *assumed* you wouldn't want to work with me.' The image of the librarian flitted through her mind as Eleanor stared back with a hint of defiance.

Raphael sounded slightly puzzled. 'If I correctly recall, you were apologising. I was merely finding out if you had really wanted to apologise. Or if you felt coerced by your friends. Then we were interrupted, after which you practically ran off. I was going to join you, but-' He paused before saying decisively, 'I got held up.'

Eleanor was unsure what to make of this new information. He looked like he was telling the truth. He had little reason to lie. Up until now, she had felt Raphael was goading her during the apology and had made a conscious effort to avoid him. It transpired that Raphael was not being truncular, but merely inquisitive.

She forced herself to think back and see the situation from Raphael's perspective. In thinking he disliked her, Eleanor had been unnecessarily rude yet again. She mentally cursed herself whilst realising that she had been ostensibly unreasonable.

A soft grin emerged on Raphael's face as he said earnestly, 'I was actually going to thank you for your apology, but then it was too late. I hoped to catch up with you later that week… but you seemed really busy.'

Feeling slightly foolish yet inscrutably euphoric Eleanor said hastily, 'I can squeeze in a few hours on Saturday afternoon. If not we'll meet sometime next week, maybe cram twenty minutes next Tuesday?'

'No, tomorrow's fine. Where would you like to meet?'

She said coolly, 'Library?'

Raphael paused for a fraction of a second. 'Works for me. 3:00pm OK? The library closes at 6:00pm giving us a good few hours. Take my mobile number. In case anything comes up.'

'Trust me, I'll be there. See you in the library at 3:00pm.'

Raphael replied with a hint of perseverance, 'Take it. In case you're running late.'

Eleanor pursed her lips, annoyed by his insistence on giving his number. There was no way she was going to miss the study session yet for some reason, Raphael seemed to doubt her.

Forcing herself to rise above his potential slight she took his number and said hotly, 'Thanks, but it totally was unnecessary. See you tomorrow.'

Raphael nodded his head in acknowledgement, a hint of a smile on his face as she continued to watch him with a mixture of growing curiosity and perturbed pleasure. Interrupted by a sudden movement to her left, she reluctantly tore her eyes away from Raphael. She noticed four army officers in khaki uniform enter the room.

A young bright-eyed cadet trailing behind the group placed a laptop bag on the nearest work-bench. He said jovially, 'I think this room should have been booked out? We're due to give a lecture on the history of the Armed Forces.'

Smiling apologetically Eleanor said, 'Sorry, we're done. Room's all yours.'

She glanced back at Raphael whose countenance had swiftly changed into a surly scowl. He dashed past the army men, flinching as he made fleeting eye contact with the leader before disappearing down the corridor.

Eleanor thought she imagined alarm in Raphael's eyes as he fled the room. Tiny warning bells were ringing, continuing to peal faintly in the background of her perplexed mind. Brushing aside her unfounded apprehensions, Eleanor headed to the Student Union bar. She couldn't help a tiny smile escape her lips. She was suddenly looking forward to the weekend.

# 4 SWEET SURPRISE

Eleanor stirred awake the following morning surprisingly refreshed. It had been another fun-packed Friday night at the Student Union which had started with Jack lining up a row of ice-cold beers. She was glad to have paced herself throughout the evening with regular glasses of water in between beers, shots and cocktails. She needed a clear head for her study session with Raphael.

Not due to meet till later that afternoon, she wanted to get a head start on the assignment. Eleanor had never been competitive, yet Raphael had seemingly awakened this spirited streak in her. Lying dormant for the past eighteen years, it flexed its new-found muscles like an eager infant who had just learnt to walk.

Raphael had an odd effect on her and she couldn't understand why. She wasn't naturally argumentative yet found herself quarrelling freely and easily with Raphael. She barely knew him yet felt strangely close to him. Closer than she did to Michael, which was weird, considering she had known her ex for over three years and Raphael a mere few weeks. She half-smiled to herself, wondering what Raphael would make of this. Not that he would ever know. Focusing on their fresh start, Eleanor finally clambered out of bed.

She very nearly jumped back into the welcoming arms of her warm duvet. She hadn't realised the room was freezing whilst lounging in her cosy bed. Hopping across the chilly floor whilst chiding herself for forgetting to switch on the heat-timer, she remembered the bedroom had felt noticeably cooler last night. Allowing her mind to stray whilst in the shower she wondered what to wear for her study session.

She visualised her ensemble of low-slung skinny jeans, fine-knit red polo and tan riding boots. Maybe she could ditch the equestrian outfit for a fitted top with cigarette pants. Finding herself in familiar yet loathed procrastination territory, she wondered why she was bothered about her outfit choice when she was only seeing Raphael.

She purposefully chose her most worn-out pair of jeans and oldest cotton blazer. Lightly spritzing herself with Chanel, she was suddenly distracted by the bellowing door-bell. Running nimbly downstairs, she opened the door to find a stranger on her doorstep.

A snowy white courier's head popped around a large gift-wrapped box swathed in cellophane. Giving a toothy smile, she informed Eleanor that her signature was needed for the parcel.

Eleanor was unsure who it could be from. She hadn't even given her full address to her Manchester friends yet. Guessing the sender to be Lucille, she returned the courier's smile and said, 'Bless Mum, wonder what she's sent!'

The courier's smile stretched wider. 'That's what parents are for. Just sign here dear.'

Eleanor scribbled her signature across the LED screen and studied the heavy package in her hands. Her suspicions were confirmed as Eleanor opened the envelope which read: *Happy House-Warming! Love L xx.*

Eleanor gave a delighted giggle as she noted the familiar crest of her favourite confectioners on the front. Tucking the signing machine away and winking, the courier said, 'I'd crack open the box straight away if I were you.'

'I might just do that! Have a great weekend!' Closing the door, Eleanor balanced the chocolates on the side cabinet near the entrance. Sprinting upstairs for her mobile phone she quickly called her mum to thank her. Eleanor babbled excitedly, 'Hey Mum, hope all swell! Just to say thank you! Your present was all kinds of awesome-'

Lucille cut her short. 'Hang on. What on *earth* are you chattering about?'

'Ha ha, very funny Mum. You knew I've been feeling down and this gorgeous gift really cheered me up, you know how much I love Sciolti!'

'I promise you honey, wasn't me. Was there a card? You don't know who it's from, do you..? Aaah, only a few weeks there and you've got yourself a secret admirer!'

Eleanor flushed, her mind flitting back to the handwritten card. She said slowly, 'Actually the card was signed "Love L" which is why I automatically thought of you. You sure it's not you doing your "good deed of the day"..?'

'Wasn't me hon. Hey, when you find out who the mystery sender is, let me know. They've just earned serious brownie points!'

Eleanor hung up, curiosity eating at her as she made her way downstairs. It took her the full length of the staircase to notice something was wrong when she finally entered the kitchen.

A small puddle of water had gathered under the sink. Running over to investigate, she noticed a leaking pipe and flung a tea-towel onto the floor over the excess liquid. Wrapping another towel around the defective pipe to stem the small flow, she wondered what to do next.

Racking her brains whilst staring at the worrying water, she remembered seeing a Yellow Pages directory in the alcove near the entrance. Six queries later, she had managed to book a plumber for an urgent call-out and awaited his arrival. Still optimistic about making her study session with Raphael, Eleanor tried to relax with a decaf coffee. Pulling The Count of Monte Cristo from the bookshelf, she perched on a breakfast bar stool whilst keeping a wary eye on the sink.

Eleanor was soon engrossed in the world of Edmond Dantès. She imagined the thrill of docking a ship after a long journey in the bustling fishing port of nineteenth century Marseilles. She daydreamed strolling through the sun-drenched village of Catalan, where an adoring Mercedes eagerly anticipated Edmond's arrival. Before long, the leaky sink had become a distant problem as it was pushed out of Eleanor's mind and replaced with a more appealing set of circumstances.

Eleanor frequently found herself getting lost in books. Reluctantly glancing at her watch, she realised with growing alarm that two whole hours had flown by with no plumber in sight. Even if he arrived *now* and *if* he managed to fix the problem expediently, Eleanor still had to get to Waterloo. Her study session was thirty minutes away and she would undoubtedly be late.

Grabbing her phone she paused before hitting dial, trying to get past the weirdness of seeing Raphael's name in her mobile. Her heart thrummed in her chest with each ring as she found herself torn wishing he would, then wouldn't answer. When he eventually picked up, Eleanor was quick to offer her explanation.

'It's Eleanor. So sorry but I can't make it today. I'm having a leaking sink crisis. Plumber's on his way, unsure how long he'll be so I guess I'll just see you some oth-'

Raphael cut her short. She was taken aback by the congenial words that followed. 'Don't worry. All that matters is that you're OK. You are OK, aren't you?'

She was momentarily thrown by his pleasant tone. He sounded genuine and Eleanor soon realised that in trying to make her point hurriedly, she had sounded abrupt. She said somewhat apologetically, 'Honestly Raphael I am so sorry for messing up your plans. If I could leave the house I would.'

He said hesitantly, 'You can't leave the house, I totally get that. What if I came to yours..?' She listened with a surprised smile as he tried to unsuccessfully backtrack. 'What I meant was... it would be good to complete the assignment. Listen, no worries if you don't-'

He sounded contrite, almost slightly embarrassed and Eleanor couldn't help but laugh as she said, 'It would be *great* to start the assignment today. I'm in Mortlake not far from the train station. How are you getting here?'

'I'll be there before you know it.'

'Cool, I'll text you the full address. Bell me if you get stuck.'

He hung up as she continued to stare at her silent phone. With normal traffic, she expected to see him within forty minutes. A short while ago she thought Raphael despised her. Now forty eight hours later he was on his way to her house for a study session. Suddenly cheery with the idea that Raphael maybe didn't hate her she found herself worrying less about the leaking sink.

Casting her eye around the spotless kitchen to ignore the incongruous tea-towels on the floor, she willed herself to be patient. A sudden creaking from the sink area grabbed her attention whilst the ensuing raucous scraping of metal broke the silence of the house. Fearing the worst Eleanor leapt off her seat and peered under the sink.

The defective pipe gushed water in sharp bursts and all Eleanor could do was grab another tea-towel to wrap around the pipe. Mid-crisis a knock on the door indicated an arrival. Only fifteen minutes had lapsed since she had given Raphael directions to her house. Hurrying to the door expecting to see the plumber, she was surprised to find Raphael on her doorstep.

'Hey,' she faltered, 'I thought you were the plumber. Not that you look like one. FYI, I digress like crazy when panicked, and I'm sort of in middle of a mini crisis here, so you've been warned.'

Raphael's cool interjection had an instantly calming effect on Eleanor. He said, 'Kitchen sinks can be tricky. Let me take a look.'

The thumping metallic noise emanating from the kitchen was considerably louder this time and its unwelcome return spurred Eleanor back into the kitchen. The cabinet door which Eleanor had left ajar to monitor the flow showed a section of piping had now fully come away from the under-side of the sink. Water flooded out at an alarming rate. The few tea-towels which had earlier been saviours lay like drowning islands, inadequacy taunting them as water poured freely over them.

Raphael followed her into the kitchen. Giving the kitchen a cursory scan he said quickly, 'Get more towels. Larger ones.'

Crouching on the floor with his back to her whilst attending the offending pipe he said calmly, 'Switched the water off yet?' He swivelled his head, waiting for her to respond.

'You can switch water off?'

Instinctively cringing at her unintelligent remark she glanced up at Raphael to notice a glimmer of a smile on his face. He said patiently, 'The switch is normally near the boiler. Where's that?'

Thankful for at least knowing that much, Eleanor pointed triumphantly to the cupboard across the kitchen. 'Hang on, I'll come with. It's like learning long multiplication at school. Even if you don't ever use it again, it's always good to know.'

His mouth twitched into another smile as they cut across the room to the boiler. The low cupboard ceiling was no match for Raphael's six foot frame. Lowering his head for a better view whilst peering into the depths of the otherwise dark cupboard, he tried to point Eleanor in the right direction. 'Can you see the water switch? It's hidden there.'

Eyes riveted near the second pipe, Eleanor leaned in further to see the exact location of the switch. Her water comment had left her mortified and eager to dispel the burning feeling of obtuse inadequacy, she examined the cupboard with renewed enthusiasm. Straining her eyes in the dark recesses of the cupboard, she suddenly spied a small rectangular switch which Raphael flicked off. Grimacing at the musty smell of the boiler and making a mental note to aerate the cupboard later, she wrinkled her nose in distaste at the stale smell.

She suddenly caught a hint of the most arresting scent. Invigorating forest fern with top-notes of bergamot was woody and bittersweet. She was still for a few seconds, breathing in the utterly intoxicating aroma before realising it was Raphael's scent. Feeling the cool leather of his jacket brush lightly on her wrist as he shifted to close the cupboard door, she was suddenly aware of their proximity. She gulped and proceeded to quickly back away.

She said hastily, 'Fancy a drink or something whilst we wait? The plumber was due two and half hours ago. And did you take a short-cut? It normally takes me double the time. You could give the Road Runner a run for his money. And what's with the Road Runner – you barely see him around. Nowadays, it's all digital animation which is great, but you just can't beat the good old cartoons, you know? I sound Amish, don't I? Not that there's anything wrong with being Amish. In fact I'm frequently fascinated by Amish lifestyle...'

She knew she was rambling and by the looks of it, so did Raphael. He watched her squirm before saying, 'No drink thank you, I'm good for the time being. Short-cut and zero traffic made it a quick journey.' Taking a step back to lean on one of the work-tops he said, 'I'll show you the route sometime.'

She wondered at his comment that seemed to be loaded with hidden promise and expectation. Her arms dropped to her side as she continued to study him leaning on the work-top, not saying a word. She found the sudden lull in the conversation simultaneously easy yet inexplicably uncomfortable.

Despite feeling tense when standing close to Raphael just moments ago, the restlessness she experienced when they first met was no longer there. It was as if a virtual cloud had dispersed and her instinct had been mollified into thinking everything was perfect. She watched Raphael take in his surroundings.

He was the first to break the silence. 'The recent cold weather could have affected the heating. That grinding racket sounded like antiquated pipes for an old heating system.'

Eleanor thought back to the morning and the unusually cold bedroom sprang to mind. 'You may actually be right. It was flipping freezing this morning and I was so sure that I had turned the heating on when I came in last night. Although I wasn't in the same drunken league as Captain Jack Sparrow, I did wonder if I had forgotten to switch it on last night.'

Eleanor smiled as she spoke, recounting the events of the previous evening as they ran through her mind like flashes of a fast-forwarded film. Jack lining up her drinks whilst Christina and Serena challenged each other to outrageous dares. Jack freeing her from the clutches of an over-zealous suitor's advances by pretending to be her boyfriend. Turning to Raphael as she spoke, she was surprised to see him staring sternly at her.

He said in clipped tones, 'Glad you had fun last night.'

There was little doubt he was annoyed and Eleanor suddenly wondered how she could have possibly offended him. Focusing on their fresh start and wanting to remain positive, Eleanor chose to rise above his pointed remark and continued as normal. 'Yeah, it's great having friends that you can have a laugh with. I suppose it's all part of growing up right? OK, I've just realised I suddenly sound dinosaur old.' Laughing lightly she said, 'Actually, I feel lucky for having a nice bunch of friends here. It doesn't stop me from missing my mum though.'

Raphael seemed to visibly soften as Eleanor continued in an upbeat tone. 'What about you. Are you close to your parents?'

Raphael answered swiftly, 'No. Rarely see them.'

Worried that her efforts for light conversation may be construed as prying, Eleanor quickly changed the subject. She didn't have to extol the virtues of the Nintendo Kinect for long as the tardy plumber finally arrived.

Standing at the door with a bag of tools slung over his shoulder he apologised in his heavy cockney accent. 'So sorry love, got held up just outside Putney. Now, where's this sink?'

The plumber waved the cabinet door open and started tinkering with the pipes. The scraping steel din made an unwelcome return which did not appear to faze the plumber. Shaking his head whilst readying himself to bear bad news, he delivered his prognosis. 'Pipes are too old, look Victorian to me. They detract in the cold and if the system isn't up to scratch, they can't handle the cooler temperature. You'll need a new heating system. The water system's interlinked so the central heating will be shot to pieces if you're not careful.'

Eleanor listened with growing alarm. Being perpetually cold-blooded, she was in the habit of sleeping with the central heating switched on during the cooler months. Staying in a large unheated house meant she would undoubtedly freeze. Her reaction to the plumber's prognosis was less a response, more of an impassioned plea. 'OK, I assume installing a new heating system will be time consuming, not to mention expensive? I know the central heating's definitely been affected as it was way cold this morning.'

The noncommittal plumber said carelessly, 'I'll be back next week once I've sourced the parts. This is one hell of a house. Should take about four or five days to get everything sorted, in the meantime you won't have any heating or hot water. Don't use the bathroom either unless you want to freeze.'

Eleanor said thoughtfully, '*Actually*, I did notice the water was cooler than usual in the shower this morning too. I just cranked up the temperature. Eventually it ran comfortably hot.'

The plumber ran his eyes appreciatively over her body. She was suddenly self conscious and instinctively pulling her jacket tighter, opened her mouth to formulate a response.

Raphael beat her to it. Upon the plumber's entry, Raphael had shifted to the far corner of the kitchen leaving Eleanor in charge. From standing behind one of the larger cabinets, he swung into full view of the plumber and Eleanor. He had watched the conversation unfold from the far end of the kitchen. Now with arms crossed tightly across his chest he stared directly at the plumber.

Raphael's quiet tone was loaded with insistence and frank hostility. 'Five days is unacceptable. I've had a brief look at the pipes. I know the problem can be fixed in two days. The hardware store in town coincidentally stocks all the items you need. It's open now. I can direct you there if you like.'

The plumber looked up to acknowledge the speaker. Noticing Raphael in the room for the first time he faltered. 'I... I did see a hardware store on the way, but I was going to use my normal supplier. A two day time-frame is pushing it mate.'

Raphael glowered at the plumber, flexing his hands into balled fists then relaxing them to remain loose by his side. He was the epitome of calm yet quietly belligerent as the wavering plumber finally capitulated.

'I suppose it's not impossible if I use the store in town. I'll have to shift my other appointments though.' Eyeing Raphael suspiciously he said, 'You seem to know a lot about the piping system. You a plumber?' His question was tinged with resentment.

'No.'

Directing his next comment to Eleanor the plumber continued, 'Guess I'd better get myself to the hardware store. I'll be back in about twenty minutes or so. *If* I get what I need.'

Eleanor was simply thankful that the repair time had decreased to a manageable two days and mentally thanked Raphael. As she followed the plumber out he commented loudly within earshot of Raphael, 'And I ain't a rip-off merchant. Tell your boyfriend to stop worrying.'

Eleanor didn't have time to rectify the plumber's mistake as she watched him stomp away. Quietened by staccato stabs of embarrassment by the plumber assuming Raphael was her boyfriend, she waited near the open door for a minute. As the cool air caressed her hot cheeks, she knew there was no way Raphael could not have heard the plumber.

Returning to the kitchen with a fixed smile she started by way of thanks, 'Cheers for that, really appreciate it. I didn't know you were a plumbing professional? And when did you check out the hardware store?'

Raphael shrugged. 'I'm no expert. The materials for a heating re-fit can generally be found in any good hardware store. The one I passed in town looked half decent. I only said all that to get him started on the job.' He paused a second to say, 'And just ignore the boyfriend comment. He only assumed that as I was being vocal.'

Eleanor cringed again, feeling like a schoolgirl being teased in the playground about her first boyfriend. Her embarrassment must have been fairly obvious otherwise Raphael wouldn't have mentioned it. She tried to change the subject by glancing at her watch. 'Hey, it's only 3:15pm, how about getting some study in? If we work in the kitchen, we can perch on these breakfast bar stools, if that's OK?'

He seemed quietly amused as he settled opposite her, taking in her slightly flushed cheeks as she fumbled for her pen. Separated by a pile of Epigraphy textbooks, Eleanor soon found deciphering the Praeneste label an enjoyable yet complicated task. Most epigrams she had seen were difficult to read due to continuous abbreviations and ligatured letters. Although this made the transcription problematic to understand, Eleanor loved the challenge and studied the label with keen enthusiasm.

The plumber returned from the hardware store with a hoard of relevant fittings. More relaxed, he happily tinkered away under the sink and the rest of the afternoon flew by.

Shooting Raphael fleeting looks, Eleanor was surprised to find he was nothing like what she had expected. Despite his unfriendly and somewhat adverse reaction to the plumber, he was polite and the antithesis of rude with her. His insightful theories made him a great study partner and Eleanor couldn't help feel ashamed as she slowly realised she had been preoccupied with petty one-upmanship. Dismissing her childishly competitive notion and even temporarily letting her guard down, she found herself quietly enjoying Raphael's company.

Whilst scribbling some notes Eleanor suddenly remembered the chocolates. 'Can't believe we've ploughed through nearly half of the assignment. Think we deserve a treat...'

He seemed intrigued by Eleanor's cheeky smile and watched her cradle the chocolate package like a sleeping child in her arms. Speaking in a reverent half-whisper Eleanor placed the box on the pile of text-books. 'Now these are *the best* chocolates in the whole wide world. Even if you're not a chocolate fan, they'll blow your mind.'

Gently pulling the ribbon to free the folds of cellophane, an exultant Eleanor flicked open the lid and paused to savour the moment. She pushed the open box towards Raphael and said, 'There's a description list here, not that I need it – I've memorised the entire selection! It took a while, then again me and Mum are hard-core chocoholics.'

Turning over the vellum card in his palm Raphael asked, 'Where did you say these were from again?'

Eleanor was waiting for Raphael to choose before she dived in. Willing him to make his selection faster as she anticipated the scorched caramel truffle in her mouth she said lightly, 'They're from my favourite chocolatiers. Only I don't know who they're from. It's a funny story actually. The card said the sender was from "L" so I assumed it was from my mum, except she swears it wasn't her. Unsure who would want to send me chocolates, but hey, I'm not complaining!'

Raphael was unable to take his eyes of the open box. As he continued to stare at the rows of confectionary, Eleanor's attention was abruptly diverted by a sudden crash on her left.

Another pipe suddenly burst under the sink and the half-drenched plumber shouted for more towels as the pipe continued to furiously spray ice-cold water into the kitchen.

The bewildered plumber shouted, 'I DON'T UNDERSTAND! The water's switched off! I had only just patched that area of piping up! Oh great, a bigger section has come loose! MORE TOWELS NOW!'

Spying a dry towel on the work-top, Raphael reached over to extract it from the pile of textbooks. Handing the towel to the plumber, his elbow caught the corner of the box. Eleanor watched in horror as the box of chocolates tumbled onto the wet floor.

The chocolates were ruined. Casting a fleeting look over the sodden box Raphael said apologetically, 'Guess the box was nearer to the edge than I thought. I am so sorry Eleanor.'

She blinked, trying not to focus on the delicious chocolates on the floor. Taking a few deep breaths to quell her growing anguish she murmured, 'Don't worry about it. It was an accident.'

As her gaze shifted to the dripping sink, the plumber finally stopped cursing after controlling the burst pipe. Eying the drenched vellum card nearby he said, 'Expensive chocs huh? What a waste. Second layer not OK?'

A disheartened Eleanor had already picked up the half-empty box and studied it. 'Nope, all waterlogged. There may be a few chocs still dry, but it's not worth it.'

Eleanor returned to the work-top where Raphael was sitting and after dismissing the thought of wasted chocolates with great difficulty, turned her attention back to studying. Raphael seemed quieter than usual and the evening wore on as they studied in near silence. Eleanor only looked up once when the plumber finally announced he had finished for the day.

Spying the ruined chocolates on the side, the plumber picked up the box. Rummaging through the second layer he said, 'Mind if I have a look at these?'

Raphael's eyes darted up. He snapped, 'They're all trashed. They belong in the bin.'

Eleanor added ruefully, 'Yup, nothing pains me more than wasted chocolate. The silver lining is that at least I won't have to spend an extra hour on the Kinect.'

Shrugging his indifference, the plumber turned his back and headed to the bin with the box in hand. He continued eying the luxurious gift-box. Fingering the heavy embossed crest, he surreptitiously slipped a dry truffle into his mouth before tossing the box away. Greedily gulping away the remnants before turning around, he gathered up his tools. Promising to return the following afternoon to finish the job, he shuffled out of the house and away into the night.

# 5 DINNER DATE

Eleanor watched the plumber pull out of the drive-way and glanced up at the navy sky. The nights were drawing in and it was only 6:45pm. She suddenly realised they had skipped lunch. Mentally scolding herself for being an imperfect host, she contemplated asking Raphael to stay for dinner.

Unable to understand her hesitation at asking him a simple question, she loitered for a few minutes near the bookshelf. Idly pulling out the Domestic Goddess Express Cookbook, she was suddenly encouraged by Nigella's smiling face. Re-entering the kitchen she opened her mouth to speak, yet her words remained silent when she saw him deep in study.

Eleanor frequently became entirely engrossed in reading to forget her surroundings. As usual she had failed to realise how dark the room had become. She watched Raphael from afar as he pored over the Praeneste inscription utterly absorbed in the extract. He seemed to have forgotten about the dark room too and Eleanor smiled to herself. They were more similar than she thought.

Flicking on the main kitchen light she said, 'Didn't realise how dark it was. You've probably got other plans, but... Wanna stay for dinner?'

Raphael looked up as the room suddenly became luminous. Holding up the extract he said, 'This is fascinating. There are so many different interpretations. One misconstrued symbol can give an entirely different meaning to the one intended.' Cracking a smile he said, 'And dinner would be good.'

Oddly elated she smiled to say, 'Pasta and salad do you? There's a new jar of yummy Tiger Tomatoes that I'm dying to open. They don't have a Franca's in London so I stock-piled before moving down!'

'Sounds cool. Can I help with anything?'

Raphael seemed pleased. Closing his note-book he awaited Eleanor's response. She was on the verge of accepting Raphael's offer when a random memory abruptly quietened her. She suddenly remembered Michael watching her cook. He would lean on the counter and be food-taster, playfully distracting her with kisses whilst she laughed and stirred the contents of a simmering saucepan. She wondered what Michael was doing now and if he missed her at all. Concentrating on her post-break-up mantra she mentally recited, '*I am independent. I don't need Michael. I don't need ANYONE.*'

With these thoughts in mind she answered coolly, 'I'm good. Dinner will be done in about ten. You can chill out in the lounge for a bit. Oh, there's a docking station there if you want to listen to music and have an MP3 to plug in.' As an afterthought she added, 'Actually, it's been a mad day — fancy some vino?'

Raphael watched her move away from him as she headed for the wine which she liberally poured into fancy stemmed glasses. He said reluctantly, 'I'll just go chill in the lounge then.'

She watched him disappear before turning her attention to the salad. She had thought of Michael just now, the first time in nearly a week. Taking a sip of wine, she was pleased her effective mantra seemed to be working. Maybe she would be over Michael sooner than expected.

Her musings were interrupted with the abruptly broken silence of the house. She paused mid-sip to listen to music that Raphael had put on. Chopin, her favourite composer of all time emanated from the lounge. The stirring melody of Nocturne in E-Flat Major gently danced its way to Eleanor's ears causing her to still in surprise as she realised she had something in common with Raphael.

It seemed their divergent personalities weren't as different as she had originally thought. His serious, intense demeanour was in stark contrast to her relaxed daydreamer stance. Trying to get a clearer idea of his personality, she ran through their previous interactions. From their initial meeting, it was his helpful nature that had initially triggered Eleanor's misunderstanding with the painting. And judging from the way he had initiated the kitchen repair-work, he was thoughtful too. Without him encouraging the plumber to start work earlier, she would have had to freeze in an ice-cold house for longer. He had also offered to help her cook; being considerate was apparently Raphael's nature.

She glanced around the spacious kitchen as she absentmindedly drained the salad. The vast space compounded the growing emptiness which gnawed at Eleanor whenever she thought about Michael. Humming to keep herself occupied, she neglected to hear approaching footsteps.

She was immediately silent when she noticed Raphael beside her. Suddenly self-conscious she cleared her throat to say, 'Finished your wine already? Want a top-up?'

He shook his head. 'Are you sure I can't help with anything?'

Chewing her lip she unwillingly conceded an extra person in the kitchen would dispel her loneliness. 'OK, you can start on the pasta. Sauce-pan's over there.'

Raphael shifted into action and the pasta was soon simmering on a low rolling boil. Watching her drizzle the salad dressing he said inquisitively, 'When did you move down? And why here? Most would prefer student digs in London.'

'I got here just over two weeks ago. The house is my mum's inheritance. The place isn't so bad once you get past the creepy factor! I actually wound up at King's College by chance. Long story, I won't go into it now.'

He watched her keenly as she sorted the salad. Oddly comforted by his presence, she voluntarily continued. 'When I first moved down, I hated London. The people aren't the friendliest. Hey, when you're a northerner, these things matter. London's sort of grown on me. And sometimes the house feels too large but in this quiet street in Richmond, I can... I can just be.'

Eleanor's voice trailed off as she stared dejectedly at the salad. Raphael said quietly, 'You'll be OK. London's not too bad. It's like any place really.'

Snapping out of her momentary misery Eleanor asked, 'What about you? When did you move to London? You seem well settled.'

'I've been here for a while now. Pasta's nearly done. Where's the colander?'

She was distracted by his question and pointed to the far cupboard. He moved around comfortably in her kitchen and it was her turn to watch as he drained the pasta. Seeing him chilled out relaxed Eleanor and she found herself opening up a little more.

'I may have sounded a little miserable earlier. I don't mean to be. Not that anyone purposefully sets out to be depressed, because that would be just plain wrong, right?' She managed a half-smile before ploughing on, 'It's a new scene. I'm close to my mum and I really miss her. Being here just reminds me that I'm... alone. Don't get me wrong, I have some really cool friends around me. Sort of makes life a lot easier.'

She contemplated talking about Michael. She hadn't told her university friends about her ex-boyfriend yet found herself wanting to tell Raphael. She reflected with a hint of sadness, 'Sometimes, you can't help but miss people you're not supposed to care about. If that makes sense.'

Raphael said evenly, 'You have people around that care about you.' Taking a gulp of wine he added quickly, 'I've seen you around with your uni friends. It is obvious they care about you. OK, this food smells great. Shall we start?'

Whilst Eleanor dished up she realised Raphael was her first dinner guest. Her friends had visited her house a few times but she had never had the chance to cook, having always succumbed to take-away at the last minute. Placing cutlery on the work-top, Eleanor realised this was the happiest she had been in some time. Not quite understanding the reason for her good mood, she muted the light to the dinner setting. They were soon seated opposite each other with food before them.

With no study, misunderstanding or other distraction, Eleanor found herself looking straight at Raphael. His face was a buttermilk canvas tinged with a hint of golden honey. Tousled dark chocolate hair framed his face to complement compelling coal-black eyes. Eyes that seemed to be observing her with curiosity and comprehension in equal measure.

Draining the remnants of his glass, Raphael asked Eleanor how she was finding university. Aglow with the warmth of the wine she replied, 'I love it! The people, the course, it's all too cool. Uni is keeping me busy, which is way better thinking about pointless things.' She raised a glass to say, 'Just want to say a quick thank you for all your help on this crazy day. Here's to you being my first dinner guest, and a *really* good study session too!'

She found his inquisitive nature weirdly charming. Although not overtly loquacious, he became more forthcoming as the evening wore on. They were in middle of discussing the debateable qualities of the current coalition government when the bellow of the door-bell interrupted them. Excusing herself whilst speculating who it could be, Eleanor ran lightly to the front door. Her eyes widened in surprise as she wondered what a nun was doing on her doorstep.

There was something about a religious person that put Eleanor slightly on edge. Feeling somewhat awed by their religious purity, any nun or priest usually sent her packing in the opposite direction. Eleanor smiled at the diminutive elderly nun who held out a battered collection box in her wrinkled hands. 'I am so very sorry to disturb you dear. I'm collecting donations for church repair work in the neighbourhood. Is there anything you can spare?'

Melted by compassion at the frail vision in front of her, Eleanor smiled away the nun's apology. 'It would be my pleasure. My purse is inside. Come in out of the cold for a bit whilst I fetch it?'

The nun followed Eleanor gingerly inside the house. Hovering near the entrance of the kitchen whilst Eleanor rummaged for her purse, the nun noticed the food on the table. She said meekly, 'I'm so sorry for interrupting your dinner dear. You see the church roof is leaking and we're trying to raise urgent funds-'

The nun suddenly stopped talking. She had moved inside the kitchen to accept the note from Eleanor's hand and had noticed Raphael for the first time. He held his glass aloft and caught the nun's gaze over the rim of his glass.

She was instantly silenced by his stare. Her face which had been a picture of smiling gratitude quickly gave way to quiet distress. She tried to tuck the five pound note into her collection box but kept missing as she stared at Raphael all the while. She continued to fumble with the money and eventually managed to shove the note into the box a few seconds later. Stammering her thanks to Eleanor, the nun quickened her pace to pause on the porch. Placing a cold, papery hand on Eleanor's warm arm she whispered, 'May the Lord deliver us from evil. Bless you my child.' She gave Eleanor's arm a lingering pat before edging away and disappearing into the night.

Eleanor wondered if she and Raphael looked like a couple. Maybe it was a vibe they gave off. First the plumber had thought they were together and now the nun had practically ran out of the house after probably assuming she was interrupting their date. Dismissing the nun's odd behaviour she returned to the table where they leisurely finished dinner. It was nearly two hours later that Raphael got up to leave and she found herself at the open door seeing him out.

Seemingly unaffected by the cold, he lingered at the door for a few seconds. 'Thank you for dinner Eleanor.' He paused before tilting his head to gesture behind him, 'I'm parked around the corner so I'll be off.' He glanced upwards at the darkening sky, continuing hesitantly, 'I know it's a new scene here. But you'll soon get used to it. As for the people you miss, well I'm sure they miss you too. See you on Monday. Hope you don't freeze too much tonight.'

Eleanor loitered at the door for a few minutes after Raphael's departure. Briskly rubbing away the goose bumps on her bare arms, she fell back on the closed door in a happy haze. Remembering the plumber's prediction of the house getting cooler, she ran upstairs to pull on a jumper. Snuggling into the warm cocoon-like confines of her bed, she murmured a quick prayer of thanks.

Eleanor wasn't overtly religious, yet she prayed when she felt the need to. It was more of an informal chat, the sort of conversation one would have with their best friend. She asked for strength not to fixate on Michael and said a quick thank you for Raphael's timely appearance.

In the dreamlike state before deep slumber, her psyche tried to make sense of an unusual day as various images floated through her mind. She saw Raphael poring over his books in the darkened room. With heavy eyelids giving in to sleep, the last thing she thought of was the way

Raphael's mouth curved into a small smile whilst she gave a thank you toast. Maybe they could be friends after all.

# 6 PEACEFUL PARK

The following day Eleanor answered the door to a different plumber. Reading her confusion he said, 'You saw Simon yesterday. I'm Jeff, his business partner.' He continued wearily, 'Simon had a heart attack late last night. I'm taking over his patch for a while.'

The strain of a doubled client list had apparently taken its toll on the lethargic Jeff. His underlying resentment at the additional workload became increasingly apparent as his mobile buzzed incessantly to claim more of his dwindling time. In response to Eleanor's shocked expression he added casually, 'He'll be OK, he's not critical thank God. Crazy how even the fittest get ill. Right, let's see this sink.'

Eleanor stayed in the kitchen whilst he carried out the necessary repair work. Taking a five minute break whilst sipping tea which Eleanor had thoughtfully made, Jeff said, 'Hope the house wasn't too cold, it was a chilly evening.'

Eleanor recalled being pleasantly warm all night. Despite being cold before drifting off to sleep, she had awoken to a cosy bedroom. The rest of the house had been particularly cold, especially the bathroom where the freezing water had reduced her usual leisurely shower to a ten minute icy blast.

Wondering aloud at her isolated warm bedroom, she watched the plumber listen in puzzled silence before he said, 'That's strange. Your room should have been the coldest. I noticed your bedroom had a separate set of heating pipes that were directly affected. Don't worry, it'll be back to normal in a few hours.' The plumber worked diligently to fix the heating, leaving a relieved Eleanor to focus on her latest assignment.

In the midst of juggling various deadlines, she spent the majority of the following week busy with lectures and researching essay questions. Most of her friends except Jack had mentioned the pressure of mounting work.

Discussing study techniques one lunch-time, Katherine waited for Jack to leave the table for a drink before saying lightly, 'The thing with Jack is that he works best under pressure. He'll just crazy cram a few days before and still get straight 'A's. I've known him since primary school. Last minute study is clearly his thing.'

Katherine watched him from afar, her fondness evident as her eyes lingered in his direction. Quickly changing the subject before Jack returned, the girls' suddenly stilted chat was immediately picked up by Jack.

Swigging his soda as he took the vacant seat next to Katherine he joked, 'Talking about me again huh? You girls simply can't get enough of me. I wasn't gone for that long, jeez..!'

His jovial retort drew laughs from Eleanor and Christina as they rolled their eyes in mock disappointment whilst Eleanor playfully slapped him. Only Katherine remained silent, fixing her eyes on her plate in mute embarrassment.

Noticing Katherine's downcast gaze, Eleanor's quiet curiosity was interrupted by an openly inquisitive Christina who paused to take a second bite of her sandwich before saying, 'Oh look, there's Raphael. I've never seen him in the canteen. He's stopped. Hang on. He's looking over. Oh. Now he's walking this way. *What the f..?*'

Eleanor looked up from her salad in surprise. With her back to the canteen door, Eleanor hadn't seen Raphael enter the room. Instead, catching Christina's running commentary whilst throwing a disconcerted look in her vocal friend's direction, she willed Christina to be quiet. Raphael strode over to Eleanor's seat. His clear, low voice quietly commanded attention as her table looked up in mesmerised interest. 'Hi Eleanor. You OK? I was just passing and thought I'd ask how the sink was. All fixed?'

Only a few seconds had passed since Christina's blow-by-blow account of Raphael's movements, giving Eleanor little time to prepare. She opened her mouth to speak, when she realised she had an audience. Not only her friends but people on the adjoining tables, mostly girls, gawked in her direction. Some lowered their conversations to listen in, whilst others simply looked on.

Trying her best to ignore the uncomfortable stares she replied, 'Hey Raphael! I'm cool and so is the sink — well, last time I checked. Thanks again for your help.' Nudging the morsels around her plate she said, 'Hey how about another study session before the deadline?'

Raphael continued speaking in his soothing voice. Even the din of clattering dinner plates had ceased as listeners in the near quiet canteen hung onto his every word. Remaining focused on Eleanor he said, 'Sounds good. How about we actually make it to the library this time? Or you could come to mine?'

Eleanor found herself trying to suppress a smile as she said, 'Cool. Saturday work for you?'

'Yes. We'll set a time later this week. Goodbye Eleanor.'

Raphael then turned on his heel disappearing as quickly as he had arrived. The surrounding tables continued to gawp at Eleanor before begrudgingly returning to their own seemingly mundane matters. No longer dumbstruck Christina chirped, 'A study session with *Raphael*? What's up with your sink? Wow Eleanor, what on *earth* have you been up to?'

It was Eleanor's turn to blush. The colour rose to her hot cheeks, refusing to shift for the next few minutes whilst Jack rocked his soda bottle back and forth in agitation. He muttered, 'You could have called me. I'd have been there like a shot.'

Momentarily lost for words Eleanor soon found herself justifying her actions. 'I would have told you guys except you weren't around – it really wasn't a big deal.' Eleanor forced a small laugh in an unsuccessful attempt to shake off her escalating embarrassment.

Refusing to be pacified Christina continued in full-on mocking mode. 'It *is* a big deal Eleanor. It's a *huge* deal when Raphael's concerned. That's the equivalent of having, like the Pope at your house. You're so luck-'

Jack's barbed comment, heavy with incredulity was enough to momentarily hush Christina. 'You're comparing Raphael to the Pope..? You've *got* to be kidding me? That's seriously crazy chat, not to mention downright blasphemous too.'

Christina playfully snapped back, 'Oh come on Jack, I didn't mean it like that! You're so easy to wind up, blasphemy's never bothered you before! And Elle, what I *meant* to say about Raphael is that it *is* sort of a big deal. The guy doesn't talk to anyone. I think someone's crushin' on someone...'

Eleanor reached over to playfully smack Christina whilst trying to refute the claim in vain. 'NO. No. Noooo. It's not like that at all, I promise. I'm not into the whole dating thing. Raphael's just a great study partner. I know we didn't hit it off to begin with, but I suppose he's alright.'

Christina chuckled. 'The lady doth protest too much methinks! And FYI, he's more than a bit of alright! Katherine, need some back-up here chick!'

Grabbing his bags, Jack stomped off towards the library. Christina continued teasing as an entertained Katherine looked on. 'Come on, it's only us girls now. What's he really like? What do you guys chat about? Come on Elle, tell tell tell!'

Eleanor wanted to make her grilling session as painless as possible whilst satisfying Christina's growing curiosity. Instead of having information awkwardly extracted, Eleanor judiciously decided to volunteer the basics. She said lightly, 'I don't *really* know him that well. He seems cool.'

Christina raised an eyebrow. 'Ohhh, he's cool now, huh?'

'He's actually pretty quiet. You were right about him knowing his stuff, he's one brainy guy. I'm talking Stephen Hawking clever. He stayed for dinner and-'

'He stayed for *dinner*..? You've gotta spill?!'

Eleanor smiled with a hint of exasperation. 'What's with you repeating everything I say?' Nonetheless she squirmed her way through the myriad questions, only half listening whilst thinking about Raphael. His unanticipated approach was the exploratory beginning of a solid friendship and Eleanor intuitively felt she had found a genuine friend. His earnest tone had filled her with unexpected warmth and despite the pressure of a few dozen staring eyes, she had felt protected under Raphael's gaze. Gathering her bags in a cheery daze, Eleanor found herself looking forward to the Friday lecture. Not only could she study one of her favourite subjects all day, but she would also get to see Raphael. Relations were no longer in the Cold War stage; they were decidedly thawed and mutual respect seemed to have been borne out of a mere misunderstanding.

She arrived early for her Friday lecture sitting on the same work-bench as Christina, Serena and Jack. Declining a Twix offered by Serena, Eleanor pulled out a throat pastille and swirled it around her mouth. Ever since her icy shower that weekend, she had been plagued with a stuffy cold and sore throat. Eleanor hated illness and considering it to be an abominable waste of time, wondered what it would be like to never be ill. Although in conversation with her friends, her meandering mind only heard various snippets of chatter.

'Oh look, Raphael's coming over to sit with us.'

Eleanor's head snapped upwards as she quickly scanned the room. Raphael was nowhere to be seen. Christina burst out laughing. 'Gotcha! Only Raphael's name caught your attention. Why oh why might that be..?'

Eleanor opened her mouth to speak but was beaten by Jack, whose light-hearted comment seemed incongruous with his unsympathetic expression. 'You should know better Elle. There is *no way* Raphael would come to sit with us. His "Lone Ranger" routine is weird but hey, each to their own. You really into him?'

Crunching on her pastille in disappointment whilst trying to sound unbothered Eleanor said, 'Nope, I'm not into anyone. Raphael's not even my type.'

Jack seemed decidedly perkier. Serena simply laughed and said, 'How can Raphael *not* be your type? Oh, speak of the devil, here he comes.'

Eleanor looked up as Mr Berlis entered the room followed by Raphael. He headed straight for his usual seat on the second row without making eye contact with anyone. The lecture was soon underway and two hours flew by as Mithraism and curse-tablets took centre stage.

Scribbling her final notes on older cults, Eleanor promised to join her friends for their usual Friday night at the Student Union bar and glanced around the room. Eager to start the weekend, most of the students had left on time, yet Eleanor hung back for a few more minutes. As Raphael gathered his books, she noticed they were the sole occupants of the lecture theatre, just like last week. Edging forward she tapped him lightly on the shoulder.

He turned around, his eyes keenly appraising her before he said, 'Hey. I was going to text you later. You still OK to meet tomorrow at mine? Shall we say 3:00pm?'

'Yep that works for me. You live in central London, right? If you just text me the address, I can punch it into my Sat-nav. My sense of direction is sort of sucky.'

'I'm not far from Westminster actually. I'll text my address later. Any problems, give me a shout.' Shoving his hands into his pockets he continued hesitantly, 'What are you doing now? I just wondered if you wanted to go-'

His eyes hovered over her bag that now held her loudly buzzing phone. Lost in thought as she wondered what Raphael was going to ask her, it took Eleanor a few seconds to acknowledge the source of the noise. Slapping the phone to her ear, she heard Jack bellowing over rowdy revellers, 'HEY ELLE, WHERE THE HELL ARE YOU?! Get your butt down to the SU, it's buy one drink, get *two* free night! I'll line up some JD for you, it'll do your cold some good! See you SOON!' He hung up as quickly as he had spoken, the loud conversation undoubtedly heard by Raphael a few yards away.

Heading towards the door Raphael said coolly, 'You need to go. See you tomorrow.'

She was taken aback by his mercurial response; he had been on the verge of asking her something, now he couldn't get rid of her fast enough. She said brightly, 'You were saying something before Jack called?'

'It's nothing. You need to g-'

Eleanor blinked, reiterating calmly, 'What were you going to say..?'

He stared at her clutching her bag as she waited patiently for his response. He seemed to check himself as he said, 'Nothing. I was going to grab a bite to eat, that's all. Your friends are waiting for you.'

Eleanor smiled and shook her head. 'The bar will still be there in a few hours time. Where are we going for dinner?'

His deep-lidded gaze swept the window and the sky suddenly seemed brighter. 'You sure? It's a nice Italian place not far from here.'

She beamed to say, 'You had me at Italian. I'll text Jack to let him know I'll be late.'

Walking out of the room together, she contemplated how much could change in a week. From disliking Raphael intensely to now accompanying him to dinner, she was filled with joyful optimism at the unexpected turn of events. Walking in comfortable silence for a few minutes, Eleanor felt paradoxically at ease, yet simultaneously on edge.

The crisp October afternoon accentuated Eleanor's chill as she found herself shivering in the cold bright sunlight. Raphael ground to a halt. Suddenly frowning he said, 'You're cold. Why didn't you say? Take my coat.'

She declined with a grateful smile, 'I'm OK thanks. This autumn sunshine's deceiving or what? My bad, wish I'd worn something warmer, especially since I think I've got a chill. The heating at home's been erratic since the crappy sink debacle. Can't wait for the summer though. Hey, what's your favourite season?'

Eleanor missed the flash of confusion on his face as he said, 'You were still cold? All seasons melt into one for me. Take my coat. I don't need it. Feel my hand, see?' His hot hand covered hers entirely, his lean fingers gently resting on her cool palm before he whisked his hand away in a flash. Eleanor immediately missed the temporary heat. Feeling as if a deliciously warm liquid had been poured onto her skin, she revelled in the fleeting moment of sheer comfort.

Peeling off his coat to drape it around her shoulders, he waited for her to button up. Her protestations remained trapped in her throat as she caught his heady scent of invigorating forest fern. Eleanor suddenly wanted to wear the coat. Pushing her arms through the sleeves of his midnight blue woollen trench coat, her goose-bumps vanished as warmth flooded her insides. Feeling as if she had just been given a big bear hug, she couldn't help but smile.

Looking down at the lapel to check where the asymmetrical buttons came together she said, 'No kidding you're warm, this coat's way toasty! These button-holes are fiddly tho-'

As she struggled with the buttons he stepped forward to face her. Pulling both sides of the coat inwardly closer to her, he found four buttons around her waist and deftly fastened them. Moving his way up, he found three more on her lapel, hooking them just as quickly. Immediately backing away he waited a few long seconds before saying, 'The restaurant isn't far.'

A suddenly flushed Eleanor murmured a grateful thank you. Making a conscious effort not to look directly at him, she glanced around instead to observe unfamiliar surroundings. The short walk from campus had brought them to a picturesque suburb across the road from a sprawling park. Instinctively feeling homesick, she recalled the open green spaces of Manchester. Quickening her step, she failed to notice Raphael had stopped in his tracks. He said somewhat offhandedly, 'It's a nice park. I think you'll like it.'

He had obviously sensed her homesickness and Eleanor wondered if she would ever stop missing home. The greenery had an immediate calming effect on Eleanor. They entered the park to wander in contented silence. Happy and free in the open space, she broke away from Raphael to instinctively make her way to a water feature up ahead. Mounds of petrol blue and biscuit coloured pebbles lay at the foot of a large spherical granite structure. Glistening water illuminated by the sunlight, flowed from the top to lightly gush over the pebbles. Marvelling at the eye-catching focal piece she said, 'It's gorgeous! Do you come here often?'

He seemed pleased by her reaction. 'As often as I can. I came across it some time ago. I find it peaceful.'

Eleanor could imagine herself whiling away the hours in the serene park. She said in breathless awe, 'Wow, this is Dalai Lama peaceful. It's like time has stood still.' Heaving a contended sigh, she looked around and spied some swings on her left. Before she could say anything, he cocked his head in the direction of her gaze to say, 'Dinner can wait, swings can't.'

She was soon sitting on the nearest swing and soaring through the sky, brimming with child-like excitement. The steadily increasing momentum filled her with a delicious thrill and she felt she had taken flight on a wondrous journey where nothing mattered. Her heart rate quickened with the sudden descent on the downward dip, whilst the wind whipped stray strands of hair onto her face. Still exultant, she closed her eyes for a few minutes to eventually slow down. She opened her eyes to find Raphael studying her from an adjacent stationary swing.

Lost in the excitement she had forgotten her whereabouts. Realising he had been watching her filled her with a thrill of a different sort. Suddenly self-conscious, she looked skywards as the adrenalin rush kicked in. She said gleefully, 'I love the swings! Even more than chocolate, it's the most natural high! For a few minutes, I'm as free as a bird without a care in the world. Can you imagine what it would be like to fly through the sky? Must be exhilarating, don't you think?'

Raphael simply said, 'I can only imagine.' Lush greenery and abundant oak trees emphasized the serene stillness of the park. She peered at Raphael who was apparently unaffected by the intense glare of the sun.

The park was one of the last places she had expected Raphael to frequent. He just didn't strike her as a park-person, although she quickly conceded she didn't really *know* what a park-person looked like. She slowly realised they had more in common than just their Ancient History degree. Apart from food, music and passion for Latin Epigraphy, she soon found herself wondering what other interests they shared.

She suddenly knew they were going to be good friends. She struggled to understand her prescient thought, all the while feeling their bond growing stronger by the minute. She likened their organic, burgeoning relationship to a newly planted seedling, brimming with promise and untold potential. Currently latent, it would blossom into something exquisitely beautiful, growing till it reached and surpassed the lofty heights of the surrounding oak trees.

She had an unexpected urge to tell Raphael about her ex-boyfriend. She always felt uncomfortable talking about her ex, mainly because she thought she should be over him. She couldn't explain why she wanted to tell Raphael about Michael when she hadn't even told her friends.

Gently swaying on the swings she said, 'Thanks for bringing me here, it's über peaceful.' She paused deep in thought whilst tracing the metal links with her fingers. 'I've not really been myself lately. I split from Michael – my boyfriend – nearly two months ago and I just *can't* get over it. Don't know why I'm telling you this. Crazy, considering we barely know each other...'

Looking ahead Raphael listened in silence. He appeared to mull something over before saying, 'You will get over him. Don't force it. The heart always wants what it cannot have. You're probably talking to me because you don't talk about Michael anywhere else. That's your release. It's easier to talk to a stranger. They won't judge you. And neither will I.'

Eleanor felt a sudden burst of affection for Raphael. Somewhere deep down, she knew he was right. Setting herself unrealistic targets in wanting to get over Michael as quickly as possible, she had found her mind and heart doing battle on a daily basis. She suddenly decided to let herself think freely of Michael and was surprised by how quickly she felt relieved. She said in a half-whisper, 'You're right. I set myself these idealistic targets, which I naively thought I could keep. The only person I wound up disappointing was myself.' She trailed off, lost in contemplation before willing herself to be upbeat. 'I'm not normally this serious. God knows what you must think. I'm usually more positive, honest. I've just not been myself.'

Raphael turned round to face her with solid words of reassurance. 'No-one's judging you. You're your own harshest critic. Give it time. And for the record, you're fine just the way you are.'

She held onto the cool metal chains for longer, which suddenly felt good in her hot hands. Catching sight of her watch she exclaimed, 'Can you believe it's been two hours? Feels more like twenty minutes!' Her announcement of the time seemed to spur Raphael into action as he quickly got up and motioned to the exit of the park. Chatting away, they made the short walk to the restaurant down the road.

It was a quaint Italian joint, busy with diners yet quiet enough to hold a conversation without having to shout. Seated towards the back, they enjoyed a dinner of garlic bread and risotto whilst the conversation was relaxed and easy. Eleanor found herself not wanting to leave the cosy confines of the restaurant. When a waiter proffered a dessert menu, Raphael looked questioningly at Eleanor. Quickly casting her eye over the menu, she was momentarily torn between trying to be healthy and give in to temptation. Eleanor hated her sweet tooth which had plagued her since childhood. When most children wished for the latest computer game, gadget or Disney doll, a young Eleanor dreamt of being locked in a bakery to eat all kinds of cakes and pastries without interruption.

She whispered naughtily, 'Ooh, Devil's Chocolate Cake thanks. Take it you're not a dessert guy?' When Raphael shook his head, the unassuming waiter nodded and whisked away the menus. Eleanor whispered naughtily, 'I know, I'm going straight to hell, I'm not even going to *think* about the calories! Hey, you sure you don't want any?'

He seemed amused as he said, 'I'm good thanks.' As an afterthought he added, 'And I can't see you in hell. You don't strike me as the sort.'

Eleanor grinned back. She reviewed her newly arrived dish and tucking into the gooey slice, took her first mouthful of decadently moist sponge. 'It's heavenly. How can something with a negative name taste this gorgeous?'

Raphael merely shrugged and motioned with an indiscreet nod for the waiter to bring the bill. They were soon outside the restaurant. Raphael glanced upwards at the darkening sky before turning to face her. A content Eleanor, warm from the glow of good food and company said with growing reluctance, 'OK, I'm off now.'

Spying his coat in his hand she smiled. 'I won't need your coat, it's only a short walk. Besides, if I get chilly tonight, I've got a foolproof exercise to keep the cold at bay. I'll just put on four layers of jumpers and pretend for an hour that I'm a conductor of an imaginary twenty one piece orchestra.' Seeing his confused expression she laughed to say, 'It really works! Those conductors burn a hell of a lot of calories frantically waving their arms around. OK I need to stop waffling. Just to say thank you for dinner. And listening. See you tomorrow.'

He was openly amused by her rambling as he slowly stepped forward. Draping his coat over her shoulders he murmured with a ghost of a smile on his lips, 'Goodbye Eleanor.' Turning on his heel he started walking in the opposite direction.

She watched him for a few minutes before remembering she had somewhere to be. Walking briskly to the Student Union, she caught the sudden aroma of forest fern. Pulling the coat tighter around herself, she smiled in anticipation of their second study session together.

# 7 RAPHAEL'S PAD

Eleanor awoke the following day and let her alarm ring through. Stretching diagonally across the full length of the warm bed, she snuggled deeper into her duvet to lap up the lazy weekend feeling.

She knew she had had the most delicious dream, yet she was annoyingly unable to remember much of it. She recalled being blissfully happy and in awe of something or someone, as fragments flitted through her mind, like flickers of road signs seen from a 200mph train. She smiled as nebulous flashbacks of the previous night bombarded her sleep-fuzzy brain. Sharing the Student Union stage with Serena to karaoke was a breakthrough for Eleanor, who had spent the past few months shying away from attention of any kind. Like a dismantled jigsaw, pieces of her were being slotted back into place and she felt a little bit of her old, confident self slowly returning.

Thinking through myriad outfit combinations whilst enjoying a long hot shower, she eventually plumped for skinny jeans and sweetheart emerald jumper. With a quick spritz of Dior, she ran downstairs for her weekly fix of *James Martin's Saturday Kitchen*. Quickly pouring herself a bowl of cornflakes, she perched on the couch and flicked on the TV to see the heavenly chef work his magic in the kitchen.

Eleanor adored everything about James Martin, from his delectable dishes to his broad northern accent which reminded her of Manchester. Usually within five minutes of listening to his dulcet tones, the routine ache of homesickness would set in. Today, his voice was simply soothing. Realising her homesickness had eventually dissipated filled her with an inspirational charge of positivity. She felt getting over Michael was a tangible possibility and suddenly felt buoyant as Raphael's words flitted through her mind. As she recalled his determined demeanour, she was instilled with delicious bubbles of optimism and was soon floating in another daydream. She failed to notice three different TV programs had passed before realising she was staring at a series of nondescript moving images.

Realising she didn't have to leave for another few hours, she wandered over to the bookshelf. Picking up her battered copy of The Count of Monte Cristo, Eleanor was soon engrossed in the tribulations of Edmond incarcerated at the Chateau D'Ilf. She loved the thought provoking narrative and wondered what it would be like to have no freedom. What would she do if she was in exile? Would it make her stronger?

She was quickly pulled out of her musings by Raphael, who texted his address and PIN code. Edmond's predicament faded into oblivion as she leapt from the couch to shove the bookmark on the wrong page before setting off for his house.

Eleanor found the drive curiously long and contemplated skipping a set of lights just to arrive at her destination faster. She was a safe driver and had never before been reckless, yet now she felt impelled to speed up her journey. She felt the pull in her gut like a magnet, but towards what she was unsure. Curiosity bugged her, like an unseen hand consistently tapping her shoulder for attention as she wondered why she was feeling more energetic with each passing minute. Trying to shake off her questioning psyche, she wound down the window to enjoy the bracing breeze.

Eventually pulling into Watling Street at Raphael's address, she glanced upwards at the imposing mammoth glass structure. Butterflies fluttered in her stomach as she paused at the entrance. The ground floor doors softly slid open and she found herself in a striking atrium.

Alternating burgundy and grey Sicilian slates lined the vast floor and far end of the wall. An OLED TV mounted above a steep vacant reception desk silently streamed Sky news, which was the only movement in the quiet building. Eleanor was still for a few moments as her eyes travelled several hundred feet upwards to rest on a gargantuan glass dome. She suddenly felt very small, as if she was being scrutinised under a giant microscope.

Entering the lift which remained motionless, it took her a few seconds to realise the PIN code Raphael had texted earlier was for lift access. Her mouth was inexplicably dry, which seemed to get drier still with her growing eagerness at seeing him. Her hand hovered over the keypad as she wondered why she couldn't wait to see him. It was only Raphael, someone who she didn't even like until a few days ago. There was no reason for her strange excitement and shaking away her silly unformed thoughts, punched in the PIN. The keypad came to life as FLOOR 40 flashed across the glossy LED and the lift silently shifted into action.

When the lift doors eventually parted, she spied Raphael at his open door. He was waiting for her. Leaning with one arm on the door-frame, he motioned her inside the flat with a glimmer of a smile.

It was an impressive apartment with ceiling to floor windows. The light streaming in accentuated the décor, a fusion of the traditional with a shot of extravagant elegance. On a minimalist white canvas, framed Italian artwork adorned the walls to provide splashes of colour. The teak flooring was covered with an enormous amber rug. Her eyes travelled around the apartment filled with contemporary bespoke furniture. Laughing lightly she said, 'Not your usual student digs then? Oh and here's your coat. Thanks very much, it kept me très toasty.'

His fingers gently dusted hers as he took the heavy garment from her. Casually throwing the coat in the direction of the stand where it landed neatly on the hook he said, 'How was the SU last night? Have fun?'

Still feeling the delightfully warm trail of his fingers Eleanor placed her bag down and laughed. 'It was pretty awesome, I actually did the karaoke, can you believe that? Next thing you know, I'll be auditioning on a cheesy talent show whilst proclaiming "singing is my life's *passion*" in the futile hope of being signed up by an amoral svengali!' She willed herself to stop rambling and said casually, 'Hey, you should come out with us sometime. The SU's fun!'

He moved further into the room. 'It's not really my scene. Would you like a drink?'

Her mouth was still dry, her uncomfortable thirst increasing by the minute as she rambled on. 'I feel like a camel, I'm that parched. Put me in a desert and I'm sure I'd fit right in. Don't know what's wrong with me. Um, yeah, water would be nice.'

He bit down a smile before disappearing into the kitchen, emerging with a pitcher of water and glasses which he placed on the granite-topped table near the window. Taking the corner seat near her, they settled down to study with their papers fanned out in organised chaos.

The evening wore on as they leant over books to study. Having finished their separate projects along with a joint report for Mr Berlis, they simultaneously closed their study books with victorious grins. Raphael stared at the cover of his book for a few seconds. He said quietly, 'Our last study session together.' He was silent for a few more seconds before continuing adroitly. 'It's been productive. And I've enjoyed myself. Listen, I was thinking-' He paused again, his gaze flickering in her direction before settling back on his book. 'What time do you have to get back? Stay- if you like..?'

Eleanor realised she wasn't actually hungry yet found herself saying, 'Yaay to food, what have you got?'

The corner of his mouth twitched into a smile as he disappeared into the kitchen, leaving Eleanor sitting in the open plan lounge. Gathering her books into a neat pile, Eleanor wandered over to the massive window. The rooftop as spacious as the floor of a small car-park, was accessible via a window panel on her left. She imagined the breathtaking view of watching a sunrise from the rooftop and wondered if she would ever see it from his apartment. Maybe one day she would. But that would entail her staying over at his place. Quickly shaking her head before preposterous thoughts could form, she ambled into the kitchen to find Raphael studying the contents of an open fridge.

Pushing the door open wider he said earnestly, 'Stir-fry, gnocchi, salad and panini. Or would you prefer something else?'

Eleanor glanced around the large showroom kitchen. An array of electrical appliances lined the spotless work-tops. Her eyes travelled over the espresso machine, bread-maker, an indistinguishable heavy-duty gadget and finally came to rest on the slick smoothie-blender. Sweeping her fingers across the cool stone work-top she said, 'Jeez Raphael, you've got enough gizmos to make Jamie Oliver proud! Oh and a panini with salad sounds great. Can I help?'

He handed her a small truckle of cheese to grate. Starting on the salad he said, 'Food shouldn't be long. What's your poison, Rosé, right?'

Eleanor usually found Rosé to be a safe option yet today she was feeling particularly adventurous. 'Hmm, I fancy a change. Surprise me Raphael.'

He regarded her with a curious smile. 'A change huh? I have a nice 1947 Château Cheval Blanc just begging to be opened. How about a drink before dinner on the rooftop?'

She nodded with an eager smile and soon they were drinking on the balcony. He propped the wine bottle next to his glass, leaning with one elbow on the balcony ledge. Glancing back at the apartment she said, 'Can I just say again how gorge your apartment is? Rent must cost you a fortune!'

Taking an elongated gulp he said, 'The place belongs to my father.'

'Well, he must *really* trust you, the artwork alone costs a fortune! I think your dad knows you well enough to think you won't pull an Ozzy Osbourne and trash the place. Don't you just love it when parents actually *get* you? My mum's like that too.'

He said tightly, 'I doubt your mother is anything like my father.' Appearing momentarily torn he continued in a more measured tone, 'This place isn't that big a deal. Money is not an issue for my father.'

Eleanor had the oddest feeling Raphael did not want to talk about his family. Deciding not to broach the subject she continued casually, 'Hey this wine's pretty good. I'm generally not a fan of red, but it's actually quite nice. Good call.'

Raphael turned around. With his back to the apartment, he held the railing with arms outstretched and looked out ahead. 'Families can be difficult.' He paused again as he said in a slightly upbeat tone, 'Thought you'd like the wine. It's very you.' Catching her confused expression he explained, 'It has an intense flavouring with a light zesty undertone.'

He moved closer. Curling his fingers around her glass so that they overlapped hers he said, 'Swirl the wine around for a few seconds. Inhale. Close your eyes and take a sip.' He lightly pushed her hand in gentle circular motions as the blood red liquid sloshed around the glass walls.

After a few long seconds his hand returned to the balcony ledge. Trying her best to focus on the wine and not his fingers, she said with a smile, 'My first wine-tasting, move over Olly Smith!'

She lowered her nose into the swirling glass. Closing her eyes, she inhaled and took a small sip. Complete darkness heightened her sense of smell and she quickly ascertained a woody base. Taking a deeper breath, she concentrated on the liquid inches away from her nose.

The sudden burst of flavours had her temporarily gobsmacked as she exclaimed breathlessly, 'The strawberries are really coming through. Oh, there's a hint of orange. And some cherries too.' She had her eyes still closed and continued to revel in her newfound sense.

Feeling increasingly mellow with the wine, she took another liberal sip and smiled to say, 'Wouldn't it be great to be a wine-taster? I suppose you'd have to have a strong constitution and not be affected by hangovers! And I didn't know you were a wine expert. This wine is amazing.'

He was now looking down over the balcony edge. His eyes flickered once in her direction. Seeing her happy he flashed a half-smile as he said, 'I'm no expert. I just read a lot. Red wine imbues the drinker with a pronounced warmth. As you're perpetually chilly, I thought... I thought it would suit you.'

Eleanor burst into laughter. 'Yeah, I'm nearly always freezing, story of my life. Being a northerner, you'd think I'd be immune to this cold weather! Although this wine is doing a fairly good job of keeping me warm. I don't actually feel cold anymore.'

Following his gaze, she peered over the stone railing and realised how far up they were. Eleanor had a love for heights since childhood. She remembered watching Hitchcock's Vertigo with horror, mainly because she couldn't understand how anyone could be petrified of heights and be denied a stunning birds-eye view.

Her eyes travelled back up to the magnificent London skyline, with the grand dome of St Paul's cathedral in the far distance and the spires of Tower Bridge towards the left. Eleanor was momentarily lost gazing at the breathtaking view. Happy and content she suddenly remembered her dream earlier that day.

In her dream, dusk had set. She was magically flying through the skies. Green mountains provided a striking backdrop whilst thick ribbons of dazzling fjords lay below. She was toasty warm in Raphael's coat and was acutely aware she was not alone. Someone was holding her hand. She realised Raphael had been flying with her. Stopping mid-air as if treading water, she smiled as he unbuttoned her coat. Pulling her closer he leaned in to kiss her. As his mouth descended on hers, she had woken up from her dream.

She was back to reality on the balcony. Taking another sip of wine she realised with growing dismay that the object of her inappropriate dream was standing right beside her. The dream had felt as real as the cool glass she held in her hand. And when he had leant in to kiss her, she had waited expectantly.

She cleared her throat and quickly shook her head. Her mind felt like the retro Etch-a-Sketch toy, where a shaken receptacle would erase the image. Except the toy did not work. The image of Raphael kissing her was frozen in her mind's eye.

Suddenly awash with stifling embarrassment, she was silently thankful that he didn't know what she was thinking. Pouring a top-up into both their glasses he said, 'Last glass before dinner, I promise.'

She mumbled her thanks and couldn't help notice he was grinning. Wondering what could have amused him, she followed him inside as they settled to eat. The food was delicious. Fresh bread loaded with tangy Wenslydale cheese made the sandwiches all the more delectable, whilst melt-in-the-mouth buffalo mozzarella complemented the crunchy salad. Eleanor said, 'This tastes yum! Take it you like cooking?'

He said with a proud nod, 'Glad you liked it.'

Conversation came easily during dinner and continued to flow long after. Suddenly glancing at her watch Eleanor said begrudgingly, 'It's getting late, I should go. Got absolutely tonnes to do tomorrow. Raphael, thank you for dinner, it was delish!'

'Hey, it was great having you over. We can still study together, you know. The only difference being, next time round, no-one will be forcing you to study with me.' Catching her embarrassed face he said gently, 'Come on, it was obvious you didn't want to work with me.'

Eleanor couldn't help but grin back. 'OK, it's true! But you're a cool study partner. I feel we know each other a bit better. And that's always a good basis for friendship, right?'

His smile didn't reach his eyes. 'Studying with you has been... fun.'

Eleanor laughed out loud and gathering her books, slung her bag over her shoulder. Following her to the door he said hesitantly, 'Wait. I almost forgot.' He disappeared into the kitchen and returned with a large brown box which he thrust into her hands. 'Here.'

When realisation struck what he had handed her she squealed, 'Woah! Sciolti chocs?! Oh Raphael, you shouldn't have!'

He said a little awkwardly, 'It's the least I could do after trashing your originals. And for the record I am glad Mr Berlis made us study together. Just so you know.' He seemed on the verge of saying something else but instead nodded curtly. 'Goodbye Eleanor.'

Genuine affection swelled inside her as she cradled the chocolates, watching him disappear as the lift doors sandwiched shut. As the lift passed different floor levels, she felt their relationship had reached a new stage too as they were slowly becoming familiar with each other.

Settling into bed that night her flying dream resurfaced. Instead of restraining herself she allowed her mind to roam free. She wondered for the first time what it would be like kissing Raphael. Eleanor was soon fast asleep. If someone had been watching her, they would have seen that she had fallen asleep with a smile on her lips.

# 8 TURNING POINT

Glancing at the calendar on her bedroom wall, Eleanor couldn't quite believe she had spent a full month at university. Having settled into a routine of studying and socialising, she rarely thought about Michael. Although the constant barrage of work and deadlines kept her busy, she was also acutely conscious of the swift passage of time. Nearly halfway through her first year, the thought of being only five semesters away from a degree filled her with an odd sense of apprehension and excitement.

She imagined her post-university life as archaeologist extraordinaire, leading a dig in a far away land. Her meandering mind placed her knee-deep in an excavation site as she unearthed historical treasures from centuries ago. She would only visit England once a year to touch base with friends and family for Christmas vacation. During her myriad musings she never envisaged a boyfriend as part of the picture. Michael too was a fading shadow as her dependency on him decreased each day.

She was hanging out more frequently with Raphael, whose reclusive attitude didn't seem to apply to her. He would catch up with her post lecture where he sometimes walked with her to her next class or to the Student Union. He never entered the Student Union and whenever Eleanor invited him, he always swiftly declined.

Studying took up a huge chunk of Eleanor's life and she was happy that her hard work was coming to fruition. The Praeneste report which Eleanor and Raphael co-authored earned them a highly respectable grade A. Glancing at the paper which Mr Berlis placed on her desk whilst doing his rounds, she read his scrawled writing with glee: *'Incisive report, wonderful in-depth study of Praeneste. Great team effort!'*

Grinning at the comment, she looked across at Raphael seated on his bench. He simultaneously cast a backward glance to make eye contact with Eleanor. With his mouth curving into the faintest of smiles he nodded his head in a congratulatory gesture, whilst an ecstatic Eleanor mouthed back, '*Well done.*'

Christina nudged Eleanor's elbow and whispered mischievously, 'Seriously Elle could you *be* any more transparent?' Serena simply smiled with an all-knowing look, while Jack seemed disinterested and continued to scribble idly into the margin of his notebook.

The exams pushed Eleanor and Raphael closer as they spent an increasing amount of time studying over weekends. She loved watching him in the midst of study and sometimes caught surreptitious glances of his face as he studied with furrowed brow. She often found herself wondering what he was thinking and also thought it odd, that whenever he flitted through her mind, he would casually look up at her with what she imagined to be a hint of a smile.

Flicking through her phone calendar during one of their study sessions at his house, she realised they were nearing the end of the first semester. She stared at the revision timetable she had just drawn up, the whole month polka dotted with numerous study sessions. She murmured in contemplation, 'Gosh it's nearly December. Manchester beckons...' Raphael's gaze broke away from his book. With an apologetic smile she said, 'Sorry, I talk aloud a lot. Must be annoying to hear my random mutterings.'

'You get used to it. What about Manchester?'

Leaning over to show him the revision schedule on her phone she said, 'I was thinking how it's nearly end of term. Can't wait to go home and see Mum. Hey, how are you spending Christmas vacation?'

Raphael said carefully, 'I don't really celebrate it. Take it you do?'

Eleanor loved Christmas and found it to be the singular aspect which made the winter season bearable. Christmas reminded Eleanor of her childhood. Remembering her first one aged six years old, she had woken up one frosty December morning and sprinted downstairs to discover a bulging stocking packed with treats and numerous presents nestled against the decorated tree. Growing up, she would help her mum adorn the gigantic tree which took up one full section of the lounge. As she got older, decorating the tree had evolved into a more grown-up affair. Her mum would have a gently simmering pot of mulled cider in the kitchen and as the delicious aroma of cinnamon and cloves permeated the house, they would spend the afternoon decking the tree. Taking a break from the festive decoration amidst much merriment, they would indulge in home-made mince pies with thick brandy cream, before surveying their handiwork in the cosy glow of the fairy lights.

Revelling in the sudden warmth of the delightful memories she answered enthusiastically, 'Yeah, we've celebrated Christmas as far back as I can remember. It's my favourite time of year actually. It's just a shame how commercialised it's become. The supermarket in town started selling mince pies in *August*, can you believe that?' She laughed lightly to say, 'Rant aside, I love Christmas and a white one would be truly fab, although that hasn't happened in a long time.'

He seemed amused by her child-like eagerness. 'So when do you head up north?'

'Not till the very last day. I've got a few weeks to cram some study sessions in. We're meeting at mine next time, yeah?'

Returning back to study, it was a few hours later that Eleanor placed her book face down with a weary sigh. Staring at the numerous books strewn across the table heightened her disquiet as she said, 'I'm all studied out and there's still a tonne to get through. Think I just need a bit of fresh air to clear those cobwebs. Mind if pop outside for a bit?'

Raphael nodded and continued reading as Eleanor stepped out onto the balcony. Thinking of the upcoming weeks, she tried not to be overwhelmed by the heavy revision timetable which filled her mind. Thinking of her imminent visit to Manchester filled her with unease; although happy to see her mum and friends, the double edged sword was the distinct possibility she would bump into Michael. Unsure if she was over him, she didn't want to find out either. She was happy for the time being living in a study bubble and didn't want anything or anyone to rock her contented existence. Slowly pacing the balcony she glanced behind to see Raphael deep in study.

An unknown emotion stirred in her chest and for a split second she was unable to place exactly what she felt for him. She was fond of Raphael, she knew that much. She now regarded him as one of her closest friends in London and thought it strange knowing very little about him. It was a niggling feeling which she almost immediately dismissed as she continued to watch him through the glass. Being in his presence made her feel protected. He tapped the end of the pen on his lips in obvious contemplation and Eleanor felt a sudden surge of contentment as she ambled back inside suddenly lighter.

She glanced around the bright lounge, stretching her arms in a bid to re-energise herself and noticed some high shelves towards the back of the room. Various books lay stacked and walking closer to them, noticed a boxed chess-set that also doubled up as a bookend. She said inquisitively, 'You play chess? I haven't played for time..!'

His eyes flickered up to the box. Threading the pen in between his fingers in dexterous downward flips he said, 'I play, but I'm no Kasparov. I haven't played in an age.' He paused as if mulling something over before venturing, 'Fancy a quick game..?'

Eleanor nodded excitedly and watched Raphael lift the dusty box from the high shelf with ease. She was in awe of the mini-sculptures intricately fashioned from marble. Turning over the heavy pieces in her hand, she suddenly felt deadly calm ebb over her. Revision, exams, and all other immediate worries vanished as she clasped the cool marble in her hand. Studying a pawn in her hand for a few seconds, she soon replaced it on the chessboard covered in velvet so taut, a penny could have bounced off the surface. She said, 'Loving the chess-set, where on earth did you get it from? These carved pieces are amazing, they look almost human.'

He said dismissively, 'It's my father's. Collector's item. He gave it to me when I first moved here. He's an avid chess player too.'

Eleanor looked up. This was the first time Raphael had divulged a detail about his father. Not wishing to probe she simply nodded as Raphael continued coolly, 'He's a decent player.'

His voice was an odd amalgam of rebellion and melancholy. Staring at the king piece in his hand he murmured, 'I rarely see him.'

Eleanor remained quiet before saying gently, 'Well, since we played years ago, I wonder who will be worse?'

Settling down on the floor facing each other, they were ready opponents for a game of friendly combat. The warm room and plush pile of the rug made an already comfortable Eleanor even more relaxed. It was a fast-paced game from the outset. Raphael's moves were well thought out and executed with precision and he frequently pre-empted Eleanor's few surprise challenges. Having lost her queen Eleanor smiled to say, 'No *Kasparov*, you lied! I thought you said you hadn't played in ages?'

Raphael said with muted smile, 'I'm nowhere near as good as I used to be. You're not too bad yourself either.'

The game continued. Within a few minutes, Eleanor unexpectedly found herself in a leading position and grasped the opportunity to check-mate Raphael. Triumphantly punching the air she said, 'Can't believe I won! I thought I was a goner after you took my queen. See, you never know what's round the corner! Ha!'

Raphael continued to look amused and shook his head to admit defeat. A victorious Eleanor teased, 'Hey, fancy losing another game?'

Five games of chess and three hours later, Eleanor happened to glance out of the window. 'It's pitch black outside! I completely forgot about study! Can't think of a better break though!'

His eyes wandered onto the chess board and over his horizontal king. 'We've done more than our quota of studying today. Fancy just… chilling for a while? We've actually skipped lunch. Aren't you hungry?'

Eleanor smiled appreciatively. 'A bite to eat would be fab. What's on the menu at Casa Raphael today?'

After a spontaneous choice of prawn and chicken stir-fry, they started cooking harmoniously in the kitchen. It wasn't long before they had plated up two steaming dishes of noodles and were sitting facing each other at the lounge table. Warmed by the glass of Merlot which Raphael had thoughtfully poured and Strauss playing in the background, Eleanor couldn't have been happier. The conversation flowed with the wine and as the hours slipped away, Eleanor wished she could capture her contentment in a box and take it home. Time seemed to fly by faster when she was with Raphael. She could feel the seconds swirling away and half imagined standing still in the vortex of a whirlpool with a hive of activity around her.

She hated looking at her watch whenever she was with Raphael. Begrudgingly glancing at her Rolex she noted it was 11:30pm and made to get up. 'I'd love to stick around, but it's getting late and-'

Whilst getting to her feet, a head-rush suddenly rendered her unsteady. Regaining a wobblier balance, she placed her hands flat on the table. Raphael was by her side within seconds, worry flickering over his face as he demanded to know if she was OK.

Raphael was inches away from her face. Trying to blink herself more awake, it took her a few seconds to realise she was enjoying looking at his eyes from close quarters. Pools of jet black fixed on her, like deep pots of a profound black ink. The grey flecks somehow added depth to his stare and she was hushed into silence as she continued gazing at him.

'Eleanor? Are you alright?' He spoke with a pronounced urgency which oddly brought a smile to her face. His eyes continued searching hers, demanding a satisfactory answer that would allay his fears.

She smiled as the fuzzy cloud started to lift. 'I'm fine, I get head-rushes all the time. I hadn't realised the wine would get to me that much. Honestly there's nothing to worry about.'

He couldn't take his eyes of her, unease evident in his usually impenetrable eyes. He spoke tersely with a palpably apologetic air, 'Sorry about the wine. Just because I have a higher tolerance to alcohol, doesn't mean everyone else does. It was remiss of me.' He said forcefully, 'And you're not going anywhere like that. I'll drive you home.'

'Seriously Raphael, it's no big deal. I'll just sober up for a short while here, if that's OK?'

He immediately perked up, although a troubled look continued to lace his dark eyes. 'That's fine. We could just watch some TV if you like?'

Eleanor nodded and dropped onto the rug opposite the TV. Raphael reappeared with a large pitcher of water and tumbler which he placed directly in front of her on the nearby coffee table. 'Drink up.' Settling onto the rug next to her, Raphael flicked on the massive TV and handed her the remote control. 'Here. Knock yourself out.'

Eleanor smiled and was soon channel flicking through the meagre offerings of late night TV. She continued surfing the channels, waiting for a programme to grab her attention when she paused on the opening scene of Gone With The Wind. Clapping her hands in gleeful appreciation at being able to watch one of her favourite films, she looked over at Raphael to see if he minded. Judging by his nonchalant shrug, he didn't seem to be bothered by her choice. She smiled to say, 'I totally rate Clarke Gable, Sean Connery and Marlon Brando, you just can't beat them. Hey, who are your favourites?'

He was quiet as he pondered his answer. 'Clarke, Sean and Marlon are certainly heavyweights in the talent department. Rock and James are pretty high up there too.'

Eleanor looked momentarily confused. 'Huh? *Rock* and *James*..?'

'Rock Hudson and James Dean. Method actors have a certain gravitas which makes their style inimitable. There are very few actors in today's age that can even compare to those Hollywood greats.'

Eleanor smiled and found herself wholly engrossed in Raphael's observation. He spoke in a matter of fact tone, yet his remark was tinged with sorrow. It was as if he lamented on a personal level the disappearance of method actors, whilst the lack of current talent seemed to be an added insult to injury. She wondered why he sounded disappointed and suddenly realised she was staring again.

It didn't take long for her to get sucked into the film. She laughed out loud at Scarlett's coquette and longingly admired the striking costumes. Imagining swishing her way through the crowds in her corseted outfit, she was suddenly very sleepy. The last scene she remembered was Rhett assisting a mistakenly drunken Ashley indoors as she drifted off to sleep on Raphael's shoulder.

# 9 HANGOVER FROM HELL

Eleanor stirred awake. Still half asleep, she clung onto the fluffy pillow and instinctively turned away from the daylight that came streaming in through the ceiling to floor window. She felt enveloped in a silky warm cloud and revelled in the feeling of heavenly bliss. Still in the dream-like state teetering between lucidity and sleep, she opened her eyes and yawned. The room was warm, and her duvet lighter than usual.

She was suddenly conscious she wasn't in her own bed. Jolting awake as realisation struck, she quickly became aware that she was in Raphael's apartment. Pushing the duvet to one side, she sat bolt upright. She found she was still in yesterday's attire with one difference. She had acquired an additional piece of clothing. The silky warm cloud was Raphael's cashmere jumper.

Slowly rewinding the events of the previous night, she vaguely remembered a study session and several games of chess. Dinner was somewhere in between. She must have fallen asleep during the film. Looking down at the over-size duck-egg blue jumper, she smiled contentedly and waved the lengthy sleeves to and fro that hung over her arms in distracted amusement. It was only when she glanced towards the source of the sunlight, that she realised Raphael was sitting at the table. Watching her.

'And she wakes. Good morning sleepyhead.'

Eleanor blinked and immediately stopped fidgeting with the jumper as her fuzzy mind began to wonder exactly how much wine she had consumed. With unkempt hair and unwashed face, she cringed at the unflattering picture forming in her mental mirror. Trying to tame her tousled locks, she combed frantic fingers through her hair. She replied sheepishly. 'Hey Raphael. So, I fell asleep huh? You should have woken me up.' Scrunching her eyes as the inconsiderate sunlight increased its intensity, she winced to say, 'Whether it's a good morning is debatable.'

He said lightly, 'Didn't want to disturb you so I just let you sleep through. Hope the jumper kept you warm.'

'The jumper was great. I... I should go home. I'm a mess and my head feels like it's packed with a hoard of dancing pixies. Doing the Riverdance. With heavy clogs.' She swung her legs over the side of the couch. Raphael remained seated on the table facing her.

He kept his eyes on here the whole time as he said gently, 'You look fine. Fancy breakfast?'

Eleanor groaned as loudly as her mind would allow. 'Coffee would be great. Really not feeling the food as I may well see it again. Got any painkillers? Those damn pixies have just upped the ante and my head feels like its going to explode. Even my eyelashes hurt. Is that possible? Totally self-inflicted hangover. I deserve zero sympathy.'

Raphael was already on his feet. 'I'll grab some painkillers from the shops. Be back in ten.' Before Eleanor could say another word, Raphael flung on his jacket and left. Eleanor was still for a few minutes. Alone in Raphael's apartment, she leant back on the couch and closed her eyes.

Her head was still blurry as the alcohol infused cloud refused to shift, like a spoilt child putting up a fight to stubbornly stay in the chocolate aisle. Fingers of guilt stroked her conscience and she suddenly thought about Raphael rushing off to get her painkillers. Whilst she was lying on *his* couch, wearing *his* jumper, *he* had gone out to get her medicine, for an ailment that was totally self-inflicted. Forcing her brick-heavy eyelids open to survey her surroundings through narrowed slits, she wondered if there was anything she could do. Not even her hangover could stop her appreciating Raphael's beautiful, uncluttered apartment. The one anomaly was the chess-board, which remained on the coffee table from the night before.

Trying to ignore her throbbing headache, she decided to rectify the minor incongruity by putting the chess-set away. Gingerly edging off the couch, she knelt by the coffee table as her hands closed around the chess pieces. The cool marble chunks felt icy to the touch.

Eleanor held the pieces closer to her eyes. They looked and felt different, somewhat heavier, like ice-cubes in her hand. Half expecting them to melt away with the heat from her unusually hot palms, she quickly slotted them back into the box.

Clambering onto a dining chair to reach the high shelf, she accidentally pushed over a bulky book which fell to the floor with a resounding thud. With the chess box still in her hand, Eleanor dropped to the floor to retrieve the fallen object.

It was a heavy ancient book bound in sepia leather. The loose spine and faded italic writing made it look like an historical artefact. A soft coating of dust appeared to be the book's only protection, leaving Eleanor momentarily horrified she had inadvertently damaged it beyond repair.

The book had fallen open face down. Cursing her clumsiness, she carefully turned it over. Striking font filled yellow pages crisp with age. Her misty mind tried to unscramble the indecipherable lettering, which looked like a foreign archaic language. Several other sheets of paper lay strewn near her feet. They had also fallen from the book and Eleanor noted with relief they were not part of the actual book. The loose sheets had a more contemporary feel and the parchment although wan, felt heavier and less fragile. Time had not yet completely ravaged the ink intensity, making the writing easier to grasp. One of the pieces of paper appeared to be a music score, whilst lyrics filled the other two sheets. Judging from the illegible handwriting, Eleanor imagined the author to have scribbled these in a hurry. One of the sheets had been simply signed *RS* and as Eleanor continued to collect the splayed pages, she heard the front door open. Raphael was at her side within seconds.

'WHAT DO YOU THINK YOU'RE DOING?!' His guttural bellow was enough to momentarily stem her pounding headache. Startled by his angered shout, Eleanor remained frozen on the floor. He snatched the book from her hand before quickly scooping up the loose sheets. Stuffing them back into the book and replacing it on the shelf, he shoved the chess-set onto a higher shelf with swift efficiency.

It took Eleanor a few seconds to find her voice. 'Um... I'm sorry. I tried to put the chess-set away and I couldn't reach the shelf, then this huge book fell down and-'

His shadow towered over her and she quickly stumbled to her feet making reluctant eye contact. Her hammering hangover returned with a vengeance and she clutched her temples in sudden pain. Seeing her wince seemed to instantly calm him. He appeared to check himself as his stony expression slowly melted away. He said tersely, 'I got you painkillers.'

Edging towards the table where the box of paracetamol lay, she gulped two tablets and dropped onto the couch. Willing the puffy cushions to swallow her whole, she wished she hadn't touched the book. Hearing Raphael raise his voice for the first time had alarmed and scared her. For that split second, she felt he was a different person. Yet with one look into his compelling black eyes, her fear had disappeared and she was at ease again. She lolled her head on the squishy backrest for five minutes and only realised Raphael had disappeared when the scent of fresh coffee filled the apartment. He emerged from the kitchen clutching a cafétiere and plate of warm croissants which he placed on the coffee table.

'Here.' He seemed repentant as he pushed the food towards her. The painkillers worked their medicinal magic and her head already felt lighter as she sat up to take a sip of the dark, steaming liquid.

'This is what heaven tastes like. The drugs are working a treat too.' She paused to whisper sheepishly, 'Sorry if I damaged your book.'

His blank expression gave nothing away. 'Croissants?'

Eleanor nibbled on her pastry and remained quiet. She considered herself to be a boring drunk and hated company when her conversational skills were at an all time low. She just wanted to go home.

Wiping away stray crumbs with her napkin Eleanor said gratefully, 'Thanks for breakfast. Hey, how much wine did I have? You had more than me and you seem to be OK. How come you're not looking like hell? How do you handle your hangovers? Any tips gratefully received.'

For the first time since entering the flat, Raphael looked amused. Gripping his coffee cup, he said with a tight smile, 'That vintage wine was potent. It's understandable how you were inebriated so quickly. I wouldn't know how to handle a hangover as I've never had one.' He paused, watching her ashen face that was still suffering from the after effects of alcohol. 'I can imagine it to be thoroughly uncomfortable.'

Eleanor blinked, his energised and alert state heightening her obvious lacklustre disposition. She said incredulously, '*Never* had a hangover? Wow. I don't know whether to be impressed or utterly envious. How much did you have to drink to build up immunity like that? Do I even wanna know?'

A roguish smile flashed across his face as he said, 'No. You don't want to know.' A hint of sorrow lingered in his eyes, yet within moments, his uncomfortable demeanour was shrouded in a blanket of pokerfaced cool. Eleanor felt as if the curtains had come down during a theatre show, the impassable barrier purposefully restricting access. Eleanor knew she was not allowed past this point. She continued indifferently, 'You're not missing much. The joys of being human.' Unaware of him flinching she continued, 'Think I'll head home, I'm feeling a little better now. Hey, do you want a hand with the dishes?'

A barely visible smile returned to Raphael's lips. 'Do you ever stop tidying? You need to go home.'

'What? It's good to be neat!'

She slipped into her ballet pumps and clutching her bag, was soon inside the lift. He inclined his head to catch her gaze just before the doors closed. 'You could never be boring. Goodbye Eleanor.'

Walking back to her car, she couldn't recall telling Raphael that she was a boring drunk. She probably mentioned something whilst sitting on the couch in hazy inertia. She glanced at her reflection in the rear-view mirror and blushed at the red eyed scruffy image staring back. What she needed was fresh air and lots of it. Winding down the window, the light breeze did little to lift her spirits. What she really wanted was to blow away the mental cobwebs. She couldn't think of a better place than a park.

The park which Raphael had taken her to suddenly popped into her head. She remembered it not being far from campus and headed towards the university grounds. Pulling into the familiar street where they had walked a few days ago, it took her five minutes to crawl along the full length of the street. There was no park in sight, yet Eleanor was sure this was the correct street.

Knowing the park wasn't far increased her frustration. Her lethargy was making an unwelcome comeback and she reluctantly decided to drive down the street one final time. Spotting one of the residents in a garden up ahead, Eleanor pulled into a vacant spot. The old lady leaning on the gate surveyed her with idle curiosity. As the wind gently nudged her white hair, she spoke in a plummy voice, 'You look lost my dear. Can I help..?'

'So sorry to trouble you. Is there a park anywhere around here?' Eleanor waited for the shrunken lady to confirm her suspicions that she was on the wrong path. The elderly lady tilted her head to one side, as if trawling through a memory bank as thick as a telephone directory. 'Yes. Of course there's a park. It has the most beautiful water feature! It's just further down.' She pointed a wrinkly finger towards her left, two doors down. 'Even I can see it from here.'

A mystified Eleanor spun round. Her eyes travelled in the direction of the old lady's gaze and Eleanor found she was looking at an empty house. Before Eleanor could verbalise her confusion, a young man emerged from the house. 'You OK Gran?' He eyed Eleanor with suspicion as he waited for his grandmother to respond.

'I'm fine. I was just telling this lost girl about the park. You can see it from here.' Craning her neck like an adventurous turtle, she pointed again down the street and looked up at Eleanor. Her crinkly face showed signs of frustration as she said more persistently, 'It's *there*. Why can't you see it?'

The young man tenderly placed a hand on her shoulder. He said gently, 'Gran, there is no park. Come on, let's go inside.'

The old lady edged further towards the gate. '*But it's there!*' She looked back at her quiet grandson and reading the customary concern on his face, whispered, 'Oh dear. I'm getting all muddled again, aren't I? I'm... I'm sorry. Can I go inside now?'

The grandson quickly nodded. Speaking to Eleanor before leading his grandmother away, he whispered, 'Advanced Alzheimers. There hasn't been a park round here since Gran was a child. Sorry we can't help you.'

A bewildered Eleanor slowly returned to her car and remained still for a few minutes. She glanced across the street at the supposed site of the park. The blank face of the empty house stared back at her, its window-like eyes quietly surveying Eleanor as she tried to make sense of the bizarre situation. Although the old lady had been lucid when speaking about the park, the grandson had said there was no park in the area – something that Eleanor knew to be incorrect. She may have got the wrong street, but she knew the park was definitely in the vicinity. *Why would the grandson lie? Unless the park really wasn't there?*

Eleanor's head was beginning to throb again. She didn't understand how a park could disappear into thin air, yet the harder she tried, the more incomprehensible the problem seemed. Craving another painkiller, she drove home puzzled and tired, heading straight for the shower when she got in.

As the unforgiving hangover loosened its grip, snippets of the previous evening replayed in her mind. The flotsam images rose to the surface of her subconscious, to gently bob into view. She visualised herself nestled close to Raphael with her head propped on his broad accommodating shoulder. She didn't remember much else apart from his scent. The forest fern with a hint of lavender had helped her fall into the most comfortable slumber she had ever had.

She remembered Raphael watching her when she had finally arisen and wondered how long he had waited for her to wake up. As her mind continued to drift, she wondered why she had been particularly self-conscious in front of Raphael. Why was she bothered that he would see her hung-over and unkempt? A flickering fluorescent light bulb in her mind appeared to be on the verge of disclosing an otherwise closely guarded secret. Instead of producing dazzling light and shedding knowledge, it continued to sputter unsteadily, leaving Eleanor pondering why it mattered what Raphael thought of her.

The mystery of the park returned to bug her. Maybe she was in the wrong street. She hadn't really paid much attention to her whereabouts during her visit and all she really knew was that the park was near university. She had simply got the street wrong. There was no other explanation. The old lady could have been talking about any old water feature. Plenty of parks had them. She would just ask Raphael for directions to the park next time she saw him.

Her mind meandered onto the upcoming Christmas vacation. She knew that an infinitesimal part of her didn't want to leave Richmond. A tiny voice whispered, '*Why? It's not just because of Michael, right..?*' Tired of questions that she didn't know the answer to, she forced her mind blank and continued enjoying the rest of her hot shower.

# 10 FIRE-STARTER

The last week at university flew by. The biting December wind was in stark contrast to the warm and toasty indoors as tutors and students alike revelled in jovial anticipation of the holidays. Christmas cheer infused the university walls, permeating the chunky bricks to swathe its residents in a convivial cloak of cordiality.

The bulging room on Friday contained high spirited students and an equally exultant tutor, ready to welcome the start of vacation. Sitting with her friends, Eleanor watched Raphael take his usual spot near the front bench. He acknowledged her with his trademark nod and when he turned away, Eleanor forced her lingering gaze to return to the books in front of her. When Mr Berlis eventually called the lecture to an end, a sea of students poured out of the door.

Serena let out a contented sigh. 'It's been a heavy few weeks, can't wait to take it easy.'

Jack said in a playful tone, 'Vacation starts right now! The end of term SU party is gonna be epic! Why are we still here? Come on guys, we've gotta leave NOW!'

Eleanor placed half of her books in her bag and carried three in her arms. Motioning to the pile she said, 'Just gotta dump these in my locker, I'll catch up with you in a mo.'

Throwing a look of mock disgust at her books, Jack shook his head to say, 'Seriously Eleanor, you're the *only* student I know who brought in extra books for the last lecture. We're headed over to the SU now, see you there in a few mins, yeah?'

She watched him disappear and looked around to realise her and Raphael were the only stragglers. Walking to the front, she tapped him lightly on the shoulder. 'Hey Raphael! The semester's comes to an end, can you believe it? It's gone wahey too fast!'

He threw her a fleeting look as he continued packing his satchel. 'Yeah. It's been interesting.'

Eleanor said cheerily, 'A good interesting, right? Can't believe how much I've learnt. This has got to be my favourite lecture. I love Mr Berlis and I love Classical Antiquity! Geek Alert – I think I'm going to actually miss uni!'

'Love Mr Berlis, huh? I'm sure he'll be glad to hear that.' After a long pause he said casually, 'What are you going to miss about uni..?'

'I'll miss the lectures and going out in London. I'll miss-' She stopped, checking herself before continuing in a more forthright manner, 'I'll miss Richmond and my friends too.' Eleanor found her books getting heavier as his eyes continued to rest on her face. He seemed vaguely pleased and clocking his growing grin she ploughed on. 'Hey, there's a huge end of year SU party. If you fancy coming along..?'

Her upbeat manner underplayed her hesitant tone. Eleanor knew what Raphael's response would be before she asked the question. She knew he would decline, yet couldn't stop herself from asking. A heavy anchor of disappointment lay at the pit of her stomach with the thought that she wouldn't see him for over a month. Silent questions flitted through her mind. *He was just a friend – why the big deal about missing him? What was so special about Raphael?* Shaking her head free of these annoyingly perplexing thoughts, she calmly awaited Raphael's negative response.

He appeared distracted as he gathered up his books. Taking a few seconds to answer, his eyes flickered from the window behind her, to her patient face. The gentle flexing of his jaw indicated he was deep in thought and for a split second, Eleanor wondered what lay at the root of his apparent conflict. Seeming to dismiss his apprehension, he said earnestly, 'Can't make it right now. Maybe later?'

Eleanor stared in surprise at his unexpected positive response. She stammered whilst her heart did a mini back-flip, 'Um... Yeah! That would... be kinda cool!'

They walked off into the corridor, each wearing a light smile. Suddenly remembering something, she quickly swivelled round. 'Hey, I keep meaning to ask you, but somehow always manage to forget.' Raphael turned around. He looked at her expectantly, although the smile on his face had vanished.

Eleanor said earnestly, 'You know that park we went to a few weeks ago? Well I couldn't find it. It couldn't have been far from uni because we walked there. Which street was it on?' Imagining a flicker of annoyance on his face, she spoke quickly. 'Sorry to keep you, it's just that I tried to find it the other day and I couldn't. It's like it had disappeared or something. And then this old lady came out who was just as confused as I was...'

Eleanor's voice trailed off. She was suddenly unsure what point she was trying to make. All the while, Raphael continued to stare at her, waiting for her to finish. She said a little more hesitantly, 'My sense of direction is crap at the best of times. I'd obviously taken the wrong turning-'

Raphael spoke quickly. 'I'll take you next time.' He lowered his gaze to the books in his hand before edging away. He said lightly, 'It's not far from uni.' Swiftly brushing off her query with a mischievous glint in his eye, he teased, 'Don't worry, I wouldn't trust your sense of direction either.'

As he disappeared around the corner, Eleanor had an overwhelming desire to run back to him. She felt a part of her was left behind and she couldn't quite understand why. Staring at the place where he had stood a few moments ago, she reluctantly continued her detour to her locker as she wondered if Raphael would come out that evening.

It wasn't really his scene so he would most likely skip it. Trying not to think about how much she would miss him, she entered the Student Union bar in a subdued state. More obscure questions filled her mind. *Why did she feel deflated at the notion of being away from Raphael? Why did she still want to run back to him when they had said goodbye only five minutes ago?* These thoughts, like tiny metallic balls in a pinball machine, whizzed around in her head. Bouncing from one surface to another without hitting an actual target, the questions remained unanswered.

She was happy when Christina came into view. Joining her friends on the dance-floor and absorbing their contagious merry state, her earlier disquiet vanished in an atmosphere charged with fun and frolics.

Mid-way through the night, Eleanor was standing by the edge of the dance-floor in animated conversation with Jack, his arm casually draped around her shoulder whilst trying to explain the off-side rule. When Serena leaned over to tap Eleanor's hand with fevered urgency, she was momentarily distracted. Turning around, she found herself face to face with Raphael.

He was looking directly at her. His eyes lingered briefly on Jack's arm around her shoulders, before flitting back to her face. His slight frown seemed to communicate the mildest of objections. Her snowballing delight etched an elated smile across her face as she realised he had come to see her.

His casual demeanour was reflected in his outfit, with his loose khaki tee and faded blue jeans accentuating his relaxed stance. Excusing herself from Jack whose arm had dropped back to his side, she stepped forward to hug Raphael. 'You made it! Didn't think you'd come! What are you drinking?'

With loud indie music throbbing from the speakers, Eleanor leaned in to listen to Raphael's response. 'Bourbon. I'm not stopping for long. I'll get this round. Would you like a drink? What about the rest of your friends?'

Eleanor looked back at Jack who had moved away, whilst Serena, Christina and Katherine were back on the dance-floor. Serena and Christina caught her eye and flashing identical impish grins, gave her a thumbs-up.

Shaking her head whilst smiling and praying that Raphael didn't see them, Eleanor quickly turned back to Raphael. 'Looks like they're all set. Come on, let's hit the bar.'

Cutting across the dance-floor and passing the fake smoke machine near the stage, they made their way to the smaller bar at the back. It was quieter and out of the way, which Eleanor knew ensured a faster service. Raphael glanced upwards and around the packed room. He seemed on edge. His lips set in a concrete hard line as his eyes flew across the bar before honing in on the bartender. She flounced in his direction and within seconds of Raphael peeling a note from his wallet, drinks appeared on the bar. Leaving a more than generous tip for the grateful bartender, Raphael grabbed the glasses and made his way to the seating area followed by Eleanor.

Sitting opposite each other in the lurid yellow booth, Eleanor sipped her JD whilst Raphael drank his Bourbon on ice. After the first gulp he said, 'I can't stay long. I just came to-' He stopped abruptly as his eyes stayed focused on his glass. He continued more determinedly, 'I thought it would be nice to say goodbye before you head back home. I won't be seeing you till after Christmas. That's nearly a month away.'

She found sweet comfort in the fact that she wasn't the only one conscious of their month apart. Cosy joy melded with the warmth of the JD as she replied, 'I know, it'll be weird not being around you. I'll miss you! Hey, if you're ever up north, you should come visit! You got any plans over Christmas? Will you be going back home?'

He swirled his glass of Bourbon, keeping his eyes fixed on the floating chunks of ice. He answered tersely, 'No. Have fun in Manchester. It'll be good for you to see your friends.'

Eleanor smiled and nodded. 'Yeah, can't wait to see them, it'll be a cool break.' She added thoughtfully, 'Uni's such a unique experience. It's like functioning out of your comfort zone without your usual support network of friends and family, don't you think?'

A harsh smile was carved onto his face as he said, 'Sometimes the absence of a support network can be a good thing. It gives you a chance to discover your true self. That's life.'

*That's life* – they were two simple words, yet his blasé intonation belied the seemingly clear-cut phrase. His response was loaded with hidden meaning and she couldn't help but wonder what he was thinking as she sipped her drink.

Eleanor's contemplative veil was perforated by a sudden blast of music. As another rock song belted out from the mammoth speakers, she looked up to see Raphael staring in the direction of the bar. There was a roguish glint in his dark eyes and Eleanor felt a sudden tug in her gut. The fake smoke machine seemed to be in over-drive too as they found themselves surrounded by a lingering acrid mist.

The music seemed to be getting louder by the minute and making conversation from across the table was now futile. As the infectious music worked its pied piper magic, the area around their booth saw an overspill from the larger dance-floor. Within seconds, they were surrounded by fellow revellers who jostled near the booths to jump, gyrate and groove to the music.

She watched him take another gulp of his drink. The glass all but disappeared in his large hands with only the rim poking out like a glass parapet. She suddenly realised she would miss him more than any of her London friends. This recurring thought annoyingly pushed its way into her subconscious, like a greedy shopper at a New Year's Eve sale, crushing logic and reason in its wake.

As Eleanor tried to make sense of why she would miss him so much, she looked up to catch Raphael staring at her. His sudden flash of a smile filled her with a delicious electric charge and she couldn't help but grin back. He leant over the table to speak and as Eleanor edged forward to listen, she caught a flare of silver around his neck. His tee concealed most of the chain that disappeared back out of sight when he casually shrugged. She had never seen the chain before. Mesmerised by its threadlike quality, it took her a few seconds to realise that Raphael was speaking to her. 'Eleanor? Want another drink?'

Before she could answer, the DJ cranked up the music to an ear-splitting level. Mouthing 'NO', she scanned the room for a quieter spot and followed Raphael's eyes to the rear exit where smokers had congregated. Motioning her to follow him, they were soon standing directly outside the door.

Awakened by the sharp blast of cold air, she breathed in the scent of tar and nicotine which hung in the air along with her icy white breath. The deep, reassuring smell of tobacco reminded Eleanor of her grandfather smoking his pipe. She smiled in fond recollection as she was momentarily transported back to her childhood.

Unsure if it was happiness of the imminent vacation or seeing Raphael, but once outside, Eleanor was on a natural high. She was suddenly more talkative and felt like her old self, whilst he seemed less distracted too. Standing opposite each other with drinks in hand, they continued chatting as the minutes flew by. When Raphael glanced at his watch, Eleanor knew he would be leaving soon. Her question was more a half-hearted request than a statement of the obvious.

'You've gotta go, right..?' He nodded as she tried to sign off on a positive note. 'Hey, thanks for coming. It was nice to say bye. Have a great holiday! Don't do anything I wouldn't do..!'

The corner of Raphael's mouth turned upwards into a wicked smile. His gaze flickered to the exit of the Student Union before resting on her face again. He seemed relieved as he said, 'I'm glad I swung by. Hope you have a great vacation too. Keep yourself out of mischief.'

Striding forward to bid her goodbye, he circled his arms around Eleanor to envelope her in a firm hug. With her face on the lapel of his jacket, she caught the lingering scent of fragrant forest fern. Feeling his warm breath above her head, Eleanor nestled closer to him as Raphael continued in a low voice, 'Travel safely tomorrow. Have a fantastic Christmas.'

Eleanor lifted her head slightly to look at him. With just a few inches between them, his breath warmly caressed her cheek. Forcing her mind to stay clear, she smiled to say, 'Have a super duper holiday. Oh, and thanks for listening to me when I was going off on one. Hey, I'll miss ya.'

Tilting his head a little lower, his lips lightly brushed her brow. She suddenly found herself voluntarily leaning into him. His voice was just a few octaves above a whisper as he said, 'I'll miss you too.' He continued quietly, 'I've really got to go. I'm not even supposed to be here-'

A thunderous bang like the simultaneous popping of ten thousand balloons sounded from the building behind them. Raphael's head snapped to attention, his body stiffening with the abrupt noise.

A startled Eleanor turned to stare at the building. Panicked students started to pour out from the mouth of the Student Union exit. Raphael suddenly grabbed her arm as he whispered urgently, 'You need to get out of the way.'

He propelled her across the road where a crowd of students had already gathered. Eleanor stared at the thick plume of smoke emanating from the skylight. Raphael's stony face was a picture of conflict. A look of dread had settled in his eyes. He remained quiet in shadowy contemplation as he watched the scene unfold in front of him.

Eleanor suddenly remembered her friends. They were still in the building. Whizzing round to face Raphael, she made to speak. Before she could open her mouth, he said quietly, 'Don't worry about your friends. They're all out.'

Her brow furrowed deeper in confusion. 'Huh? How do you know that?'

His voice was deadly quiet. 'I can see them.' He nodded across the street. 'They're coming over.'

Serena led the way followed by Jack, Christina and Katherine. Weaving their way through the crowd they quickly found her. Standing on the pavement in a huddle Eleanor said, 'You guys OK? What on earth happened?'

Christina's clear voice was carried over the babble of voices and the piercing shrill of a cavalcade of ambulances. 'One of the pyrotechnic machines malfunctioned, which set the stage on fire. Then all hell broke loose.'

Serena added, 'All the flimsy props didn't help either. It was pretty scary actually. The initial blast got one of the bar-tender's in the face when she was taking a break near the stage.

Eleanor stared in shock. 'That's awful! Is she alright?'

Jack's red bull-alert eyes flitted over Eleanor and Raphael standing inches away from each other. He said flatly, 'She was cute too. I saw her working the smaller bar.'

Rubbing away her goose-bumps in the chilly air Katherine said, 'We saw her being stretchered into the ambulance just now. Hope she makes it.'

Glancing at the heaving crowd a resigned Jack said, 'The party is well and truly over. Unless-'

He was interrupted by an irate Katherine who snapped, 'I'm heading home, my coat was left in the cloakroom and I'm flipping freezing! There's a bunch of taxis out front.' She started walking away before pausing to shout, 'Elle, I'm staying at a friend's in Putney, wanna share a cab?'

Raphael answered for her. He barked, 'Yes she'll go with you.' He was preoccupied again as he said quietly, 'Travel safely tomorrow Eleanor.' She found herself nodding as Raphael, his arms crossed over his broad chest in moody contemplation, continued to stare at the smoky building. Within seconds, he had disappeared into the crowds as blaring ambulances sped past Eleanor and away into the night.

Running to catch up with Katherine, Eleanor turned around to see if she could catch a final glimpse of Raphael. Furiously rubbing her arms in a futile bid to keep warm, a smiling Katherine said, 'I know that look. You've got it bad. Come on missy, I've got a cab waiting!'

# 11 BACK HOME

Eleanor indulged in a lengthy daydreaming session during her drive back to Manchester. Sitting in the lounge three hours later, she waited for her mum to arrive from work whilst glancing around her recently decorated home.

Earthy terracotta replaced the neutral colour palette, beautifully offsetting the oversize canary yellow cushions strewn across the sofa. Eleanor smiled as she likened the room to herself; it was still the same, yet it felt more alive and effervescent. Her mum's arrival saw them exchange hugs and descend into an excited flurry of conversation. Running to her daughter with handbag still on her shoulder, Lucille said, 'Oh Elle, it's sooo good to see you, I've really missed you! Have you stopped eating – there's nothing left to you!'

'Missed you too Mum! Can't believe it's been nearly three months since we last saw each other. Love what you've done with the house and good call with the new Hirst painting! The Christmas tree is looking fabulous too.' She paused to continue a little crestfallen, 'Can't say I'm not gutted that I couldn't help do up the tree this year.'

Lucille narrowed her eyes and gave Eleanor a mischievous smile. 'Well, it *is* tradition that we decorate the tree together...'

Clutching the base of the tree, Lucille carefully twisted it round. With the rustling of the tinsel and the light tinkle of the glass baubles, the front of the decorated tree disappeared out of view as a completely bare side was slowly revealed. Eleanor squealed with delight. 'You only decorated half! I officially have the coolest mum! Oooh, can we decorate it now? Have you stocked up on the mulled cider and mince pies too..?' She quickly added, 'Silly question, huh?'

'Oh ye of little faith! I couldn't break the twelve year tradition of you and I jointly decorating the tree, could I? I'll start mulling the cider, the mince pies will be hot from the oven in twenty minutes and we can finish the tree together whilst you fill me in on uni.'

The next few hours were spent decorating the tree and catching up, as animated conversation was interspersed with sips of cinnamon-infused cider and mouthfuls of hot mince pie. Eleanor didn't mention the Student Union accident last night; it was futile and would only worry Lucille. Draping the last strand of golden tinsel on a protruding pine branch, Eleanor finally switched on the lights. Both stood back to review their joint work of art. The eight foot tree decked with candy, ruby red baubles and twinkling fairy lights was a sight to behold. Giving a high-five in celebration of their handiwork, they settled down for a light supper of chicken salad whilst A Christmas Carol played on the TV in the background.

Retiring to her room at nearly midnight, a tired and contented Eleanor dropped onto her bed. Nearly everything was the same as she had left it, except for a brown envelope on her study-desk. She soon realised it was the weeping willow painting which she had posted out in a fit of frustrated anger a few months ago. Discarding the envelope, she cast her eye over the artwork as a small smile escaped her lips. The painting now reminded her of Raphael. Propping up the painting on the desk she quickly unpacked and changed. Her university life was hundreds of miles away, yet in her home-town of Manchester, she oddly felt closer to it than ever. Today had been a reminder of how much she had missed her mum. It was good to be back.

Eleanor had given herself a week off before getting stuck into revision and was excited to see friends whom she hadn't seen for months. Lunching at The Retreat Bar with Valentina, Steven and Gabrielle on her second day, Eleanor concurred enthusiastically, 'Uni is awesome! The learning curve is steep, but it makes you really come into your own. I love King's College!'

Valentina nodded excitedly to say, 'It's so cool! You can rock in and out whenever you please. Plus, my timetable isn't so heavy – I *love* being a student! Which reminds me Elle – it's so good to see you back to your old self, especially after the whole Michael thing.'

Clocking her fading smile, Steven paused, unsure whether the mention of Eleanor's ex was wise. He ploughed on as he saw a gentle smile emerge on her face. 'Yeah Elle, it's great to see you happy. Not that Michael's a bad person, but the break-up was a little off.' He whispered conspiratorially, 'You can do better, we all said that.'

Eleanor found this comment mildly amusing, more so, coming from Michael's best friend. Her mind flitted back to that dreadful summer. Eleanor shuddered as she recalled the very public break-up. The colour red flashed through her mind. She remembered the oxblood red chequered table cloth of the restaurant. She remembered the flushed red face of the embarrassed waiter when he realised she had been dumped on her birthday.

The deep red wine splashed on the table was just the end to an unforgettable evening. Shrugging away the negative memories Eleanor said, 'Thanks for the vote of confidence guys. In the words of Ms. Morrisette, you live, you learn.'

Valentina chipped in, 'Michael would have got a lot more than just a glass of wine in his face, if I hadn't popped out for a cig. Good on you for chucking it on him!'

Eleanor smiled serenely to say, 'I didn't throw it over him. I *poured* it over him...' Her friends burst into laughter as Eleanor said dryly, 'What a waste of perfectly good alcohol.'

They chatted away before Steven glanced at his mobile. Quickly shoving his chair back he said, 'Right, girls, it's been a pleasure as always. Blackpool's playing and I can't miss the match. Elle and Valentina, I'll see you before you head back to uni. Gabi, see you tonight?' Casting Gabrielle a lingering look, he disappeared into the car-park.

Within moments of him leaving, Eleanor turned to Gabrielle and said playfully, 'Well..? What's the deal with you and Steven? I saw the way he looked at you.'

A beetroot red Gabrielle said, 'Don't know what you're talking about, we're *just mates*!'

Eleanor nodded her head in disbelief, laughing all the while. 'Oh come on Gabi, it's sooo obvious! Can't you see the signs? I'm surprised he hasn't told you yet. Even so, why haven't you said anything to him? It's the twenty first century hon!'

Valentina chirped, 'You should totally tell him Gabi, you and Steven make a cool couple!'

Gabi chewed on her lip, staring distractedly at the floating marshmallows in her hot chocolate. She said hesitantly, 'You *really* think he likes me..? I just don't see it. There has been the odd occasion when I think that maybe he *does* like me more than a friend, but then the moment passes along with the insane thought...' Switching her gaze back to Eleanor, she said with playful defiance, 'And you're *really* telling me that you'd tell a guy how you feel *before* he told you? Yeah right!'

Eleanor thumped her Americano on the table in mock outrage. 'Come on Gabi, "carpe diem" baby! It's all about female empowerment! Someone needs to bump your heads together, seriously! And yes, I would tell a guy that I like him, before he told me.' Giving the thought more consideration, she said lightly, 'Or I'd try to anyway. Yup, I'd *definitely* try.'

Gabrielle seemed amused. Narrowing her eyes she said, 'You're just saying that to shut me up! I think it's hilarious we're having this conversation, since you yourself remain clueless when people like you.'

Valentina nodded to agree with Gabrielle. Smiling she said, 'Gabi's got a point. Before I forget, any hot guys on the scene?'

'No *Valentina*, there aren't. I mean, I'm sure there are, but I just don't notice, if that makes sense. And I *can* tell when someone likes me! Look, let's raise a drink to seizing the day and not being afraid to tell people how we feel. OK?'

Both Valentina and Gabrielle shouted, 'Yes!' in unison and it wasn't long after that Eleanor waved goodbye to her jovial friends to continue Christmas shopping for the remainder of the afternoon.

Three months away had seen Eleanor change a great deal. She was much happier, yet despite her increasingly positive outlook, she knew that deep down she still loved Michael. Forgetting him had been marginally easier in Richmond. Now, as she passed places where they had spent time together, she felt maudlin knock on the door of her subconscious.

Finishing coffee with another school friend the following day, Eleanor popped into The Arndale Centre for some wrapping paper. The teeming shopping mall decked in myriad decorations and lights was packed to the rafters. People laden with bulging carrier bags crammed last minute shopping in the few days before Christmas. Lunch-time office workers eager to sate their hunger whilst making the most of their precious, gold dust lunch hour scurried past Eleanor. Although she loved Christmas, she wasn't a fan of the swarming throng that pushed, shoved and jostled her as if she was invisible. Edging her way through she stopped abruptly outside Reiss.

As the crowd milled around her, a window display caught her eye. A familiar blue cashmere jumper was draped on the shoulders of a mannequin towards the back. It was identical to Raphael's jumper, which she had fallen asleep in. She recalled the soft downy wool on her skin, its velvety smoothness embracing her in a cloud of contentment. Smiling whilst preoccupied with thoughts of Raphael, she failed to notice someone lightly tapping her shoulder, nimbly commanding her attention.

It took her a full five seconds to notice the steady tapping. Still smiling she turned around to find herself face to face with Michael. Snapping out of her reverie, she stared dumbstruck at her ex.

'*Elle*..? Hi, I thought it was you. How are you?'

Eleanor had pictured this scenario a million times over in her head. How she would be witty, cool and charming when she bumped into Michael. How she would appear nonchalant with zero trace of heartbreak. How he would see her in self-assured radiant glory. How she was over it. Well, sort of.

Eleanor drank in his appearance, not knowing when she would see him again. Perfectly styled sandy brown hair framed his smiling face whilst questioning bronze eyes hovered over her. He wore his Abercrombie tee and blue jeans with aplomb, oozing self-confidence and not in the least bit awkward. That unfortunately seemed to be Eleanor's department. The faltering words that eventually plopped out of Eleanor's hesitant mouth did not feature in Eleanor's myriad scenarios, but tumbled out regardless. 'Hi... Michael. I'm good. Yeah, good. How- How are you..?'

'You were miles away there.' He laughed lightly as he pressed on, 'Glad to hear that you're good. I'm good too. How's uni?'

Eleanor made reluctant eye contact before continuing awkwardly, 'Um, uni is busy, but fab. Richmond's gorgeous, and London's cool too...'

'Yeah, bright lights, big city. I never thought it was your scene. Glad you're enjoying yourself. It must be awesome living in London. You're looking well, by the way. Really well.'

'Thanks... I've gotta dash- Bye Michael.' Marching off in the opposite direction she dare not look behind and was suddenly appreciative of the lunch-time throng that had annoyed her earlier. Safe in the belly of the crowd, her mind replayed the scene of a few moments ago. So much for wanting to appear cool and relaxed; she had been the antithesis of what she had intended Michael to see.

The scene continued to play an eternal loop in her mind. How he had been friendly and chatty, whilst she had been tongue-tied and thoroughly ill at ease. She couldn't help analyse their short dialogue. *He* had stopped to talk to *her*. He had said that she looked well. He was glad that she was enjoying herself. Did that mean he still cared about her? She recognised that look in his eyes. He had wanted to continue their conversation. *Why?* What could he possibly want to say to her?

She needed to get away from the shopping mall and Michael. Suddenly craving tranquillity, she found herself jumping in her car to make the short journey to Heaton Park, arriving at the park twenty minutes later. Making her way to the central conservation, she slumped on the bench overlooking the weeping willow trees. The bright afternoon sun bore down on Eleanor, giving brief respite from the cool December air. It was an invigorating amalgam, a delightful mixture of hot and cold that Eleanor found strangely pleasant. All was quiet bar the distant chatter of a couple and their two children up ahead.

Eleanor gazed at the weeping willows. The tall, stately trees possessed a sagacious, philosophical air which instantly put her at ease. Lush greenery was the calming blank canvas to Eleanor's overactive mind, her swirling thoughts slowly halting, like a washing machine winding down on its last cycle. Nothing mattered here on this little green island. She felt immediately calmer, as if she had just had a triple shot of Valerian.

Eleanor had discovered this quiet spot one warm evening in June. She had then found herself visiting the spot more frequently after her break-up with Michael. Yearning inner peace during those despondent weeks, the park had lovingly provided a calming backdrop to the incessant whirring in Eleanor's mind. Today, like those dark days a few months earlier, the park presented a poignant antidote to the maelstrom in her mind. She tried to think with a clear head. Being away from Manchester had lulled her into a fall sense of security of Michael's significance in her life. Without all the distraction of moving and university, she was slowly beginning to realise how much she had actually missed him.

She recalled an indescribable sensation during their earlier encounter and put it down to weirdness seeing Michael after so long. Her first deep relationship was always going to be the hardest to get over. Yet a peculiar awareness pricked her consciousness and left her openly curious.

From seeing Michael every other day to abrupt zero contact, had been a trying transition for an emotional, vulnerable Eleanor. She remembered how immediately after the break-up, she would picture him in her mind's eye; if she couldn't physically see him, she would imagine him instead. Trawling through her memory bank, her mind would piece together an image and conjure up a temporarily pacifying vision of Michael.

Eleanor considered the oddly cruel nature of a break-up. Enforced separation had the effect of magnifying otherwise dormant emotions. Paradoxically, top of the list was the intensified need to be loved in the face of obvious rejection – how brutally inconvenient. The break-up had exposed a raw, needy gene in Eleanor, which surprised her, as she had always been self-sufficient. She recalled feeling utterly powerless, as if her heart and mind had not been her own.

That was then. She thought she was stronger now, yet despite seeing Michael less than twenty minutes ago, her mind cried out for a "Michael fix". She would summon her ex in her imagination, just this once. Closing her eyes she steadied herself, expecting to see an image of Michael in her mind's eye any moment now.

She braced herself and imagined to be on the brink of the dangerous slippery slope to heartbreak. She knew she couldn't afford to go there again. Yet in a twisted way, she pushed herself nearer to the precipitous edge. She exhaled as an image came together in her mind and flashed in front of her closed eyes.

As he had his back to her, she saw his broad shoulders first. He was wearing a cashmere jumper with sleeves rolled up half-way to reveal his muscular forearms. He turned around and fixed his eyes on her. Jet black flecked with slate grey. It was Raphael.

Her eyes popped open in surprise and the image vanished. *Could she be over her ex?*

An inner voice shouted a resonant, *'YES YES YES!'* All this time, she had convinced herself that she still loved Michael. Yes, she cared for him a great deal. But she didn't love him.

Her heart seemed packed with sunshine that she could no longer contain. Seeing Michael had been cathartic. She knew for certain she was over him when she realised she hadn't wanted to kiss him, or hold his hand. A delighted Eleanor leapt up from the bench in a fit of happiness as she waved her heartbreak goodbye. As if the elements were in acquiescence, the afternoon sun suddenly intensified on the spot where Eleanor was standing. Since the break-up, her exhausted heart had felt like a deflated balloon. Bursting with positivity, she was buoyant with optimism and ready for the next chapter in her life. Standing in nature's very own spotlight, the world was a more beautiful place.

Driving home elated, she ignored the small voice in head. *Why did you picture Raphael..?*

# 12 CHRYSALIS

Apart from a surprisingly white Christmas Day and New Years Eve, Eleanor spent the bulk of vacation revising. Texting her friends of her imminent return before leaving Manchester, her phone buzzed intermittently during the course of her frosty drive to Richmond. All her friends texted back and made plans for a catch-up. Only Raphael hadn't replied. Waiting for his text made her three hour journey feel considerably longer. When she eventually flung open the creaking door to the Richmond house, she was oblivious to the icy cold air. She was just happy to be back. Glancing around the dark, unwelcoming house that she didn't think she could ever miss, she realised she had grown accustomed to it. For better or worse, she now considered it to be her secondary home.

The sudden buzzing of her mobile shattered the cold silence of the gloomy house. Dropping her bags at the entrance, she dug into her pocket to see a text from Jack. Her heart sank a few millimetres into her chest as she realised Raphael still hadn't replied. Focusing on her own plans she looked forward to seeing Jack the following day in Richmond.

Pulling up outside Patisserie Valerie on a bright Sunday afternoon, she noticed Jack sitting at a window seat engrossed in a book. Entering the bustling café, she crept up behind him. Placing her hands over his eyes, she whispered, 'Guess who?'

His hands automatically flew up to rest on hers. 'Couldn't stay away, could ya?' Jack was on his feet within seconds and turned round to greet her with a huge hug. Smiling he said, 'I've missed you!' Surveying her whilst still holding her, he said with a curious smile, 'You seem different, what's changed? You seem care-free, like Atlas has reclaimed the world to bear on his shoulders and not yours.'

She laughed to reply in mock protest, 'I figured Atlas needed the world more than I did so I returned it without a fight. Life's too short baby! I'm going to be super positive from now on. Hey, what are you drinking? And when did you get back?'

'Few days ago. The whole family landed at ours for Christmas, which of course meant zero revision. Don't get me wrong, I had a blast, no-one can pack away the port like my gran! Now I'm slightly panicked by the thought of six exams, plus three essays. I figure if I cram solidly this week then I'll be OK.' Stifling a yawn, he said, 'Double-shot espresso would be good. I feel I should be surrounded by six short men who call me Sleepy.'

Chatting over coffee, she glanced up to catch Jack looking inquisitively at her. He said smiling, 'You've changed. Whatever you're on, give me some!'

'I'm high on life! Hey, before I forget, could you remind me later to pop to Tesco before I head home? I haven't had a chance to refill my embarrassingly empty fridge.'

'Cool, I need some stuff too. I figure I can't exist on just espresso and Frosties.'

Jumping into her car later, they drove to the nearest Tesco. Sharing a trolley, they ambled through the aisles before Eleanor paused to grab three large chocolate bars. Staring into the trolley with a grin, Jack said, 'What's the big deal with chocolate? I'll never get this fixation girls have with it.'

Turning to face him with a cheeky glint in her eye, she picked up a bar of Green & Blacks. Adopting a mock scientific tone she said, 'Recent studies show that the higher cocoa content of dark chocolate is beneficial, increasing attention and "feel-good" hormones in subjects.' Returning Jack's grin she said, 'ALWAYS respect the chocolate.' Throwing the bar back in the trolley she continued, 'And why is that boys never seem to understand the significance of chocolate? I couldn't live without it. The only downside is the calories, sooo not good for the waistline.'

With a lingering glance over Eleanor's skinny jeans, Jack said lightly, 'You're tiny. In fact, I *encourage* you to eat more.' He threw another five bars into the trolley whilst Eleanor doubled up with laughter. 'You're as light as a feather, trust me. Jump on the end of the trolley and I bet I won't even feel you. Go on, I dare you!'

'Fine. Don't blame me if you do your back in!' She hadn't done this since she was a child. She hopped onto the back of the trolley, gingerly positioning her feet above the wheels. Facing Jack at the helm, she squealed with delight when the wheels gathered speed. Deftly steering the trolley down the bread aisle, she heard the satisfaction in Jack's voice. 'See, there is absolutely nothing to you. C'mon, say I was right!'

They were school children for a few minutes, and for once, Eleanor didn't care. Drawing disapproving glances from quiet shoppers, Eleanor tried in vain to suppress her giggles. With the wheels spinning at full speed, she suddenly remembered the iconic flying scene in Titanic. In homage, she tentatively raised her arms on either side and declared in mock breathlessness, 'Jack! Look, I'm flying!'

Jack groaned, increasing the pace of the trolley. 'Wow, Titanic and chocolate, killer combo – literally!'

Eleanor continued laughing, not noticing that the trolley had slowed to a stop until she caught sight of Jack's unsmiling face. Wondering at his sudden mood change, she hopped of the trolley and turned around.

Raphael was standing a few metres away. He was busy perusing the shelves and suddenly looked up, his concentration momentarily broken to see them nearby. Eleanor stared at Raphael's bare arms and his dark blue cotton tee as she wondered how he wasn't freezing. Picking up a small box which quickly became engulfed in his large hand, he gave her the softest of smiles and started to walk towards her. Filled with a sudden swell of happiness, Eleanor bounded over to Raphael as he caught her in his arms.

'Hey Raphael how have you been?! What are you doing here? It's sooo good to see you!'

Raphael let go of her within seconds as he turned to briefly acknowledge Jack who responded with an equally curt nod.

'I'm good Eleanor, I was only passing through. Just picking up a few light-bulbs for the flat. How was Manchester?'

'Yeah, I had an awesome time. Back to uni and exams though! How's your revision going?'

'Well. Sorry for not texting back sooner.' He glanced briefly at the boxes in his hand as he said distractedly, 'I was tied up. Listen, how long are you around for today? We could catch up later?' He gave Jack the most cursory of glances as he said, 'That's if you don't have other plans.'

Eleanor shook her head and smiled. 'Actually, I was going to head home straight after shopping, so yeah, I'm free this evening. Jack, would you like to join us-'

Jack took a millisecond to answer. 'No, it's been a hectic few days. You go on ahead, I'm gonna go home and cram some more.'

Eleanor faced Jack to say unsurely, 'Revision can wait for just a bit longer?'

Before Jack could answer, Raphael said coolly, 'Don't let us keep you.'

Addressing Eleanor directly to ignore Raphael's cold stare, Jack said, 'Nope I've gotta dash.' Placing a lingering hand on Eleanor's shoulder Jack continued in a softer tone, 'Revision can wait huh? Looks like we've swapped roles. See you at uni.' Jack didn't hang around and shortly after paying at the checkout, promptly headed home.

As Eleanor and Raphael walked to the supermarket car-park, he suddenly stopped by a gleaming navy Alfa Romeo 4C. Looking at the sleek car then back at Raphael, Eleanor said, 'Nice chick magnet. Isn't parking a pain?'

Raphael grinned as the doors softly unlocked automatically. 'I very rarely use it. Let's get your car loaded up. We can go drop off the shopping at your house now. You drive and I'll follow, yeah?'

After pulling up in her drive-way, Raphael carried six bags, whilst Eleanor struggled with the three that weighed her down. Standing outside the front door for a few minutes whilst rummaging in her handbag for the keys, she realised it would be easier to use the hidden spare set above the door-way of the porch. Raphael saw her reach overhead and beat her to it. Quickly switching all six heavy bags to his right hand, he deftly located the key from the ceilinged porch. They were in the house within moments and after placing the bags in the kitchen, Eleanor turned to Raphael and said gratefully, 'Thanks for your help, you saved me three trips in the freezing cold!'

'No worries.' He gently dropped all the bags on the work-top in one swift movement whilst Eleanor unpacked. Watching her from afar with enquiring eyes, he didn't verbalise whatever had piqued his curiosity. Instead he said lightly, 'Good to see you Eleanor. Looks like Manchester agreed with you.'

Eleanor's tinkling laugh echoed through the hollow kitchen. 'I think it wasn't just Manchester. I also realised a few things when I was there too. Self-realisation is pretty cool you know. It's great when things click into place.' She smiled and turned around, briefly making eye contact with him before turning back to the fridge.

His dark eyes keenly followed her around the kitchen. 'Self-realisation..?'

Eleanor chuckled whilst unpacking. 'I realised I was finally over Michael. I was sooo happy. I have moved on! I realised when-'

She was on the verge of saying realisation had struck in the park when she suddenly stopped herself. Since that day whenever her mind questioned her motives for imagining Raphael and not her ex-boyfriend, she automatically suppressed the inquisitive voice into oblivion. She couldn't help but feel slightly embarrassed and swiftly changed the subject. 'Anyway, um, Manchester was a lovely break and it was great to see everyone.'

She looked up whilst piling clementines in the fruit bowl, to catch a glimpse of a satisfied grin on his face. He casually leant against the larder with an air of contentment about him, before sweeping a small parcel from the nearby work-top. He held out the package. 'I know it's late. But you're big on Christmas. It's been in the car this whole time.'

A huge smile broke on Eleanor's face. 'Noo, you shouldn't have! I feel bad for not getting you anything. Thanks Raphael!'

The parcel felt as heavy as a pound of sugar. Tearing away the thick brown paper to reveal a book, she saw it was The Count of Monte Cristo. Puzzled by its antiquated appearance, she gently flicked past the first few pages.

She stared at the faded book, remaining speechless for a few moments as it dawned on her that she held the first edition. Looking firstly at the precious book then Raphael, she finally opened her mouth to let out incoherent garbled thanks.

'This is a first – a FIRST edition! Crikey Raphael. When did you- I mean, how... It's awesome! *You're* awesome! Thank you times a trillion! Quadrillion even!'

Still clutching the book, Eleanor threw her arms affectionately around Raphael to express her obvious gratitude. He in turn held her close, encircling her in a solid hug. Standing in the quiet kitchen, they were locked in an embrace that saw each party too comfortable and unwilling to move away.

Eleanor had two initial thoughts as she hugged Raphael. She felt complete and content as she remained wrapped in his arms. Secondly, she was reminded again how much she had missed him. Nestling closer, she closed her eyes. Lost in the moment, Eleanor was still leaning on his lapel when she suddenly realised they had been standing together for the past few minutes.

Glancing up to catch him staring at her rendered her speechless. Charged with exhilaration, happiness surged from her heart to the rest of her body, pricking it awake in one deliciously spine-tingling sweeping motion.

He lowered his head a fraction of an inch. Instinctively, Eleanor raised her head. Only a few inches separated them. Abruptly breaking eye contact, he cleared his throat before backing away. He exhaled and when he finally spoke, it was in a low, guarded tone. 'Glad you like the book.'

Eleanor was still for a few moments, not quite knowing what had just happened. Or what hadn't happened. One moment they were two friends hugging. The next, he had held her tightly, close enough so she could feel his warm breath on her cheek. A mystified Eleanor had been expecting something. Quite what she wanted, she wasn't entirely sure.

When Raphael had stepped away from her, she had felt oddly disappointed. Trying to figure out why she felt let down, she suddenly remembered where she was. Rambling thoughts tugged at her mind, wanting to digress and explore the possibilities of what could have, would have, maybe should have been, had Raphael not moved away from her.

Forcing her mind to disregard these wandering thoughts, she grounded herself to the spot in the kitchen. She said casually, 'Coffee before you go? I could murder a cappuccino. What about you?' When he nodded his acquiescence, she smiled and sauntered over to the coffee-maker. Pulling out the coffee packet she joked, 'I know, I know, I drink too much coffee. This would be my fourth cup. Still, if it's any consolation, that is my one and only vice. God knows how many you have, I'm not even going to ask.'

He seemed amused by her joke as he sat down. They were just two best friends again, joking and hanging out over a cup of coffee. Eleanor was aware of the discernible switch from best friends, to something else, then back again. The switch, no matter how slight, existed all the same, seemingly being triggered by Raphael when he had moved away from her, and sustained by Eleanor, through her teasing, glib remarks.

Eleanor breathed in the ground coffee scent as she packed the filter with the coarse brown powder. She felt as if the strong aroma of freshly brewed coffee had dissipated the potential fog of awkwardness as they continued to chatter and joke as if nothing had happened.

It was late evening when Raphael left. She thought about their earlier embrace with a mixture of curiosity, pleasure and restlessness. This intriguing hybrid awoke an unfathomable emotion in Eleanor. Unsure whether to be extremely happy or upset by Raphael pulling away from her, she remained mystified as she attempted to decipher the reason for her agitation.

Snuggling down in her duvet later that night, she looked over to her bedside cabinet where Raphael's gift had taken prime position. Falling into a deep slumber, she ignored the small voice in her head which returned to taunt her. *You enjoy being close to Raphael, don't you? What if he hadn't moved away? What if...*

# 13 POWER CUT

The weather got progressively colder, several inches of snow falling each night to cover the roads in a treacherous mix of slush and black ice. The snowfall was the heaviest in nearly forty years and worse weather was predicted over the coming weeks.

With exams firmly underway, university was officially a taxing, tense place to be. After her third exam, Eleanor frantically worried that she had performed inadequately. Serena, Christina and Jack too were weary whilst an anxiety-ridden Katherine officially rued the day she had decided to become a student.

Raphael's attitude throughout the exam period was in direct contrast to Eleanor's. He was seemingly unaffected by the cloud of exam stress which hung over most of the university. Whilst Eleanor worried about the first term exams, Raphael breezed in and out of the examination halls in a detached manner, leaving her slightly in awe of his candid insouciance.

The second semester started a week later. Eleanor stirred awake on Thursday morning, instinctively snuggling lower under the warm duvet. Peering over the quilt edge, she stretched and yawned as her mind invariably meandered to Recommended Reading Lists and plans for the weekend.

For a split second she thought the room looked brighter than normal. As her sleepy gaze fell on the window, she thought the magenta curtains appeared more transparent. She was momentarily puzzled. A dreary grey sky would usually greet her when she arose at 6:15am every morning, yet the daylight streaming through the curtains was definitely more pronounced. As her brain kick-started awake in realisation of the impossibility for curtains to increase their transparency overnight, she wondered what time it was.

Eleanor was suddenly aware that her mobile phone alarm had not buzzed her awake. *How late could she be?* Rolling over and grabbing her mobile phone which she had left charging the night before, she noted the blank screen with growing dismay. Stumbling out of bed, she picked up her wrist-watch that told the time to be 8:23am. She had overslept. With growing panic, she realised that her phone hadn't charged and she was now late for university.

Leaping out of bed to check why her phone hadn't charged, she noticed the absence of the indicator light on the adaptor plug. The flashing LED on her hi-fi displayed a frozen time of 11:02pm and she slowly realised that the house had suffered an electrical power cut. Eleanor was temporarily grateful that it wasn't her mobile phone that was faulty. A broken phone was the last thing she needed, and it was going to be one of those days. She could just tell.

Eleanor always caught the train to university. Yet with a lecture less than thirty five minutes away, she contemplated driving to avoid being late. Moaning when she caught sight of the thick blanket of snow, Eleanor realised she had no choice. She would have to drive to university. She told herself it wouldn't be so bad. Besides, if she had the car, she could do a larger food shop after lectures, instead of just picking up a handful of items from the local grocery store.

The roads were worse than she had expected. Throwing frequent glances at the dashboard to keep track of time, Eleanor hoped she wouldn't be late. The snow disguised layer upon layer of perilous black ice; as it increased her driving time, Eleanor's punctual arrival was looking more and more unlikely.

Waiting at the traffic lights, a fresh snowfall caused her to smack her steering wheel in frustration. Her windscreen wipers did not alleviate the problem either. Within minutes, the light dusting became a steady swirl, and Eleanor quickly realised she was caught up in a snowstorm. She remembered the local weather report from the previous night. The stern news anchor in his sombre stone suit had issued severe weather warnings, advising against driving unless absolutely necessary. The report also included details of the last snowstorm which had lasted nearly three hours causing further chaos on the roads. She had to get out of the snowstorm quickly and wondered if things could get any worse.

They could. A mustard Range Rover hurtled towards her. Spinning out of control, it smashed into her Peugeot with a sickening crunch. The last thing Eleanor saw was the mustard bonnet protruding through her windscreen before everything went black.

Christina joined Serena and Jack who were already seated at their usual work-bench. Glancing at Eleanor's empty seat, Christina said, 'Where's

Elle? It's nearly nine and she's been early for all her lectures this week. Seriously, wish I had her enthusiasm!'

Jack chuckled to say, 'It's probably the weather keeping her away. Not that I'd ever use the weather as an excuse. Not straight away, anyway. I'm saving that till next week when it's really bad and getting out of bed is way worse!'

A smiling Serena shook her head lightly. 'Seriously, has *anyone* heard from Elle? Maybe I should text-'

Jack had already whipped out his mobile. 'I'm on it. I'm sure she'll call if anything is wrong.'

Raphael had resumed his place near the window. Being seated near the front of the room, he only heard snippets of Jack's conversation. Raphael thought Eleanor's absence odd too. Calling her now would be of no consequence if she wasn't picking up. Forcing himself to concentrate on the lecture, he pushed aside his growing disquiet and couldn't help but wonder where Eleanor was.

# 14 PLEASURE AND PAIN

Eleanor's eyes flickered open. It was white. Everywhere. Unrecognisable surroundings increased her disorientation. Confused and overwhelmed, she struggled to place where she was. She was definitely not at home. Or university. Which reminded her – didn't she have a lecture to go to? A hazy memory streaked through her mind and she remembered driving in the snowstorm.

She suddenly realised she was lying on a stiff bed in an unfamiliar room. Cold panic crept over her. As she made an effort to get up, a dull ache swept across her chest and abdominal area. She continued her painful endeavour to sit upright, slowly edging her legs over the side of the bed. A sharp paroxysm of pain engulfed her left leg and she automatically winced. *Where the hell was she?* As if in answer to her question, the door suddenly opened. A man wearing a white coat glided into the room. He had kind eyes.

'Eleanor Hudson?'

Eleanor blinked before nodding. She had numerous questions, but before she could verbalise any of them, the white-coated man spoke. A shiny stethoscope hung from his neck. He spoke slowly, his soothing voice pacifying Eleanor as she temporarily curbed her curiosity.

'I'm Dr Quinn. You were involved in a minor accident earlier today. Don't worry, you're going to be fine. You have two broken ribs, slight concussion, a sprained elbow and what I suspect to be a torn ligament in your left calf. Any questions so far?'

Eleanor shook her head and remained silent. She remembered the Range Rover careering towards her followed by distant shouting in a thick French accent.

Dr Quinn gripped his stethoscope, watching Eleanor all the while. He said, 'You're a lucky girl, Eleanor. You'll be right as rain in a few weeks. The interim period may see you experience slight discomfort, which is what the painkillers on the side of your bed are for. I am also going to suggest that we keep you in overnight. Just a precautionary measure. Is there anyone you would like to contact? Family or friends?'

She contemplated calling her mum but swiftly decided against it. Why bother her or indeed anyone else when she would be home the day after? It was pointless worrying them unnecessarily. She slowly shook her head. Heading towards the door and his next patient, the doctor informed her of a few key points. He advised Eleanor to notify her car insurers if applicable, and that her handbag which had been retrieved from her car, sat on the corner chair opposite her.

'That's it for now. I know it's only 11:15am and I'm unsure how hungry you are. Lunch is served at 12:30pm and dinner at 7:00pm. If you get hungry in the meantime, just ask one of the nurses. Is there anything else you would like to know?'

Again, Eleanor found herself slowly shaking her head. She watched him leave and shifted on the bed, grimacing as she accidentally leant on her sore leg. The shock of being in her first accident was starting to sink in and the feeling of utter helplessness compounded the pain. Losing the will to probe, she craved solitude, thankful that she was the sole occupant of the room. Forcing two painkillers down her dry throat as she settled into the least painful position on the bed, she closed her eyes and welcomed the seclusion of the next few hours.

When Eleanor arose the following morning at 6:45am, it took her a few seconds to remember where she was. She felt oddly calm as she glanced around the cool, dark room. Stirring in bed with the realisation that she had spent her first night in hospital, she placed a light hand gingerly on her sore abdomen. Her raw muscles ached with the fleeting touch. So, this is what having broken ribs felt like.

She remembered the doctor's words. *You're a lucky girl.* As optimism slowly filtered through her bruised body, she realised she had emerged from a near fatal accident with minor souvenir bruises. Suddenly thankful to be alive, constructivity kicked in and a *To-Do List* began to form in her head. She had a few phone-calls to make, first to her insurance company, then to the other driver involved in the accident who had apparently left his number with the ambulance attendant. Heaving herself off the bed, she leant forward and caught her handbag in a limp grasp. Rifling through her satchel, she found her back-up battery and discarded the flat one. Deciding to check her messages after eating, she washed her face and eagerly awaited breakfast.

The painkillers seemed to accentuate Eleanor's hunger, yet the hospital food did nothing to sate her appetite. Cardboard toast and anaemic coffee propelled Eleanor to leave the hospital at the earliest opportunity.

Once breakfast had been cleared, Eleanor made her way to an outside area which permitted the usage of mobile phones. The icy February air pinched at Eleanor's face and hands as she switched on her phone in the quiet square.

Eleanor felt strange not having checked her phone for the past twenty-four hours. It was easy to become addicted to the latest mobile gadget. Prior to becoming a mobile phone aficionado herself, she had relentlessly teased her other friends who had embraced technology before her. Now, she viewed her coveted Samsung with admiration, a super-tool essential for life in the twenty first century.

The screen flickered to life and within minutes, texts and voice-mails came fluttering through. Tackling her inbox first, she came across texts from Jack and Christina, sent a few minutes before the lecture started. She tried to form a nonchalant reply, blasé enough not to raise concern yet informing them of her mishap. It was pointless mentioning the accident for now. Her friends would worry unnecessarily and attention was the last thing she wanted. Texting a simple reply, Eleanor said that she had been tied up and would see them on Monday.

Swiftly moving on to her voice-mails, the first one she picked up was from Valentina. As her friend had simply called to touch base, Eleanor decided that conversation could wait till later. The second voice-mail was from Raphael:

'*Raphael here. Where are you? You didn't show for lecture. Call me.*'

He spoke casually, yet the staccato message gave his seemingly indifferent enquiry an edgy undertone. The voice-mail was stripped bare of superfluous detail and lasted less than five seconds, yet Eleanor suddenly found herself wanting to speak with Raphael. It was the oddest sensation and one that she could not shake off.

The time on her mobile flashed 7:15am. She knew Raphael's first lecture wasn't till later that afternoon, and not wanting to disturb him, sent a text instead. She tried to keep the missive short and uncomplicated, saying she was OK, how she had got tied up, and that she would see him on Monday. She wasn't technically lying to him, simply being economical with the truth. The odd sensation she experienced earlier returned with unexpected intensity; now she not only wanted to hear him, but see him too. Within seconds of texting her reply, her phone buzzed an incoming call. It was Raphael. He sounded tense then relieved when she answered on the second ring.

'You OK? What happened to you? You never miss a lecture.'

He was edgier than usual. She didn't really want to tell him the specifics; the reality of an accident always sounded much worse than it really was. She tried to play down the situation and subtly change the subject.

'I'm fine Raphael. Just a tiny mishap. Hey, how was the lecture, did I miss anything?'

He said in a low voice, '*Mishap?*'

She didn't want to lie to him. Eleanor reluctantly capitulated. 'Just... Well, it was only an accident. A teeny tiny one. I'm fine now. I'll be discharged later today and-'

Raphael's voice was spiked with curiosity and incredulousness. '*Accident..?* Hang on, *where* are you now..?'

His voice had become increasingly strained as the conversation progressed. The last thing she wanted was to worry anyone and here was Raphael, doing the exact thing she didn't want. She *was* glad that he had called. Her heart had pounded with joy when she had seen his name flash across her mobile screen.

Yet a small part of her wanted to pull away from him. She was autonomous and fiercely valued her independence. Michael was her lesson learnt. She would never get attached to anyone and rely on them completely. Thinking of Michael (even though she hadn't done that in a while) brought out her self-determined, tenacious streak and she found herself answering Raphael more forcefully than she had originally intended.

She snapped, 'I'm in hospital. I don't *know* when I'll be home, should be a couple of hours. You've got lectures today, right? You better go, wouldn't want you to be late-'

'Hang on. You're in hospital and you expect me to *go to my lectures?*'

His evident defiance startled her. Suddenly guilty, she realised he was just trying to be a friend. As if he guessed her train of thought, he continued in a softer tone, giving Eleanor the distinct impression that he felt slighted.

'I get it. You're independent. Friends help each other though, right? *Let* me help.'

Eleanor frowned, bothered that she had inadvertently affronted Raphael and for a moment, she hated herself. The crazy thing was, she *wanted* him to help. She wanted to see him. She wanted to feel safe and protected in his arms after the accident. Slowly lowering her barriers like a descending drawbridge, she relaxed her stance and shifted position.

Exhaling, she said, 'I appreciate your offer of help, really I do. There's no need to worry though. And I do value your friendship. You don't need me to say that, because you must know how much I love that we're mates.'

They were both silent for a few moments. Raphael wasn't ready to give up. 'Fine. I'll go to uni. FYI – I'll be passing through Richmond anyway. If you need me to drop anything off at your house, let me know.'

Eleanor couldn't help but smile at his audacious intonation. He was going to be there for her whether she liked it or not. Suddenly remembering she had no food in the house, she hesitated a moment and cautiously decided to take up Raphael on his offer. He wanted to help, and she needed it.

'OK, I just need some basics picking up. If you could grab some milk, cheese, bread and butter that would be great. No worries if-'

She heard him smile, a contagious grin which she couldn't help but reciprocate. He said quickly, 'I'll do it.' He paused. Although fresh from the triumph of finally getting Eleanor to accept his help, he was treading slowly. He said tentatively, 'So you don't know when you're returning home?'

'Probably by two-ish. Not that I expect you to be there. You know where the spare key is, right? Just above the porch door. If you let yourself in and drop off the stuff, that would be great. I'll sort you out with money when I see you next.'

'OK. Text me if you need anything else. And Eleanor – take care.'

Then he was gone. Eleanor remained standing in the cold for a few more minutes before remembering where she was. Hobbling back indoors feeling oddly content despite her present circumstance, Eleanor waited for Doctor Quinn to deliver his prognosis. He gently explained that her left wrist needed a cast due to a hair-line fracture. She would also experience localised muscular aches, which was apparently normal as the torn muscles began their restorative process. Handing her extra medication in case of severe muscular pangs, she was free to go.

She couldn't have been happier to see the grey silhouette of her house fall on the taxi as it pulled into her drive-way. She shivered, drawing icy puffs of air as she limped onto the porch. Suddenly remembering that the thermostat needed altering daily, she braced herself for the cold indoors. Keys in hand, she noticed a note pinned to her front door. It read:

*Didn't want you to struggle in the kitchen. R.*

She read the cryptic note twice, her eyes lingering over Raphael's hastily scrawled missive. Mounting confusion hastened her entrance into the house. The sweet scent of freshly cooked food hung in the air, temporarily alleviating her pain as she entered the kitchen a few seconds later.

The heated kitchen having seen recent activity over the past few hours, warmed Eleanor's icy cold skin within seconds. She balanced her handbag on the work-top, peering into the various sauce-pans on the stove, which were still warm and filled with steaming hot food.

He had cooked for her. Bewildered, she remained still for a minute before wrestling a fork from the cutlery drawer. Sampling each dish,

Eleanor considered this heavenly recompense for the tasteless hospital food. In a large pan, pillows of pasta lay nestled in a rich tomato and basil sauce, whilst fat prawns enveloped in a white wine cream concoction clung to ribbons of velvet soft tagliatelle in an adjacent pan.

A dumbfounded Eleanor opened the fridge. Not quite knowing what else to expect, she gaped at the contents in delighted disbelief. Cartons of her favourite chicken soup and other groceries filled the top two shelves whilst a nearby basket contained a loaf of farmhouse bread, flaky croissants and fist-sized muffins from Carluccio's.

She gingerly leant back on the work-top to survey the feast in front of her. He had skipped university to cook for her. All the hot food was home-made. He would have had to start shopping and cooking pretty much as soon as he had got of the phone to her.

Eleanor's stubborn independence could not detract from Raphael's compassionate gesture. Not even Michael had cooked for her, and he had been her boyfriend. Overcome with grateful happiness, Eleanor pulled out her mobile and dialled his number. Her heart stopped in her chest with each ring, yet there was no answer. Redirected to voice-mail, she decided to text him instead.

**Eleanor: I can't believe you did all that! TY! Everything looks AWESOME! Come round tomorrow for late breakfast, say 11-ish..?**

Polishing off a croissant within a minute, she contemplated the next dish on her hit-list. She smiled as she read Raphael's swift reply.

**Raphael: Can't talk at the moment. Glad you liked the food. See you at 11 tomorrow.**

Crawling into bed that night, Eleanor was thankful she had returned home to the comfort of her own bed. She mentally replayed sections of her day, like CCTV footage stored in her mind. It was surprising how enlightening a painful experience could be. If she hadn't been involved in an accident, she would have remained oblivious to the extent of Raphael's feelings towards her. Her arm hurt like hell, but she didn't care. She was seeing Raphael the following day. And that's all that mattered.

# 15 BREAKFAST

He was punctual as usual. A smiling Eleanor slowly pushed open the front door at 11:01am. His black vintage Triumph jacket gave him a darker edge and Eleanor got the distinct impression he was angry. Quickly dismissing her irrational thought, she chirped, 'Hey Raphael! Good to see you!'

His eyes flickered over her and came to rest on her sling. They remained there for a few prolonged moments before moving up to her neck, where a large purple bruise had bloomed overnight. He said tersely, 'Not just a mishap huh?'

He continued to stare at her in quiet dismay, leaving Eleanor wishing she had chosen to wear a polo neck that would have hidden the contusions. When he eventually spoke, his voice was detached, as if he was willing himself to be composed.

He stepped forward and for a split second, Eleanor thought he was going to hug her. Yet he appeared to restrain himself, instead pushing his hands deep in his pockets whilst stepping into the house. It was that awkward moment where a hug was expected which somehow didn't transpire.

Eleanor waited expectantly for a few seconds before saying lightly, 'The bruises look worse than they feel. It's great to see you!'

She wanted to hug him and was a little unsure why he was particularly hesitant today. Guessing that he may be concerned about hurting her bruised body, she smiled conspiratorially to say, 'You don't have to worry about hurting me.'

His eyes flashed up at her. Those perfect black pools seemed blacker today and Eleanor was distracted for a few seconds before she said, 'Anyway, I *need* a hug. It's been a mad few days.' Leaning in whilst placing her good arm around him she said, 'Thank you for the food, I really appreciate it. You're a fricking life-saver!'

Quickly removing his hands from his pockets he caught her in a gentle hug, as if suddenly aware of her fragility. She pressed into his pleasantly cool jacket, revelling in his butterfly-soft embrace. When Raphael spoke, his voice was barely audible. 'I worry. About you. Can't help it.'

'Well don't, seriously. I'm a big girl, I can look after myself.' Adding as a humorous afterthought she said smiling, 'Although recent circumstances refute this! Coffee?'

He let go of her almost immediately when reminded of the accident. Following her into the kitchen, Raphael's eyes swept all corners twice before he glanced into the lounge. As she switched on the coffee-maker, Eleanor wondered if she was imagining his disquiet.

He seemed miles away, visibly relaxing whilst giving the empty kitchen a third cursory glance. He said calmly, 'Does your arm hurt? At least you've got a bit of time off uni.' He paused before saying hesitantly, 'You *are* going to time off, right?' She met his disapproving gaze as he pressed, 'Tell me you're going to take a few days off?'

With a guilty smile Eleanor said, 'Nah, I've already missed one day, and I've got the long weekend to recuperate. Hey, that reminds me. Could I possibly borrow your notes from Thursday's lecture? I can catch up this we-'

He had already pulled out a thin wad of folded paper from his back pocket and placed it on the work-top in front of her. 'Knew you'd ask for this.'

Eleanor chuckled and pouring coffee said, 'You star!' He seemed to take heart by seeing her move around the kitchen independently. She said somewhat distractedly, 'The food was an awesome surprise. And there's nothing like a good old accident to bring some clarity back into your life. Life really is too short, don't you think?'

She suddenly looked up questioningly at Raphael sitting opposite her. His eyes, two fascinating shadowy pools of immeasurable depth were fixed on her and she found herself unable to move or look away. It was the most delicious sensation, peculiar and hypnotic. Even if Eleanor could pull her eyes away, she didn't want to. Having uncovered the bread-basket, her hand hovered mid-air, whilst the question she had asked Raphael flew out of her mind. It was only when he spoke that she blinked and the fog started to clear.

He spoke flatly, his voice suddenly devoid of emotion. 'Clarity is always good. And life, existence, or whatever you want to call it, is too short. You should always make the most of what you have.'

His final sentence was tinged with sorrow that had stealthily crept into an otherwise objective opinion. His mouth was set in a firm line and for those few moments, he was totally unguarded.

She was suddenly struck by his vulnerability. For those fleeting seconds, he seemed exposed and he had unknowingly let Eleanor get a step closer to him. An unidentifiable emotion swelled in her chest and she wanted to embrace him again. She was acutely appreciative of his presence, yet for a reason unknown, she was unable to voice her obvious delight.

'Nice philosophy for a Saturday morning! Right, what would you like?'

They both reached into the basket at the same time and their hands descending on the same croissant. As their fingertips touched, Raphael quickly withdrew his hand to place it on the adjacent loaf instead. He started to saw off a hunk with the bread-knife that lay on the counter.

Eleanor's hand hovered over the croissant. It was an awkward moment, yet she didn't know why. They were best friends and frequently made platonic contact as best friends frequently do. It was fleeting moment heavy with promise, yet try as she might, was unable to pinpoint the reason of its potential. She knew she was on the cusp of something gargantuan, but for the time being, it remained incomprehensible.

Eleanor felt as if she was standing close-up to a gigantic billboard. The letters were painted in a massive bold font, yet due to the size, she was unable to read what was directly in front of her face. Something had happened since the accident, which was a trigger for the discernible shift in their relationship. Like the seismic shifting of the Earth's plates before an earthquake, everything appeared to be fine on the surface. Yet deep in the Earth's core, something had moved with the potential of life-changing consequences.

The swirling thoughts in Eleanor's mind accelerated ten-fold and she closed her eyes for a moment before grounding herself. Dismissing the bothering questions which were starting to pile up in her mind, she picked up the croissant and placed it on her plate. She said casually, 'I had my eye on this. I would have fought you for it.'

'Would have liked to see you try.'

Raphael flashed a roguish smile and Eleanor burst out laughing. The awkward tension vanished just as quickly as it had appeared. She hit him playfully with her good arm and once again, the Earth's plates shifted and a subtle transition had occurred. They were now best friends again and after a chatty breakfast, Raphael asked if he could sign her plaster.

Catching her smile, he took a seat beside her and bent his head closer. He was inches away as Eleanor sat transfixed, watching him write on her cast as he gently held her hand.

He suddenly looked up to catch Eleanor watching him. Moving closer to her, those inches slowly, slowly disappeared. He wasn't touching her anymore, having moved his hand onto the adjacent table. Yet she felt the intensity of his gaze like hundreds of beams of a concentrated sun. Eleanor felt as if she was floating in mid-air and convinced herself it was the potent painkillers that were having a crazy effect on her. She found herself fractionally moving in closer to Raphael and closed her eyes, not quite knowing what was going to happen.

An abrupt ringing startled her. Her eyes popped open to see Raphael throwing his buzzing mobile a dark glance. His face clouded over as he perused the caller display and picked up.

Whoever was on the other end didn't have much to say. Raphael replied curtly that he would leave immediately and quickly hung up. Raphael's countenance was now deadly serious as he announced in a sombre tone, 'I have to go away for a few days. My father needs me home.'

The promise of a few moments before had now disappeared with the ringing of the phone. They were back to being friends again. Eleanor was quiet, unsure exactly what to say. He still didn't talk much about his family, and she hadn't broached the subject either. She said lightly, 'Everything OK?'

'Nothing I can't handle. I have to leave.'

She wanted him to stay. Raphael too seemed reluctant to go, almost forcing himself to get up.

She said a little awkwardly, 'OK. See you soon?'

'Definitely.'

Now at the front door, they were opposite each other. He remained standing for a few seconds before leaning in to hug her goodbye. She smiled contentedly as his arms gently closed around her in a protective circle. She was unsure if the telephone call had relayed bad news. The content of the call had displeased Raphael and all she wanted to do was cheer him up. She said lightly whilst still in his arms, 'You're a legend Raphael, thanks for all your help. Who would have thought a power cut had advantages! Bell me when you get back, yeah?'

She felt his body tense as he looked directly at her. 'Power cut..?'

'Yeah, on Thursday. Long story, I won't keep you, but my phone didn't charge, then I ran late for uni and had to drive in, hence the accident. If it's any consolation, I'm not really hurt, *and* I got a load of luscious food.'

He stared at her, practically barking, 'No Eleanor. It's *not* any consolation. Take care of yourself. OK?'

In a sudden rush to leave, he let go of her and had slammed his car door shut within seconds. The loud revving engine broke the silence of the winter evening. Watching Raphael's car rocket away to be swallowed up by the dark, Eleanor couldn't help but feel a sense of foreboding. Judging from Raphael's telephone conversation, it was obvious something was wrong. Eleanor hoped that Raphael's dad was alright.

He wasn't. Several miles away in the heart of Westminster, Lucifer had disconnected the call and awaited his son, Raphael's arrival.

# 16 UNYIELDING FATHER

Raphael entered his father's study. The heavy oak door slid ominously shut behind him. Lucifer was standing by the window. He turned around. His impeccable dark suit gave him an air of international statesmanship, whilst his crisp white shirt with the top two buttons open denoted a casual look. His ivory complexion offset his profound pitch-black eyes as he stared at Raphael.

The crackling fire in the gilded grate gave the slightly dimmed room an added intensity. The dancing flames hungrily licked the wooden logs, eructating slender shadows on nineteenth century artwork that adorned the endlessly tall walls.

The air was thick with tension as father and son stood opposite each other. With nothing but a large teak table and a tonne of silence separating them, a few seconds passed before Lucifer broke the silence. He said in a cool, smooth voice, 'Did you get here OK? It's been some time since you've been back home.'

Raphael was quiet for another few moments before he answered. He tried to keep cool yet had difficulty keeping his temper in check. He did not want to stay longer than necessary. Forcing himself calm, he replied, 'You asked to see me.' He made fleeting eye contact with his father before staring past Lucifer's shoulder and out of the window. Raphael continued flatly, 'And it wasn't my idea to leave home in the first place. Your rebuke is uncalled for.'

Lucifer's lips curled upwards into a small smile, yet his eyes remained unsmiling. He shifted away from the window and started to move around the huge table. He walked slowly as he pondered, appearing deep in thought. Now standing by the drinks cabinet, he poured himself a Hennessy on ice. The clinking ice-cubes against the glass seemed much louder, as the sound was magnified ten-fold in the near silent room.

'Yes, I know it wasn't your idea to originally leave home. But that's a subject for another day. I don't wish to waste time revisiting tiresome ground. Talking of humans, how is Earth treating you Raphael?'

Raphael knew the signs. His father's chalk-smooth voice had acquired a harder edge, reflective of the severity of his thought process. Drink in hand, Lucifer moved slowly closer to his son. He stopped a few yards away.

Raphael was as still as a statue. He knew he was being goaded. He was also acutely aware that a potential outburst could harm innocent people who he cared for. He wasn't prepared to let that happen. Raphael answered as evenly as he could, 'Earth is fine. There is still much to learn. Humans are truly fascinating creatures.'

'All humans? Or just *one*?'

Lucifer looked directly at his son. His pointed question was uttered gravely, bitter disdain evident in his voice. Raphael's eyes flashed upwards whilst Lucifer continued in an unyielding voice. 'That human. I know you're close. I hadn't realised you were that close. You continue to break the rules. No change there then.'

Clenching his fists into tight balls by his side, Raphael stared ahead, angry rebellion clouding his eyes.

Lucifer watched his son from afar. Sipping his Hennessy, his eyes glossed over Raphael's balled fists. Lucifer continued in his silky voice. 'You're quickly racking up a list of misdemeanours. The park is a good one to begin with. No human has ever set foot in a port-hole. Yet you had no qualms taking her to the park. I *wonder* why.'

As Raphael opened his mouth to speak, Lucifer said sharply, 'I wasn't asking.' Draining his glass, Lucifer placed the empty tumbler on the table with a dull thud. Continuing to slowly pace around his study, Lucifer continued, 'Then there's the pathetic business at the student bar. You must know it's a former military site. Why would you *knowingly* go to a place that's strictly off-limits?'

Lucifer's ice-cool veneer seemed on the verge of cracking as he said somewhat forcefully, 'Then you *cooked* for her. I thought only stupid humans did that sort of thing.' Recollecting himself, his aggravation gave way to a slick smile. 'Great performance of pyrotechnics at the student bar by the way. You made me proud.'

Anger slammed inside Raphael's mind, yet the thought of one person kept him from reacting. He said evenly, 'Eleanor. That's her name. She's just a mate.' Shoving his hands into his pockets, he continued coolly. 'I took her to the port-hole in a moment of boredom. It won't happen again. And I was curious to see if the SU building was really as painful as they say. Turns out it wasn't too bad.' Glancing around, he said flatly, 'There are worse places to be. And friends cook for each other, it's no big deal.'

Lucifer topped up another glass with Armagnac. Swirling the alcohol around the glass, he remained silent for a few moments. He continued with a smile, 'You have to tell her about yourself. Once she knows, she won't want to be near you. I guarantee that. But then, that won't matter, if she doesn't mean anything to you. Let's see how great a friend she *really* is.'

Lucifer didn't like humans. And Raphael had seen what happened to those who didn't meet his father's approval. Raphael knew he had to conceal the fact that he cared about Eleanor. It was with difficulty that Raphael kept a firm grip on the simmering lid of emotion that was by now dangerously close to boiling over.

Raphael spoke defiantly, yet his forcibly level tone suggested that his vexation was down to being dictated to, and not the actual action of potential separation from Eleanor. He replied vehemently, 'I'll tell her. Whilst we're on the issue of transparency, any thoughts on staged accidents?!'

It was Lucifer's turn to flash his eyes at Raphael. He was quiet for a split second. When he spoke, he reciprocated Raphael's earlier defiant tone. Looking his son squarely in the eye, he shrugged to say, 'No one was majorly hurt. A few tests never killed anyone.'

Raphael had suspected foul play with the poisoned chocolates and fairground accident, yet hadn't imagined his father being involved. There was no reason for Eleanor to be on Lucifer's radar. Ever since she had moved to Richmond, he had suspected Eleanor was in danger. He had tried to discover who was behind the strange attacks and unbeknownst to Eleanor, rarely left her side. Yet he had automatically known that his father had engineered the power cut. Lucifer's presence scrambled signals in electromagnetic fields and Raphael had been furious and horrified at the thought of anyone hurting Eleanor, especially his father.

Raphael could keep quiet no longer. This information overload was too much for him to handle and the bubbling emotion now spilled over. He bellowed, 'HOW DARE YOU! You hurt Eleanor, you hurt me. Don't forget that!'

Lucifer jerked his head up at Raphael's outburst. He had finally elicited a confession, something that although he had triumphantly acquired, was cacophony to his ears. He said in smug irritation, 'I thought she was nothing to you? As much as I am fond of lying, I hadn't expected my own son to lie to me.'

'She's my friend. And what the hell was it a test for? It makes me almost happy that I'm in exile. Away from you.'

Lucifer gulped his Armagnac, staring at Raphael like an infuriated parent chastising their difficult child. 'They were tests to see if you really cared about her. Which is obvious that you do. Raphael, I need you to listen to me. I will only say this once.' He spoke quietly to accentuate the significance of his order. 'You haven't got long left on Earth. You need to steer clear of her. Got that?'

His final sentence was more an intimidating statement than harmless question. It was a father telling his son what to do. Striding over to the drinks cabinet, Raphael poured himself a tumbler full of neat Bourbon. Anger which had previously bubbled over, was still fresh and effervescent in Raphael's mind. A bewildering amalgam of fury, rebellion and confusion bombarded him, plunging his mind into fresh chaos.

Taking a large gulp of the deliciously burning liquid, Raphael answered as steadily as he could, 'Eleanor is a friend, nothing more. But you cannot hurt a friend of mine. And I am very much aware of my imminent return home. I look forward to leaving Earth, trust me. Even if that does mean being back here.'

Lucifer held the glass in his hand, still not taking his eyes of Raphael. He wanted to believe his son. Raphael had spoken so convincingly a few moments ago. Lucifer appeared to briefly surrender. 'I shall have to trust you then. She is just a friend to you, I accept that. And you *will* leave Earth by the end of the year.'

Raphael nodded curtly. He said boldly, 'Fine. Anything else?'

'No. You may leave.'

Lucifer watched his son disappear, yet his eyes remained fixed on the door after Raphael's exit. He shook his head in silent incredulity. He would have to monitor the situation closely. Eleanor was trouble. He would not stand anyone hurting his only son. Especially a human.

# 17 WHAT IF

The following day Eleanor tried to sort out her car insurance. The car languished in temporary holding having been towed away after the accident. Getting a taxi to the car lot, she surveyed the car with sadness. Both driver and passenger doors were now twisted lumps of metal whilst the bumper was smashed beyond recognition. The impact of the head on collision had caused instantaneous reversal and extensive damage to the rear. Although the car needed major work, it wasn't a complete write-off.

The insurance company was like a duty-bound doctor, asking perfunctory questions before seeing off the patient in an efficient and impersonal manner. She had already spoken to the other driver involved. Having begrudgingly admitted culpability in his heavy French accent, he had facilitated an easier conversation with her insurance people. She still didn't have to worry her mum, which provided Eleanor with some comfort. The holding lot had a directory of garages that undertook car maintenance, and having chosen a local company, was informed that her car would be fixed within four weeks. She didn't particularly want to drive so soon after the accident and considered the month long hiatus a healthy break from driving.

Eleanor was feeling much better after the long weekend. Although her ribs and elbow were still sore, her left leg had nearly healed. She walked slowly into her lecture the following Tuesday and was immediately surrounded by friends. A stunned Serena was the first to exclaim, whilst Christina and Katherine took a few moments to provide their shocked input.

'Jeez Elle, what *happened* to you??'

'Are you OK?!'

'*That's* why you weren't in lecture last week. Why didn't you call us??'

Smiling weakly Eleanor said, 'It's nothing really, I look a lot worse than I feel.'

A worried Jack said, 'You're limping, bruised and sporting a cast. I can't believe you say that's nothing.'

Eleanor had taken a seat on her usual work-bench next to Jack. His eyes fell on her sling and narrowed in on Raphael's signature. He was quiet for a few moments before saying, 'What's with the fancy signature?'

Not understanding Jack's accusatory tone, she answered slightly confused, 'Raphael-'

Still staring at the cast, Jack was in no mood to be mollified. 'Came round straight away, did he?'

Jack's voice trailed off whilst Serena grabbed a pen from her bag. She chirped, 'Ignore him Elle, he's just sore he wasn't the first person to sign the cast!'

Pulling out her pen Serena said, 'That reminds me, is everything OK with Raphael? He wasn't in his earlier lecture.'

A puzzled Christina said, 'Oh yeah, he seemed a little tense on Friday too. I mean weirder than usual. I remembered because when he bumped into me on his way out, I realised just how delicious his black and grey eyes were.'

Jack made a mock nauseous sound causing Christina to reply, 'What..! We've never been that close before for me to notice this yummy fact!' She let out a delighted giggle and continued. 'Aaanyyway, he seemed to be in a hurry on Friday too and couldn't leave fast enough after the lecture had finished.'

Jack turned to her and added, 'Yeah, we were worried when you didn't show last week. Next time *anything* like that happens, call us, OK? We worry about you.'

It was now Christina's turn to make jocular nauseous sounds and the class eventually quietened when the lecturer started the lesson. Christina's comments however, stuck in Eleanor's mind. Instinctively reaching for her mobile, she scrolled to her missed call register. Eleanor didn't know why she was checking her phone. Something was wrong, she could feel it. Flicking through the call log to the date of the accident, she noted the times of registered missed calls. Jack and Christina just ten minutes into the lecture, her mum at noon, then Valentina shortly after. Raphael's missed call was at 11:01am and the lecture had finished at 11:00am. He had been in a rush to leave, yet it appeared he had tried calling her as soon as the lecture finished.

Eleanor was unsure what to make of this information. Her brain descended into a hazy fog and the lecturer's voice became a background murmur. Trying to grope her way through the confusing blur to common sense, she reasoned that Raphael may have called her whilst en route to wherever his emergency was.

She found herself furtively replaying his voice-mail. It was a curt message. Did she imagine there to be a hint of urgency to it? She contemplated asking him but quickly decided against it. What would she say to him anyway? *Why did he call her straight after leaving his lecture?* Swiftly dismissing the line of neurotic questioning, she floated her way through the Classical Studies lecture.

The rest of the week flew by and still there was no sign of Raphael. Expecting him to be back by now, she noted his week long absence with a growing sense of disquiet. She tried to forget about him and focused on her friends to keep herself busy, finally managing to return Valentina's phone-call on Friday evening.

Eleanor quickly apologised for her delayed response and was about to explain why, when Valentina sullenly declared, 'I feel crap Elle. I was thinking if I could come visit you for a few days..? I've split up from the boyfriend. A fresh scene would do me good. Seeing you would be a much needed bonus.'

Eleanor immediately agreed. 'Oh hon, I'm so sorry! You OK? Break-ups are totally sucky. You're welcome around anytime. When do you want to come?'

'Tomorrow..? Or is that too early?'

Eleanor knew only too well about the sorrow and distress that followed in the wake of a broken relationship. With the long weekend ahead, Eleanor saw this as an ideal opportunity to cheer up one of her oldest friends. She smiled to say, 'Brilliant! Will be good to see you too! Ciao baby!'

Eleanor's break-up with Michael had been one of her most trying times. In one of her now humorous bids to cheer herself up, she had made a *Break-up Box of Guilty Pleasures*. A secret stash of chocolate, an assortment of Spice Girls and Backstreet Boys CDs, and Sunset Beach and Supernatural DVDs formed part of the collection. The box had helped her through some dark times and in a bid to cheer up Valentina, Eleanor scoured the lower cupboard in the lounge for the box. Her sore arm hindered her search and when she finally located it with a sigh of relief, placed it triumphantly on the side cabinet ready for Valentina's arrival. Making a mental note to pick up ice-cream and popcorn tomorrow, Eleanor looked forward to spending all weekend doing nothing but relaxing.

Valentina arrived from Derby the following afternoon. Quietly clutching her weekend holdall, she was withdrawn and unusually introverted, heartbreak evident on her wan face. The weekend saw the girls talking and laughing at the over-the-top plots of Sunset Beach whilst munching on toffee popcorn and eating strawberry cheesecake ice-cream straight from the tub. As both girls relaxed for the full weekend, Valentina left on the Monday looking decidedly cheerful.

Seeing Valentina put Eleanor's life into perspective. She realised how vulnerable she had been, and how much she had changed and moved on. Love was a funny thing, inspiring a rainbow of emotions. It could make you exceedingly happy, so that you felt your heart was going to burst with joy. At the other end, it could also break your spirit, ruthlessly draining you of all positive emotion and replacing it with bitterness, anger and resentment. Looking at Valentina had been like looking into an old mirror that showed Eleanor's previous self. Now, she was fully healed and couldn't be happier.

Raphael's prolonged absence still bugged her. She thought about calling him, but each time she scrolled to his number, an inner voice stopped her and she snapped her phone shut to shove it in her bag. By the end of the second week, she couldn't help herself. At home one late Friday night with the TV blaring in the background, Eleanor found herself texting Raphael. Punching the message in quickly before she could change her mind, she casually asked him how he was and when he was returning to university.

Her phone rang immediately after she had sent the text. Assuming it was Raphael, she didn't even bother to check the caller display and answered within seconds. She was momentarily thrown by her mum's effervescent voice. 'Elle! How are you hon? Just touching base. It's been a while!'

'*Mum*? How are you? I'm good. And yeah, it has been ages.' Eleanor tried to sound upbeat despite being beaten by waves of disappointment. She said lightly, 'Nothing much happening here, just studying and chilling, you know me. How's work? It sounds busy, where you are?'

'Just grabbing dinner from Sou's. I know, I know, it's a bit of a late one.'

'Mum, it's half eleven, I hope work isn't keeping you too busy that you forget to eat? Let me guess, another crazy busy day in the life of Lucille Hudson, hotshot PR!'

'It's all systems go with a deluge of new accounts! You know the footie player who'd tweeted his transgressions? Well I've been head-hunted by his wife to do her PR instead! Can you believe that? Course I had to decline, that is totally unethical. On the flip-side I'm steadily building a reputation so it's great news that she personally asked for me!'

Eleanor couldn't help but be drawn into Lucille's PR world. She said proudly, 'Way to go Mum! Hey, tell me about those new accounts. I'm not one for schadenfreude, but I'm still intrigued by the actions of those lacking good judgment!'

Lucille laughed to say, 'Now now Elle, without sounding totally mean, it's those people that keep me in the job! Last week I took on a bank chairman under fire for not returning his billion pound bonus, huge uproar about that at the minute. Then there's the politician embroiled in an expenses scandal – taxpayers are livid at being charged for his extortionate gardening bill. Actually, there are quite a few of those politicians. It's a busy, immoral world out there! And don't you worry about me honey, I thrive on this sort of thing.'

Both mother and daughter were silent for a few moments in quiet reflection, oblivious of their noisy backgrounds. Lucille said perceptively, 'It's simple. Humans are never satisfied. They always want more. Greed is scary, and some people, possibly the weaker, just don't know when to stop. And honey, they're not stupid... they're just human. Anyway, who am I to judge? I'm only human too. Listen, I'm being handed my chow mein so I really must dash. Take care sweetness, love you lots!'

Eleanor stared at her quiet phone for a few minutes. She had been so sure that Raphael would call back and try as she might, was unable to dispel her increasing apprehension. He had been gone for over a fortnight when he had said he'd be back within a few days. Shaking off her paranoia, she forced herself to abandon all thoughts of Raphael and was suddenly glad to have a busy weekend ahead of her.

Eleanor had invited her friends round for a pizza and DVD night on Saturday. Katherine, Christina and Jack were already seated on the couch, whilst Eleanor let Serena in and promptly curled up on the rug by the floor.

Entering the lounge, Serena excitedly waved the Seventeen Again DVD in her hand and said breathlessly, 'Got the DVD! My bus was crazy late and so was the flipping Tube, sorry! God I hate public transport!'

Eleanor said, 'Not to worry, we don't mind waiting for the sublime Zac Efron! Grab a beer, pizzas are on the way.'

It was a funny, sweet film that drew plenty of laughs and which continued to be the subject of debate after the credits had rolled. Sipping a bottle of Bud whilst surrounded by her friends, Eleanor said, 'Hey guys, here's an age-related "what-if" for you. I know that we're only eighteen, but what advice would you give to your fifteen year old self?'

Jack, quick off the mark was the first to answer. 'It would be: "Don't worry about the girls Jack, they'll come flocking to you!"'

Everyone groaned whilst a preoccupied Christina said, 'Hmm, that's a difficult one. I'd probably say that things aren't as dramatic as they seem, and to just enjoy being young.'

Eleanor laughed to take another sip of beer. 'Totally agree. Thing is, at fifteen, because you don't know any better, even the most trivial situation is magnified forty-fold and blown waaaay out of proportion. Yup, I'd say just enjoy life. Oh, and that you're never gonna get it so good!'

That particular "what-if" spawned other hypothetical scenarios, and the rest of the evening was spent amidst merriment, inquisitive conjecture and bottles of beer and wine. Jack and Katherine left at the end of the evening as they lived close to each other, whilst Christina and Serena stayed the night at Eleanor's. She saw them off on Sunday morning after a breakfast of doorstop toast and coffee. Curling up on the couch soon after with Shakespeare's The Tempest and a top-up of steaming coffee to wake her up, she opened the book at the first page before her phone buzzed an incoming text.

Raphael's name flashed across her mobile. Snatching up her phone, she quickly scrolled to his message.

**Raphael: Sorry for late reply. You busy? Need to talk. Could I come by later?**

Eleanor re-read his text as the underlying urgent tone sent her mind into overdrive. She frowned, trying to analyse the text. She dissected each sentence and studied the cumulative meaning of the words. He was sorry, but he didn't offer any explanation. It was obvious he wanted to see her. He did want to see her, didn't he..? As fuzzy questions brought her mind to a near standstill, she grabbed her phone to text back.

**Eleanor: Just chillin at home. Come round, be nice to see you!**

He said he'd be there within the hour. Intrigue and anticipation kept her from enjoying one of her favourite Shakespearean pieces and when the door-bell rang fifty minutes later, she hastily flung the book down and ran to the door.

Raphael was a vision in black, his tee and inky black jeans shrouding him in a shadowy cloak of obscurity.

'Eleanor.' His hands remained in his pockets as he stared past her shoulder and into the house. 'Wasn't sure if you were busy.' Switching his gaze back to her face, he continued awkwardly, 'How have you been?'

He seemed more guarded today. Unable to conceal her joy at seeing him, she smiled to say, 'Hey stranger, I'm well! How's it going! Come on in!'

He gave her a tight smile, avoiding prolonged eye contact. He spoke quietly, offering an apology almost immediately. It was as if he had a to-do-list in his head, and was ticking off the things to be done, one by one.

'Sorry for not texting you back. It's been pretty manic at my end. How's the arm? You're looking much better.'

Tapping her cast she laughed to say, 'The plaster is irritating the crap outta me, but I'm on the mend. Uni's good, busy as always. Come, let's veg in the lounge.'

He followed her into the house and seated himself on the couch. Sinking into the seat next to him she said lightly, 'Hey, how's your dad?'

Raphael said curtly, 'He's fine.'

He seemed preoccupied. As she wondered what was wrong, she said casually, 'Fancy a drink? There's a fresh pot of coffee?' She paused to say inquisitively, 'Or maybe something stronger?'

He seemed to come alive as he replied, 'Brandy would be good.'

Fetching him a glass of Courvoisier and a coffee refill for herself, Eleanor settled back onto the couch. His gaze fell on The Tempest as he flicked distractedly through the book. Sheets of loose paper lying on the coffee table momentarily distracted him. He seemed genuinely interested when he asked, 'What are these papers? Sorry, I don't mean to be intrusive.'

It was the *What If* list from the previous night which her friends had drawn up, with various scenarios having a brief, albeit humorous pro and con list.

Eleanor smiled to say, 'Nothing, much. It was a bunch of us being silly after watching a film yesterday. We were just talking about hypothetical *what if* situations. You know, like what advice would you give your fifteen year old self? What would you rather be, divinely beautiful, or extraordinarily clever? What would happen if you won a massive lottery? Serena made me laugh though. The first thing she said she'd buy was a whole bunch of suitcases, then go shopping and actually fill the empty trunks with her new wares. I think Aquascutum was her first stop. She's crazy but I love her..!'

Reflecting on the list for a few moments, he turned to face Eleanor and said, 'Here's a "what if" for you.' He paused for a few long seconds before saying, 'Do you believe in life outside Earth?'

Eleanor stifled a chuckle. 'What do you mean, like the X Files? I don't expect aliens to descend to Earth and *"Phone Home"* or anything!'

She was silenced by his sombre stare. He wasn't impressed. Trying to take his bizarre question seriously, she answered lightly, 'Well, I *do* think there's life out there, not sure exactly what though. I did believe in UFOs like a decade ago. I was eight and had rubbed my eyes too hard when I thought I was seeing spinning discs in a kaleidoscope of crazy colours.'

His grave look was in stark contrast to her cheeky grin. His thoughtful eyes continued to rake over her face as he contemplated a different tack. He pressed on, 'What if you could live forever? Someone handed you an elixir which guaranteed eternal life. Would you drink it?' Raphael's resolute voice amplified the unusual question.

Eleanor tried to be serious. She answered with a small smile, 'Hmm, not sure. You've got to look at the positives. With eternal life, I assume you'd never be ill? That would be sort of cool. Hey that reminds me. Did you ever see Mork and Mindy? Robin Williams was out of this world!'

She was teasing him. A sense of urgency crept into Raphael's determined voice. 'I'm serious Eleanor.' He waited for her to respond, his eyes never leaving her face.

Twirling a few strands of hair whilst deep in thought, Eleanor pondered Raphael's question. 'Nope, I wouldn't drink it.' Shaking her head lightly, she said, 'I just couldn't. I'd rather grow old gracefully with my loved ones around me. I mean, what's the point of a life with no friends or family? It would be an isolated existence. I can imagine it to be a thoroughly lonely time. What about you?'

Raphael continued to stare at her. Something was amiss, Eleanor could feel it. His eyes flashed up at her. He said flatly, 'I'm no fan of eternal life.' He continued glaring through the dull window as he continued with conviction. 'I don't rate eternal life either. What if-' His momentary hesitation gave way to terse questions. 'What if you didn't have a choice in the matter? What if it was preternatural? Something you were born with?' He paused for the briefest of seconds and exhaled deeply before saying, 'And you're right, it *is* a lonely place to be.'

Eleanor smiled and shrugged. 'Well, if it's inherited, then there's not really anything you can do about it, is there? And-'

Eleanor's chatter came to an abrupt standstill. The conversation trailed into silence. In sharing banter about incredible situations, a serious tone had somehow infiltrated the conversation. Raphael was the most concise person she knew and just a few seconds ago, he had agreed that having eternal life meant being lonely. It suddenly dawned on her what he was saying. Those few moments of self-realisation seemed to take forever to pass, yet weirdly flew by with lightning speed. The confession afforded lucidity as she realised Raphael was immortal.

Eleanor was stunned into silence. She mentally replayed Raphael's last sentence. She didn't know how long she was quiet for. She tried to formulate a sentence, but was unsure what to say. She started questioning herself; maybe she had heard incorrectly? When she finally spoke, she said, 'OK, backup. I'm not entirely sure if I got this right. Correct me if I'm wrong, but you're saying... you're saying that you're... *immortal..?*'

It was an outrageously peculiar notion, yet somewhere deep within, Eleanor knew he wasn't lying. Raphael wasn't the sort of person to joke around, and looking at him now, he appeared to be in a state of shock. His jaw flexed in hard concentration. He looked up at her with those bottomless black eyes which today, were tinged with sadness and defiance in equal measure.

'Yes.'

The one syllable confirmation was devastatingly simple yet profoundly obscure, as Eleanor attempted to consider the intricate details of this weighted reply. Her mind had ceased to function in protest of receiving a significant, life-changing piece of information. She sat on the couch wondering what the next steps were. Trying to adopt a logical approach to an otherwise nonsensical situation, she said hesitantly, 'OK.'

She paused again, before continuing with more confidence. 'You're immortal.' She was silent again before saying in a daze, 'I'm just trying to understand. Could I ask how? What makes you–'

Raphael slowly shook his head, the air of despondency around him becoming heavier by the minute as his eyes darted in her direction. He seemed to take heart from Eleanor's initial response and said, 'Here goes. I'm immortal because it's inherited. My father... He's not your conventional kind of guy.' He paused again, before restarting reluctantly. This time he spoke more determinedly. 'Lucifer. That's my father.'

Raphael had said what he had to say. He continued looking ahead, out of the window and beyond. After a few minutes, he turned his head towards Eleanor. When he eventually made eye contact, he saw that she was looking at him steadily. Her face was expressionless. Not happy, not sad. It gave nothing away.

The only discernible noise in the room was the rhythmic ticking of the dusty clock. Raphael waited patiently for a response. After about five minutes, Eleanor appeared to register some sort of emotion. Taking a sip of her now lukewarm coffee, she said quietly, 'So. Lucifer. That's your dad huh...'

Eleanor didn't know why, but saying out loud the seemingly preposterous statement lent much needed gravitas to the otherwise bizarre situation. Her mind remained a void for the next few minutes. She finally said, 'I... I don't know what to say Raphael. I'm... I just...'

Worry had settled on his brow as he scoured her bewildered face for the slightest reaction. She chewed her lip and eventually murmured, 'I don't get it... Help me understand, Raphael.' She turned towards him and listened intently as he started to speak.

# 18 RAPHAEL'S STORY

My father created me in a mirror image of himself. Hell is my home. It's where I was raised.'

He started tentatively, slowly discarding caution as he offered his explanation to a silent Eleanor. 'Hell's a busy place these days. Once the dead leave Earth, their souls have two main trajectories. Good souls ascend to Heaven. Evil souls descend to Hell.'

His eyes flickered up to her face. 'Hell-bound souls go there due to their negative earthly actions. I'm not going to go through the list, but particular deeds guarantee a place in Hell. This is where souls are tortured for eternity.'

He watched her sitting in silence. Encouraged by her composure he went on. 'Before my existence, a different policy was in place. Souls were tortured for a thousand years, before being cast out to return to Earth. Here, they had one final chance to redeem themselves. If they repeated their mistakes, they would find themselves permanent residents of Hell. If however they atoned for their sins and rectified their mistakes whilst embracing the learning curve, they found their pathway to Heaven after death.

'After my father created me, he adopted a hard-line approach. A new strategy of zero tolerance became rule. Once in Hell, souls had no chance of redemption and remained a permanent fixture. My father also wanted me to be as involved as possible. I worked the full spectrum, from choosing which souls were Hell-bound, to devising specific torture programs. Capital punishment was my principal duty.'

Raphael was silent for a few long seconds as he recalled his time in Hell with a shudder. Forcing himself to relive untold horror, he continued in an unsteady voice. 'Torture was my job. I despised it with all my being. The activities were gruesome, to say the least. I didn't want to be involved. But I felt obliged. I had been doing my job for a few centuries and had remained silent with growing discontent.

'When younger, it is easier to accept situations as they are. I frequently found myself questioning my father's ideologies. Did souls really deserve permanent torture? What about second chances? No one is infallible, I truly believe that.

'One day, I challenged my father's principles. Gravely displeased, he believed that humans deserved just the one chance, and that they held their destiny in their own hands. If they were too foolish not to act in their best interests during their time on Earth, then they simply deserved to be in Hell for eternity. Whilst my father felt he was merely redressing the balance, I believed the opposite and stuck to my guns.

'We had reached a stalemate with neither one of us willing to back down. I remember he was absolutely livid. I had never spoken up against him. For once, when I raised an issue which I felt strongly about, my opinion was scorned and dismissed. My father failed to see how reinstating the thousand year rule would make a difference. He considered Earth to be no better than Hell and that my "perceived compassion" for humans was unnatural. My father argued that humans were unwise creatures, deserving to be tortured in Hell and on Earth. His word was final.

'Although I was created in my father's mirror image, I held a totally opposing viewpoint. I had opinions and thoughts of my own, which were exceedingly dissimilar to his. This was a point of contention for a number of decades. Although I had voiced my concerns, I remained in Hell. I didn't see any another option.

'The breaking point came one day when a fresh batch of newly departed souls arrived in Hell. They were sentenced to eternal damnation whilst watching their loved ones suffer from afar.'

Raphael stopped. The room fell silent for the next few minutes, as he deliberated on if, and how he should continue. The soothing ticking of the clock was in harsh juxtaposition to Raphael's alarming admission.

'As the souls were herded together to watch their loved ones undergo the most horrific of tortures, the head of the family cried out. I was used to hearing last minute pleas, yet this one was different. He begged for his family to be released, asking instead for himself to remain in Hell. That was an altruistic act, and the thoughts of a truly repentant soul.

'I was at a loss. It was my job, my duty to torture these souls. Yet, his self-sacrificial cry for help awakened something in me. It was the first time I had encountered selflessness – and I couldn't ignore it. Most souls beg for mercy for themselves, so the heroic act of the father wanting to save his family from unspeakable torture beguiled me.

'He did not deserve to be in Hell, I was aware of that much. I knew what I had to do. I made a decision to free him and his family, to give them a second chance. I took it upon myself to liberate them. Using the simplest magic, I transformed them into doves. Somehow, my father learnt of the plan. He was infuriated. Just before I could set the doves free, he caged and hurled them into the fire.'

Raphael's voice dropped to its lowest point. His shock was mirrored in Eleanor's face. Try as she might, she could no longer remain impassive. The story was horrifyingly macabre and it took her a few seconds to slip back into the role of objective listener. Focusing on a spot through the window, he didn't even look in her direction as he continued his wretched tale.

'There is something appallingly sick, seeing terror blaze in the eyes of one who is facing a fate worse than death. As flames engulfed the cage, the doves realised their time was near. Crying out and fluttering wildly, they beat their wings in futile hope. I was unable to save them. That moment still haunts me.

'It was a critical moment and a significant juncture in our relationship. My father was angry on two counts. Firstly, because I had gone against his wishes. Secondly because I had shown compassion to what he considered to be unworthy human souls. A huge showdown followed.

'His view is that humans are little more than self-destructive creatures powered by greed. He also asserts that God shares his perspective. When death, destruction and suffering are prevalent on an Earth ravaged with war and disease, he marvels how God can allow his beloved humans to lead discontented lives filled with affliction and distress.

'When I refused to back down, my father said there was only one way I would learn. That was to observe humans firsthand. He truly thought that I would come to see what he saw, that humans deserve castigation and ultimate condemnation.'

He was watching her again as he said with a resigned air, 'That's the reason I'm here on Earth. I'm in exile. Sent to learn a lesson. And now you know.'

They were both silent for a few minutes. His eyes searched her face as she remained quiet. When she eventually spoke, it was like someone else was talking. She felt numb. Her brain that usually went into overdrive simply puttered to a stop and refused to function. She whispered, 'That's... That's really...'

Fear and dismay made a temporary home on Raphael's face. His balled fists accentuated his anxiety, as he wondered what Eleanor would say. She continued hesitantly, 'OK, let's break this down. You've been on Earth for how long..?'

He whispered, 'Nearly five hundred years. You're the first human... Person I've told.'

Eleanor gulped, her throat suddenly dry. 'Woah. That's some exile.'

They were silent again as Eleanor struggled what to think and say. Common sense was staying away for now. The ticking of the clock now seemed much louder. Eleanor exhaled to say, 'I appreciate you telling me. Really, I do. I don't know what to say to you. I just...'

He slipped off the sofa. Standing a few feet away from her, he said, 'I know it's a lot to take in. I'm going to go now. Call me when-' He paused and quickly changed tack. 'Call me if you want to chat.'

There was a poignancy about his last sentence. He spoke hesitantly, unsure if she wanted to see him again. Eleanor looked up. Nodding her acknowledgement, she was about to say that she would call him. Before she could get her words out, he had already headed to the door and was gone.

She sat reeling on the couch for the next twenty minutes. Not moving or thinking, her mind was blank, like a single white sheet of A4 paper. Then came the blizzard of questions, filling up the paper with frantic scribbling like a court transcriber speed-writing a lengthy conversation of a meaty case. She tried to make sense of the illegible writing whilst sitting in a cloud of disbelief, yet Raphael's admission left her stunned.

He was the son of the Devil. She repeated the sentence a few times in her head, to familiarise herself with the phrase. If she said it often enough, it may register some form of understanding. *Son of the Devil. Son of the Devil.* Each time she said it, the words appeared in front of her, painted in stark blood red font and she shook her head to dispel the wording with growing astonishment. She was no closer to understanding the situation. Lucidity evaded Eleanor, which for once did not bother her, as she remained in an oddly comfortable mist of bewildered confusion.

It was an unbelievable revelation, yet as soon as he had uttered those words, she had known it was true. He wouldn't lie to her. On some level, his uncanny admission had made sense and she hadn't even questioned the validity of his declaration.

She attempted to make sense of the bizarre state of affairs. Starting from the beginning, she recalled the early days of their tentative friendship. She had experienced an unsettling feeling whenever she was near him. She had known something was wrong then, yet after getting to know Raphael, her disquiet had gradually vanished. He had always seemed different from the crowd. He never talked about his family and had no earthly connections that she knew of. Then there was the peculiar incident of the peaceful park. A park, which try as she might, could not locate. It was as if it had disappeared into thin air. She suddenly remembered Raphael's missed call on the day of the accident. He had called her immediately after the lecture ended. Almost as if he had known she was in danger. As the little tell-tale signs slowly became clearer, Eleanor realised she had subconsciously known all along that Raphael had a secret to hide.

She wondered about the implications of Raphael's confession and the impact on their friendship. Eleanor wasn't overtly religious. She didn't pray every day. But she *did* believe in God and tried to be a good person. The Devil was the antithesis, and one would assume, the son was too. A double-barrelled question flared in her mind. *Was Raphael evil and could he ever hurt her?* As quickly as the question had appeared, her mind automatically shouted a reverberating '*NO!*'

Raphael was not evil. She knew that. He had been contrite during his confession and the harrowing subject of torture had affected him to such a degree that he couldn't speak of it without wincing. Whatever he was, he wasn't evil.

Telling her had not been an easy task, yet he had ploughed on with his difficult confession. She was the only person he had told. That meant something. She suddenly recalled a recent conversation with her mum who she remembered saying, *'Who am I to judge, I'm only human.'*

She realised she had been sitting on the couch for the past hour. She wasn't hungry and spent the rest of the day preoccupied with thoughts of Raphael. As ambivalence gave way to curiosity, Eleanor found herself wanting to know more. If he had been on Earth for the past five hundred years, how long was his exile? If he visited his dad a few weeks ago, how did he get there? How *different* was he to his dad? The most important question of all, was why had he felt the need to tell her in the first place?

These questions and many more whirled through her mind like a full speed tornado. When she finally fell asleep that night, she resolved to call Raphael in the morning. He was her friend and she cherished his friendship, regardless. Besides, she wanted answers.

# 19 FRESH EYES

Having fallen into a fitful sleep, an exhausted Eleanor awoke in the early hours of a dull February morning. Through gummy eyes she noted it was only 3:15am. Sleep continued to evade her as she dragged herself out of bed for an early morning decaf coffee. Thankful it was her day off university, she sat in the draughty kitchen whilst waiting for her coffee to brew.

She yawned, stretching her good arm above her head. A fortnight after the accident, she was nearly as good as new. Most of her bruises had disappeared, her leg had fully healed and although her wrist remained in the cast, she no longer needed the sling. Gazing out of the window at the expansive grey sky, she suddenly wondered what Raphael was doing.

She had planned on spending Sunday finishing her theology, yet she was in no mood to study. Reaching for her phone, she was on the verge of texting Raphael to arrange a meeting. Realising it was only 3:30am and not wishing to disturb him, she abruptly stopped. Sipping her hot coffee, she wondered if he was sleeping before a question popped into her head. *Could he even sleep? If he wasn't human, what else could he do?* Surreal questions fell on deaf, sleepy ears. She eventually decided to text him at a more considerate time. Just in case he *did* sleep.

She whiled away the next few hours sitting through diabolically dull early morning TV. For once, it suited her purpose by providing a nondescript canvas to her overactive mind. As soon as it hit 7:00am, she texted Raphael if he was free to meet later that afternoon. His immediate reply gave her the impression that he was already awake. As they arranged to meet in town at 2:00pm, Eleanor anticipated the meeting with curious excitement, listlessly channel flicking all the while.

Despite the sunshine, it was a chilly afternoon. Sensibly wearing her black skinny jeans and yellow jumper, she made her way into central London. Arriving a little early, she waited outside Café Prinzi sipping her hot Americano. As the slender twirls of steam rose to fix themselves on the cold February air, she inhaled the delicious coffee aroma and curled her cold fingers around the protective collar of the coffee cup.

She looked around a densely packed Oxford Street. The lunch-time rush saw people spill onto the streets in hectic chaos, jostling past her on the pavement, too wrapped up in their own world to pay attention to anything else, let alone the numerous homeless tramps who dotted the two mile stretch.

The streets of London were notorious for the homeless that came out in droves in the winter months, nestling at cash-points and entrances of restaurants and cafés. Although used to seeing them beg, the crawling guilt was fresh every time she saw a vagrant, and she always gave money whenever she could.

A tramp had settled a few metres away from Eleanor's feet. She heard his forceful call through the cacophony of beeping cars, thrum of traffic and a hundred simultaneous shouted conversations. He hollered, 'CHANGE PLEASE! Anyone spare some change please! Just for a cup of tea! GOD WILL BLESS YOU! If he doesn't, I will!'

Eyeing his empty flat-cap on the floor with sympathy, he continued his rousing call for change. Digging into her pockets, she fished out a few pound coins and ducking down, gently dropped the money in. His ears pricked up, expertly zeroing in on the melodious chink of coins above the din, as his hungry eyes rested on the money. Staring at Eleanor's still outstretched hand, he stared into her hazel eyes and gave a wide toothy smile to say, 'Bless you love! May all your dreams come true!' Snatching the coins from the floor, he dismissed Eleanor with a sideways glance and continued his unrelenting plea for cash.

Happy to have fulfilled her good deed of the day, Eleanor switched her gaze to the teeming mass of people. She suddenly spied Raphael walking towards her. In the blurry grey crowd of hundreds of people, she saw only him. Her heart thrummed in her chest as she watched him with fresh eyes. Everything yet nothing had changed. She knew he had a good heart, irrespective of his background. The only difference was that she respected him more.

He was now less than fifty metres away. She suddenly couldn't wait to tell him that it was all going to be OK. Part of her wished that she could have been more supportive during his confession, yet her debilitating shock had prevented any coherent speech. She could no longer wait to be near him. Edging her way through the crowds which annoyingly hampered her speed, she finally came face to face with Raphael.

She was slightly out of breath, having half-run the five blocks that separated them. He wore his vintage Triumph jacket and charcoal jeans combo. He looked expectantly at her, anxiety worrying his face. Without a word, Eleanor flung her arms around him. She didn't care about her slightly sore elbow, as she rested her face on his cool jacket. He caught her quickly as his strong arms folded around her, securing her in a tight embrace. The crowds melted away into an irrelevant jumble as she remained in his arms for the next few moments. Looking up at him, she said, 'Hey. You're my best friend. That's *never* going to change, got that?'

His face was awash with relief. A smile slowly spread across his face as he leaned in towards her and said in a hushed voice, 'Thank you.'

She whispered back, 'Thank *you* for being you.'

His eyes swum in gratitude. With an exquisite smile he said, 'Want to go some place... not so manic?' Reading her shining eyes he said, 'Cool. I know just the spot.'

Manoeuvring their way through the back streets, they walked to Raphael's parked Yamaha. Jumping on the back without a single word, the engine roared to life. They pulled up outside the Victoria & Albert Museum twenty minutes later. Eleanor contained her mystification at the chosen venue; although it was quieter than Oxford Street, it was still a tourist hotspot and not the quietest place to have a private conversation. She remained silent as they passed the main entrance and made their way to the garden courtyard of the museum. Raphael said casually, 'Want to grab a coffee first?'

Eleanor nodded appreciatively and after waiting in line at the coffee cart, they were soon walking away with hot Americanos. Settling on the steps under the small archway, Eleanor watched people milling around the packed courtyard enjoying the bright winter sunshine. Raphael said calmly, 'It'll be less busy soon.'

Eleanor enjoyed the comfortable silence. The tight archway perfectly seated two and rendered a conversation private without difficulty. She started, 'Central London is going to be busy practically anywhere. Anyway, I just-'

She stopped talking to hear the unmistakeable rumble of thunder in the distance. A perplexed Eleanor looked up at the gathering clouds. The skies were clear and bright when she had left and she had neglected to pack an umbrella. As she thought about her inevitable soaking journey home, the few raindrops swiftly transformed to a full-on downpour.

As the drenched tourists made a run for the dry indoors, Eleanor suddenly looked at Raphael. He had cryptically said a few moments ago that it would get less busy. Raphael cocked his head to one side and smiled. Eleanor gulped to stammer, 'You... You made that happen, right..?'

He simply nodded, his smile increasing as Eleanor looked on in awe. 'How..? That's crazy. That was one of the things I was going to ask you. So... you can... *change* weather patterns..?'

He spoke with ease. In the wake of yesterday's confession, a more assured, less diffident Raphael had emerged. He was starting to open up to her. Finally, she would get to know him better and get some answers in the process. Glancing in her direction he said, 'Not change weather patterns. I can manipulate the weather. I do it mainly to get about.'

He put his coffee cup down and was on his feet in one agile movement. She wondered why he was suddenly standing and laughing lightly said, 'Okaaaay. Now I'm officially confused. You do it to get about..? What do you mean?'

'This.'

One moment he was standing in front of her. The next, he had disappeared. Eleanor was momentarily startled. She blinked in bewilderment, tentatively taking a sip of coffee. It was a full minute before he reappeared. He was standing in the exact same spot. It was as if he hadn't been away for those sixty seconds. The only clues of his departure were his dripping wet leather jacket and his head to foot soaking body. Eleanor shook her head in disbelief.

'Ohhh. OK. Now I know what you meant. Sort of. Hey, aren't you going to get cold in the rain-'

She suddenly remembered a snippet of a conversation from what seemed like an age away. As it clicked that he was unaffected by the cold, Eleanor stopped herself from uttering a seemingly irrelevant sentence.

Raphael grinned to say, 'I'm perpetually warm-blooded. I'll dry off in a few minutes.'

An apologetic Eleanor whispered, 'Sorry, I keep forgetting you're not human.'

His eyes shot up to hers when she said the last two words. The smile that appeared on his face was suddenly hollow and Eleanor guiltily mumbled an apology. 'Sorry. I... I didn't mean for it to come out like that. What I meant was-'

'Don't worry. You were simply stating the obvious. There's nothing wrong with that. And I'm not human. You *can* say it out loud. It really doesn't bother me.'

He had now taken a seat next to her. Peeling off his drenched jacket, he placed it to one side and inadvertently shifted a few inches closer to her. Taking a swig of coffee, he threw her a furtive glance over the edge of his cup. Playfully shaking rain from his dripping wet hair onto her, he said, 'Any more questions? Shoot.'

Here was Eleanor's opportunity. She had carte blanche to ask him anything. The huge obstruction that had previously blocked intimacy had been partly demolished by a large bulldozer powered by the energy of the confession. The wall which she had felt between them since the first day they met, had now crumbled away. She had a number of questions to ask him. Questions which had plagued her till the early hours of the morning. She wanted to know more, yet she remained quiet for the next few moments.

She was glad he was being open with her, and sitting next to him under the archway, remained contentedly cheerful. Reluctant to rock the happy equilibrium, she started hesitantly. 'OK. You have special powers. I mean, you can *do* things. What else can you..?'

She watched him serenely gulping his coffee, as if having this surreal discussion was one of the most natural things to talk about. He grinned to say, 'I was wondering how long it would take you to ask that. I can influence the weather, which you know. My method of getting about is somewhat different to humans too. I can become airborne quite easily. Again, you've seen that.'

She said slowly, 'Except I didn't actually *see* you. You can... *fly*..?'

He smiled at her perplexed face and explained, 'I move fast so that I'm usually not visible to the naked eye. Sometimes I forget that you're human.'

Eleanor looked up and he suddenly fell silent, dismayed at potentially causing her offence. Before he could say anything Eleanor laughed to say, 'I am human. You *can* say it out loud. It *really* doesn't bother me.'

They looked at each and burst out laughing. It was an odd scenario. Just as she had forgotten about his supernatural abilities, he too had forgotten about her human state, each considering the other's background irrelevant to their friendship. Smiling he continued, 'OK, as I was saying, I can fly. I can also read humans.'

'*Read* humans?'

'I'll try to explain, hang on.' He paused, trying to find the words to best describe his extraordinary powers. 'Humans have an aura, almost like a vibe, which is invisible. It is projected by the soul and is indicative of one's earthly actions. I can see an aura, which I use as a sort of yardstick to gage a person's positivity. I have a heightened sense of perception. Being highly intuitive, I can usually sense things before they happen.' He added as an afterthought, 'Oh, and I can read minds too.'

Eleanor listened transfixed. Their conversation had taken on a dreamlike quality as she had been pulled deeper into Raphael's magical world. As she slowly digested the information, she realised the impact of his last sentence. He could read minds. That meant he could read hers too.

She suddenly remembered how much she disliked him in the early stages when they were mere acquaintances. He had known what she was thinking. She thought of the time when she had dreamt of kissing him and quickly averted her gaze. He bent his head whilst shooting her a surreptitious glance.

'Don't worry, I don't know what you're thinking now. I mean, I can guess, but my conjecture would be as good as any human. My telepathic abilities are a little... erratic at the moment.'

Eleanor looked on mystified. Raphael appeared lost in thought for a few moments as he gazed ahead into the empty courtyard. In response to her confusion he said, 'I don't quite understand it either. Recently, it's been more unreliable. You're one of the few I can no longer read. Which is bizarre. Maybe it's because I'm nearing the end of my exile, or some other reas-'

Eleanor's eyes instantly flitted up to his. Trying to keep her voice level she asked, 'End of exile? When... When do you go back..?'

Eleanor's embarrassment vanished, concern edging its way to the forefront of her suddenly panicked mind. Her cool enquiry held an undercurrent of apprehension and he switched his gaze to look directly at her. He seemed troubled for a split second as he said evenly, 'I return at the end of this year. I can't believe I've been here for nearly five hundred years.'

Eleanor exhaled as she continued to absorb the incredible scenario which she found herself embroiled in. It was utterly unbelievable, yet nothing had ever felt so real. As she sifted through the myriad pressing questions she asked inquisitively, 'So, you've been on Earth for nearly five hundred years. How have you done it? I mean, I get impatient waiting a week for something as trivial as exam results. Five hundred years is a loooong time to wait. What on earth have you been doing for this long? Sorry, no pun intended...'

He finished his coffee and leant casually back on his elbows. The inadvertent pun seemed to amuse him and a small smile escaped his lips. He spoke candidly with the weight of experience behind him. 'It's been a learning curve. It was difficult at first. Earth is a complicated place. And humans are such complex creatures. It took a while to get used to it here. I've travelled the whole world. I've had a tonne of jobs in heaps of different places. My CV would be hundreds of pages long. From working in a sixteenth century poorhouse to a twentieth century prime ministerial cabinet, you think of a job and I've probably done it. In the process, I've met people from varying walks of life; as the environments have varied greatly, so has my experience. To see first-hand how humans interact with one another and how they function has been the whole point of my exile. I've spent the last century in Europe and here I am today.'

Hearing Raphael speak of life in the sixteenth century only added another bizarre dimension to their surreal conversation. As her mind pieced the random jigsaw pieces of fantastical information together, she suddenly wondered how old he was. Curiosity tugged at her, like a small child incessantly plucking at its parent's coat for attention. She said quietly with a hint of reverence, 'So... you've been here for some time. Exactly um, how old are you?'

'Considerably older than you are.' Sitting upright again, he laughed lightly as he said, 'Over six hundred years old.'

The mere mention of his age reminded her all over again that she was in the presence of a paranormal being. In a bid to appear unaffected, she shrugged to say, 'Guess I should respect my elders!'

He grinned as they burst into reciprocated laughter. Slipping back into comfortable silence, they each continued to absorb the enormity of the situation. Eleanor was still taking stock when she suddenly thought of the situation from Raphael's perspective. She wondered what he was thinking and had a sudden thought.

Did he handle situations differently as his genetic make-up was different? Did paranormal beings have a different perspective and as a consequence, did he *feel* differently? Had he told his secret to anyone else? She imagined the relief that he probably felt, finally being able to speak the unspeakable, something that had not been verbalised for centuries. She imagined not being able to talk to her friends or family and bearing a secret which was bizarre and enormous to render it almost unfathomable. As she contemplated this train of thought, Raphael continued looking at her puzzled face.

By way of explanation she said, 'I was wondering how you did it. I mean, not talking to anyone about it. Did you want to tell anyone? I know I'd go stir crazy if I didn't have people to talk to. Then I thought, maybe it would affect you in a different way, you know, as you're not... Sorry, I'm not making much sense...'

His voice acquired a hardened edge when he eventually said, 'It's curious you mention that. When I first came to Earth, I was used to being by myself. Not having a confidante was of little consequence to me. I thought nothing of it. Then I started observing humans. I saw how they built relationships. How they confided and communicated with each other. I saw trust being built and how through nourishment and maintenance, it grew to powerfully bond people together. I noted this with amused interest from afar. It was a remarkable aspect of human behaviour and I spent many years exploring the different facets and studying it. I could never be part of it. I couldn't touch or feel it. And that was absolutely fine. Then you came along.'

He paused as his eyes fixed on a heavy cloud in the grey sky. He continued more fervently as he explained, 'Don't get me wrong – I have spent time with other humans.' His eyes flickered in her direction as he quickly said, 'Not much time, because I never stayed in one place long enough. Being close to anyone was of no consequence because I simply didn't care enough. Then I met you. Suddenly, I wanted to be part of the trust equation. It was something I had never wanted before. It was an overwhelming desire where I wanted to trust you and have it reciprocated. I don't quite understand why, so I can't explain.'

Running his fingers through his hair, his eyes continued to scour the sky as if looking for answers there. 'It was the oddest sensation. Something of which I had little control over, had been kick-started deep within me. I was used to observing humans from afar, so to get to know you, let alone get close to you, was a wholly interesting experience for me.'

Eleanor listened in curious silence. Raphael had wanted to trust her. She felt her heart do a variation of mini-cartwheels and back-flips like a first class Olympic gymnast. Yet with the amount of crucially significant information being ferried to and fro, she was unable to ascertain a reason for her growing delight.

He said eagerly, 'I just had to get to know you. I tried to be as normal as I could. From living a certain way for a number of years, to embracing change was difficult. Yet, I *wanted* to undergo this change. If it meant getting to know you, then I'd do it. It was a slow process. Some days, I found the futility of the exercise simply frustrating. I found myself seeing humans in a new light. I started to respect them. All this time, they had been merely intriguing objects of amused interest. Suddenly, I was observing them for an entirely different reason. I wanted to see how they built rapport and interacted with one another, so I could learn and use them as a working example. Once I had mocked humans from afar. Suddenly I found myself empathising with them.'

Eleanor felt as if she was having an outer body experience. She was just starting to wrap her head around Raphael's magical qualities, but one other aspect was too incredible to believe.

He wanted to get to know *her*. She was quietly comfortable in her own skin, yet she knew that there were plenty of others more beautiful and intelligent than her. Apart from a lifelong crush on Nicholas Cage, she thought she was really quite normal. It didn't make sense for him to be interested in her.

She continued to listen in dumbfounded surprise as he said, 'No matter how hard I tried, you didn't seem to want to know me. Many days, I cursed myself for wanting something I had little experience or knowledge of. But the desire to get to know you was too strong for me to dismiss. It was something I tried to ignore. I was pulled headlong, like a magnet against my will. I had to continue trying, so I listened to your thoughts whenever I had the opportunity. I know you're a private person, so I tried not to listen in too much. Yet I couldn't help myself. I didn't choose this particular power. It's just the way I'm built.'

Eleanor couldn't keep quiet a moment longer. She turned around to face Raphael, forcing him to look at her. Although she spoke with certainty, her heart was a sandpit of doubt and indecision. Deep down, she wanted the answer to be something so profound, she couldn't even bear to think of it, let alone verbalise it.

She said as evenly as she could, 'Why me, Raphael? You've been around for some time. No doubt you've had the opportunity to get close to far more worldly, not to mention interesting people than me. I'm the very epitome of normal. Why confide in *me*?'

Raphael hooked his eyes on her. For a few moments they were still, staring at each other in the heavy silence of the archway. He said quietly, 'Because I have never felt affinity to anyone or anything. The first time I saw you, I knew I had found a true friend. And friends don't keep secrets from one another. That's why I'm telling you. I trust you. Implicitly.'

An unnamed emotion swirled in Eleanor's chest as she reluctantly pulled her eyes away from him. If he had a heart, he had laid it bare. His pure sincerity aroused a sudden swell of tenderness which she didn't know she was capable of. The intensity rendered her speechless. She loved and doted on her friends and family, however the emotion that overwhelmed Eleanor was new. She felt as if she was drinking stars, which floated in her stomach before whooshing back up and shining out of her mouth in an exultant smile.

Silent exhilaration overwhelmed her as the gravity of his words sunk in. She whispered, 'Thank you for trusting me.' As an afterthought, she smiled to say, 'I'm glad you persevered. I know I was being difficult and I didn't make it easy for you. I was going through a tough time. I know that's no excuse. And hey, for the record, I trust you too. Implicitly.'

Worry flickered across Raphael's face as he seemed to be mulling something over. Eleanor suddenly wished she knew what he was thinking and realised she didn't blame him for listening in to her thoughts. She knew she would have done the same had she been in his position.

They continued sitting peacefully together. A gargantuan amount of significant information had been divulged, some of which she was still digesting. She had a tonne of questions to ask him. For now though, it was enough. The remaining questions whizzing around her head could wait for some other day.

The silence was abruptly broken by the sudden buzzing of her phone. Fumbling in her bag, she read a text from Katherine, who was organising Jack's surprise birthday party. A smiling Eleanor quickly confirmed her attendance to the bar on Thursday and dropped the phone in her bag. Glancing up to catch a flash of Raphael's sardonic smile, she said brightly, 'It's Jack's birthday this Thursday. A whole bunch of us will be going out then. Wanna come along?'

He said coolly, 'Can't make it. Besides I don't think Jack will be pleased to see me. He'd rather I kept my distance.'

'Huh? Why wouldn't he be pleased? You guys don't talk much as you don't have common ground, that's all. Jack likes everyone.'

Raphael took a moment to answer. A wry smile crept onto his face as he said, 'He doesn't want me around. You – he likes. That's the one thing we have in common. *You.*'

Eleanor couldn't think of a single reason why Jack would dislike Raphael. Frowning she said, 'I know he likes me, just as I like him. We've been mates since the first week of uni. And how do you know he doesn't-'

She stopped talking as she suddenly realised that Raphael's assertion had probably come about by reading Jack's thoughts. 'Ohhh, you *know*. That's sort of a handy trick. Wish I could read minds. Actually, scratch that. My mind is a minefield of random thoughts anyway, and to add thoughts of others into the mix, would just tip me over the edge into full-on insanity mode.'

Shaking his head Raphael chuckled to say, 'OK, it's nearly 5:00pm. What are you doing now?'

'I've got Serena coming round later. I can't cancel, we've already rearranged twice over. So yeah, it's home for me.'

He was suddenly on his feet. Extending his hand to her, she grabbed hold of it and pulled herself up. His hand lingered on hers for a few seconds before he pulled away from her and grabbed his jacket. As they started walking out from under the archway, it was suddenly bright again. The sun streamed out onto the courtyard, throwing shimmering rays onto the central pond. Tilting her head to catch Raphael's eyes, she joked, 'What, no rain now?'

'I've got the bike today, no rain needed.' He smiled and added as an afterthought, 'This is nice. Being able to be myself around you.'

A small bubble of happiness bobbed in her chest, making her feel slightly giddy. Having dipped into Raphael's phantasmagorical world for the past few hours, she felt detached from reality. She was a part of Raphael's incredible world and she had never felt safer.

The ride home took less than thirty minutes as Raphael expeditiously ploughed through the central London rush hour. She clung to him as he swiftly manoeuvred the sharp corners and cramped in-roads, the chilly wind whipping strands of hair across her cool face as she melded deeper into his leather jacket. He didn't stick around as she watched him speed away after dropping her off outside her house. Crossing her porch to enter the cold house in a daze, she felt the past few hours could easily have been a dream.

She had to really focus on Serena and a tiny, guilty part of her couldn't wait till her friend had left. She just needed time to think and properly digest Raphael's confession. Later that night when snuggled in bed, Eleanor found herself thinking about Raphael's parentage. Just as her mind would start to accept this crucial piece of information, she would question the fantastical scenario and convince herself that she had somehow misheard or misunderstood the situation. In a mental sparring match between doubt and common sense, the latter emotion would prevail, leaving Eleanor convinced she was going mad. She knew deep down, that this implausible yet extraordinary situation was actually very real. Things would never be the same again. She valued Raphael's friendship. That would never change. Her heavy eyelids weary with over-thinking welcomed sleep like a long lost friend. She ignored the light whisperings of her inner voice as she drifted off into the arms of a peaceful slumber. *Raphael is the son of Lucifer. Be careful...*

# 20 LUCIDITY

For the first time since Eleanor had started university, she wanted to skip lectures. She wanted to see Raphael now, not three days later. So when he texted if she was free that afternoon, she quickly agreed.

She rushed out after her final lecture to find him waiting outside the university gates. Leaning casually against the wall, he cut a striking figure in his loose cream jumper and black jeans. She slowly realised that his confession had zero negative impact on her opinion of him. Yes, she was still curious about various aspects of his life. Yes, it had been a lot to take in. But, he was still the same person and her admiration for him had intensified a hundred fold.

Eleanor's smile grew as each quickened footstep brought her nearer to him. He said with a smile, 'Want to go some place quiet? Lots to catch up on.' Eleanor nodded as they made their way to a near-empty café down one of the side-streets.

The chatter of a few students and low background noise of the TV provided decent cover. Ordering two coffees from a bored waiter, they took a seat at the rear where they had little chance of being interrupted.

It was a neat but fairly nondescript café. Pushing aside a six month old tatty magazine which lay on the formica table, Eleanor was suddenly thoughtful. Sighing at the headline which shouted *"KING OF POP FOUND DEAD IN L.A MANSION!"* she said, 'Can't believe he's dead. I grew up with the guy. I mean, not actually *with* him, but you know what I mean. The world won't be the same.'

There was a cryptic glint in his eyes as Raphael murmured, 'You shouldn't believe everything you read.' Eleanor stared at him. Ignoring her incredulous look, he said swiftly, 'I'd much rather talk about interesting things. How was uni? Enjoy your lectures?'

'*Hang on.* You can't say something like that and not explain. Besides, you don't have to ask me details about my otherwise mundane life, I think we're past that. My life is fairly routine and dull in comparison to yours. No need for small talk-'

Raphael's eyes clouded over. He snapped back, 'It's not small talk Eleanor. I am genuinely interested in you. And your life is far from mundane. A thought to consider. Just like you want to know more about me, I want to know more about you. I find you-' He paused for a split second before continuing, 'I find humans fascinating. So to be up close to one for more than a few hours is extraordinary. I'm overwhelmed by this minefield of information. I... I couldn't ask for more.'

An astounded Eleanor smiled to say, 'That's exactly how I feel about *you*! Crazy world huh? We're the same but different, if that makes sense..?'

Radiating tension he said, '*We are very different.* We're worlds apart Eleanor. Yet I feel this connection with you, which try as I might, I'm unable to understand or dismiss.'

Eleanor suddenly remembered that she too had felt drawn to Raphael in their first encounter when he had tried to help her with her painting. And in their subsequent meetings, the allure had been too potent to ignore. She nodded in agreement to say, 'I feel it too, this connection... it feels so right. Oh, and before I forget, uni was fine, although the lectures seemed to drag a little. I couldn't wait to see you actually.'

She glimpsed a muted smile on his lips as he said, 'Couldn't wait huh? Well, go on, shoot. I know you want to continue probing. Although I must admit that I find your method of questioning amusing. You seem almost embarrassed to question me. Don't be reluctant. I won't take offence.'

Eleanor said slowly, 'You're right. I want to know so much more about you. I've surpassed the initial shock, so now, one enquiry snowballs into another, and before I know it, a whole avalanche of questions are piling up in my head.' She chewed her lip in concentration. 'OK, here goes. There are loads of myths, surrounding the Dev-'

She paused, wondering how to proceed without sounding facetious or insulting as her accelerated speech led into a full-on ramble. 'There are so many myths, legends about Sat- I mean your- Sorry, what would you *prefer* me to call him? Gosh, I really suck at this...'

Raphael interjected to quell Eleanor's growing embarrassment. 'He's my father. Lucifer. Satan. The Devil. Pick one. Any. He's not fussy.' He smiled to add as an afterthought, 'And you're doing OK... considering the context of this crazy conversation.'

Buoyed by his vote of confidence, Eleanor went on. 'Are there any places you can't visit, with Lucifer being your father?'

She felt strangely apprehensive acknowledging Raphael's relationship. It was a bizarre concept to understand. Although she was slowly accepting the idea, to fully understand the gravity of Raphael's parentage would take a little longer. Hours. Days even. Possibly weeks. She spoke more decisively and started with a neutral opening gambit.

'I'm interested to know your take on good and evil.' Although she tried to remain objective, her mind vacillated onto the age old debate of good versus evil. She continued, 'I've seen the films. I've read the books. Although my memory is sort of hazy on the Bible front, having read it years ago when I was at school. Can you go to religious places, like church? Not that you'd *want* to go to church... Or would you? Have you ever been? I mean, what would you do there anyway? What would happen if you touched a Bible, would you be hurt? See, told you I had lots of questions...'

Raphael watched her with quiet amusement. He took a few seconds to respond as he weighed up his answer. 'That is a minefield Eleanor. I could spend days discussing every argument expounded on this exhaustive topic. I'll try to give you a snapshot. For many centuries, myth has intermingled with the truth. Extensive debate surrounds the concept of good and evil. However a lot of it is open to interpretation. Over the years, humans have construed this good versus evil concept with varying degrees of success. It's been very hit and miss – what one person considered evil in the sixteenth century may not necessarily be thought wicked today.'

Catching sight of her perplexed frown he said, 'An example may help. Adultery is classified as one of the cardinal sins and has been since time began. Centuries ago, death by stoning was the punishment for an adulterer. Nowadays, most societies are accepting of one who has committed this sin. Although the act of adultery is frowned upon, the individual in question is no longer vilified or considered to be an abhorrent character.'

Heartened to see confusion dwindle on Eleanor's face, he continued in a forthright manner. 'About those books and films. Most literature written about good and evil adheres to stereotypes. Characters are usually severe caricatures of what is deemed good or evil. Films like that amuse me. I understand that certain things are said and written for the sake of entertainment, but I have yet to see something that is an accurate representation of how it really is. That's when I realise how clueless humans are. Either clueless or just incredibly naive.' He said with a stoic smile, 'And yes, I can go to church – if I wanted to. I choose not to. It holds nothing for me. And I won't... spontaneously combust if I come in contact with the Bible or any other religious artefact. It'll take more than the Bible to do that.'

Fleeting fear clutched at her heart as she said, 'Good to hear that you can't be hurt.' Her evident relief bolstered his subdued smile to a full-on grin. She said with increasing confidence, 'It's nice to know basic info like that. Not that I'd ever thrust a Bible on you. I don't carry one around or anything. I mean, I'm not a Bible basher, but it's just nice to know basic, um... house-keeping rules.'

Her comment drew a contented laugh from him. 'Not many people leave me dumbfounded – you're the exception.' He paused a moment before saying, 'Your question about church is an interesting one. I have been, but only once. I was curious. There was a time when I couldn't go anywhere near a church. Nowadays, I can enter one with zero problem.'

Clocking her perplexed frown he continued more determinedly. 'It's simple. I am unable to enter places filled with hope and happiness. Up until the beginning of this century, church was a no-go area. I couldn't be in the vicinity of one without experiencing severe repercussions. One day, I passed a derelict building not knowing it held consecrated ground. This shocked and surprised me, as I had no adverse reaction. My curiosity got the better of me and I found myself tentatively making my way into the church. It was 1907 and my first and only visit. Since then, I can pass and enter a church without experiencing pain.'

As the gravity of his words sunk in, she asked inquisitively, 'OK... So what happens when you *do*, inadvertently or otherwise, enter a place that is technically *out of bounds*?'

He tore his eyes away from her and drained his black coffee. Just as he placed his empty cup down, a passing waitress asked if he wanted anything else. Eleanor's cup was now empty too, yet the waitress seemed to only notice Raphael. He acknowledged the over-attentive waitress with a faint smile before saying, 'Eleanor, would you like the same again? Americano?' As Eleanor nodded he said, 'And a black coffee for me. Thank you.'

The waitress seemed to be in a loitering mood. Placing her toned arm on her hip she purred, 'Oh, I am sorry. I hadn't realised the other cup was empty. I'll get refills for both you and your *girlfriend..*?'

As the waitress waited expectantly, Eleanor ignored the fleeting pang of irritation exacerbated by the increased time the waitress stared at Raphael. She knew why the waitress annoyed her. They were in the midst of a serious conversation and Eleanor wanted to know more about Raphael, not watch some random girl hit on him. She waited for Raphael to respond, who seemed amused by the waitress and her obvious advances. He said coolly, 'Yes. My girlfriend and I would like those refills. Make mine a double shot.'

Quietly happy as she watched the waitress slink away, Eleanor said wryly, 'You don't have to be a mind-reader to know what she was thinking. So I'm your pretend girlfriend huh? Keeps the baying fans at arms length I suppose.'

Her sarcasm was not lost on him. His eyes flickered up to hers before his face broke into a grin. Shrugging he said, 'Just makes for an easier life. Now, where were we?'

Seeing Raphael dismiss the pretty waitress filled Eleanor with an odd satisfaction and she didn't know why. Her heart and mind were engaged in a tussle; her psyche trying to wrangle an explanation as to the exact reason why she was suddenly pleased. Like steam evaporating into thin air, her cheery disposition was short-lived, as her mind suddenly returned to the serious conversation topic. They were in tune with one another as Raphael too, mirrored her serious demeanour.

He said soberly, 'There are a number of places that are out of bounds. Hope and happiness are a toxic fusion. I can just about handle one or the other. But both together... have a debilitating effect on me.'

Eleanor held her breath. She was torn between curiosity about his fascinating situation and wilful ignorance in her refusal to know that he could be hurt. Her mouth was suddenly dry. Thankful for the cup of coffee that appeared courtesy of the sullen waitress, she took a gulp of the hot liquid to try and melt the growing lump of dread in her throat that refused to be dislodged.

Raphael now spoke in a matter of fact tone. 'My genetic make-up, if you can call it that, is vastly different to that of a human being. I don't eat, sleep, rest or breathe as a normal person would.' He paused for a gulp of coffee. 'I have a voracious appetite. I can eat and drink twenty times the normal amount and still my appetite will not be sated. It took me a while to keep my cravings under control. When I first came to Earth, I had no idea of what was considered "normal". I could get through gallons of drink and tonnes of food without feeling remotely satisfied. Now, I can get by on a regular sized dinner.' He continued with a sly smile, 'I think humans call it "portion control". Of course it took time to curb my appetite as I learnt to eat and drink in proportion, which is essentially nothing more than a "blending in" exercise to avert suspicion that I am anything other than human. One of the few things I can taste is alcohol. It fortifies me.'

Eleanor said with an incredulous smile, 'So you can eat and drink anything you want and *still* look like this? If the flying and mind-reading wasn't enough, it's safe to say that I'm officially envious with this whole "eat-anything-you-want-and-still-look-hot."'

She hadn't realised the impact of her words until she clocked his astounded face. His eyes widened with surprise as she gently conceded, 'Oh come on, you know what they say about you. People think you're easy on the eye...'

He stared at her for a few long seconds before saying, 'People in general? *Anyone* in particular..?' His eyes never left her face.

She blushed, bursting into laughter. 'You seriously want names? Lecture theatres filled with near swooning females not enough for you? You know all that stuff anyway. Besides, I'm not into ego massage.'

He grinned before saying, 'What were we talking about now? That's it – blending in exercises. I may not be human, but I'm not infallible. Should I enter a prohibited place, I experience something akin to torture.'

With his gaze fixed firmly on his coffee cup he said quietly, 'I feel shrouded in a miasma of pain. Relentless stabbing covers every inch of my skin, igniting a ferocious fire in my body. It fuels my inner angst and I am swiftly drained of any other feeling. The raging inferno coursing through me has a violent undertaking, urging me to commit despicable, reprehensible deeds.'

Avoiding eye contact he chose to focus on the notice-board behind her instead. His voice had dropped a few octaves as he continued the conversation with obvious difficulty. 'It's an inner struggle. I have to battle to keep these grotesque thoughts under control, which is somewhat difficult when I am devoid of emotion and energy. It is a furious pain unlike any other. I am glad you will never know what it feels like.'

Eleanor had stilled in silent distress as Raphael continued in a low voice. 'I am forbidden to enter places filled with hope and happiness. Army base camps and hospitals are the two main ones, although there are others. This rules out sites of former military or hospitals too.' As an afterthought he added, 'It's complicated. These places have a high concentration of bad energy too, with both places being a hub of death and destruction. Yet the good energy outweighs the bad. Never underestimate the power of hope. Army personnel are amongst the most hopeful people I have ever encountered. Their propensity for optimism in the face of horrifying adversity astounds me every time.'

Eleanor suddenly remembered Raphael's reaction when he had practically ran from the army general at university. She was suddenly filled with stone cold fear at the thought of Raphael being hurt. Trying to remain calm she murmured, 'You mentioned other places?'

He said dismissively, 'There are various places, yet in the past few decades the numbers have dwindled. Sporting grounds are perennially difficult areas. Some football grounds are out of bounds.' Her brows pulled together as she struggled to understand what he was saying. He explained, 'Think about it. Sporting grounds are frequently filled with legions of fans, fervently wishing and hoping their team wins. Crazy as it sounds, I have to steer clear of these places.'

Comprehension dawned on her as she suddenly remembered an article from a few years ago. She said slowly, 'Tell me about it, English footie fans are the most fanatic in the world. I read this newspaper column ages ago that reported these fans were more afraid of watching England lose penalties than lose their wallet, job or hair. Mental huh? I only remembered that because it was one *bizarro* article.'

He was silently amused as he said, 'Some football clubs are more accessible than others. The northern teams are the worst – I can't get anywhere near Manchester City Football Club. The devotion of their fans is absolutely crazy. They're one of a kind. But not all football is out of bounds. I can watch most other clubs with ease – there's not much hope there. Just extreme self-confidence and assumption.'

She smiled but couldn't forget the notion of him being hurt. She said quietly, 'You mentioned an internal battle of sorts. What did you mean by grotesque thoughts? Do you only have them in these "forbidden places" or just, generally?'

Running a hand through his hair, he continued to stare over her shoulder at the curled up flyers on the notice-board. Switching his gaze back to her face he said firmly, 'I was created in the mirror image of my father. He is technically pure evil. So am I. My primal instinct is to harbour ill-feeling and drive death and destruction. This is not my choice. It's the way I am built. The main difference between me and my father, is that I seem to have this inexplicable over-riding concern for humans.'

His eyes flickered back to the notice-board behind her and hooked onto an old Christmas card emblazoned with glittery snowflakes. After a beat he said, 'I liken humans to snowflakes – both are fragile, unique and easily destroyed. I don't think humans should be harmed, whereas my father does. That's where the whole problem stemmed from. My father doesn't understand how this came to be. To be brutally honest, neither do I.' He paused again, tracing a finger over his hot coffee cup whilst deep in thought. 'Although I was built to be pure evil, I have a sense of right and wrong. I am something of an anomaly, a strange amalgam of evil smashed through with a shot of virtue. Conflicting emotions I know, which makes it all the more... complicated being me.'

He was silent again. The subject matter was now so personal that he was looking into himself to explain his very being. Eleanor suddenly wondered if he had a soul. Could paranormal beings have a soul, or was it *"pre-damned"*? Did this term even exist? She would ask Raphael later.

She smiled encouragingly as he faltered, 'For the most part... I keep the negative side of my character under control. Sometimes... the evil is too strong to ignore. I revel in wicked actions and thoughts. It's a constant struggle for me. Being in the presence of hope and happiness is a bizarre sensation too. In order to counteract the positive emotion that surrounds me, I feel a trigger within go off. I suddenly have an aching desire to address the balance of good and evil. It is with great difficulty that I curb my powers to exert evil actions. Being in forbidden places only accentuates my malevolent thoughts and the ultimate need to be immoral, hence me staying away from these places. It's a stark reminder that I am not human.'

He was quiet for a few moments before repeating vehemently, 'I am not human. I AM NOT HUMAN. Sometimes, I forget that.'

Eleanor couldn't comprehend the notion of Raphael being pure evil. She refused to believe it. To fight against oneself and do battle on a daily basis to suppress negative characteristics was incredible. She was suddenly filled with awe. He had persevered, trying his utmost to go against the grain whilst keeping in check whatever destructive thoughts he had.

Placing her hand lightly on his and looking directly at him she said, 'I don't care about your bad thoughts. We all have them. It's part of being human.' She reluctantly pulled her hand away and said a little more determinedly, 'You're more human than you think you are.'

He returned her gaze in thankful relief before they were interrupted once again by the waitress. This time, she was efficient and did not loiter. Picking up the bill, they soon found themselves outside the café.

It was now 6:30pm. Standing on the pavement Eleanor watched stray students make their way home. Refreshed by the bracing air, she knew she wasn't ready to leave Raphael just yet. He glanced up at the rapidly darkening skies. With a wicked grin he said, 'Fancy a ride home?'

# 21 JOYRIDE

Eleanor stared at the charcoal sky. Pregnant clouds edged into view as overwhelming anticipation filled her with delicious elation. Taking a few gulps of cool air to calm her crackling nerves, she turned to Raphael and said, 'Ready when you are.'

He led the way around the rear of the café which opened onto a secluded area. Amongst the debris, panels of discarded corrugated steel lay strewn on the ground. It had started to rain. Eleanor thought the bursting rainclouds sounded like a magical maestro, with the pattering raindrops playing a light prelude on the steel before switching to a full-on concerto. With the subtlest of smiles he said, 'Hold tight.'

Engulfed in sheets of rain, Eleanor draped her bag across her body to ensure it wouldn't fall off mid-flight. Shivering slightly as she zipped up her now rain-saturated jacket, spine-tingling exhilaration over-rode the cold as she edged closer to Raphael.

He swept her off her feet in one swift movement. His arms were a protective block on her back and under her legs as she realised with an embarrassed thrill that he was carrying her like a child. Her arms automatically found their way around his neck, where they stayed clasped in a tight circle. Before she could think of anything else she felt a mighty whoosh.

The ensuing moments were a blur. One minute, Raphael was standing on the corrugated steel, the panels crunching loudly beneath his feet. The next, she felt she had been propelled head first in a blustery gush of air and half imagined she was being sucked into a giant hand-dryer. Alarmed, she squeezed her eyes shut. She no longer felt the rain, just the comforting hot mass which she clung on to. After a few moments she tentatively opened her eyes.

All she could see for miles around was a near black blanket speckled with glitter. As the ecstasy of the adventure kicked in, it took her a few moments to realise that the blanket was a star-spotted sky. She peered below, stunned by the view of tiny rooftops dotted on the ground. The houses were barely discernible, like pieces of earthly Lego which oddly seemed to be within arms reach. Aware that they were several hundred feet above ground, Eleanor revelled in this dreamlike birds eye view for a few minutes, not wanting to move, think or blink as her erratically beating heart leapt into her mouth.

Suddenly overwhelmed, she nestled closer to him. She felt his arm muscles flex as he gently tightened his hold in a protective grip. With his chin nearly touching her hair, he whispered to say, 'I've got you. Don't worry.'

Eleanor couldn't stop staring at the star-spotted sky, exhaling as apprehension and fear melted away. When she eventually managed to speak, it was a choked, awe-struck whisper. 'This view is beyond cool. You can do this anytime you want? Do you realise how *awesome* that is..?'

She continued staring at the twinkling stars. Avoiding making eye contact at the prospect of being so close to him, Eleanor hadn't seen his face since they had taken flight. She could feel him smile as he said, 'Pretty cool, huh?'

Hovering mid-air in a delicate bobbing motion, Eleanor felt as if she was afloat in a cool lake. With Raphael as her warm, solid anchor, she had never felt safer. Which was odd, considering she was hundreds of feet above the ground. He seemed pleased by her exultant expression as he said, 'Hold tight. Just a quick detour before I take you back home.'

Nestling closer to him, she smiled as he began the downward descent. The wintry air had little effect on Eleanor as she held onto Raphael's warm body. Although the rain had abated, a fresh drizzle provided the necessary camouflage for them. Flying lower, Eleanor noticed the colours become more vivid. The greenery of the leafy treetops was stunning against the ground dotted with twinkling evening lamps.

Peering over Raphael's arms, Eleanor gasped at the spectacular view of London by night. The length of London Bridge was packed with moving dots which she quickly realised were hundreds of commuters making their journey home. Watching people from afar who were oblivious to their presence rendered their excursion as all the more special. It felt deliciously clandestine and Eleanor revelled in the fact that it was her and Raphael's secret. She glimpsed the murky waters of the River Thames on the left, snaking under the bridge and beyond. As they moved further north of the City, she suddenly spied St. Paul's cathedral. The mottled grey exterior tempered with age gave it a beautiful antique marble effect. The magnificent dome stood boldly like a revered army general exuding hushed authority.

Passing over the cathedral filled her with serenity and she suddenly wondered what Raphael thought about her religious convictions. Did he know she was religious? Maybe it didn't bother him.

A random thought flitted through Eleanor's mind. Where was Raphael's *real* home? She still had so many questions to ask and was glad he had given her carte blanche to ask away. She earmarked another question for him as they continued their magical journey across London.

The London Eye with its packed unhurried carriages was fascinating to watch, whilst Nelson's Column cut a striking stance as virtuous signpost in Trafalgar Square. Across Westminster Bridge the bright lights of Oxford Street twinkled in the dark, whilst a sea of shoppers flooded the perennially crowded street. Savouring the view of her exclusive sight-seeing tour, she sighed in satisfied delight. She normally experienced this level of exhilaration after four cups of strong coffee. This was a natural high.

She felt a sudden rush of affection for Raphael. He had given her the opportunity to see into his world, an enigmatically private existence that no one else was privy to. As Raphael's sole confidante, Eleanor felt as if she wore a temporary visitor's badge which currently granted her fettered access to his world. Curiosity returned with a vengeance as she suddenly found herself wondering if her badge would ever be upgraded to bona fide inhabitant. A sudden thought darted through her mind which sent shivers of expectation through her body. *What would it be like to be a permanent resident in Raphael's world?*

She didn't know why she thought it. Maybe his enticing world seemed so new and exciting in comparison to her humdrum human existence. That had to be the only reason.

He was fast approaching the end of his exile. She knew he wasn't going to be around for much longer and to want to be part of his world was senseless. Not to mention idiotic. Chiding herself for letting a ridiculous thought ever cross her mind, she shook her head to dispel the embarrassingly foolish notion. Her subconscious however had other ideas, refusing to back down by its unwillingness to dismiss this particular train of thought. Her mind was like a Catherine-wheel firework. As it continued gently spinning, a question was fired after each temporary lull, forcing Eleanor to address the questions being asked. Could she ever be part of his world? She felt she was, yet the reality of the situation was far from straightforward. More importantly, did he consider her to be part of his world? As these thoughts occupied her she failed to notice that they were no longer in the air.

He had set her down gently and she hadn't even realised. As her feet touched a hard stone surface, Eleanor thought for a few seconds that they were back on the ground. They weren't. She had been airborne for the best part of an hour now and her legs suddenly felt stiff from being in the same position. Stretching and smiling, she looked around.

They were standing in an open air turret. The terracotta stone structure was approximately twenty square feet with four main pillars and an overhead darker stone roof. Cool air swished through the glassless windows. She was still for a few moments, trying to establish her location. With peaking curiosity, she turned to him and said, 'Where are we? Looks familiar..?'

Running to the edge of the building, she looked out ahead. It was a clear view from the turret. Her eye level gaze fell on the distinctive crown of the building opposite. Recognising it as the roof of Westminster Abbey, she realised with mounting shock that she was standing in the uppermost roof of the Houses of Parliament directly opposite the Abbey. She had studied pictures of the turret and the adjacent buildings for one of her history projects back at college. Textbook pictures didn't do the buildings any justice. She whispered, 'I'm- I can't believe... And I thought the evening couldn't get any better!'

She felt like an overwhelmed child who had been handed the best present in the whole world. Keen to share this moment with Raphael, she called out to him.

She hadn't realised he was already behind her. As she stood looking out, he gently placed his left arm inches away from hers. Unaffected by the chilly February air, he was the warm wall that she gently leaned on whilst staring in awe ahead. They stood lost in thought for what seemed like a few minutes, yet when the Big Ben clock chimed 8:30pm, Eleanor realised they had been standing together in quiet contemplation for over half an hour. She felt the gentle vibration of his voice as he whispered, 'Hope you had a nice evening.'

A laughing Eleanor said, 'It was a brilliant evening! Nice is a major understatement! It's like saying Churchill was an average prime minister. I've had the best time ever!'

Raphael said with a low chuckle, 'Glad you had fun. Better get you home, it's getting late.'

Reluctantly tearing herself away from the side of the turret, she peered over the edge for one final look. The low hum of the odd car speeding past was the only distinct noise. Bar the twenty-four hour police patrol stationed at the entrances of Parliament, there was minimal activity on the streets below. Eleanor was suddenly conscious that they were in forbidden territory. If the police noticed them, she knew they wouldn't hesitate to make use of the large guns that hung ostentatiously on their arms.

She spun round to face Raphael and whispered, 'Can't believe I'm here! Suppose we've gotta go. I'd hate to think what the policemen would do if they found we were chilling out twenty metres above their heads. I know we're probably trespassing here, but this is sort of cool!'

Raphael said with a devious glint in his eye, 'Don't worry about the policemen. They've never noticed before. And it's only *technically* trespassing if you get caught.'

He was beside her in a split second, lifting her up as if she was as light as a bag of candy floss. With her arms around his neck again, they had soon taken flight before Raphael whispered in her ear, 'Just a quick pit-stop. Hold tight.'

Eleanor was briefly woozy as the unexpected change in speed threw her off guard. She heard a swish before his speed dialled back down to normal. They continued travelling in silence, as Eleanor's mind was side-tracked by the fleeting images of the landscape flying by. She felt flying in Raphael's arms was the most natural thing to do. She couldn't think of a better place to be. She didn't want to be anywhere else.

Twenty minutes later they were outside Eleanor's house. She hadn't realised until she spied her porch behind Raphael. She gushed, 'Thank you for the best time ever! Words cannot describe how much... you rock!'

His chest puffed out with unspoken pride as he slowly extended his arm to hand her something. She strained her eyes in the dark and glimpsed a section of coloured fabric. Surprise on her face turned to mystification as she looked down at a Union Jack flag in her hand.

Raphael grinned to say, 'Just a little souvenir from your first flying trip.'

Still confused, Eleanor stared firstly at Raphael, then back at the flag, its cool damp cotton increasing the chill in her fingertips. She said lightly, 'Where did you...'

'From the pit-stop.' He seemed to revel in her confused surprise. Slowly stepping away from her and now openly grinning, he said, 'It was a great evening. The pleasure was all mine. See you at uni on Thursday?'

'Yup. Goodnight Raphael. Sweet dreams!'

The rain resumed and Eleanor waited till he had disappeared. She practically skipped into the house. She loved every second of her incredible, whimsical, out of this world journey. As she fell asleep that night, her inner voice managed to get in one final pot-shot before she fell asleep. *Today was brilliant. But did you love flying or who you were flying with..?*

# 22 BEST OF BOTH WORLDS

Eleanor awoke the following morning in a contented haze. For a few moments she questioned whether she had actually flown across London, before her eyes fell on the large flag draped across the dresser. She smiled, stretching leisurely in bed whilst mentally replaying scenes from the previous evening. The wholly unreal experience of flying was in stark contrast to being in Raphael's arms, which had felt as natural as breathing.

Eleanor intuitively felt a hidden depth to their relationship. It was that odd grey area, the next step up on the relationship ladder covered in clouds of confusion. Currently balanced on the friendship rung, she was unsure what the next stage was. Recently she had felt the urge to step up and feel for the next rung, however something always stopped her.

She loved Raphael as a friend. Convincing herself that it was a purely platonic relationship, she had found herself ignoring her inner voice that hinted at something more. Her subconscious ineffectually harangued her on numerous occasions, wanting her to recognise a fact that was too obscure to comprehend or believe. Unsure of the mixed signals which bombarded her brain on a disturbingly frequent basis, she gently shook her head in amused futility as she skipped into the shower.

Dressed and now ready for university, she flicked on the TV, wanting to quickly cram some news over breakfast. She managed to catch the back-end of the weather report. The bored weather anchor reported the unpredictable recent weather. Warning of freak storms driven by winds entering the hemisphere via the Atlantic, he sternly advised of potential localised flooding and damage to external property. His report was nondescript, but his final throwaway comment caught Eleanor's attention.

Looking into the camera with a fixed smile to unsuccessfully draw attention away from his sleep deprived eyes, whilst trying to inject a touch of humour into an otherwise anodyne report, the anchor said, 'And a word of advice to Her Majesty The Queen and everyone else. With more stormy weather ahead, take special care of yourselves and your homes too. Otherwise it will be disappearing flags and garden gnomes all round. Have a great day all and see you at 9:00am for your next hourly update!'

It took Eleanor a few seconds to realise the Buckingham Palace flag was now draped across her dresser. She shook her head in quiet disbelief at the absurdity of royal property now being in her bedroom. Conceding that it barely constituted grand larceny, Eleanor told herself that the Palace probably had a few extra flags anyway. It had been a spontaneous if not audacious gift. Raphael had given it to her with a good heart and she loved it.

She walked into university with an extra bounce in her step. The sun was out on a crisp February morning and Eleanor felt as if she could conquer the world. Spying her friends from afar, she remembered she had been looking forward to discussing Jack's birthday preparations all week. Yet the nearer she got to the group, she felt an unexpected sense of emptiness tug at her insides.

All she could think about was Raphael. She wanted to spend time with him and mull over their dreamlike conversations in peace, instead of standing here in university. Although she loved hanging out with her friends, she wanted to see Raphael more. Baffled and mildly irritated, she told herself to focus on the friends in front of her as she walked with them into lecture.

Eleanor's mind wasn't her own today. She mistakenly imagined passing Raphael in the corridor, who turned out to be some random ginger-haired guy who incidentally looked nothing like him. Great, she thought to herself; she was also seeing him everywhere now. A double-barrelled question flitted through her mystified mind as she wondered why she thought of him so frequently, and why it bugged her in the first place. The fruitless search for answers seemed to be part of an ingenious never-ending circle which continued to fuel Eleanor's curiosity. On any other normal day this would have frustrated her. Today, she was in too good a mood to be annoyed.

Her mobile suddenly buzzed an incoming message. She flicked open her phone, thinking, hoping it was Raphael. The text from the car garage was good news all the same. Her car had been repaired ahead of schedule and was ready to be picked up. She decided to go straight after university, conceding that driving would decrease her overall travel time, meaning more time for study. And Raphael.

Listening absentmindedly to her friends chatter in the canteen, she felt guilt echo through her body and prick her penitent conscience. It was Jack's birthday and all she could think of was spending more time with Raphael. She knew she wasn't being paranoid when Serena's faraway voice came to holler in her ear, 'Earth calling Elle! You were miles away! Isn't it a shame about the bakery? Damn this flipping recession!'

Snapping to attention, Eleanor quickly tried to grasp the gist of the conversation whilst feeling sheepishly unhelpful and unintentionally rude. Attempting to rectify the problem, she asked if there were any party preparations that she could help with.

Katherine had organised everything except the cake. Leafing through the various alternative bakery flyers, she dejectedly lamented the ill-timed closure of the chosen bakery. 'We paid for the cake upfront too. No chance of a refund. Crap or what! Guess it'll have to be a Tesco job.'

Serena's comment now made sense. Eleanor piped up, 'I'll do it! It won't be a masterpiece, but I make a mean sponge!' Eleanor swiftly volunteered to shoulder the cake-baking duties with gusto as her friends nodded in appreciation. Savouring the sweet sense of gratification, Eleanor was happy that she was contributing something to the party. She also loved cooking, so her gift to Jack would have a personal touch too.

Deciding to spend a constructive evening baking and not think about Raphael, Eleanor left university on time to make her way to the repair garage. Looking at her Peugeot as she signed the discharge paperwork, she realised how much she had missed driving. Calm and in control as she climbed into the driver seat, she was a little shaky when the engine came to life. Within fifteen minutes she was driving normally again, winding down the windows and blasting Anathema to keep her company on her drive home. Telling herself to focus on the cake and that thoughts of Raphael were strictly out of bounds, she pulled into her drive-way and ran into the house to start on Jack's present.

Eleanor loved baking and considered it to be therapeutic, an art form and hobby all rolled into one. Baking reminded Eleanor of her childhood and she couldn't help but feel the warm buzz of familiarity as she assembled the paper packaged ingredients on the work-top. More significantly, cooking was something she had control over. She knew exactly what the end result would be. Life was so much more complicated. With no concrete recipe for success, what it ultimately came down to was trial and error. Sometimes it was just nice to be in control.

Creaming the butter and vanilla sugar together in regular circular motions, she contemplated the gravity of Raphael's confession. Once it was said out loud, there was no retracting of words, no going back. It had obviously been a difficult confession and his very act of confiding in her filled her with an appreciative thrill. Additional thoughts entered the mix along with the flour and eggs, as she wondered what Raphael really thought of humans.

Placing two deep batter-filled tins in the oven, she leant on the washer still deep in thought. There was something supremely comforting about standing in a warm kitchen, with the delicious aroma of vanilla spreading throughout the house. Whipping the buttercream, she wondered about Raphael's first few days on Earth. What exactly had he done in nearly 500 years? He had mentioned that he had known other humans for a short while. How close did he get to them? And were any of them girls?

She had spent the best part of the evening thinking about him. For a split second, Eleanor wondered if she crossed his mind as much as he did hers. Suddenly embarrassed, she quickly dismissed the thought as wilfully childish. Why would he think of her when he had more pressing issues?

She was aware that she had become attached to Raphael, something she tried to ignore as she clocked Raphael at the university entrance the following day. Arriving earlier than usual meant they were the only inhabitants of the otherwise empty car-park. Waiting as she parked up, he was by her side within moments and swiftly opened her car door. He looked content and relaxed in his green tee and dark blue jeans as he leant on the door. He eyed her car to say, 'How are you? Good to see that your car's OK.'

Smiling in the glare of the sun she said, 'I'm great! How are you? Good news about the car huh? I wasn't going to drive in, but I had Jack-' Suddenly remembering the stolen flag, she chirped, 'And before I forget, thank you for the unique souvenir! Oh Raphael, it's going to be a cool day, I can feel it! It's Jack's birthday too, plus I get to bug– sorry see you!'

Raphael grinned back at her cheeky comment as Eleanor slammed her car door shut and dropped her keys into her bag. As she moved away from the car, his gaze fell on the large white cardboard box on the passenger seat. He eyed the package with quiet interest, saying casually, 'What's with the box?'

Eleanor beamed, 'Remember I told you it was Jack's birthday? Well, turns out he very nearly wasn't going to have a cake. So I baked him one. Reeeeally hope he likes it.'

Raphael flashed a tight smile. The grey flecks in his eyes had all but disappeared as he replied coolly, 'That's nice. He will like it.'

'That's the plan! Hey, have you got time to grab a quick coffee from the canteen? Some of us can't function without caffeine!'

He nodded as they walked, Eleanor chattering away whilst he remained quieter than usual. Although people were now used to seeing them hang out together, there was still the occasional double-take, mainly from girls, who firstly stared at Raphael before superficially glancing at Eleanor with a vague dismissive look. As a laughing Eleanor grabbed her coffee, she whispered conspiratorially to Raphael, 'Even *I* know what they're thinking.'

Leaning in he said vehemently, 'They can think what they like. It doesn't concern me.' His cavalier remark was heavy with distaste. Eleanor wondered if he was being more offhand than usual, but didn't have time to ask as they had now reached the lecture theatre. They parted ways when Serena waved Eleanor over to discuss Jack's surprise party and Raphael took his usual seat near the front.

Eleanor and her friends were soon engrossed in party talk, their spirited conversation ending abruptly when Jack appeared at the door. Strutting into the room with a huge grin Jack said, 'Come on girls, form an orderly queue. I'm waiting for my birthday kiss!'

Everyone burst out laughing. They watched Jack crack a pseudo-corny smile as he worked the room, eliciting chaste kisses from a few female class-mates. Eleanor, Christina and Serena jumped up to hug him before each planted a kiss on his cheek too. A beaming Jack finally sat down and the lecture soon commenced, but not before the visiting lecturer, Mrs Seymour had commented on the lip-gloss marks on Jack's cheeks.

'Morning class. Mr Jack Brennan, is there a reason *why* you're covered in lip-gloss? Actually, I don't want to know. Just make yourself presentable and we'll start.'

'It's my birthday Mrs Seymour. I'd hate for you to be left out and would be happy to get a birthday kiss of-?'

A ripple of laughter spread through the room. It was a cheery start to the lecture and the next two hours whizzed by with Eleanor trying to pull her stray mind to attention. Whilst taking notes, she wondered when it was Raphael's birthday. He was over 500 years old, but exactly when was he born, or *created?* Her musings were cut short as the shrill bell signalled the end of the lecture. Telling her friends that she would catch up with them in the canteen, she sprinted to the front where Raphael had finished packing his bag.

She smiled to say, 'Hey, we're going to the canteen now, wanna tag along? I think Katherine wants to see the cake, but Jack's there already so she'll just have to wait. It's going to be an awesome night, I just wish-'

'No. Can't make it.'

She was puzzled by his curt response, yet convincing herself that she was being paranoid, she ploughed on regardless. 'Jack's so funny, did you see Mrs Seymour's face when he asked-'

Raphael barked, 'Yes. It was entertaining. To see him ask, and get what he wanted.' He paused before saying sharply, 'You're in back-to-back lectures now, right? I'll just see you at the weekend. If you're free.'

Eleanor flinched at his brusque response. Their earlier two minute conversation barely counted as catching up and Eleanor couldn't help but feel crestfallen. With her face suddenly lighting up she said, 'I can do tomorrow? My weekend starts early as I don't have lectures on Friday. We can spend the day just chilling out..?'

She couldn't wait three days to see him. He eyed her, carefully venturing, 'OK, I'll come round to yours at 11:00am tomorrow?'

'Cool, see you then!'

There was a big turnout for Jack's birthday. Katherine won the humorous accolade for officially silencing Jack, who upon entering the bar, stood agape with surprise. The cake had gone down a treat too as the bar-tender carried it out alight with nineteen candles. It was an entertaining evening as Eleanor danced the hours away with her friends.

Eleanor decided to call it a night at 2:45am. Edging through the crowds towards Jack, she shouted over the pumping music to make herself heard. 'HOPE YOU HAD A GREAT NIGHT JACK! HAPPY BIRTHDAY AGAIN HON!'

Hugging him goodnight once more, she turned to leave. Jack grabbed her hand. She turned round and smiled, having seen him stop all their other friends from leaving in a bid to keep the party going longer. He leant in to say, 'Don't go.'

Kissing him on the cheek, she replied, 'I have to! Hey, I managed to stay till nearly 3am – that's something, right? Night Jack!'

She made to leave, yet Jack continued to hold fast onto her hand. 'Elle, what's the deal with you and Raphael?'

She laughed to say, 'Too much dancing juice Jack! A solid nine hours of partying can do that to you!'

Although he loosened his grip, his hand remained on hers as he continued to stare at her with misty blue eyes. She was suddenly sober as she said gently, 'Me and Raphael are just mates. Friends, like me and you, yeah? And Jack...' She paused to gently extricate her hand from his, 'Katherine rates you. She's cool, but you know that anyway, right?'

He blinked, briefly kissing her cheek before disappearing onto the dance-floor. Recognising the look of desire in Jack's eyes, she had found herself secretly hoping that he wouldn't verbalise his feelings. She hated the idea of unrequited love, lust, or whatever it was that Jack felt for her. Eleanor was forever sympathetic towards people in the *Unreciprocated Feeling Camp* having been a fully fledged member since Michael. She continued looking with guilty concern at the dance-floor where Jack had walked off. She knew Katherine liked Jack and putting in a good word for her quickened the evaporation of her guilt. With a final glance in Jack's direction, she ran to the exit and hailed a taxi home.

# 23 PEBBLES AND SUNSHINE

Eleanor awoke the following morning with a mild hangover. By 10:30am, she had showered, breakfasted and chosen a casual ensemble of pale blue skinny jeans and fitted green jumper.

Raphael was prompt and seemed more preoccupied than usual. Watching her make a fresh pot of coffee he casually ventured, 'How was last night? You left your car at uni so I assume you were drinking. No hangover?'

Rolling her eyes she teased, 'Hey! I don't get hangovers every time I go out!' He flashed her a knowing grin, causing her to concede sheepishly, 'Actually, I *did* get a hangover, that's why I left the car there. But, I'm feeling absolutely fine now. And yes, it was a great night! Actually, speaking of birthdays... When is it yours?'

The curveball question seemed to throw him off track. After a beat he said, 'I don't acknowledge my birthday and never will. I don't see the point in celebrating myself.'

'That's cool, I was just curious. With me it's just a ritual, although I prefer helping friends celebrate their big day instead. Jack had a blast, he loved the cake too!'

He listened to her happily chattering away as she regaled him about the previous night's activities. He asked evenly, 'How was Jack?'

For a reason unbeknownst to Eleanor, she felt compelled to tell Raphael about Jack. She said light-heartedly, 'Jack had a great time. He was a little worse for wear towards the end of the night. Nothing major, he just needed reminding that I see him as a friend.'

Eleanor imagined a restrained smile on Raphael's lips. She continued somewhat dejectedly, 'I just don't like disappointing people. You should have seen his face...'

He continued looking at her in masked delight. As Jack's downcast face flashed through her mind she said lightly, 'Part of me feels guilty. It's like I've somehow given him the wrong impression. I just feel bad, like I've led him on somehow, you know?'

Raphael's smile shrank as he moved forward to grab his coffee cup from the work-top. They were quiet for a minute with only the background hum of the TV in the otherwise silent house. Catching a glimpse of the Snooker championships on TV, he said, 'Fancy hanging out in town? Do things you humans do. A game of pool maybe, or catch a movie?'

Eleanor laughed to say, 'You can't get more human than that. There's a pool hall not far from here. I haven't played in ages, so you've been warned!'

As they drove through Richmond on his Yamaha, the chilly February air blew away the last remnants of her hangover. Her refreshed mind however, didn't help her technique. A part of her had been looking forward to showing Raphael how to play pool, yet she quickly realised after a series of impressive first shots that he was a master pool player. He tried to even the games out as he conceded points with a discreet smile, yet Eleanor knew this was deliberate. He could so very easily clear the table within minutes, yet he chose to humour her instead.

Eleanor tried not to hold up the game with her awkward shots and vacillation as she debated the best angles. Mid-way through the fifth game, her clumsy cue smacked the ledge and she watched in horror as the white ball flew off the table. Raphael tried to disguise his amusement as Eleanor stared dumbfounded at the rolling ball on the floor. Her humiliation slowly gave way to a fit of giggles and the pair were soon laughing at Eleanor's futile attempts to play a decent game. Refusing to be embarrassed furthermore, Eleanor eagerly suggested lunch and they were soon settled at the pizza place across the way. Munching on her garlic bread, she smiled to say, 'I never thought I'd spend three hours playing pool. I still suck at it!'

Taking a slug of coke he said, 'You weren't that bad. Hey, what are your plans now? Fancy just- What's the word you use, *vegging*..?' Returning her smile he said, 'I feel a spot of rain coming on. Fancy another flying visit?'

By the time Raphael had paid the bill and opened the door for her, the sky was already overcast. The car park rapidly emptied as the handful of people scuttled away like ants seeking shelter from a torrential downpour. He swept her off her feet amidst sheets of rain. Nestling closer to him with her arms around his warm neck, they were soon airborne.

She didn't know where they were headed and she didn't care. The now gentle patter of raindrops was perfect for contemplation. Just like her mind would digress whilst driving, she wondered if Raphael needed to concentrate whilst flying. Keeping quiet lest she disturb him, she nonetheless enjoyed their exhilarating twenty minute journey.

He set her down gently. Suddenly conscious of an odd crunching underfoot, she quickly realised that the gravelly surface was part of an empty beach. Following Raphael's gaze, she saw a large expanse of deep blue about forty metres from where they had landed. Smiling in delight, Eleanor took a few steps towards the swishing sea and spun round to find Raphael looking directly at her. Before she could verbalise her curiosity, he answered with a mischievous smile, 'Brighton Beach.'

'You flew all the way here in under half an hour? Woah, Richard Branson would be envious! Hey, I've not been here for years!'

Eleanor sprinted towards the sea as childhood memories flooded her mind. Brighton, Bournemouth, Dorset and Blackpool were regular beach hotspots, the visits only waning as Lucille's diary had become increasingly busier. As the water lapped her boots, Eleanor felt like a child again. With flushed cheeks cold from the bracing air, she stared out ahead. The sea was an exquisite royal blue cloak with delicate white foam piping. Returning to Raphael's side, she noticed the rain had now stopped. Although the sky was still overcast, Eleanor revelled in the beauty of the scene ahead. She was unsure how long they had been standing when Raphael gently said, 'Take it you like the sea?'

Eleanor whispered in awe, 'I LOVE the sea! I feel so at peace, here. I haven't been here for years!' She knew Raphael was well travelled. He had undoubtedly seen countless beautiful countries. Her structured and sheltered human life was in stark contrast to his worldly or even otherworldly experience. Suddenly curious she said, 'What's your favourite place Raphael?'

He threw her a sideways glance. His eyes seemed to whisper something to her, something so alien yet reassuringly familiar. He paused for a fraction of a second before saying, 'Too many places to mention. Earth is cool and definitely up there.' Peeling off his jacket whilst talking, he dropped it to the floor. He settled down next to the splayed garment, motioning for her to take a seat beside him.

Dropping to her feet she snuggled down into his still hot jacket. Looking out ahead he said, 'Your turn. What's your favourite place or thing? Is there anything you dislike?'

'Ooh, where to start? I have a huge "Favourite List!" I love the sea, the snow, Christmas and all things festive! I love the smell of freshly baked bread, the colour green… Want me to go on?'

He was openly amused by her childlike glee, her infectious enthusiasm prolonging his grin as she chattered away. 'It's a bit of a random list, here goes. I love Sou's up north, they do the BEST fish and chips! I love my lie-ins! I love my friends and family. I love uni too which sounds a tad geeky, but I don't care! Although having said that, studying feels a bit tedious at the mo.'

Her last sentence seemed to catch his attention. He quickly switched his gaze back to the horizon as she swiftly added, 'It's dull because this semester's a little more intense, you know? I don't get enough time to do things I like doing. Life gets in the way! OK, more favourite things. Umm... I love the start of a brand new day. I love Sean Connery and Hillary Clinton who might I add, was the original architect of girl power. I love sunshine too! I used to love painting, but I'm not feeling it so much anymore.' She pondered, 'There's not much I dislike. I mean, I don't *really* hate anything or anyone. Except our ex Prime Minister, but that's only because I'm against war-mongering pillocks.' She was lost in thought for a few moments as she said, 'When I was younger, I hated thunder. I was *petrified* by the sound of it. Mum used to calm me down by saying that it was just the sound of God moving his beer barrels across the floor of the sky. It's a silly explanation but it worked – I've not really been afraid of it since.'

He said thoughtfully, 'You should take up art again if you enjoy it.' They were sitting in comfortable silence before he said hesitantly, 'Talking about painting...' He seemed momentarily torn as he murmured, 'That day. When your painting fell from your bag...'

She said with an embarrassed smile, 'I know, my behaviour was CRAP with a capital C. Talk about bad first impressions! I just-'

His swift reply was even more perplexing than his sudden mood change. 'It wasn't a bad first impression. Thing is...' He paused again, before saying quietly, 'That wasn't the first time I saw you.'

Recalling their first meeting which was imprinted in her mind she laughed to say, 'Yeah, we met at uni. I think I would have remembered seeing you-'

Mystification softly engulfed her brain as she realised that was not what he meant. She looked at him for an explanation which he offered almost immediately. 'I *had* seen you before. Only for a few seconds. I was en route back to Central London. Via Richmond. It was raining. You were caught in the downpour.'

Eleanor cast her mind back to her first day and the rainstorm. Raphael's face seemed to be riddled with conflicting emotions, none of which she could fathom. Squirming with humiliation, she laughed lightly to say, '*You were there*?! Why didn't you say anything?? You saw me doing a mini rain dance and everything... Jeez Raphael, why didn't you say "Hi" or something??'

She was silent for a moment as she realised it would have been impossible for Raphael to suddenly pop up out of nowhere and initiate a friendly conversation without arousing suspicion. Flashbacks of her twirling in the rain like a moron caused a fresh wave of mortification.

He said quickly, 'I wanted to say something, really I did. My sudden appearance would have seemed odd. I wanted to tell you sooner. I just didn't want to bombard you with additional crazy information.'

Mollified by his earnest tone she gently said, 'I'm just embarrassed more than anything. Don't worry about not stopping. That'll teach me not to act like a first class idiot – you just don't know who's watching you!'

Although Eleanor burst into peals of laughter, Raphael remained quiet. He said gently, 'You didn't look like an idiot Eleanor. Besides, it was your aura that caught my attention.'

Still amused she suddenly remembered Raphael's ability of reading people. As her laughter gave way to curiosity she said, 'Gosh, I forgot about the whole aura thing. Just when I think I've honed my question list, up pops another one. Go on, what about my aura? It better be good!'

She listened intently as he explained, 'I can read people. I can hear their thoughts. The constant torrent of information is like thousands of live radio stations streamed directly to my mind. The auras are more visual. It's an inner human energy that manifests itself in a hazy, ethereal glow. Like a halo, but all around the body. Each aura is unique to a person. Like spiritual DNA, if that makes sense.'

Eleanor nodded transfixed, listening more attentively as tidal waves crashed in the background. Staring at the sea he said, 'An individual's aura is dependent upon their thoughts and earthly actions. Incidentally, examining the aura was one of the tools I used to determine a human's location in the after-life.' He exhaled as the thought of home flitted through his mind.

Glancing at his captive spectator he said, 'After centuries of practice, I am now able to drown out the random babble and glowing visions of auras. The voices are always with me but on a much lower volume setting. It is easier to manage when I am flying hundreds of feet above the ground. For those few hours I am at peace. I don't usually think of anything when flying. Having forced my mind clean, it is a blank canvas. I actually prefer the solitude of the skies.'

Surprised by his introspective musing, she placed a reassuring hand on his shoulder before returning it to her lap. Encouraged by her fleeting touch he continued firmly, 'I was passing through Putney via Richmond with a clear mind. Suddenly hundreds of feet below, a luminous object caught my eye. Curious, I flew closer. I had seen plenty of auras yet this was a unique sight. A burnished orange orb glistened with amber rays. The rain did little to mask the immense energy that emanated from this unusual sphere. As I neared the object, I couldn't help but be drawn to it.' He paused to look directly at her. 'It was you.'

She hadn't realised that Raphael had come to the end of his explanation. She tried to make sense of what he had said. Raphael had been right to wait to tell her. This was definitely information overload. She said uncertainly,

'You sure that was me? I mean, I'm just normal. Although this point is sometimes debateable. I don't get it..?'

She realised she wasn't the only one puzzled on the beach. Raphael too appeared mystified as he said, 'That makes the two of us. I don't quite understand it either. In all my 499 years on Earth, I have never seen anything like it. I just put it down to you being an anomaly.'

She laughed to say, 'Great, I'm an anomaly now! Still, there are worse things to be called!'

Picking up a pebble whilst deep in thought he said, 'Thoughts of Manchester filled you with hope and despondency. I was only there for a short while. Yet those few seconds were momentous. All my preconceptions about humans suddenly seemed superficial and one dimensional. Although I had lived alongside humans for nearly half a millennium, I had never wanted to be close to one. You changed all that.'

He stopped again, clutching the tiny pebble which was swallowed up in his hand. She stared at the blue wall of the sea growing taller as the tide crept in. Eleanor felt the crashing somehow grounded the surreal situation.

Dropping the pebble by his side, he continued earnestly, 'You intrigued me. Don't ask me why. As I watched you from the skies in the downpour, I remember having this sudden desire to tell you it was all going to be OK. Except I couldn't. It was so frustrating.' He fidgeted awkwardly with another pebble. 'Seeing you at uni the following day was bizarre. I couldn't quite believe it... I'm glad we're friends.'

Giving him a friendly nudge with her elbow, she said gently, 'I can't imagine you not in my life. Look at us now, vegging on this bright beautiful day. Well, not bright, but you know what I mean.'

Glancing around the empty beach with a playful glint in his eyes, he grabbed a handful of pebbles. Suddenly he was on his feet. Extending his left arm to her, he pulled her up in one swift movement.

'You wanted a bright day,' was all he said as they edged closer to the sea. Taking one of the pebbles in his hand, he hurled it at the sky. Eleanor looked on mystified, unsure of the rules of the strange game which Raphael was obviously playing.

Although the temperature had remained fairly cool throughout the afternoon, Eleanor thought it was unexpectedly brighter. Casting her eyes upwards, she gasped as she realised that the grey sky was being punctured by pebbles. Eleanor stared dumbstruck at the miniature spotlights thrown on the beach where they were standing. Raphael seemed pleased, evidently enjoying her gobsmacked expression. He continued hurling the stones towards the sky for a few minutes longer, grinning all the while. 'Bright enough for you?'

She whispered, 'That was- WOW... It's like having a personal weatherman.'

They stood in hushed silence for a further few minutes, each engrossed in private thoughts before Raphael said gently, 'We should get you indoors soon, aren't you cold? Besides, I think that's enough weather manipulation for one day.'

'We could stay out for longer, I never get cold when you're around. See, you *do* have your uses!'

'Good to know that you hold my friendship in high regard. Come on cheeky, let's get you home.'

She gushed, 'But I don't want to go, I love our excursions!' Suddenly remembering the park she said, 'Before I forget, any chance you could show me en route where that park is? You know, the one we went to near uni? Can't believe I still haven't managed to find it yet. Well actually I can, taking into consideration my diabolical sense of direction!'

Flicking a pebble away he said carefully, 'I can't show you. It's not a regular park.'

For a split second she thought she had misheard, before realising that her conversations with Raphael had a habit of falling outside the realms of reality. He said with a mischievous smile, 'Being me has few advantages. I can perform the most basic magic to enter places that *used* to exist.'

She swivelled her head in his direction. She said in a half whisper, 'You can do magic..? *How*? Just when I think I've got you figured out, you go pull a Marty McFly..?'

His rumbling laugh made her smile as he said, 'It's only the simplest of enchantments. I've memorised a handful. There's a book of spells which I very rarely use. Actually you've seen it in my flat.'

Recalling the ancient book, she nodded in remembrance as he said, 'Technically the park doesn't exist. It used to in the last century. What you saw was my projection.' He said with a muted smile, 'And it's not time travel. That's way beyond my capabilities. It's not about rewinding time. It's *retreating* to a place that is hidden to the human eye. There are very few places that I can really be myself and the park is one of them. I can fluidly enter these hot-spots, although there aren't that many here in England. When I crave peace, I go there. It's my personal safe-haven.'

Jigsaw pieces were beginning to slot together to form a more cohesive picture in her mind. She remembered Raphael's agitation when she had stumbled upon the book in his flat and immediately understood his annoyance. She also recalled trying to unsuccessfully find the park and the old lady who had remembered the park from her younger days. She suddenly wondered what constituted basic magic. He interrupted her thoughts as he gently said, 'If you really want to go, I'll take you sometime. Now, ready to go home?'

Filing away another question in her mental folder already bursting at the seams she said, 'Ohhh, I've just remembered another question. I'm just curious why- I mean how come you're named after an archangel..? I don't know the "ins and outs" of the Bible, but that's definitely a religious name. Did your dad um...' Unsure how to continue she said exasperated, '*See?* Each day brings a hundred different questions and I *still* don't know enough about you!'

He was suddenly serious, his jaw flexing in moody contemplation. 'I *was* named after an archangel. My father and Raphael are as close as brothers but- There is so much to tell. It's impossible to cover in one afternoon. It's… complicated.'

Chastened by his stone cold demeanour Eleanor said gently, 'Hey, questions can wait. You're not going anywhere right now. I'm gonna lock you in a room one day and just sit there questioning you about spells, magic, flying and everything else in between.'

With a roguish glint in his eyes he said, 'Locked up huh? I look forward to it.'

Now used to the ritual of flying, they stepped towards each other. Within seconds he was carrying her and moments later they had taken flight. The cooler evening air was of little concern to Eleanor as she snuggled up to Raphael. Thirty five minutes later, they were back outside Eleanor's house. The steady rainfall had now subsided to a gentle patter as he said softly, 'Thank you for your company Eleanor.'

'Thank *you*! Every day is an adventure with you! Just when I think I've had the best day ever, another one tops that.'

Grinning he said, 'Best day ever huh..? And just so you know, you're pretty cool to hang out with.' Walking backwards, he seemed reluctant to leave. 'I have to pick up my bike from the pool place before they tow it away. Breaking and entering isn't really my thing anymore. Goodnight Eleanor.'

The rainfall increased to a heavy downpour and Raphael disappeared. Eleanor remained standing in the rain for a further few moments looking at the sky. He was letting her be a part of his world and she loved him for it. She suddenly felt elevated as if she was soaring through the skies, which was odd considering she was on terra firma. Abruptly grounded by gloom when she realised she wouldn't see him for a full four days, she ran inside the house to focus on the long relaxing weekend ahead.

# 24 LIKE GLUE

During her Theology write-up, Eleanor wondered what her mum would say about Raphael. She considered him to be an important part of her life and felt guiltily evasive for not telling Lucille about him. Eleanor had always treasured their close relationship and wondered how she could possibly broach the subject.

She felt the growing distance between them, like a yawning chasm growing wider by the day. What would she say to her mum anyway? She and Raphael were only friends after all, and his supernatural confession wasn't really her secret to tell. There was no half-way measure for an admission like that; once it was out, there was no going back.

She knew that she could never tell anyone about him. Raphael was a separate part of her life, a beautiful magical secret that may not be understood or appreciated. She suddenly realised that she didn't *want* to tell anyone else and revelled in the knowledge that she was Raphael's sole confidante.

Life was good for now. She had a solid social circle, she had nearly finished her first year of university and the world was filled with endless possibilities. She would focus on the present and not even think about Raphael or how she would feel when he left. The first step was to free herself from thoughts of him. She scoffed at the impossibility of not thinking about Raphael and threw herself into study with renewed vigour.

From finishing the steady stream of assignments to seeing her friends, Eleanor found her weekly schedule packed jam tight. To her relief, Jack was normal with her too. He had probably forgotten about their conversation on his birthday and Eleanor put it down to a drunken moment not worth mentioning.

A week after seeing Raphael and acutely aware of their time apart, Eleanor walked out of university post lecture and pulled out her phone to text him. She battled with herself; it had been a few days and she missed him already. *What the hell was she going to do when he wasn't around?* Gulping away the uncomfortable thought she continued procrastinating; to text, or not to text, that was the question. As she stood frowning in contemplation, she glanced up to make out a familiar figure waiting at the university gates for her.

Raphael looked up as saw her appear, lounging casually on his bike. Although the car-park was now packed with students rushing to leave, Eleanor saw only Raphael. Her smile grew to a full-on grin as she walked closer to him. Gently waving her phone, she said, 'Hey! I was just about to text you! How are ya? You don't have lectures today, what are you doing at uni?'

'Hey Eleanor. I was just-'

'Passing through.' His smiling eyes caught on hers as she laughingly finished his sentence. Starting up his engine he said, 'Fancy a bite to eat before you head home?'

She had already placed her handbag across her shoulders. Climbing onto the back of his bike she said, 'I'm starving. Food would be great!'

They sped off as she hugged him tightly from her passenger seat. She noticed he hadn't worn his usual leather jacket today. Clinging to his sculpted body under his fine-knit crimson jumper, nervousness eventually gave way to comfort as she nestled closer. Despite the cool February air she was no longer cold as she luxuriated in the comforting heat emanating from the warm wall in front of her.

Riding through Westminster, they pulled up outside The Cinnamon Restaurant twenty minutes later. Seated and having ordered food and drink, Eleanor glanced around at the opulent surroundings. The inspired décor was a fusion of contemporary meets archaic and she was silent for a few minutes before saying, 'I've never been here before, it's beautiful! Apparently the food's pretty hot too!'

He smiled, glancing upwards at the golden concave roof and the luminous lamps that gave the vast room a cosy ambience. 'I like what they've done to this place. It's not much different to when it first opened. They've embraced their heritage. Not many places like this around. It reminds me of home.'

A question bobbed to the surface of her mind. She said gently, 'Talking about Hell... what's it like? And where exactly is *home*?'

The careful smile on his lips disappeared. Fixing dark eyes on his Bourbon he said, 'Hell is my home. In the heart of Westminster. Hell feels much like Earth, just without the label.' He said with a sardonic grin, 'The commute home is easier than using the London Tube. That's logistics out of the way.' He stared at his glass as he said coolly, 'Hell is where I was born. I have mixed feelings towards it. It's part of me, whether I like it or not. Besides, it's all about interpretation.'

Speaking with the air of a diplomat attempting to explain a difficult political situation he said determinedly, 'There are aspects of my home which I like and abhor. I've already told you about work, which I loathe with every fibre of my being. My interpretation of Hell is therefore different to that of a *non-resident*, whose experience is infinitely worse than mine. For a hell-bound sinner, it's constant torment and anguish. Although I never ,experienced pain like those tortured souls, the frustration and sorrow that tore at me whilst-' He paused again before resuming quietly, 'Whilst undertaking various duties is something I will never forget.'

He stopped when plagued by images of his life in Hell. He no longer looked at her. His obvious anguish ripped through her like a tsunami and it took every inch of her not to leap up and hold him in a comforting embrace. They picked up their drinks in one inadvertent synchronised movement and each took a sip, glancing around the busy restaurant to make sure their conversation remained private.

Placing his Bourbon back on the table, Raphael continued firmly, 'There are many parallels between Hell and Earth. One gets judged in both locations. Both are also places of extreme pain. Each has a high concentration of sinners, although the number of sinners in Hell is marginally higher. The number of misdemeanours being committed on Earth is increasing daily. That's another reason why my father ratified the zero tolerance decree. Capping numbers of an over-populated Earth which is currently his territory, whilst simultaneously expanding his underground realm is his top priority.'

Eleanor stared with eyes as wide as saucers. She whispered, '*He rules Earth...?*'

Catching her reaction he paused for a split second. He continued unapologetically, 'Yes. He controls Earth. There-'

He was quiet when he saw an approaching waiter, who placed their platters on the table and disappeared within seconds. Staring at the steaming plates of food, she tried to make sense of what Raphael had told her. She knew Earth was filled with good and bad energy, yet to hear Lucifer governed her world filled her with a queasy sense of alarm.

The fleeting sense of disquiet vanished as she made eye contact with Raphael. Watching him surveying her filled her with unexpected tenderness. For now, she didn't want to think about the consequences. She just wanted to spend time with her friend. Picking up her fork to dig into the monkfish curry, Eleanor was struck yet again by her bizarre situation. Here she was, discussing Hell with the Devil's son over dinner.

He appeared thoughtful as he said, 'There is however, one major difference between Hell and Earth. With Hell, you know exactly where you are. Nothing takes you by surprise. Being on Earth is such a mixed bag. I've watched humans experience extreme pleasure and raw pain, all in the space of a few moments. Sometimes I wonder how humans can live like this. I suppose this is what you call *life*.'

A sad smile flitted across his pensive face. 'Nothing makes sense here. Although my stint on Earth has been an enlightening experience on certain levels, I still find humans difficult to understand. It certainly makes it easier that I can- *could* read their minds. I'm a little off my game at the moment.'

He seemed preoccupied by an alternate train of thought before he continued in a semi-trance like state. 'Humans are such complex creatures. There are good and bad humans, but the majority of people here seem to be in self-destruct mode. They never seem to be happy, constantly striving for a better existence, no matter at what cost they want *their dream* or whatever the hell it is that they wish to achieve.'

He paused for a split second and flashed a grin to say, 'See, I can use *humanisms* too.' Catching her smile he said, 'Don't get me wrong. It's good to have goals and aspire for a better life. The majority of humans however, forget that their time on Earth is finite. They believe they're invincible. Westminster is a haven for these sorts of people.' He paused to take a gulp of Bourbon before saying, 'At first, their hubris astounded me. Now I know that's just how some humans function.'

He spoke with a detached air as if reflecting upon his time on Earth. 'It's little wonder that humans think like this. Money seems to be the crux of a supposed happy earthly existence. Most humans equate money to happiness, which is so very far from the truth.'

Raphael stopped talking abruptly. A waiter emerged from the corner to whisk away their empty plates before saying in a silky smooth voice 'Would you like any beverages? Perhaps a nice after-dinner coffee?'

They both shook their heads in unison as the waiter disappeared to leave the coffee menus on the table. Raphael threw a quick glance around the slowly emptying restaurant. 'My father vehemently believes that humans are powered by greed. He says Earth is filled with self-destruction and violence – the root of which is money. Although I don't fully agree with him, part of me understands where he is coming from. Sometimes, I wonder how one can stay sane here.'

Eleanor laughed quietly to say, 'Hey, it's not all bad! Yes, money does play a huge part because life is certainly *easier* if one has money. Some people forget that money is merely a physical currency, not a famed panacea to worldly troubles. And you're right. Some do confuse having money to being happy. However, in the defence of humankind, it's easy to fall under this misguided notion. No-one's perfect, I know I'm not. We're human after all.'

They were silent for a few minutes as the dying buzz of conversation and faint clattering of plates sounded in the background. Raphael said, 'Earth is a remarkable place. The human spirit too, is infinitely fascinating. Who knows, by the time my exile has ended, I may actually understand how humans operate. And by the way Eleanor, perfection lies in imperfection. Just remember that the next time you say you're not perfect.'

Taking a quick sip of wine to hide an embarrassed smile, she said quietly, 'I'm totally aware of my imperfections and-'

A growing grin on Raphael's face accentuated the grey in his eyes. He teased, 'You don't believe me? Can't you even take a compliment..?'

She said with a half smile, 'Well, it just sort of makes me feel a little weird, that's all. My mum's the life and soul of a party and can handle a million compliments with such finesse. I'm the opposite. I wish I could be more like her. I never knew my dad, so I guess I must get that from him.'

She realised she had digressed and fell silent. His prolonged gaze seemed to amplify her slightly awkward state. She blushed again as he continued to tease her. 'I never realised you were this shy. See, you learn new things everyday.'

He was laughing at her again and Eleanor leant over to playfully hit him. As her hand practically bounced off his solid arm, she laughed to say, 'Ouch that hurt! And the moral of the story is that violence doesn't get you anywhere.' Rubbing her sore hand, she glanced at her watch to say, 'Hey, I can't believe we've been chatting for the past two hours!'

'And you've not had a single cup of coffee.'

'I think the riveting conversation just blew the thought of caffeine right out of my mind. See, having you around does have its uses. Hey, you can be my caffeine substitute!' She grinned, and the two friends continued to chat before Raphael picked up the bill.

When he dropped her home she found herself standing with the front door ajar. She hated watching him leave and always hung around to see him off. Pushing the heavy door shut, she stood in the silent, dark house for a few minutes. The more time she spent with him, the fonder she grew of him. Living without one of her best friends would be difficult. One question returned to haunt her even when she was settled in bed. *He WILL leave. What then..?*

The following weeks marked another shift in Eleanor and Raphael's relationship as they sought each others company on a more frequent basis. It seemed both were conscious of his imminent return home. She had even taken to sitting at his work-bench in lecture. The first time it had happened, Raphael looked up from his desk when she entered, held her gaze and looked back down at his book. Maybe it was the sun streaming through the broad windows that beautiful March morning. Or maybe Eleanor was becoming acutely aware of their limited time together. It was probably an amalgamation of both. Like an hour-glass filled with inconsiderate sands of time, she felt the grains slipping through too fast. As the floating hour-glass flashed through her mind, she had placed her bag on Raphael's work-bench instead of walking towards the back of the room. With a growing grin, Raphael had pulled out the adjacent chair and turned to ask her about the assignment.

The room had plummeted into stunned silence as people stopped mid-conversation. A few girls in the room merely gawked whilst trying to figure out Eleanor's secret. Suspicious, envy stained stares thrown in Eleanor's direction quietly questioned how she had managed to bag a seat beside the elusive Raphael, who for once, did not seem to mind the company. Jack tried to appear unbothered as he fumbled for his notes. Only a smiling Christina and Serena seemed genuinely pleased, as they both winked at her surreptitiously to mouth, *'Finally!'*

By mid-March, the exam dates had been finalised. By now Eleanor felt like an expert plate-juggler, being preoccupied with exams, research deadlines and spending the bulk of her time with Raphael. During any other exam period, her socialising would have been significantly reduced. However with the hour-glass imprinted in her mind, she factored Raphael into her timetable without fear of guilt.

She knew she was attached to him and she hated herself for it. She tried to imagine a life without Raphael, but her mind was as blank as the empty back pages of her calendar, imbuing her with a growing sense of inescapable anxiety. Unable to shake off cloying claustrophobia, she forcefully told herself, *'He will leave. He will leave.'* Keen to take her mind of the inevitable, she invited Valentina down to Richmond and was filled with happy relief when she accepted. Seeing her friend would be a minor distraction, giving Eleanor time out from exam worry and the Raphael situation. Reluctantly cancelling her plans to see Raphael, she looked forward to Valentina's arrival for a nice long weekend.

# 25 EPIPHANY

The person emerging from the taxi on Friday evening looked nothing like the old Valentina. Sporting a healthy tan and bright smile, she had left behind the gaunt, cheerless shadow from a few months ago. Both girls exchanged hugs in a flurry of excited conversation and were soon settled on the sofa playing catch-up on the past few months. Cracking open a bottle of wine whilst tucking into their Chinese takeaway, the girls continued their catch-up chatter late into the evening.

Munching on the last mouthful of her chicken chow mein, Eleanor said proudly, 'You're looking really well hon. It's soooo good to see that you're over... stuff. God I've missed you!'

Valentina twittered, 'Ditto girlfriend! Thankfully I'm past the wallowing stage. It's Friday and we're both free and single! OK, so you going to show me London town or what?'

Heading into Camden on their girls' night out, they eventually ended up at Koko where they danced the hours away in a happy haze. The following day saw them recover just in time for another night out, as they frequented a new bar in Richmond, which boasted a ten foot long cocktail list. Encouraged by Valentina's renewed passion for life, Eleanor barely had time to think about Raphael and enjoyed the weekend of fun and frolics. After two nights of consecutive partying that could put *The Who* to shame, the girls embraced Sunday as the calming antidote to a non-stop weekend.

Arising on Sunday morning with a steaming hangover apiece, Eleanor eventually crawled out of bed to prepare breakfast. The smell of freshly brewed coffee drew Valentina into the kitchen like a lethargic bee to honey. She slowly padded downstairs clutching her head, running glazed eyes over scrambled eggs, toast, tumblers of orange juice and the large cafétiere. She whimpered, 'Can't believe you started on breakfast already. You should have woken me up. How's the head Elle..? Rocking night huh? I don't think we had loads to drink, did we..?'

Eleanor simply blinked. It felt like someone was using her head as a drum, pounding away with no consideration for its owner. Mustering up enough energy to speak, she replied, 'Head. Hurts. Need. Food.' Taking a few tentative sips of water she answered after a minute, 'Was a fun night. And check you out, getting numbers of those yummy guys. You were on fire. And we didn't have much drink, must be those shots. What was it now, *Squashed Frog*..?'

Clutching her mouth, Valentina mumbled queasily, 'Don't. It's all coming back to me. There was some other concoction. *Flatliner*..?'

Both girls were quietened by their debilitating hangovers. Perching on the kitchen stools in their nightwear, they nibbled on breakfast. Eleanor chewed a tiny bite of toast. Catching Valentina do the same she groaned, 'It's all self-inflicted. We deserve this. Ohhhh, my head....'

The sudden bellow of the door-bell broke the comforting silence of the house, causing both girls to simultaneously cringe. Valentina's hands flew up to cover her ears. Staring imploringly at Eleanor she said quietly, 'Who is that? Send them to a galaxy far far away...'

Eleanor replied with a tired smile and a hint of sarcasm, 'My psychic abilities are hindered by this stupid hangover. I *dunno* who it is, I'm not expecting anyone.' She remained seated for a few moments. 'I wish the room would stop spinning. Think I'm still a little drunk from last night.' Spreading her hands flat on the cool work-top as a first step in getting up, she said, 'Right, I can do this. Hopefully they'll take one look at me hung-over and leave. If that's not enough to scare them away, I'm calling you for back-up so you can just charm them away.' Rolling her eyes in mock horror, she continued, 'You make me sick Val, you still look gorge when hung-over.'

Eleanor thought the walk from the kitchen to the front door took hours. Not even bothering to check the identity of the unwanted visitor through the magnifying peep-hole, she sluggishly swung the door open to find coal-black eyes staring at her.

It took her nearly half a minute to realise she was looking directly at Raphael. His eyes flitted across her face then over her dressing gown and the loose knot on her waist. It took her an extra few seconds to realise that he was smiling at her. He sounded contrite when he eventually spoke, yet his playful smile belied any apology. He said, 'Sorry to drop in on you like this. I forgot my book in the lounge the other day.' After a beat, he said, 'Heavy night?'

He was now openly grinning at her and all she could do was smile weakly and slightly shake her head. She could almost feel the contents of her head being shifted from one end to the other and she automatically winced. She dare not look at her hung-over reflection in the hallway mirror. As she looked down, she realised she was wearing her oldest and comfiest pyjamas emblazoned with miniature elephants. Flushing hotly, she said whispered, 'Yeah. It was a heavy... night. I hate hangovers. I'm sooo never drinking again. I...'

Suppressing a grin he said lightly, 'Elephants..?'

Suddenly hot from a second wave of embarrassment, she pulled her dressing gown tighter around her. She barely felt human, with her tousled hair and tired, puffy eyes. She wanted him to stay. She wanted to spend more than a few snatched moments with him. Above all, she didn't want him to see her like this. In a futile bid to divert attention from her embarrassing attire, she mumbled, 'Yeah, elephants. They're beautiful creatures. Your book. You do know where it is, right..? Go right ahead and grab it.'

The smile on his lips was inches away from becoming a full-on grin again. It appeared he was trying his best to keep a straight face as he walked into the lounge. If only her head wasn't so fuzzy, then she could have asked him to stay. Unwilling to inflict her uninteresting, half-drunken ramblings on him, she hoped he would quickly disappear as she closed the front door and made her way into the kitchen.

Valentina yawned, watching Eleanor perch back on the stool opposite her. Disinterested, she said, 'Bible basher? We get loads of those. Take it you sent them packing...'

Before Eleanor could respond, Raphael strode into the kitchen. Valentina stopped mid-yawn to stare. The contagious yawn latched onto Eleanor who took a few seconds to answer. Fighting off her lethargy, she said groggily, 'Valentina, this is Raphael, my mate from uni. Raphael, this is Valentina, one of my oldest friends from Manchester.'

Valentina blinked and gave a half-wave. With a charismatic smile Raphael said, 'It's a pleasure to meet you Valentina. Did you have a good weekend? Judging from the hangovers, it sounds like you had great fun.'

All Valentina could do was nod and smile back. She couldn't stop staring at Raphael, who in turn seemed both amused and intrigued by Eleanor's friend. A suddenly self-conscious Valentina brushed away imaginary toast crumbs from her silk camisole. Readjusting her dressing gown, she said with an unexpected burst of enthusiasm, 'Yeah, we had a fab time thanks. If you were in town, you should have come out with us. Maybe next time..?'

Raphael moved past Eleanor and a few centimetres closer to Valentina, observing her with curious fascination. Looking directly at Valentina he said, '*Definitely*, that sounds great. I'm sure Eleanor will let me know when you're down. We can do drinks or something? Maybe steer clear of the shots though.'

His disarming smile however fleeting, drew a breathless chuckle from Valentina. 'Won't you at least stay for coffee?'

Raphael hesitated for a split second before saying, 'No, I'll leave you girls to it. Great seeing you Valentina. Eleanor, thanks for the book. I'll catch up with you next week. Once again, I'm sorry to disturb you.' He caught Valentina's extended hand in a farewell handshake, his hand holding hers for a few prolonged seconds. A soothing smile seemed to have found a permanent residence on his face as he said, 'See you soon Valentina.' Without even looking at Eleanor he said, 'I'll see myself out.'

Eleanor remained quiet during their exchange, her head slowly shifting between Valentina and Raphael as if she was watching a tennis match in slow motion. Before her brain could kick into gear to formulate a response, Raphael had disappeared. The house was quiet again. As Eleanor cradled her bowl of scrambled eggs, she heard Valentina say, 'Can't believe you didn't tell me about the dish.'

Eleanor stared quizzically at the bowl in her hand, drawing tinkling laughter from Valentina. 'Not that dish, silly. *Raphael.* You never mentioned he was so very yummy.' Eleanor shrugged whilst swallowing a mouthful of scrambled egg. Valentina continued, 'I could have died when he walked in. I look terrible hung-over. Next time I'm down, invite him out. He seems really cool.'

Eleanor stopped munching. A few minutes ago, the scrambled egg had felt like buttery pieces of velvet. Now, it felt like pieces of cardboard, dry and floppy in her mouth. She said somewhat defensively, 'I *did* tell you about him. It was ages ago, when I flipped out over my painting. Remember, I said we didn't get on-'

'And now you do?' Valentina eyed Eleanor enquiringly. Seeing Raphael had somehow boosted Valentina's conversational ability and she seemed to momentarily forget about her painful hangover. Eleanor's head however remained fuzzy. More peculiarly, she felt annoyance nag a reply out of her as she said a little grumpily, 'Yeah, we do get on now. He's one of my best friends actually.'

'Best friends huh? So... how long have you known Raphael for? Are you guys-'

Eleanor didn't wait for her to finish. She said a little too quickly, 'Noooo, I just don't see him like that.'

Her response was enough to spur Valentina into a humorous mini tirade. 'What's wrong with you? You sure you're not dead? How can you not see what's in front of you? Seriously Elle, he's not your average guy, very Brando circa Waterfront. You *sure* there's nothing going on with you guys?'

Eleanor wasn't sure where Valentina was going with her line of questioning, but she didn't like it. Answering in a level voice, she replied,

'Honestly, there's absolutely nothing going on with me and Raphael. We're best mates, that's all.'

Flashing Eleanor a knowing smile Valentina said, 'In that case, you wouldn't mind if I ask him out next time I'm down? I mean, he practically asked me out *anyway*, so it won't be that big a deal. Hey, why don't you set us up?'

Valentina's words sliced through Eleanor's hangover. She was suddenly lucid as she grabbed her coffee cup to take an elongated sip at the mental image of Valentina and Raphael together. Suddenly queasy yet forcing herself to remain unbothered, Eleanor said, 'Cool. I'll talk to him. Next time you're down, we'll lock a date in the diary.'

'Elle… why are you grimacing?' A soft smile graced Valentina's pretty, upturned mouth.

Eleanor answered as nonchalantly as she could. 'It's just the hangover. No more shots for me. EVER. Come on missy eat up, you've got a train to catch.'

Eventually bidding Valentina a fond farewell at the train station, Eleanor's mind was preoccupied with random thoughts during her drive back home. Plagued by unease since Raphael's visit, the mere prick of agitation earlier that morning had morphed into a fist-sized ball of knotted discontent bouncing in the pit of her stomach.

She couldn't even be bothered to make breakfast the following morning. Everything seemed an effort and as she boarded the packed bus, her mind returned to Valentina and Raphael's conversation. She recalled Valentina perched elegantly on her seat like a nineteenth century porcelain figurine. She cut a striking silhouette, with her black hair piled loosely on her head and button nose that could charm even the coldest of hearts.

Valentina and Raphael were two people she had never imagined together. She rolled the idea around in her head, trying to get accustomed to it whilst ignoring her inner voice that protested against the pairing. She tried to think of other absurd unions to justify her point. Suddenly weary from thinking about her friends together, she focused straight ahead and through the crowds of students plugged into their iPods.

Normally, Eleanor loved people-watching yet today it failed to interest her. Catching sight of the windscreen wipers over the bobbing heads of the people on the bus, she realised it had suddenly started to rain. Even the rubbery swish of the wipers put her on edge. She felt their black spindly arms taunting her, waving a crucial piece of information near her fingertips which remained frustratingly just a few millimetres out of reach.

She practically floated her way through her lectures, but nothing really sank in. For once, she didn't want to see Raphael. That would mean asking him out on Valentina's behalf. She didn't want to do that. At a loss as to why she considered the thought of her best friends together as oddly offensive, she tried to understand the reason for her weird discontent.

Lost in thought whilst only half-listening to her friends, Eleanor spied Raphael from afar. Greeting him with an awkward half-wave, she continued her conversation with Jack and Christina on either side of her. As he walked directly towards her with a smile on his face, Eleanor knew she could no longer avoid him.

Reluctantly breaking away from her friends, she slowed her pace. Now a few yards away from him, Eleanor noted how the dark blue of his shirt brought out the exquisite grey flecks in his eyes. She was struck how his eyes reminded her of glimmering stars in a midnight sky. *Great.* Just when she didn't want her mind to digress, it did, and onto a subject she was striving so very hard to dismiss.

Feeling cornered she willed something to happen. Anything. Big or small she didn't care, *something* that would delay the conversation that she was now dreading to have. As the space closed between them she was suddenly startled by the buzzing of her mobile phone. Mentally thanking her caller, she breathed an invisible sigh of relief. On any other day, she would have ignored the phone-call and focused on Raphael. Today her phone was her ally. Pulling the ringing mobile out with renewed gusto, she stuck it to her ear and mouthed to Raphael, *'Busy. Chat later?'*

Confusion clouded Raphael's face as he watched her take the call whilst she quickly turned away. After a few seconds she cast a surreptitious backwards glance. He had stopped in his tracks to study her with curious surprise, before turning on his heel to walk away. She waited a full minute till he was out of sight before trying to listen to the random caller who continued droning in her ear. With her mind in the university building, she nearly tripped on the steps of the campus. Steadying herself, she could barely make out what her caller was saying. She managed to grasp "insurance" and "renewed contract" from the otherwise incoherent babble, before quickly and politely hanging up.

Her friends had disappeared inside, yet she loitered in the bright afternoon sun, horrifyingly at odds with herself. She realised with growing dread that she would have to speak to Raphael about Valentina. That conversation could wait till tomorrow. Or another day. What if Raphael and Valentina really hit it off? Then–

Taking a few gulps of cool air, she reluctantly made her way to lecture. The hours slipped by and she felt as if she was listening to the random telephone caller again. Words were being said yet nothing sank in. Like water flowing off a saturated sponge, Eleanor's mind refused to absorb any information as the minutes floated away in a hazy blur, whilst thoughts of Raphael took centre-stage. Unable to forget his bewildered face when she had unwillingly spurned him a few hours ago, she realised she could no longer delay the inevitable. She had to set up Valentina and Raphael. There was no way out.

The following day she decided to drive into university. She had been prolonging her food shopping for the past few days in her state of sluggish inertia and her empty fridge had spurred her to decide on a Tesco trip after her lectures finished. She planned to use the outbound commute to prepare herself for the conversation she was dreading to have.

A permanent lump of dread seemed to have found an uncomfortable home in Eleanor's throat as she pulled out of her drive-way. It was a beautiful March morning with warm sunshine spilling through the trees in her avenue as she made her way through Richmond. Road works near Westminster altered her route and she was soon stuck in the Blackwall tunnel waiting for the traffic backlog to clear.

She hadn't slept properly as surreal dreams swirled in her subconscious by night and continued to taunt her in the day. Tired and mildly frustrated, she wondered why the thought of Valentina and Raphael bothered her so much. It wasn't as if Valentina was *bad* for him. So what the hell was the problem?

She edged her car further into the tunnel as the traffic crept forward. She could see daylight ten yards away. Drumming her fingers impatiently on the steering wheel, she waited for the traffic to shift. Eleanor tried to think of someone who would make a good girlfriend for Raphael. She racked her brains. She couldn't think of anyone.

*There must be someone, surely.* Raphael was decent looking. OK, he was very good looking. Naturally beautiful and inherently cool too. She grinned as she thought of his smile and his coal-black eyes.

Her car edged a few more yards towards the end of the tunnel. It seemed as if the whole world had chosen to take Eleanor's route. As she continued to ponder the subject of Raphael's potential girlfriend, she huffed in annoyance whilst hoping the dawdling traffic wouldn't make her late.

She was uncharacteristically irritable today. She cast a lethargic eye over the trapped fly on the windscreen as it banged against the glass before increasing its loud buzzing. Despite winding down all four windows, the insect was still unable to find the exit. Cursing its stupidity, she was momentarily distracted by the Renault in front with a sticker on its bumper which screamed *Baby on board! Drive Safely!* She muttered, 'Shouldn't everyone drive safely anyway, regardless of there being a baby, cow or alien on board?' Attributing her frustration to the traffic which had never seemed slower, she begrudgingly continued thinking about Raphael's potential girlfriend.

There had to be *someone* who would be a good match for him. She wondered if he had a type. Maybe that's how she would broach the subject when she spoke with him later. She would force herself to appear happy and wear a fixed smile whilst her fuzzy brain would formulate those awkward words. She imagined her stilted monologue, the words falling flat from her panic-stricken mouth and wondered how she would speak, when just thinking of the impending conversation filled her with revolting dread.

The traffic started moving again and she was now leaving the tunnel. As the brilliant rays of sunlight fell onto her car, she was struck with a realisation. She didn't want Raphael to be with Valentina. Or anyone else. She suddenly realised that *she* wanted to be with him. *She* wanted to be the one to hold his hand. And hug him. And kiss him. And-

In one heart-stopping moment, she realised she was in love. She felt the sunlight had found its way into her very core, dancing a nifty waltz before skipping from her stomach and shining out of her into a mega-watt smile. She caught her reflection in the mirror and noticed her face was aglow with elation. Her tingling spine could no longer avoid the obvious declaration that flashed through her mind in bold lettering. She was in love with Raphael.

She had been in love with him since the moment he had rescued her painting nearly six months ago and she hadn't even realised until now. She was in love with kind, considerate, totally gorgeous Raphael.

She repeated the words a few times in her head as she tried to get used to the astounding idea. *I LOVE RAPHAEL. I LOVE RAPHAEL.* Each time she said it, her smile grew a fraction more. Clarity hit her like a twenty stone truck. She loved him. There was no going back.

So *this* is what it felt like being in love. It was a deliciously foreign emotion, comparable to nothing else. She understood now that Michael had been an infatuation. A foolish obsession. She had convinced herself that she was in love with her ex-boyfriend and had failed to see what was right in front of her. Her full heart brimmed over with a love so pure that she thought for a split second she was going to burst. Right now, she just wanted to see Raphael. She wanted his arms around her. She wanted that exquisite mouth on hers.

Blushing at the thought, she wondered if she could ever divulge her recent revelation. Her inner voice was running riot as a hundred questions, like exploding kernels of popcorn burst in the pressure cooker of her mind. What would he say? Yes they got on, but did he care for her more than a friend? Of course he didn't care for her like that. She wasn't his type. So who was? He didn't have time for meaningless complications anyway. He didn't have time for her... *right?* What if he didn't go back straight away? But why would he stay?

She tried to contemplate Raphael's impending departure with a clear head and found herself clutching the steering wheel tighter as her knuckles grew whiter. Her heart slammed to a rubbery stop in her chest and she forced herself to take deep, even breaths to calm her nerves. With each pacifying breath, she reminded herself that she still had the best part of a year with him. Doing a quick mental sum she calculated his time on Earth. Nine months. Thirty two weeks. Or nine hundred and sixty days was what she had left with him. Unappeased, she forced herself to think positively. Nine months was better than nothing.

Suddenly Valentina's face popped into Eleanor's mind. She nearly stalled her engine as she recalled her promise. Momentarily torn, she pulled over into a quieter side-street and contemplated her next step. She had to speak to Valentina to gage how much she liked Raphael. Lowering the radio, she was still for a few moments in the quiet of her car before slowly pulling out her mobile.

First impressions were that Valentina and Raphael liked each other. Her overactive imagination was going crazy as she pictured them holding hands. Clutching her phone to stare at the blank screen, she knew prolonging the conversation wasn't going to make it any easier. Like ripping off a plaster in one swift movement, she forced herself to make the call.

Scrolling to Valentina's number, she realised that if her friend expressed a continued interest in Raphael, she would have to step aside. Slick waves of nausea washed over her as she quickly wound the window right down whilst waiting for Valentina to pick up. It rang only three times, yet the duration seemed to last an age, her heart rate increasing as each millisecond trawled by.

A sleepy Valentina mumbled, '*Elle*? That you? It's only half eight. Who's died..?'

Eleanor's finger hovered over the disconnect button. She wished she hadn't called. Too late now. She would get the dreaded conversation out of the way and get ready to set up her best friends.

Jabbing jittery fingers on the steering wheel whilst trying to sound casual, Eleanor said as brightly as she could, 'Morning hon! So sorry to wake you, hadn't realised you'd be asleep. I'll be super quick, promise. I haven't had a proper chance to speak with Raphael about your date yet. Do you still-'

Valentina's swift interjection indicated she was suddenly wide awake. She practically shouted down the phone. '*Don't you dare*! Oh my God, I don't believe you!'

Before Eleanor could voice her puzzlement, Valentina continued, 'Seriously Elle, what's wrong with you!? You blatantly like him! And judging from the way he couldn't keep his eyes of you, I'm pretty sure he likes you back!' With an exasperated sigh she said, '*What am I going to do with you*?'

'But... I thought you liked Raphael and-'

Valentina yawned, taking a few seconds to answer. 'I only said that to provoke a reaction out of you. But you're so flipping stoic. Vintage Elle, you never realise when someone likes you. As I sat there in your kitchen, all

I could think was how obvious it was you like him. Can't you see that?'
With another sleepy yawn she said, 'I still stand by my observation that he's
a dish. Carpe diem Elle...'

Relief flooded through Eleanor as she practically shouted into her
phone, 'Yes! Carpe diem baby!!! Valentina – thank you for being utterly
fabulous!'

'That's me. OK, I've only had like four hours sleep so I'm signing off.
Ciao hon.'

The car was quiet again with only the delicate murmur of the radio.
Adrenaline surged through her veins as she cranked up the upbeat music to
fill her with a prolonged blast of euphoria. She knew life was never going to
be same again. She had to tell Raphael that she loved him.

She would seize the moment. She wouldn't procrastinate over hiding
this beautiful emotion. Of course there was the very distinct possibility that
he may not like her back. That was probably a given and something she was
prepared to accept. Taking a few extra minutes whilst the incredible idea
marinated in her mind, she dared to imagine the impossible. Maybe, *just*
maybe he saw her a little more than a best friend?

The dashboard clock Eleanor spurred into action. Unwilling to waste
another second, she quickly shifted into gear and drove the remaining few
miles to university in a blur of electric ecstasy. She had to talk to him
straight away.

Pulling into the car-park, she killed the engine and was still for a few
seconds. The enormity of loving Raphael hit her again. She had never felt
more alive. It was as if she was seeing the world for the very first time. It
seemed more vibrant and full of exquisite opportunities ready to be
explored. Maybe it was the warm sunlight against a cloudless blue sky, or
the fact that Easter vacation was a few days away. She revelled in the warm
air deliciously full of promise and untold potential. She had changed and
the world had too. Everything was different. Even the dull orange
brickwork of the campus building suddenly seemed brighter. She could
barely contain herself in her final lecture of the semester, as the excitement
of her recent epiphany and impending holidays ensured a permanent smile
on her face.

She was surprised not to see Raphael at their normal meeting spot near
the entrance. Assuming he had arrived earlier, she dropped him a quick text
in the first few minutes of the lecture to ask where he was. He texted back
straight away.

**Raphael: Studying at home today. You OK? You seemed a little tense
yesterday...**

**Eleanor: Soooo sorry about that, will explain later. PS where are you? Need to speak!**

**Raphael: All lectures finished, could meet up later..?**

**Eleanor: I fin today too (hope Mr L lets us out early). Will be home by 5.30. PS can't wait to see you.**

**Raphael: Let's meet at 6. I've got news too. See you then.**

One minute into her first lecture, an agitated Eleanor couldn't wait for it to end. As the elongated hours stretched out in front of her, Eleanor's impatient eyes flitted constantly between Mr Lorre and the clock above the smart-board. Time taunted her as she willed the syrupy slow clock hands to move faster. Two minutes felt like two hours and she had difficulty suppressing the urge to run to the front of the class, grab a chair to reach the clock and physically wind it forward so she could leave earlier.

Mr Lorre's never-ending monotone voice seemed at one with the unhurried clock. As he finally tied up his lecture ten minutes later than schedule, a happy throng of students spilled onto campus ready to celebrate the beginning of vacation. She chatted briefly to her friends in the sunlit forecourt, making plans to see them over Easter and practically ran to her car in anticipation of seeing Raphael.

Pulling out her phone along with her car keys, she scrolled to Raphael's number. It went straight to voice-mail. She hated leaving messages at the best of times, yet today was different. Undeterred by her propensity for leaving rambling voice-mails, she tried to leave a short message regardless.

*'Hey Raphael, just finished uni and I'm heading home now. Unsure why I'm calling you, I know we're meeting at 6. Just so excited... about stuff! Don't know what you'll think but can't wait to tell you! It's been a long time coming... Um, see you SOON! Oh, and by the way, it's Eleanor!'*

She drove home in a state of edgy delight, the slightest buzz from her phone causing her to peer at it whilst resisting distraction during the drive. She was home within forty minutes and grabbing herself an orange juice, plumped onto the sofa. Sipping the cool liquid, Eleanor wondered how different her life could be within the hour. She felt the old house almost welcoming and it oddly seemed to be waiting with her in a state of inexplicable tension.

Glancing at her phone balanced on the sofa arm, she suddenly wondered what Raphael was thinking. What if he knew what she was going to say? He had previously said that he could read people, although he was having trouble doing that. If he couldn't read people now, that meant he didn't know what she was thinking. Or maybe he did. In a bid to stop herself from being sucked into a never-ending torturous circle, she tried to focus on the upcoming vacation.

She couldn't quite believe all her lectures had finished. The next three weeks would mean more revision and even more study sessions before the onslaught of exams started. Not even the packed study timetable could dampen Eleanor's spirits. Her excitement mounted with each passing second. She would see Raphael soon.

His face floated through her mind. With just over an hour before she divulged her love for him, she could barely contain herself. Sitting on the couch, she tried to keep herself occupied as she surfed through myriad TV channels. Nothing captured her attention.

On tenterhooks, she mooched around the house for something to do. She picked up a book, but not even the magic of Harry Potter could keep her occupied. She needed to keep herself busy and rambling around the house in a state of restlessness, passed the treadmill. She eyed the dust-speckled handlebars with guilt, realising it had been some time since she had worked out. From now on, it was all about seizing the moment.

Already buzzing with energy, she hastily stepped into her trainers for a quick thirty minute work-out. Running upstairs to slip on her work-out gear before she could change her mind, she was soon running on the treadmill, happily watching the minutes melting away along with the miles.

The booming door-bell caught her off guard. For a split second, Eleanor thought she had forgotten the time. The LED clock on the treadmill flashed 5:21pm and she was momentarily confused. Not expecting anyone else for the rest of the evening, she realised with growing dismay that Raphael had arrived early.

Jumping off the treadmill out of breath with her vest plastered to her, she stumbled into the lounge. This was not how she wanted him to see her! Pushing the loose strands of damp hair away from her sweaty face, she tried to remain as calm possible. The onslaught of panic rendered her more breathless as she realised Raphael would be standing on her doorstep. Endorphins from the mini work-out surged through her veins, forming a powerful alliance with the anticipation of seeing him. With pounding heart and trembling hands, she ran to the door and clasped the cool brass handle. This was it. With a huge smile on her face, she closed her eyes and swung open the door.

# 26 HISTORY

She blinked. The smile slowly disappeared from her face. She was quiet as her eyes grew accustomed to the unexpected visitor on her doorstep. She said incredulously, '*Michael*..?'

His bright eyes took in her gym outfit and reluctantly returned to her face. He said cheerily, 'How are you Elle? Hope you don't mind me dropping in like this, but I was in London anyway when I realised Richmond wasn't far out. Can I come in..?'

A confused frown spread across Eleanor's face as she slowly nodded her acquiescence. She tried to formulate a response but remained taken aback by the unanticipated appearance of her ex-boyfriend. As she passed to let him in, her brain kicked into gear and she was hit with a sudden realisation.

She wanted him to leave. She had always thought she would have time for Michael, yet was startled to find herself surreptitiously glancing at her watch wondering how long he would stop for. She didn't have time for him. She had relegated Michael to the realms of *acquaintance category* and a small smile escaped her lips in recognition of the fact that she was very much over him.

She led him into the lounge. Taking a seat on the sofa whilst quickly organising her thoughts, she faltered, 'I'm great. Listen, it really isn't a good time.' Not wanting to appear rude she added as an afterthought, 'You OK? What brings you to London?'

Michael's eyes narrowed in on her as he flashed a charming smile. Once upon a time, she would have killed to know what he was thinking. She had spent numerous hours wondering why he hadn't called when he said he would, amongst a myriad of other now pointless musings. She smiled again as she realised that Michael's thoughts didn't concern her. Still clutching a bottle of Evian from her work-out, she took a sip and eyed him sitting on the couch beside her.

He hadn't taken his eyes of her since he had arrived, yet Eleanor didn't care what she looked like in front him. All she could think about was grabbing a quick shower and getting ready to see Raphael. Michael licked his dry lips as if suddenly nervous and said, 'A bunch of us went out for Steve's birthday last week and Gabi mentioned that you'd had an accident. You're looking well though. It's good to see you.'

Eleanor smiled and took another sip of her water. 'Ditto, it's nice to see you too, I just wasn't expecting you.'

She tried not to sound flippant, but a huge part of her didn't actually care for his response. She chided herself for being unfeeling. Despite everything, he was still her friend. A sobering phrase flashed through her mind. *Treat others how you wish to be treated.* She tried to feign enthusiasm and turning to face him, waited patiently for his response.

He was silent for a minute as he mulled over what to say, his eyes travelling around the room before returning to her face. Eleanor couldn't dismiss her growing impatience at Michael's inopportune presence. Raphael's imminent arrival filled her with a renewed sense of urgency; it was now 5:25pm and she still had to shower and choose an outfit. She couldn't help smiling as she thought of Raphael and imagined running her hands through his thick dark chocolate hair.

'Hello..? Earth calling Elle! You were miles away. Some things never change, always the inveterate daydreamer. I've... I've missed you.'

Eleanor snapped out of her reverie and glanced back at Michael. He was wearing a blue denim jacket and the stone crew tee which she had given him for his birthday last year. She met his gaze and he cleared his throat as he broke eye contact.

Eleanor was unsure what to say. She had missed Michael like crazy. It had been torture not having her best friend to talk to in the first few months of university. Not only had she lost a boyfriend, but her best friend too. She remembered feeling stranded as it had dawned on her that Michael did not want her to be part of his life. However difficult it had been, she had grown accustomed to his absence and the void in her life was no more. She simply didn't have space for him in her life. Choosing her words carefully she said, 'I miss- I *used* to miss you. We were so close. I guess we've drifted.'

'Yeah, I've been thinking of you since bumping into you in Manchester. I just wanted to see you to say a quick hello. I don't know what propelled me to come here. But here I am.' His eyes flitted around the room then up to her face. 'This is one hell of a house. I remember we were meant to visit here one weekend but just didn't get round to it. Remember..?'

Eleanor tried to recall the conversation which seemed a lifetime ago. Her past had come knocking on her door, insistently begging not to be forgotten. Except she had locked away those memories, conversations and everything else related to Michael in a deep box and thrown away the key. She hadn't allowed herself to think of him and now, at Michael's request she felt almost coerced to confront her past.

Michael's throwaway comment imbued Eleanor with a sense of positivity; she had accepted the change in circumstance and moved on. As she looked at him sitting beside her, she wondered what she had found attractive about him. He was a regular guy, pleasant, witty and a fantastic friend. Her mind latched onto those final two words. *Fantastic friend.* The thing she had missed most was hanging out with him. It was whilst she was studying his face that she fully understood that she had confused friendship with love.

This was another realisation that took her breath away. She knew she was over Michael shortly after bumping into him. Yet it was only now that she understood her true feelings for him. She had *always* seen him as a friend. Boundaries of their friendship had become blurred with the mistaken first flush of potential romance. Michael had been her first boyfriend yet she had never truly loved him.

As she stared at him on the couch, she realised she would always love him as a friend – nothing more, nothing less. She said lightly, 'No, I don't remember. We used to be best friends then all of sudden we weren't even speaking. They were diffic-'

She was unable to speak further. It happened so quickly. One moment she was trying to explain the situation from her point of view. The next, Michael was kissing her. As his insistent lips grazed hers, she automatically flinched. '*What the..?*'

Michael's reflex action caused him to pull away from her. He spoke apologetically with just a hint of reproach. 'Sorry for that. It's just that I've missed you. I know I could have timed the break-up better. You must really hate me.'

He looked confused, his embarrassed eyes awkwardly resting on the books on the nearby table. His eyes sought comfort everywhere apart from her face. All of a sudden Eleanor was reminded of a scolded child who had had his candy bar snatched away from him. He seemed bewildered and she was immediately sorry for him.

It suddenly dawned on her that she would never have been in Richmond if it had not been for Michael. She would never have met Raphael. That very thought made her stomach turn. For this point alone, she could never hate Michael.

So much had changed in the past few minutes. The dramatic shift in the balance of power had left Eleanor feeling oddly disconcerted for a full minute, before empowerment kicked in. She was back in control and stronger than ever. She said gently, 'I don't hate you. I could never hate you. Everything happens for a reason. Maybe in the future we'll be close again, who knows. Remember one thing – 1 will always love you as a friend.'

A hesitant smile formed on his lips as he continued staring at her. She jumped off the couch and said, 'I *really* must make tracks. I need a shower and I'm running late to see a friend. How long are you in town for?'

Michael answered hesitantly, 'I'm visiting my cousin and Richmond was only half an hour away so I thought...'

Eleanor looked down at Michael. He wanted to stay and Eleanor wondered if maybe he wanted to work on their friendship straight away. She knew she would be busy with Raphael, but it wouldn't do any harm for Michael to stay over. He was after all one of her oldest friends. Her face softened as she said, 'Listen, feel free to stay tonight if you want. The couch is comfy, sort of! Although I don't know what time I'll be back.'

Eleanor knew she was right offering him a place to stay when she saw a triumphant smile emerge on Michael's face. She returned his grin and practically sprinted up the stairs. Pausing mid-flight before running upstairs, she exclaimed excitedly, 'Michael – it *is* good to see you. Your visit's been enlightening!'

Michael watched her run upstairs. She looked good. He knew that he still cared for her ever since seeing her in Manchester. She hadn't fallen apart without him. When re-evaluating their relationship, he realised he still missed her. Although he was surprised by how much he wanted to see her. Since their break-up Eleanor hadn't really featured in his thoughts. Yet the past few weeks filled him with an overwhelming desire to see her and rekindle their relationship. It was an odd feeling that came out of nowhere. Suddenly, he found himself distracted whilst thoughts of Eleanor flooded his mind. Succumbing to this unexpected urge, Michael had found himself on a surprise road-trip to London to see Eleanor.

He tried to figure out what she was thinking. She had been pleasantly surprised to see him. Distracted at first, but pleased nonetheless. It was obvious she had missed him by the way she couldn't stop smiling. Granted, he had caught her unawares with the ill-timed kiss; in retrospect it was too early in the conversation. However she had hinted at rebuilding their relationship.

She had told him she still loved him. And she had asked him to stay over. These signs pointed to one thing. He could think of no other explanation – she wanted him back. It was just a matter of time; by the end of the night, they would be a couple again. A happy, satisfied smile spread across his face as he pictured them together. It would be different this time round. He was more mature. He was ready for a serious relationship.

Settling back on the couch preoccupied with thoughts of Eleanor, he considered himself lucky that he had a second chance with her. It was an empty house and they had the rest of the evening to reacquaint themselves.

Her lips were just as he had remembered them, soft with a hint of a candy flavoured lip gloss. She looked well, her gym outfit clinging to her curves with her vest flashing a sliver of toned midriff. Suddenly, his amorous musings were interrupted by a knock at the door. He shouted for Eleanor. No answer. The soft running water in the background indicated she was still bathing. Michael knew she could be some time and smiling at the thought of Eleanor in the shower, went to open the door.

# 27 SO CLOSE

Raphael waited on Eleanor's porch. He had been standing there for the past few minutes. Glancing at his watch for what seemed like the hundredth time, he noted he was nearly twenty minutes early. He had waited a long time for this moment. Clock watching in his apartment was no fun as he endured the agonizing wait.

He had to at least try not to be around her all the time. He had spent the day willing the hours away, pacing his apartment in a state of nervous restlessness. Yet standing on her doorstep now, he found himself unable to move.

His mind was a tornado of tumbling thoughts and emotions, jostling for prime position, adamantly wanting to be addressed. *Should he really be here? What would he say to her? How would he start the conversation?* Bittersweet knife-edge tension clouded his judgement. He smiled, finally appreciating what humans must experience prior to confessing their love.

He was going to tell her that he loved her. She was the one for him. A part of him had known ever since he had seen her in the rain all those months ago. As her face flitted through his mind, a wave of pure, absorbing love swept over him. He had known she was different from the very beginning. Since her first day in Richmond, he had found himself wanting to know more about her. It was an insatiable curiosity which refused to be quenched. They could spend hours together, yet somehow it was never enough. Time apart left him feeling incomplete and oddly restless. The thought of being away from her filled him with inexplicable anxiety and he was reminded of the fact that he had fought so hard to suppress – he was in love with Eleanor.

He had watched her from afar to begin with, attributing his actions to simple curiosity for humans. With time, he had reluctantly conceded that his feelings for her ran deeper than regular friendship. Friends didn't have such an intense effect on each other. And friends didn't secretly break into each others houses just to check if everything was OK.

It was the first and only time he had entered her house without Eleanor's knowledge. Still, he knew it was one time too many. He was acutely aware of his already long list of misdemeanours. Not wanting to add crazy stalker to the ever growing list, he had told himself that was the only time he would break in. He knew humans didn't approve of that kind of behaviour although he didn't quite understand why. Surely, to watch someone for their own safety was a good deed? He realised that despite spending centuries on Earth, he still didn't know everything about humans.

Her resistance to him was an unforeseen difficulty which had originally surprised him. Most humans coveted his company. He knew by the way they stared at him. He had grown accustomed to their looks filled with longing and desire, which over the centuries he had grown bored of. Yet Eleanor was different.

His mind flitted back to the break-in night. When Eleanor's central heating had broken down he had intuitively known something was wrong with the house. For some bizarre reason, the thought of Eleanor in discomfort troubled him and he had sat for a few moments watching her sleep.

She was shivering gently as he watched her from the darkest corner of her bedroom. He suddenly didn't care about the *Non-Magic Rule* that banned the performance of magic on Earth. He figured as long as humans didn't see anything, he was OK. And it was only a tiny enchantment. Using the simplest of spells to conjure a *Warmth Orb*, he had sat observing her on that freezing night. The silence was broken only by her gentle breathing and he had suddenly become aware of how delicate she was. Her fragility rendered him speechless and he had had an overwhelming desire to take care of her and be her shield.

It had been difficult at first. Prolonged contact with a human was unchartered territory for him. He had had more than his fair share of liaisons, never spending longer than was absolutely necessary with anyone. Sex was one thing. Getting to know someone and spending time with them was a whole different ball game that he wasn't sure how to handle.

He wanted to get to know her more but his deplorable secret was always lurking in the shadowy recesses of his mind. During his time on Earth he had learnt that humans universally regarded honesty as the basis of friendship. Yet he had found it almost impossible to truly bond with her as his leaden secret had forced him to be constantly guarded. The burden seemed to get heavier as his feelings for her had intensified. Watching their friendship blossom had filled him with jubilant exultation.

He was glad when she finally knew about his parentage. He was filled with a sudden rush of love as he recalled how she had so readily accepted him. The very thought of her disowning him filled him with sickening horror. He hadn't known how she would react when he told her. It could have gone either way.

Now he was glad it was out in the open and his love for her had increased a hundred fold. She was selfless and kind, possessing a rare quality which Raphael had found difficult to dismiss. He had attempted to walk away from her numerous times, yet she had continuously drawn him back to her. Like a reckless moth to a clear burning flame he would return, telling himself that it was for the last time. However, one look from those large hazel eyes would set his nerves on fire. His conviction to stay away would vanish in her luminous presence as he continuously ignored the warning bells and arranged to meet her time and time again.

The more time he spent with her, the more he had found it difficult to back off. He was unable to stay away from her, the person he had grown to love with all his being. She was unique yet couldn't see this, a fact that never failed to astound Raphael. It was a human trait and Raphael had been reminded again that he was in love with a human.

She was too good for anyone, himself included. She was the complete antithesis to him; her pure, good heart in stark contrast to his evil one filled with impure, often dangerous thoughts. He also knew that his alliance with a human would go against everything that he had been brought up to believe.

In theory it was a thoroughly preposterous idea. The son of Lucifer and a human. Together. He had weighed up the pros and cons for such an alliance, and although the myriad negatives far outweighed the one positive, he didn't care. He loved her. He couldn't exist without her. His father would have to get used to it.

There wasn't just his father to consider. It was the bigger picture. He hadn't even thought about the future. Everything hinged on her response. He conceded it would be easier for her to refuse him. He was half crazed at the thought of not being able to see her face and knew he would fight to stay on Earth to be with her.

He had decided to stay on Earth if she loved him back. Struggling to fathom what she was thinking, he wondered what her reaction would be when he confessed his love for her. In the beginning, reading her mind had been like delving into a library with a free pass. He had easy access to a space chockfull of interesting information and random thoughts. As he tried to figure her out, he had learnt in particular, of her love for her ex-boyfriend.

He wanted to protect her from the world and seeing her heartbroken had saddened and infuriated him. Yet he had forced himself to listen to her in the capacity of a friend whilst reassuring himself that this was the best for all concerned. Now, he wanted more. If Eleanor didn't love him, he would have to accept her decision and walk away.

He sometimes thought she liked him more than a friend. She had even dreamt of them kissing once. It was just a dream, besides, humans dreamt of all sorts of weird things. *It meant nothing, right..?*

He ran his fingers through his hair in fervent frustration as he realised he didn't know what she really thought about him. Helplessness gnawed at him and for the second time that evening he realised what humans must feel like. If Valentina's thoughts were a benchmark, then Raphael's doubts were unfounded.

His fleeting meeting with Valentina had been insightful. He was glad he had deliberately left a book at Eleanor's house on the pretence of seeing her. He had been secretly thrilled to overhear Valentina's thoughts, who was certain that Eleanor loved him. Of course it wasn't definite. Nothing on Earth was definite. He realised that despite his stint on Earth, he still didn't know how humans really functioned. Especially girls.

She had practically ran away when he had seen her a few days ago, yet now she couldn't wait to see him. He listened to her cryptic voice-mail for the seventeenth time that day, her mellifluous voice sending fresh fire through his veins. He detected an eager undercurrent to her message as she said that it was a long time coming, whatever *it* was. Maybe, *just* maybe she loved him back..? He dare not hope and shook his head in vexation as he wondered for the millionth time what Eleanor was thinking.

Since the accident, Raphael was unable to read a handful of humans. Eleanor included. The steady stream of random thoughts that had flowed so readily from her mind seemed to have suddenly stopped overnight. He recalled it was the morning of her accident when he had suspected something was untoward. His disquiet had blasted into full-on fury after discovering his father had orchestrated the terrible mishap.

Danger seemed to follow Eleanor around and he was grateful for his sense of curiosity when he had followed her to the fairground that night. He had seen flashes of the accident shortly before it happened. Stealing her token had been easy. He wished he could have stopped others from getting hurt but Eleanor was his priority.

The chocolate incident was another close call. Again, he had literally brushed aside the toxic box and attempt on her life when he had seen chilling images of Eleanor on her deathbed. The fairground accident had awoken a fiercely protective streak and since then unbeknownst to Eleanor, he had rarely left her side.

The car accident was the one thing off his radar. He should have known something was wrong when he couldn't see her in his mind's eye. He shouldn't have waited till the end of the lecture to call her. Still cursing his ill-timing on the day of her accident, he remained racked with remorse when he came to know that she had been injured. When it dawned on him that he had brought harm to her, he had been crushed.

How could he tell her all this? Would she understand? He just had to relay his feelings in the best possible way but was unsure how to start off. For centuries he had seen humans fall in love. Some fell apart, whilst others went on to lead perfectly happy lives. A part of him had found it humorously entertaining how humans became besotted. It was such a peculiar emotion. Now standing on Eleanor's doorstep and able to empathise with the previously mocked humans, he didn't find their predicament as amusing as originally thought.

It was a delicious thrill all the same, being on the cusp of something amazing whilst under the spell of a passionate, fiery love. He couldn't wait any longer. Wishing himself calm he rapped twice on the door.

He automatically squared his shoulders and straightened up. The door swung open yet Eleanor was nowhere to be seen. Raphael eyed the stranger inquisitively, who had a friendly upbeat voice. 'Hi, can I help?'

Raphael took a few seconds to answer. 'Is Eleanor in?' He paused to say, 'You are..?'

The stranger smiled, extending his arm to offer a handshake. 'Hey, I'm Michael. Me and Elle, we're sort of...' He laughed lightly to say, 'It's a recent development, so you may not have heard about me. Wanna come in and wait? Elle's in the shower, she won't be long.'

Raphael simply stared. He shook Michael's hand and just as quickly let it go. The chilly evening air was shattered by a string of flashing images as he read Michael's mind. Michael kissing Eleanor. Michael thinking of Eleanor in the shower and the night they were going to spend together.

It took all of Raphael's strength to keep his hands by his side. His first impulse was to rip off Michael's head. Eleanor had obviously rekindled her relationship with her ex. That is what she had been so excited about. *She loved Michael.*

Raphael's quick recovery came within seconds. He said through gritted teeth, 'Not to worry, I was just passing through.' He said a little more stiffly, 'Congratulations by the way.'

Michael seemed pleased and beaming a boyish grin at Raphael said, 'Thanks man. Sorry, who are you again? Can I take a message?'

Raphael glared at Michael. He said with quiet vehemence, 'Nothing important.' He didn't wait for a response, turning on his heel to stride away. The panel of light spilling from the house behind him onto the dark lawn had now disappeared and Raphael knew Michael had closed the door. Eleanor was now with Michael. And there was nothing Raphael could do.

Dusk had set. Raphael stormed off in silence, his mind numb whilst his chest was quickly filled with a ferocious flood of stabbing notions. This is what real pain felt like. This is what humans must feel.

His buzzing mobile indicated an incoming text. Maybe it was Eleanor wanting to share her exciting news about Michael. He was thankful when he saw it wasn't her. His relief was short-lived as he read his father's text.

**Lucifer: Come home Raphael. We have to talk.**

# 28 CASTLES IN THE SKY

Eleanor was in and out of the shower in record time, a personal best of seven minutes. She had little time to waste in choosing an outfit and literally stumbled into her jeans and green top whilst keeping a steady eye on her phone clock. After a quick dab of moisturiser and lick of nude lip-gloss, she ran downstairs clutching her mobile phone.

Part of her wished she hadn't asked Michael to stay, but she couldn't change that now. She would see Raphael in a few minutes and she could barely contain her effervescent excitement which fizzed inside her like a glass of Prosecco. Giddy and drunk on being in love, she focused on Raphael's imminent arrival and skipped into the lounge.

Michael was channel flicking on the couch and smiled as she entered the room. He appeared to be in good spirits and Eleanor's initial disquiet disappeared as she gave him credit for trying to rebuild their currently tenuous link. She softened as she wondered that maybe time apart had made him realise the significance of their friendship.

She beamed at him and plumped down on the sofa, having a few minutes to kill before Raphael arrived. Drumming her fingertips on the chunky arm-rest and looking over at Michael she said, 'Just waiting for a mate, unsure what time I'll be back, don't think I'll be longer than a few hours. If you're not up by the time I get back, we'll catch up tomorrow. I've just remembered you'll need spare bedding. Hang on, I'll grab some.'

She ran upstairs and reappeared with a duvet set. It was now 6:03pm. Raphael was always on time and she found herself wondering why of all days, he was late today. She could barely keep still. Forcing herself calm she sat back down and glanced at Michael. It was odd being next to him. She felt as if she was sitting next to a stranger on a bus. Although she had known him since school, she knew very little of his present life. They had drifted onto different paths since the break-up and just as she had changed as a person, no doubt he had too.

She suddenly realised Michael was not part of her life. She didn't even know where he lived in Edinburgh. They had to get to know each other again and in a bid to kick-start their re-acquaintance she smiled to say, 'I feel like I hardly know you! So come on, what's been happening with you lately? How's uni? What's hot, what's not – any girlfriend on the scene? And how's Edinburgh? It's a beautiful city.'

Eleanor wondered at the look of surprise on Michael's face. He seemed confused as he faltered, 'Girlfriend..? What do you mean..? I thought...'

His voice trailed off and he looked to Eleanor like a lost puppy dog. They both sat in puzzled silence for a few seconds before Eleanor said gently, 'You don't have to answer if you don't want to. I'm just trying to get to know you again, you know. We're mates after all, right? You *can* tell me about who you're dating though, I promise there will be no ick-factor. And hey, you must recommend some bars in Edinburgh, I've been meaning to see the castle for some time now.'

Michael simply gawked. An unexpected wave of understanding washed over his face as he said casually, 'No... course you can ask. We are... *mates* after all.' He was silent for a few seconds before speaking through a pursed smile, 'Uni's great. Edinburgh's a fantastic city... You'd love it there.' He paused again. 'What about you? How's uni?' Clearing his throat he said, 'Any... boyfriend on the scene?'

Eleanor couldn't help but grin as she thought of Raphael. She said, 'Well... Actually, I sort of do like this guy at uni. It's early days yet. I haven't even told him that I like him, let alone love him.'

Michael remained silent. He no longer gazed at Eleanor, who had now pulled her mobile phone closer to inspect the time. Unease fluttered over her as she realised Raphael was nearly fifteen minutes late. This was a first. Before she could call him, a text from Raphael buzzed through.

**Raphael: Can't make it. Sorry.**

She re-read the message. Those four words offered no explanation. Mystification edged out disquiet and before she could call him, a second text buzzed through.

**Raphael: Can meet tomorrow instead. 2pm?**

She clasped the phone in her hand, wondering about the sudden change in plan.

**Eleanor: Everything OK? PS tomorrow works for me.**

**Raphael: Can't talk now. See you tomorrow at the park near your house at 2pm.**

She just wanted to see him. Something wasn't right, she could feel it. Her train of thought was broken by Michael who said lightly, 'Everything OK?'

Pulling her eyes away from her mobile she mumbled, 'Yeah… I think so.' Smiling encouragingly, whilst trying to disregard the nagging feeling that something horrible loomed on the horizon, she said, 'Change of plan. I'm not going out tonight after all. Right, we have the full evening ahead of us. Vegging over a Chinese, waddaya think?'

A crestfallen Michael gave a small smile and nodded, 'Sounds good to me.'

Eleanor lay nestled in bed the following morning. She had just seen Michael off and having had a late night, had slunk back upstairs to grab a few more hours of coveted sleep. It was still only 8:30am and she had nearly five hours before she saw Raphael. Her mind wandered onto the previous evening. It had been an unusual night full of surprises. Michael's unexpected appearance had been on top of the list. She had been taken aback when she saw him on her doorstep, yet having spent an enjoyable evening together, felt encouraged with the possibility that their friendship could be salvaged. Things between her and Michael would never be the same again – she had changed too much for that. She realised now that her feelings for Michael had been nothing more than a juvenile infatuation and she imagined the relief that Michael would be feeling to know that she was finally over their relationship.

His kiss was another shock, awkward embarrassment sweeping over her as she recalled his advance. She put it down to nostalgia; he probably didn't even mean to kiss her. For a short part of the evening, she thought he was acting weird. It was almost as if she was seeing a different person when she returned from her shower. He had suddenly seemed a million miles away, yet as the evening had progressed, he had relaxed a little and they had spent the evening chatting and catching up over a few beers and take-away.

Raphael's no-show had been the final surprise and biggest disappointment of the night. He would explain soon enough and closing her eyes, Eleanor fell asleep with a smile on her face as the image of Raphael rested in her mind.

She awoke a few hours later fully refreshed and skipped into the shower, spending nearly an hour at her wardrobe choosing an outfit. She wanted to look her best. Nothing had happened between her and Raphael yet. He hadn't even heard her confession of love. If he didn't reciprocate, she would have to be OK with it. She would still be his friend. She exhaled and smiled as she thought of his reaction, hoping for the millionth time that he would love her back. After finally deciding on a blue dirndl skirt and white sweetheart top combo, she settled in front of the mirror and set to work. As she carefully applied her new pink lipstick and mascara, she realised how happy her smiling reflection looked. Things could be very different after a few hours. She could be *with* Raphael. The very thought sent delicious shivers down her spine as she continued to get ready in a state of delirious joy.

Gulping down her coffee and taking a few hasty bites of a granola bar, she glanced in the hallway mirror before leaving the house. With a nervous smile, she made her way to the park to see Raphael.

# 29 LUCIFER'S FURY

Raphael waited outside his father's study for a few moments. It had been over an hour since the text and Raphael had taken his time to arrive. He was in no mood for confrontation. He had been close to disregarding the text, yet even he knew that would exacerbate a potentially volatile situation. Ignoring Lucifer was not an option.

Raphael knew he had been summoned for a reason. Lucifer must know. Raphael paused at the door. He didn't want to feel anything. He craved oblivion as his frenzied mind replayed images of Eleanor and Michael together. He thrust the heavy oak door aside and stormed into the study.

The leaden door smashed against the wall. Raphael cast a quick glance around the room. The black curtains were drawn. Raphael immediately felt confined. The dense velvet folds of the curtains accentuated the oppressive atmosphere, which Raphael felt bearing down on him like an invisible, suffocating hand. The stifling air heightened Raphael's unease and he immediately knew that a difficult meeting lay ahead.

Lucifer was standing at the far end of the room by a bookshelf. Noticing Raphael was already inside the room, Lucifer said with a hint of sarcasm, 'Do come in.' He paused, his hand hovering over a book as he continued in a steely voice, 'What a fine evening it is turning out to be. Trust you are well?'

Raphael braced himself for a confrontation; this was just his father's opening gambit. Raphael tried to focus on his present predicament. Dealing with his father would require all his attention yet he still couldn't get his thoughts in order. His jealous mind returned to the bitter images in an unrelenting sadomasochistic streak, causing him to flinch with pain. Raphael said in a level voice, 'I'm fine. Why shouldn't I be-'

'Raphael.' Lucifer's voice remained calm. Deadly calm. 'I hate to say this. But I told you so. Humans... will be humans.' Lucifer's words were tinged with razor-sharp condescension. His swift interjection caused the loop playing taunting images of Eleanor and Michael in Raphael's mind to momentarily stop. It was as if someone had paused the channel of streaming images, their finger hovering with wicked intent over the play button as Raphael struggled to remain in control. Keeping calm was not Raphael's forte.

Raphael remained quiet for a few moments in the futile hope that the respite from seeing disturbing images would appease the dangerous rage that whirled like a destructive tornado inside his head. He said quietly, 'I don't know what you're talking ab-'

Lucifer's previously veiled antagonism shot abruptly to the fore like a deadly bullet from a Smith & Wesson. 'You know *exactly* what I'm talking about. I saw you earlier. At her house. With her boyfriend.'

It was Raphael's turn to cave. His reserve exploded into smithereens giving way to searing red wrath. He roared back at his father, 'YOU'VE BEEN WATCHING MY MOVEMENTS?!'

Raphael clenched his fists into tight balls. Lucifer looked directly at Raphael for the first time. Casting his son a savage stare he said, 'No different to what you have been doing with *her*.' He pressed on, 'I know you're upset-'

Raphael replied tersely, 'I am *not* upset. Eleanor's actions do not affect me.' Eleanor's face flitted through his mind. He continued after a beat, 'And yes, I have been keeping an eye on her. But it was only because I care... cared about her.'

'Care, cared, same difference. To bring a human into the equation is unthinkable. You're a sinking ship Raphael. Why do you think I watch you? Go figure.'

Lucifer's grave tone was in stark contrast to his relaxed stance by the bookshelf. Lucifer removed his jacket, throwing it casually on the back of a luxurious leather chair.

Lucifer's eyes continued to scan the myriad books as he said slowly, 'Why so quiet today? Not in the mood for talking? You seem perfectly verbose when talking to humans. Or one human in particular.' He paused for a few long seconds before continuing, 'You'd be terrific at sponsored silences, anyone ever tell you that? Still no answer? I'll tell you why I watch you. Parental concern. Or whatever the hell you want to call it.'

Lucifer's biting response could not disguise a hint of anguish that had crept into his voice. This was the first time in centuries that Raphael had heard his father express concern for him. The unexpected admission hit him hard. As he questioned his father's ulterior motives, Raphael was numb with the realisation that his father cared for him.

Frustration, shock and anger formed a curious combination and Raphael felt the bewildering side-effects almost immediately. Surprise had temporarily stemmed the volcanic rage in Raphael's mind. Like a balm, comprehension slowly soothed ill-feeling towards his father as Raphael said firmly, 'I have nothing more to say about Eleanor.'

Both Raphael and Lucifer remained in a stand-off, quietly staring at each other. Lucifer said smoothly, 'That's perfect. Because I have plenty to say on the matter. And you *will* listen.'

Lucifer's mask had slipped earlier when he had admitted to caring about his son. Now, the mask was super-glued firmly back on again. Drumming his fingers lightly on the bookshelf ledge he said, 'I sent you to Earth to teach you a lesson. If I had known things would get this complicated, I would never have banished you.' He muttered, 'I recall mocking God... Sacrificial lamb to the slaughter and all that crap. I appear to be none the wiser.'

Lucifer continued pacing near the bookshelf, crushing footprints into the blood red rug nearby. He said, 'I wanted you to see humans for what they really are. Self involved inconsiderate creatures powered by greed – that's on a good day. I have known them much longer than you have. I have watched them for centuries go about business in their small-minded way. Yet, they remain the same. Stupidly oblivious of the bigger picture and too foolish to change their ways. This is what I wanted you to see.' Half talking to himself and Raphael he said, 'Never did I imagine that you'd actually grow to like these humans, let alone love one. Because that's what you've done Raphael. You've fallen in love with a *human.*'

He uttered the last word with contempt as if the very word caused him severe offence.

Raphael was unable to keep quiet any longer. He declared vehemently, 'I *never* loved her. And for the record, you don't know what humans are really like. They can hurt each other, I'm not denying that.' He paused a while, his flashing eyes cautiously watching his father as he said, 'But they can love one another too. Everyone has a good and bad side. Even y-'

Lucifer thundered, 'DON'T YOU DARE! I did not call you here to listen to your flawed understanding of humans. Your empathy towards them is incomprehensible. I had thought a stint on Earth would have ironed out that abysmal moral compass of yours.'

He turned his head a full ninety degrees to face Raphael. Lucifer's dark eyes were full of untold terror as he said quietly, 'And Raphael, *never* compare me to those loathsome creatures again. Understand?'

Raphael flinched. Lucifer pulled a slim burgundy tome from the shelf and poured himself a drink by the cabinet. He seemed to be mulling something over as he sipped his neat Bourbon. He said nonchalantly, 'I haven't even offered you a drink, how thoroughly remiss of me. Would y-'

Raphael was at the drinks cabinet within seconds. Pouring himself an extra large Hennessy, he drained half a glass in one gulp. Father and son were standing side by side at the cabinet. Raphael sloshed some more alcohol and tumbled a few blocks of ice into his glass before moving away. Lucifer's eyes flickered over his son's glass. He said harshly, 'I drink when disgusted with human nature. What's your excuse?'

Raphael lowered himself into the seat by the broad table, staring at the glass of alcohol in his hand. A sea of shady amber liquid surrounded glistening ice-cubes that floated like miniature icebergs in the deep glass. Within five minutes, the ice-cubes would be gone. Raphael wished he too could disappear and be oblivious to the raging tornado that beat a destructive path in his mind. Emboldened by the dark fluid that burned a trajectory down his throat. Raphael said, 'I don't understand your vitriol towards humans.'

Lucifer stared in silent incredulity. He paused mid-sip to viciously say, 'I can't believe I'm hearing this. Humans are weak, despicable creatures. The road to Hell isn't paved with good intentions. That's just a cliché used by self-serving humans to gratify their immoral actions.'

Glass in one hand and another clutching the burgundy book, Lucifer edged nearer to the table. There was a faint smirk on his lips as he said in a wicked whisper, 'I want nothing to do with humans. Apart from when I am handling their souls.'

Raphael said flatly, 'Not all humans deserve to be punished.'

Lucifer tossed the book aside where it landed with a small thud on the table. He was seven feet away from his son. Lucifer slowly circled the table, still clutching his drink. His vigilant eyes watched Raphael take another gulp of alcohol as Lucifer continued his anti-human diatribe.

'Humans. They all deserve to be punished. Why do you think they're on Earth in the first place?' Lucifer continued circling the table. He was now five feet away from Raphael who remained seated seething in silence.

'There's Hell and Heaven, with Earth being something of a level playing field.' Lucifer smiled deprecatingly. His eyes travelled the enormous study and upwards to the lofty ceiling. He continued, 'All this is God's creation. I'm in no mood to give a history lesson. Suffice to say, I'm not alone in despising humans. God too recognises his folly. In a moment of recklessness, he created humans and placed these ungrateful creatures on Earth. They're destroying the world and themselves. I will give, begrudgingly of course, credit where due. God had tried in the early years to show these pathetic humans the right way, but his attempts were met with brutal indifference. He couldn't quite believe how much his beloved humans had messed up. He now views humans in the same way I do – a dreadful inconvenience.'

Raphael stared at his father in disbelief as Lucifer continued with a flourish, 'And that's where I come in. We reached a truce some time ago. I would have free reign over Earth, in return for keeping the gates of Hell perpetually open to facilitate the easy movement of souls. God could no longer watch his humans destroy the Earth he so lovingly created and decided he would merely speed up the destruction of Earth. And its ignorant humans.'

Lucifer mused, 'I like to call it free trade, a balance that needs to be regulated at all times. Of course the free trade deal struck with me wasn't an easy agreement to reach. God is one complex character. If you think I'm tricky, you should meet him. Dealing with a Libyan dictator is much easier.'

Lucifer was now two feet away from Raphael. Lucifer set down his heavy crystal tumbler with a deep clink next to Raphael's near empty glass. Leaning on the table with hands outstretched, Lucifer towered over Raphael.

He glowered at his son, whispering, 'I hope now you understand my position. I see no reason for you to stay on Earth any longer. That's why I summoned you. Come home Raphael.'

Raphael drained his drink, his eyes fixed on the burgundy book. He replied in quiet defiance, 'I'll be glad to come home.' Running his hands through his hair in repressed frustration he eventually met his father's cool gaze to say, 'I just need to return to Earth one more time.'

Lucifer's eyes searched his son's face for a tell-tale sign that would give him a clue to what he was thinking. Raphael's face was a picture of imperceptible calm and Lucifer curtly nodded his acquiescence.

'Say your earthly goodbyes then. I'll expect you back shortly.'

Lucifer watched Raphael stalk towards the exit. Now alone, Lucifer's gaze fell on the burgundy Bible on the table. He stared at the seemingly harmless tome for a few minutes with a contemplative, troubled look. He was glad his son was coming home.

# 30 BOMBSHELL

Eleanor paused at the gate. Smoothing down her skirt for the fortieth time, she glanced nervously at her shoes. Bright afternoon sun peeked out from cotton clouds as she waited in nervous excitement. Up until a few days ago, the thought of loving Raphael had been alien to her. Now her love for him seemed so natural, she wondered why the thought hadn't crossed her mind sooner.

*I love Raphael.* She mulled over the delicious sentence in her head, unable to stop thinking about him. She found herself dreaming of his warm, accommodating embrace and the way his hair curled ever so slightly at the tips. She realised she could look into his hypnotic eyes for eternity. She didn't care about anyone or anything else. She half laughed to herself as she realised how corny she sounded. But she knew there was no escape. She couldn't leave even if she wanted to, because she loved him.

She practically skipped into the park, slowing down as she spied Raphael approaching her, her smile growing as the distance between them slowly dropped away. He wore his black jeans and black tee combo and Eleanor couldn't help but stare. He looked different now that she knew she loved him. Now, he was more than just her best friend.

Normally she would have greeted him with a hug. Instead, she said with hesitant exuberance, 'Hey Raphael! How... are you? Gorgeous weather, huh?'

Shielding her eyes from the harsh sunlight, she was blinded for a few seconds as her eyes grew accustomed to the glare. She said, 'Hey, it's a shame you couldn't make it yesterday.'

Raphael moved slightly to block the sunlight from her eyes. They were now standing directly opposite each other. Eleanor glanced around the empty park as the sun continued to warm her skin. She exhaled and likened the giddy feeling of being in love, to walking on air. She couldn't stop herself from rambling. 'I'm glad we're meeting today though. How was your evening anyway?'

Raphael stared at her as she fidgeted with her bag. She cast him occasional furtive glances as they walked in silence. Trying to keep the conversation as natural as possible she smiled to say, 'I'm knackered! I barely slept all night, but managed to get a few ZZZs this morning.'

He didn't even look in her direction. His downcast eyes were fixed on the path below. She said quickly, 'Honestly Raphael, it's been a crazy few days, I have sooo much to tell you. Hey, is everything alright? I figured something was wrong when you didn't come round last night.'

The silence between them grew heavier as Eleanor waited expectantly for his response. Nearly thirty seconds later, he said flatly, 'I was called away. Sorry.'

She waited for him to expand. He remained silent. Shooting him another surreptitious glance, she said, 'Here goes. I didn't realise something up until a few days ago. Deep down I always knew.'

Raphael's eyes rested briefly on her face before fixing on a cluster of trees ahead. Her cheeks flushed a deep cherry red in response to his fleeting look. It was now or never. Clearing her throat, she said, 'It's been a long time coming. On some subconscious level I guess I *always* knew—'

For the past 24 hours she couldn't wait to see him. Now that he was in front of her, she had regressed into a tongue-tied ten year old. She could barely get the three tiny words out. *I love you.* She just wanted to step forward and kiss him, yet she remained rooted to the spot hindered by her tangled mind and jittery nerves.

Willing herself patient she ploughed on. 'I'm probably not making any sense. OK, I'll start from scratch. I have a confession. You may think it weird. Well, it's not weird, but you know, you may think that... Crap, I'm rambling again. OK, here goes. Raphael, I lo—'

'I already know.' Raphael remained tight-lipped.

She blinked in disbelief. Overcome with shyness then blooming anticipation, a surprised smile slowly formed on her flushed face. She looked at him with shining eyes as she gently said, 'Okaaaay, how did you know? So you can mind-read again..?'

He practically barked at her. 'I met him. Michael. That's his name, right?'

His terse reply threw Eleanor off guard as her smile slowly faded. Why was Raphael talking about *Michael*? And more importantly *when* did they meet? Surely Michael would have mentioned something to her? Maybe he forgot, he had seemed preoccupied all evening. But why hadn't Raphael mentioned that he had visited her in their text conversation? Her brain like a frenetic radio, struggled to make sense of a hundred scrambled frequencies that continued to bewilder her. Nothing was making sense.

Raphael's brusque response heightened her confusion as she heard him curtly exclaim, 'I came by your house last night. I spoke with Michael then. You were in the shower.' He paused for a few seconds before saying with thinly veiled ferocity, 'Congratulations. On getting back with him.'

Eleanor was about to protest but was unable to form a cohesive sentence as she gaped in astonishment. She had been on the verge of baring her soul and divulging her love for him. Instead, he was offering congratulations on her supposed rekindled relationship with Michael.

Raphael stepped forward to hug her. His strong arms were suddenly around her as she melted into him. He said roughly, 'I'm happy for you. That's great news.'

Tears pricked her now smarting eyes which were dangerously close to betraying her. Quickly blinking back her tears, she tried to gulp the smarting rejection away. She had been so wrong. Not only did he not love her, he was congratulating her. *HE DID NOT WANT HER.* He wanted her to be with Michael.

She mentally cursed herself as she realised she hadn't really been prepared for his negative response. How could she have been so stupid? *So very, very stupid?* She wasn't going to force herself on him. At least he was still her best friend. Just because she was in love with him didn't mean that he had to love her back.

As self-preservation kicked in, she tried to keep her mind on track. At least she hadn't made an idiot out of herself by confessing her love for him outright. Caught up in a maelstrom of conflicting emotions, she knew she had to pretend that she was OK. It would save an awkward conversation and spare her further embarrassment.

She had to recover fast. She felt as if she was being pulled one way then another, the shared property of two rival master-puppeteers; her astute mind engaged in a bitter tussle with her rapidly beating, drastically disappointed heart. Her mind gently cajoled her that Raphael had done nothing wrong. Yet her wounded heart revelled in painful rejection at his encouragement of her apparent new relationship. It hurt. Bad. It was a harsh reminder that he saw her as a friend. Nothing more, nothing less.

She was momentarily distracted by Raphael when he spoke. She heard the gentle vibration of his voice above her head as he continued to hold her in his arms. He whispered, 'My father has graciously cut short my earthly exile.' He paused for a few long seconds. 'I will be returning to Hell today. I just wanted to thank you Eleanor. For being a friend.'

There. He'd said it again. The dreaded *F* word – *friend*. His words cut like a sharpened knife on freshly salted flesh as her mind was thrown into fresh panic. He was leaving.

For the second time, she wanted to shout her disapproval yet felt as if someone had rammed a chunky towel down her neck. Her airless throat felt packed tight and she felt like gagging. Panic suppressed speech and she simply blinked as she stood stock still in his arms.

Her mind jarred to a stop as her heart refused to listen to her coaxing mind which pleaded with her to be positive and in control. With her head resting on his shoulder, she looked upwards. The fluffy white clouds had now morphed into dense, angry pockets of a depthless grey.

She welcomed the gentle drops of rain whilst a breeze whipped her hair to and fro. The abruptly chilly temperature cooled her cheeks and kept her complexion ruddy, providing camouflage to the now obvious pain that enveloped her.

Raphael suddenly let her go and stepped back. She immediately felt unprotected. They watched each other in silence.

He said quietly, 'I have to go. My father is expecting me.'

Her brain kicked into autopilot and she felt someone else was speaking on her behalf. Her voice sounded distant and unfamiliar. The words fell flatly from her mouth as she said quietly, 'Take care Raphael.'

An inexplicable emotion flitted across his face whilst a shell-shocked Eleanor continued staring at him. This was the last time she would see him. She wanted to drink in his image and capture every single detail in her mind's eye.

He stepped further back. Within seconds, he had disappeared in the sheets of grey rain, leaving Eleanor frozen to the spot in the torrential downpour.

# 31 LIKE EATING GLASS

And then it was quiet. She was alone. The silence was deafening. Like crashing waves, throwing her world into watery chaos. The now chilly temperature did not bother her. Her insides hurt with a dull ache. Rolling waves of nausea swept over her as she remained motionless.

She felt trapped on an emotional rollercoaster. She closed her eyes. The shock of Raphael's departure had momentarily stemmed the urge to cry. She no longer fought to keep the pain at bay. The tears came slowly at first, welling up her eyes with a familiar sting followed by unstoppable torrents. She finally stumbled onto a nearby bench and sat down.

She was unsure how long she stayed there, for it was now late evening. She sat in silence in the steadily pouring rain. She felt like a lone survivor of an earthquake watching her life slowly collapse around her. She was unsure how to function in this new, harsh world. A place without Raphael. Her world continued to crumble, and then in an abrupt dip, her mind screamed out. A silent scream charged with pure anguish.

She felt her heart plummet, falling with ruthless speed into a bottomless pit with nothing to hold on to. Suddenly she was suffocating and needed air. She felt her oxygen supply had been cut off and she gasped, closing her eyes and willing herself calm.

In the open space of the park, Eleanor suddenly felt claustrophobic. She felt trapped in a brick wall with no space, room, air or light. The normally soothing patter of the rain failed to placate her today. She exhaled a lungful of air and tried to gulp away the pain, which remained a thick knot in her now desiccated throat. She watched the rain. Falling. Slowly. Solidifying her pain and enveloping her in a continuum which was rapidly starting to fill up with more questions that she didn't know the answer to.

Through the tumultuous haze, specific questions bubbled to the surface and harangued her like bullies in a school playground. How could she have been so *galactically stupid*? How could she have even considered that Raphael could love her, an ordinary and nondescript human? How could he leave so easily? Did she really mean that little to him? Her body was still yet her mind was a hurricane of distress. She just wanted to lie down before she collapsed.

She didn't know how she got home. The journey was a blank for her. A mere twelve hours ago, her world was overflowing with happiness, promise and light. Now, it was packed tight with an indelible blackness.

She found herself standing in the hallway of her house. In her rush to leave the house that morning, she had left the light on. She caught a reflection of herself in the hallway mirror. That Max Factor lipstick certainly lived up to its boast. Twelve hours later and it was still as vibrant as a fresh application. She swept an angry hand over her lips, scrubbing them hard so that the lipstick smeared. Rubbing her sore eyes so that her mascara smudged into dark circles, she backed away from the mirror. She had wanted to look nice for him. And he didn't even care. She slammed a palm on the light switch and the house descended into darkness.

Moonlight streamed through the curtains, casting gloomy silhouettes across the breadth of the lounge. Surrounded by near darkness, the shadows were her only company.

She shifted back on the couch, her clothes soaking wet from sitting in the rain. She hadn't eaten all day but she wasn't hungry. The waves of nausea had now abated but the ache remained in her chest, a series of shifting knots that twisted and turned every few minutes.

She swept a few wet strands of hair away from her tear-stained face and continued to sit in silence. The only discernible noise was the muted hum of electricity that surged through the walls. The house felt bigger than ever, its emptiness compounding her loneliness whilst filling her with growing despair.

It was a pain like no other. She revelled in it, a small part of her secretly thinking she deserved it for actually thinking that Raphael may love her back. She was sickened by the fact that she was never going to see him again. And she couldn't do anything about it. Shackled by helplessness and frustration, she continued staring into the darkness.

She didn't know what time it was. She had forgotten to wear her watch in a hurry to leave the house. She guessed the time to be about 1:00am. Her mouth was dry and her throat felt grainy, as if she had swallowed a mouthful of sand. She continued sitting in silence in the dark lounge before she gave in to her thirst.

En route to the kitchen in the dimmest part of the lounge, she bumped into the free-standing cabinet. Something crashed to the floor. She was still for a few seconds before calmly stepping aside the broken vase and slowly continuing to the kitchen.

She didn't bother turning the light on. Finding solace in the quiet and soothing dark, she groped for a tumbler and filled it with cool water. Three glasses later, she made her way back to the lounge, remembering just in time to circumvent the broken vase in the lounge.

She sat on the couch again. She didn't want to think about anything. Impossible. Her mind hadn't fully processed the fact that Raphael had gone. She had accepted it verbally, yet the thought of him being permanently away from her brought her world to a juddering standstill.

She told herself he was no longer part of her life. Seized by gut-wrenching desolation, she clawed at her stomach to stem the sudden wave of queasiness. She looked upwards at the roof of the room and found comfort in the ceiling of darkness. She didn't know when she fell asleep. The last thought to cross her mind was the upcoming three week Easter vacation. It couldn't have come at a better time.

Eleanor awoke the following morning to bird-song. Her neck was stiff. She blinked a few times as she wondered where she was. For a few optimistic moments she lay still, praying that it was all a horrid nightmare from which she had finally woken. As the realisation of yesterday's events played in her mind, she was hit with a fresh wave of panic that made her sit bolt upright.

The sun-lit lounge was too bright for her and she scrunched her eyes in the face of brilliant daylight. Every muscle in her body ached with an odd sort of pain that came from deep within. Gingerly standing up, she swayed for a few seconds as the feeling of faintness washed over her. Slowly making her way upstairs, she crawled onto her bed and drew the curtains. She slowly drifted in and out of consciousness before finally succumbing to exhaustion.

It was still dark when she awoke. She sat upright and studying the alarm clock through squinted eyes, noticed *SUNDAY* in small black lettering. It took her a full minute to realise she had lost a full two days. She didn't care that she hadn't eaten since Friday. That was forty-eight hours ago. She didn't want to do anything. She would give anything for the unrelenting pain to stop.

She shifted her legs over the bed and sat upright. Everything looked and felt different. From her tear-stained damp pillowcase to the harder than concrete floorboards under her feet, Eleanor felt as if she was suddenly living a different life.

Everything and nothing had changed. It was crazy how much impact one person could have on her life. Raphael had no idea how much she loved him. He obviously didn't think much of her. Sometimes, it felt as if he had cared about her, yet *why..*? Her mind had started the dreaded probing loop. She just didn't have the energy to follow through the difficult questions that her mind inconsiderately flagged up.

She had to find a way out of the vicious circle and tried to formulate a plan. She didn't want to eat, yet her body was crying out for fuel. She didn't have the energy or inclination and for a split second, she hated herself. She was a human. Just a regular human. One of seven billion others who went about their daily business as usual.

Cruel questions darted through her harrowed mind. Would Raphael have loved her if she wasn't human? Would he have stayed if she was like him, one of his *kind..*? There were a thousand whys, and what ifs. But her mind was in no fit state to delve into the heart-breaking reasons behind Raphael's abrupt departure.

She needed to erase Raphael from her mind. The first few steps were always going to be the most difficult. Maybe after time, the pain would somehow miraculously stop. She argued with herself that she had gotten over Michael. He never even crossed her mind anymore.

She knew she had lost the argument before starting it. Her feelings for Raphael were in an entirely different league and elevated beyond compare. She had mourned the loss of her best friend with Michael with whom she had never been in love. She loved Raphael with her heart and soul; to think that he was no longer part of her life sent her mind into a rapid downward spiral again. As if experiencing turbulence on an airplane, her mind and world swayed in a sickening lurch as she wondered when the jolting hurt would stop.

She forced herself downstairs to the kitchen, her faintness growing each step of the way. Padding through the dark house, her dull throbbing headache propelled her towards the medicine cupboard. Swallowing two painkillers, she gulped down another two tumblers of water. She wished there was a medicine for heartache, a simple pill that miraculously erased all memories and pain. She prayed someone would find a formula, patent it and make heartbreak extinct.

Standing for a few minutes in the darkness, she pulled open the fridge door, blinking as the fluorescent light threw a yellow slice onto the cool tiles of the floor. The harsh light nudged her awake as she pulled out a slice of quiche. She willed herself to pick at the triangle on the plate in the darkness. She couldn't taste anything and might as well have been eating sawdust.

She found sitting in the dark oddly peaceful, a weird antidote to the frenetic activity in her mind. She regarded the darkness as an ally that provided a dense, protective cover. It shielded her from the pain whilst providing her with a source of comfort and relief. The moon had risen and was now streaming creamy panels into the kitchen. She no longer felt dizzy. Slightly energised by the food, she shifted off her seat and made her way to the kitchen window.

The luminescence of the moon brilliantly offset the velvet blue sky. Thoughts of Raphael peppered her mind as she wondered what he was doing, thinking and if he missed Earth. As she continued to stare at the buttery orb in the sky, she realised she would never lay eyes on him again. The moon quickly became a smudgy beige ball as she tried to gulp away the tears but they continued to fall freely over her burning cheeks. She leant her hot head on the cool glass of the window for a few seconds. Engulfed in pain, she rocked in the silent dark whilst feverishly wishing that Raphael hadn't left.

But he had gone. And there was nothing she could do. Was it really better to experience love like this when it hurt so much? His face flashed through her mind for the millionth time and she shook her head and exhaled. She didn't want to think anymore.

For now, she would just have to endure. Multiple waves of tiredness crashed over Eleanor as she realised the after effects of another night of broken sleep. Rummaging in the medicine cupboard, she soon found what she was looking for. She still had some tablets from her accident. They were heavier dosage painkillers. One of these and she'd be knock-out. She gulped three down for extra measure. Making her way upstairs, she collapsed on her bed and was soon fast asleep.

Splinters of sunlight fell on her bed as Eleanor stirred awake. Fleeting hope filled her heart before quickly evaporating like mist in the early morning sun. She had slept for nearly twelve hours. More rested, she thought today might actually be better. She just had to remain focused and not think of Raphael.

She felt better after a long shower. The hot jets of water beat down on her neck and shoulders to ease the tension of the past few days. Her mind was quiet and she revelled in the stillness whilst swathed in a mist of steam. Thankful for the momentary peace that came to her so unexpectedly, she felt more alive when she emerged from the shower half an hour later.

She was feeling hungry too. She ruminated over a light breakfast of tea and toast and wondered at the resilience of the human spirit. Maybe it would just take time. She would go through the motions; hurt, rejection, disappointment, and everything in between before Raphael would become a distant memory. She gulped as she forced herself to think positive, upbeat thoughts. She didn't have a choice but to get on with her life. Nothing was impossible. She could do it.

Careful not to lose momentum of her positive mindset, she slid off her seat and decided to give the house a quick tidy up. She loaded up the dishwasher with the few dirty dishes and wiped down the work-tops. Clocking the broken vase on the floor, she grabbed the dust-pan from the kitchen and knelt to sweep up the debris.

She had bought the vase from one of the Christmas markets in Manchester. It looked like a regular vase, but there was something unique about its composition. The vendor had explained a different type of glass had been used, rendering it more fragile and eye-catching than the rest. Now, all that was left of it was a pile of broken glass.

The shards glistened in the afternoon sunlight and she couldn't help but stare transfixed at the smaller pieces. It couldn't be fixed or super-glued back together. Damaged beyond repair, its only destination was the bin. She picked up a few fragments and gently turned them over in her palm. Light reflected off the larger piece and Eleanor's eyes were immediately drawn to its jagged edges, beautiful and dangerously sharp. The pieces of broken glass were reminiscent of something that she struggled to place.

She winced as soon as she made the connection. Black eyes flecked with jagged silver. The pieces of glass reminded her of Raphael's eyes. The cutting memory accentuated her despair and she felt her eyes welling up again. She willed herself to be strong as tears hung back in her eyes. The torturous ball of anguish wasn't going anywhere and slammed right in the middle of her chest to remind her that he had left.

The pieces of glass in her hand were now blurry crystals dashed with rainbow colours as light continued to bounce off them. She had been battling for the past few hours to remain positive, yet her resolve abruptly came crashing down. Her eyes were fixed on the blurry pieces of razor-sharp crystals. She would do anything for this heartbreak to go away.

She couldn't think of anything more painful. Not even eating glass. She didn't think it would be as excruciating as the hurt and despair that pervaded her soul. She considered the trajectory of the glass, the pointed edges slicing her mouth and tongue open in tiny incisions before carving their bloody way down her throat.

*What the hell was she thinking?!* Flinging the pieces of glass in the bin, she ran into the lounge. Preoccupation was key and grabbing the hoover with added vigour, she started vacuuming the lounge. She finished the room and hallway, reaching the top of the sweeping staircase when she stopped in her tracks.

She quickly switched off the hoover. The house descended into a short-lived silence as her ears pricked up at the unmistakable sound of distant rumbling thunder.

A rainstorm was brewing. Eleanor's mind flew to the only conclusion that she knew and craved. Raphael was coming.

Throwing the hoover aside and fleeing downstairs, she narrowly missed tripping on the cable, that snaked from the hallway to the top of the stairs. By the time she had reached the doorway, a full-on downpour met her eyes.

Fuelled by a singular thought, she ran headfirst into the rain. Raphael had returned. He had realised that their goodbye wasn't enough. This time, she would tell him she loved him. She wouldn't let him go so easily. He had returned. He had come back to her.

Her hungry eyes scanned her surroundings. The porch, the drive-way, down the street and back up again. She stood in the rainfall, the cool water like a chilly electric shower pounding her skin as her heart sank ten feet deeper into her chest.

He was nowhere to be seen. Her eyes swept upwards, staring at the sky as she tried to catch any irregular movement. He would be too fast. But still, *just* in case, she may be able to see him arrive. She was still for a few minutes. He had to appear. Any second now, she would see him.

Seconds turned into minutes. Drenched in the rain, water bounced off her soaked jumper and jeans as her eyes frantically swept the grey sky for Raphael. All the while pitiless rain came pouring down, cruelly washing away hope that Raphael had come back.

She continued standing in the downpour for a short while. A soft sob escaped her lips. Rainwater diluted her salty tears and her stomach lurched in another sickening twist as she realised that Raphael wasn't coming back.

The rainfall eventually stopped and she was still standing outside. She stumbled inside the house in a daze and leant back on the closed front door. She felt pathetic to be back to square one. She hated square one.

It was going to take more than a few days to get used to the fact that he was no longer a part of her life. She felt like a fool running into the rain. She didn't mean anything to him. She suddenly felt as insignificant as a speck of dust and wished she could be hoovered up and vanish into a vacuum where nothing mattered.

As the thought of his face bombarded her fragile mind for the billionth time, she craved sweet oblivion. Running to the kitchen she gulped down four heavy duty painkillers. Her eyes were soon heavy with sleep. She willingly stumbled into the arms of a deep, drug-induced slumber and the memory of the past few days melted away as if a bad dream.

# 32 SANCTUARY

The rest of the Easter vacation was a blur. Each day melted into one, an obscure mass which compressed and accentuated Eleanor's distress with each passing hour. She was a melancholy inhabitant of a world she didn't care about as the days trickled by.

So much, yet so little had happened. She practically drifted through the three weeks in a state of non-committal self-belief, telling herself it would get easier with time. Except that it didn't. The pain was still there, a constant ache that pulled her deeper into the depths of despair. She didn't want to see or speak to anyone. She remained holed up in her safe-haven house, a private cocoon protecting her from the rest of the world.

She spent most of her vacation indoors and only left the house when absolutely necessary. Stocking up on a handful of imperative food supplies and taking out the garbage were her two main outdoor activities. The five minute walk to the local grocery store was sufficient exposure to the outside world. She was awash with relief as the door closed behind her every single time she returned. Being outside reminded her that nothing else had changed, except for the huge gaping hole in her life.

She found herself on a mission to tidy the house, as if decluttering would somehow help clear thinking space in her mind. It worked for the first week, where she scrubbed, hoovered and dusted every inch of the house. It was whilst scrubbing the skirting board downstairs, that she noticed some loose carpet near the lounge entrance.

Bending down to polish the dusty wood, she tried to slip the carpet back into place. The small bump refused to be flattened and in a bout of frustration she grappled with the chunky pile. To her dismay it came away in her hands and Eleanor found she was looking at an uncharacteristically slack floorboard.

She tried to press the hard wood down, yet something underneath seemed to be obstructing the panel. Prising the floorboard up slowly, Eleanor found herself peering into the dark recesses of the floor. She could just about make out a rectangular shape in the dark. The old mansion probably had a whole range of creepy crawlies which Eleanor preferred not to think about. Her hand hovered over the shadowy crevice as she suddenly remembered Kate Capshaw's ordeal in The Temple of Doom when accosted with a trillion spiders, cockroaches and everything else in between. Gingerly lowering her hand into the gap, she grabbed the object and lifted it into the daylight.

It was a faded grey book. She shook off the thick dust layer which quickly disintegrated to envelope her in a dusty cloud. Spluttering, she noticed a hanging pendant bookmark nestled in between the pages. For the first time in weeks, she felt something other than gut-wrenching pain. She was curious as she stared at the book in her hands.

Sneezing as the dust tickled her nose, she knelt on the floor and flicked through the pages as her fingers curled around the hanging pendant. It was a large key, the silver tarnished with age and dull with grime. Still clutching the key, she opened the first page of the book. The font in fancy calligraphy read:

## Diary of Florence Winter.

It took Eleanor a few minutes to realise she was holding her great great grandmother's diary. Eleanor peered into the hole where she had found the book. It was empty. Suddenly emboldened, she stuck her hand in the gap to make sure she hadn't missed anything. She was satisfied when she found only handfuls of dust and dirt encrusted ground. Shoving back the floorboard and adjusting the carpet, she quickly washed her hands in the kitchen and clambered onto the couch to study her new find.

Before she could turn to the second page she abruptly stopped. She realised it was someone's diary. Judging from it being hidden, it probably contained personal and intimate memories. Did she really want to read someone else's private thoughts? She was torn for a few more minutes as she tried to justify reading it. Grappling with her conscience, she finally figured it would take the focus away from Raphael. Peeling open the pages, she started reading the diary.

She didn't know much about her great great grandmother, having never met her before. Eleanor had built the vaguest of pictures in her mind via the odd snippet offered by her mum. According to Lucille, Florence was tough, majestically beautiful and very stubborn. In her hey day, she also looked like Lucille. Staring at the musty book filled Eleanor with a curious thrill that she was about to discover more about her family's history. Taking a deep breath, she started to read.

Eleanor quickly found herself engrossed in the privileged, opulent life of a fifteen year old in the turn of the century England. The diary was packed with Florence's thoughts and ambitions. One entry, dated 17th February 1917 described an automobile accident and Florence's lucky escape as she had walked away unharmed. Eleanor held the key in her palm whilst immersed in reading and when she turned another page, an idea suddenly popped into her head. Clutching the book in one hand and key in the other, Eleanor sprinted upstairs to the locked room.

She paused a moment, unsure if she was doing the right thing and speculated why the key was hidden in the first place. She had often wondered what multitude of secrets the old house held. She also realised she hadn't thought of Raphael during the past hour. The diary and key were a welcome distraction that spurred her on. As curiosity got the better of her, she calmly inserted the key and turned it clockwise.

Nothing happened.

She tried twisting the key anti-clockwise. With a slight grinding and discernible click, the key turned in her hand. The door was now open.

Eleanor's heart rate quickened. Gingerly turning the stiff brass handle, she gently pushed the door open. It wouldn't shift. The hinges were probably tight with age and welded by dust and oil. She shoved with all her might as the heavy wooden door slowly swung open.

Hit by a wall of stale air, she paused a while before tiptoeing inside. The bleak room was filled with gloomy shadows. By the light coming from the landing, she could make out the dim outline of a window. Walking towards it, she bumped into a heavy wooden table on her left. Finally reaching the window, she felt for the curtains and brushed them away. She coughed as a heavy cloud of dust flew around her. As sunlight eventually streamed in through the dust mottled window, she looked around to observe a large room with grey sheets covering the furniture.

Pots of dried ink and old fountain pens lay on the desk. Eleanor was silent for a while, unable to move or think. She felt as if she had stumbled into a room where time had stood still. Perching on a hard chair by the table, she continued to stare at the dusty room. This was her great great grandmother's room.

She pulled out the book, fingering the leather bound cover as she wondered if Florence minded her coming into this private room. *Of course she would mind*, she argued with herself. *The key and book were hidden for a reason.* Eleanor knew she wasn't supposed to be in the room. Her mild unease disappeared with the crazy realisation that for the first time in weeks, she felt at peace. In the east wing of the large sprawling house, she could forget Raphael existed.

She spent the afternoon in the room just sitting on the chair, bereft of thought and emotion, something which Eleanor relished with great comfort. Eventually she looked at the diary and started to read again. It would take her a good few weeks to get through it.

When she eventually glanced at her watch, she realised it was nearly 10:00pm. Reluctantly pulling herself up from her newfound safe-haven, she crawled into bed, tired and elated by the welcome distraction.

This was the first of many days Eleanor would spend in the room. She would devour the diary whilst being drawn into Florence's world of lavish luxury and turn-of-the-century politics. Eleanor was fascinated with the authentic historical detail and in losing herself in another world, was able to temporarily forget her own troubles. Eleanor frequently wondered why the diary and key were locked, yet when she found herself in the room, the questions from her mind vanished as she sank into the comforting arms of the welcoming, non-judgmental room.

Whenever she was away from the room, she felt that life went on as normal. The sun and moon continued to rise. The Earth hadn't stopped turning, even though it felt like it had. The world would never be the same. She would never be the same.

In the final week of vacation, she awoke one morning and glanced sideways at the adjacent pillow on her bed. Her eyes hooked onto the two items that lay there; the folded Union Jack flag and The Count of Monte Cristo novel. Apart from these two items and notes she had borrowed, there was nothing to indicate Raphael's existence in her life.

On some days she felt she had dreamt him up, a beautiful figment of her overactive imagination and hated herself for not having any photos of them together. The thought of never seeing him again sent her heart plummeting into a chasm filled with black distress. As she struggled to keep her simmering feelings under control, she wondered what her mum would make of her crazy situation.

She was thankful for Lucille's case-load that took her to France for the upcoming Cannes Film Festival. She didn't want to explain something to her mum that she couldn't really explain to herself. What could she say anyway? *'Mum, I realised too late that I was in love with my best friend, but I before I could tell him, he disappeared. Oh and by the way, he was also the son of the Devil.'* Some things were best left unspoken.

She planned a Manchester visit to catch up with her friends yet couldn't face leaving the house or seeing anyone. She didn't want the questions. She decided to stay put and sort herself out.

She found herself listlessly floating through each day. The pain was an aching void, constantly hungry and refusing to be sated. She didn't really miss food and frequently left most of her dinners untouched, as her stomach filled itself instead with sickening knots of twisted misery.

The house was a quiet haven. The radio was always off and she muted the TV to watch meaningless pictures in silence. She only started revising on the Wednesday of the final week of vacation after remembering that exams were less than two months away. She didn't really care anymore and it took all of her limited strength to focus on studying as she purposefully surrounded herself with stacks of books and papers.

At first the hollow words on paper were nothing but a jumbled mass and it took her a few hours to really concentrate. What usually took twenty minutes, took triple the time as she pulled away from thoughts of Raphael to focus on the pages in front of her. She left the TV on in the background whilst studying, a stream of silent images that somehow made the room feel less empty.

One time in the midst of a bout of revision, her eyes wandered onto the muted TV to watch The Big Bang Theory in silence. The lovable nerds' antics always had her in stitches, yet on that day, she remained unmoved. Placing her book down, she cranked up the volume to listen to the canned, raucous laughter. It felt sickeningly empty and she quickly muted the volume to return to her book. Getting used to a life without Raphael was a painful, unhurried process. She knew she had to be patient.

She no longer leapt up at the sound of rainfall. The first few times she ran to the door, her eager eyes scanning the grey skies for a hint or sign that he had returned. Each time her heart thudded with expectant hope, yet within minutes it would be callously dashed to smithereens and washed away with the rainfall as she realised Raphael wasn't there.

Eleanor noted the increased frequency of rainstorms with bitter amusement. If she'd been paranoid, she would have thought that Mother Nature was conspiring against her by not letting her forget Raphael.

The last weekend of vacation saw a particularly heavy storm brewing, yet she forced herself to remain seated on the couch. Sitting rigidly with her legs curled up under her on that cool evening, she desperately tried to ignore the rumbling thunderstorm.

Suddenly remembering flying through the skies with Raphael, she closed her eyes, praying for the prohibited thoughts to vanish. The storm's stubborn refusal to pass prompted Eleanor to grab the remote control and crank up the volume to full blast. Disney's Bambi had been silently playing in the background and as the storm raged outside, she continued sitting quietly as high pitched animated song filled the dim lounge.

The storm bolstered by deafening cracks of unrelenting thunder produced an unnatural medley with Disney's background music. Throwing down the book and remote control, she slapped both hands on her ears in a futile attempt to drown out the thunderstorm. It felt like the longest storm she had ever heard. When it finally passed, she slowly dropped her hands into her lap and reluctantly returned to studying.

Eleanor wondered if she would ever be unaffected by the sound of rain. At least she didn't run out into the rain anymore. That had to be a good sign. It had to get better. It just had to.

Eleanor stared at the view from her windscreen. The university seemed eerily empty on her first day back. She was in no mood for the commuter crowds during rush hour and had decided to drive in instead. She glanced into her open tote and saw Florence's diary. She couldn't explain why, but she felt stronger with the book. She felt it understood her pain and wanting to keep close to the source of comfort, Eleanor now carried the diary with her everywhere.

It was going to be weird not seeing Raphael around. Being at university without him was the real test. She could feel the familiar knots of misery starting to form in her stomach. Her eyes flickered to the entrance. The now empty archway was their usual meeting spot where he would wait for her lectures to finish.

Quickly blinking away her tears, she looked in the mirror to give herself the once-over. Breaking down was not an option. She had to face facts. He had left. She had to readjust to Raphael not being there. She would build new memories. She had to.

Her inner voice told her that it was a foolishly futile attempt. She couldn't *not* think of him. He was part of her whether she liked it or not. She ignored this small voice which gnawed at her resolve like a shoal of ravenous piranhas taking sharp, tiny bites. *She had to try.* Buoyed by an unexpected hit of positivity, she focused on her surroundings objectively and looked on at the main campus. She would not associate university with Raphael. She had to forget him.

The building looked somehow larger and unfamiliar on this crisp April morning. The campus was starting to come alive from its three week hibernation as students trickled through the corridor. A small part of her expected to see Raphael as she pulled out her mobile. Waning hope still flickered unsteadily like a dying candle. He *may* have returned to university. Although he would have called to let her know, right..? She glanced at her mobile again. No messages or missed calls since five minutes ago.

She had contemplated ringing him over Easter numerous times. Every time she had picked up the phone to make the call, she stopped herself. Through red-rimmed eyes, she conceded the blurry digits on her phone being as senseless as the very action of calling him. It was obvious he didn't want to be on Earth. Eleanor didn't feature in his plans. She had to be as nonchalant about the situation as he had been.

The first day back was always going to be difficult. Walking into the canteen, she ordered a double shot Americano before making her way to her first lecture. Being preoccupied by a million thoughts, she walked straight into Serena and Christina outside the lecture theatre.

Serena piped excitedly, 'Hey Elle! How are you? How was Easter? Get many Easter eggs?'

Christina smiled and leaned forward to hug Eleanor before saying, 'Or if you did, you obviously didn't eat them! My God, you're wasting away hon!'

Serena edged closer to say, 'Don't tell me you had the 'flu? My sister had it over Easter and she must have dropped two dress sizes. She didn't realise how lucky she was. I'd kill to lose weight that quickly. I tried *so* hard to catch her germs and you know what? Zip. Nothing.'

An unimpressed Christina scrunched up her nose in distaste. 'Eeww! That's gross!'

Eleanor couldn't help but smile. It was easier to go along with the illness story and thinking on her feet she said, 'Yeah, it was the 'flu. I was bed-ridden for the best part of three weeks. Feeling much better now though.'

They were soon joined by Jack shortly after. Clocking his late appearance the lecturer said, 'Late again Jack Brennan. Some things never change.'

Jack playfully nudged Eleanor whilst grinning at Serena and Christina. Everything was the same. Except Raphael wasn't there. At first, Eleanor dare not look at his empty seat. As the lecture progressed, she had found her eyes being pulled in that direction. She was surprised yet thankful tears didn't come to her eyes. She was already stronger than ten minutes ago.

Eleanor floated through the day in a state of indifference. Seated in the canteen later that day, Eleanor realised she could never confide in anyone about Raphael. In a room full of people noisy with the hubbub of clattering plates and jovial conversation, Eleanor had never felt more alone.

She didn't realise Serena was speaking to her until Katherine said, 'Earth calling Elle! Hey, you were miles away there! I don't think you're fully recovered from this 'flu. Maybe you need to rest it off? You're still looking a little peaky.'

Eleanor shook her head distractedly and smiled. 'No, I'm fine, really. Sorry Serena, what were you saying?'

Sipping her soup Serena said, 'I didn't see Raphael today.' She smiled suggestively to say, 'Hey, did you see him over Easter?'

Eleanor was quiet, unsure what to say. She knew she would be asked the million dollar question. Eventually speaking in a controlled voice she said, 'He's had to leave uni. Family issues, I think.'

Silence fell across the table as four pairs of eyes swivelled across to look at Eleanor. Serena placed her spoon down and looked up quizzically at Eleanor. It took her and the rest of the table a few seconds to understand the link between Eleanor's disconsolate demeanour and Raphael's departure.

Serena said gently, 'Oh... He'll come back though, right?'

Eleanor fixed her gaze on the salad in front of her, her eyes taking in every detail of the shiny plastic bowl. If she concentrated on mundane detail, she may be successful in remaining cool. She picked at her salad. There was no celery today.

The rest of the table waited. Eleanor's silence provided the answer, prompting Christina to suddenly say, 'Do you mean he's gone for good? That's crazy. What the hell happened?'

Serena chipped in, 'He *can't* be gone for good, first year is nearly ending.'

Christina was quiet for a moment before saying in an upbeat tone, 'Hey, I'm sure he'll be back.'

Eleanor nodded as she grabbed her water, gulping the cool fluid down her hot parched throat whilst shrugging casually to portray her nonchalant acquiescence. The conversation soon switched onto what everyone had done over Easter. Only Jack remained half-distracted, leading the conversation whilst keeping a watchful eye on Eleanor. Unable to face small talk she made her excuses to leave the table early for her next lecture.

The day passed relatively slowly. By her third lecture, she was close to skiving off and wished she had eaten more than salad to sustain her concentration. She knew a healthy diet was imperative during exam period and realised she wouldn't be doing herself any favours by subsisting on just salad, coffee and the occasional half granola bar. She needed fresh groceries and deciding to be constructive and do a big shop, excused herself from the evening drinks and drove to the nearest Tesco.

Shopping had never felt so tedious. Piling her trolley with food she had no desire to eat, she made her way to the chilled foods aisle of the moderately busy supermarket. The stereo pumped out dated chart hits, its tinny sound from the antiquated speakers considerately providing anodyne background noise to Eleanor's overwrought mind. Picking a box of vegetarian burgers from the tall chiller cabinet, she froze for a full five seconds as she caught Raphael's reflection in the glass door behind her.

The supermarket was the last place she had expected to see Raphael. She spun round, heart thrumming in her chest. He was nowhere to be seen. Her eyes trawled the cold aisles of the supermarket in confused anticipation. Right, left, then right again.

Her suspicions were unfounded as her pounding heart conceded to devastating defeat. She knew she was losing her slender grip on reality by imagining him everywhere. She had to snap out of it, yet she couldn't stop thinking – *what if he came back?*

Stepping away from her trolley, she ran a few yards towards the central section. *He* wasn't there. As her head swam with images of Raphael, she was suddenly lightheaded and very cold. She just wanted to get home.

Walking to the check-out slightly dazed, her mind ran over the previous three weeks. They might as well have been non-existent, a blank period in her diary. Since Raphael's departure, she had been trying to convince herself that she should forget him. That was the way of the world. People got their hearts broken all the time but they would eventually move on. She would do the same too. Whilst unloading the food onto the chugging conveyor belt, a singular question harangued her, something she had never asked herself before. *Did she want to forget him?*

She knew the answer before the question had popped into her mind. She never wanted to forget him. She would hang on to those memories like precious gold dust and stash them away forever. She was unable to forget him. She couldn't.

During the drive home, she tried to imagine life before Raphael. It was impossible. She was acutely aware she would go through the pain of heartbreak a million times over if it meant knowing Raphael for a few measly seconds. Technically, he had done nothing wrong, except leave without a proper goodbye. She had to stop thinking about him. He never cared about her. She had to accept that.

# 33 UNDER MY SKIN

Eleanor found herself slowly getting caught up in university life again. Studying was a welcome distraction and she compensated for her anaemic concentration in class with concerted study at home. From self-imposed exile during Easter, to being thrust in the midst of a hectic study schedule was a shock to her system. It also reminded her of her priorities. She had only managed to cram in a few days of revision over Easter and keen to redress the balance, read more zealously than ever. She still carried Florence's diary around with her. It was her talisman, her protection from future heartbreak. She dare not tell anyone else about the book. They wouldn't understand anyway.

Weeks melted away and before Eleanor knew it, June exams had arrived. She would sit with her friends in the canteen in between study sessions. Amongst the chatter, she would invariably withdraw into her world where she wondered what Raphael was doing, before battling with herself to get over him. She felt as if she inhabited two separate worlds; the metaphysical one that she frequently retreated to for comfort, in pugnacious conflict with Earth and all its harsh realities.

One afternoon whilst waiting for an exam to start, Eleanor was flitting in between these two worlds when Katherine's excitement caught her attention. Katherine said excitedly, 'Can you believe uni ends in a few weeks? It's gone by way too fast. Listen, who's up for the end of year Ball? It's a Bollywood theme and there's a really cool retro line-up. It sounds like a tonne of fun!'

Serena chirped, 'I think we should *all* go. Don't you dare back out Elle. You rarely come out with us anymore.' She continued a little more gently, 'I get if you really don't want to, but it'll be fun..?'

Jack said determinedly, 'Yep, I think we should all go. You're coming Elle whether you like it or not.'

Before Eleanor could protest, Jack grinned at her and she couldn't help return his smile. Serena playfully said to Jack, 'Oi! You can't tell Elle what to do!' Turning back to Elle she whispered, 'It would be great to have you there, just not under duress.'

Jack rose to the bait and a playful banter between them ensued. 'What Serena, don't you *want* Elle to come?'

'Yeah but-'

'Well, my point exactly-'

'No but-'

'Carry on like that Serena and you'll give Vicky Pollard a run for her money!'

Eleanor listened to their humorous exchange and was filled with a sudden warmth for her friends. Smiling she hesitantly said, 'Count me in. It... it sounds fun.'

It had been nearly three months since Raphael had left. She didn't want to wallow anymore. Being with her friends was a comforting, sobering experience. This was her life and where she belonged. Natural order had been restored. Her love for Raphael was a blessing and a curse; something that was so pure, but which could devastatingly never be realised.

She was momentarily torn. With a twisted pang she became acutely aware of one key fact that glared at her square in the whites of her eyes. She had forgotten she was human.

She had forgotten about their very different backgrounds and for a brief period had believed she belonged with him. That was the root of her problem. She would *never* forget she was human and vowed to keep herself grounded by surrounding herself with fellow humans, people who she loved and loved her back.

She was suddenly pulled back to the conversation in the canteen as she heard Katherine excitedly say, 'Cool, I'll book tickets. It's gonna be beyond awesome, I can just feel it!'

Eleanor didn't want to go to the Ball. She preferred spending the evening indoors indulging her meandering mind whilst it traversed forbidden territory. She swiftly recalled her promise to herself. She needed to surround herself with humans. Attendance at the Ball would entail mingling with other humans. Conceding that it would also be a positive note to end the year on, Eleanor walked into her next lecture slightly happier with a sense of achievement that she was on the right path.

She awoke early on the day of the Ball. Sleep still evaded her, yet she had managed to get a decent five hours. She stretched in bed as she automatically pushed the first embryonic thought of the day from her mind before it had time to form. Today was a fresh start. She knew she would never forget Raphael and she had accepted that. He was a part of her past. Nothing more, nothing less.

Sunlight streamed through the curtains and fell on her morning-warm skin, various thoughts flitting through her mind as she continued to lounge in bed. This was the last day she would see her friends before returning to Manchester for summer vacation.

The passage of time over the past few months had been extraordinary, a paradoxical mixture of super fast and lethargically slow. Having completed her final exam last week, she couldn't quite believe she had finished her first year at university. She recalled anticipating exams with mixed feelings. On the one hand, she was glad they were over, because it meant she could chill out and see her mum and friends in Manchester. On the flip-side, the end of semester meant more time to think about one prohibited topic in particular. She could almost hear her heart rejoice at the prospect of having more time to ponder thoughts about the forbidden topic which she had unwillingly consigned to the past.

She needed to be strong. Imagining compelling role models and channelling her inner Debbie Harry, she promised herself not to waste time wallowing. The first thing she would do in Manchester would be to immerse herself in painting. And sign up for any other hobby she had ever fancied. Fencing, pottery, calligraphy, synchronised swimming. Anything, which meant her mind would be engaged in something rather than the one topic she now thought as unthinkable and mercilessly unrealistic.

Her eyes travelled across the sun-lit room and rested on the floor-length ruby red frock hanging from her dresser. Serena had picked it out after she had come to Eleanor's house along with Christina and Katherine a few days beforehand. The girls bought a clutch of costumes and had spent the evening deciding what to wear for the big night. Eleanor knew it was a subtle ploy on her friends' behalf to get her excited about the Ball. It hadn't worked, although privately she appreciated their concern.

She found having the girls round had been a pleasant change. The chattering of people was no longer white noise to her. Jack's presence too imbued her with sudden shots of positivity, like a quick-fix of energy from a chocolate bar. It was a happy coincidence that he appeared to be free whenever she was and Eleanor had found herself returning to her more upbeat self.

On the day of the Ball, she curled up on the faded velvet sofa in Florence's room whiling the hours away. Out of reverence she had refrained from touching anything in the room apart from the window which was now wide open, to let in fresh air. She was half-way through the diary and loved how the engaging narrative temporarily transported her back in time and away from her heartbreak. Dragging herself away from the room at just after 5:00pm, she had a quick few bites of a bagel. Getting ready these days took half the time. After a quick application of clear mascara and magenta lipstick, she shoved the diary in her bag and was seated in a taxi within thirty minutes.

As the taxi wove through the central traffic, she wound down the window to enjoy the balmy June evening. It was the perfect end to a difficult few months and Eleanor's spirits lifted as she spied Jack sitting on the steps of Shoreditch Town Hall. Clusters of students in fancy gear waited for friends to arrive as faint music filtered out of the giant open doors.

Clocking a grinning Jack she said, 'You scrub up quite well Mr Brennan. Nice tux.'

He flashed a mega-watt smile. 'Just something I had lying around.' He said earnestly, 'I'm glad you came. Listen Elle there's something-' Spying Christina approaching with Katherine in tow, Jack whispered, 'Chat later?'

Serena and a few other classmates rolled up in a separate taxi and soon a whole crowd had congregated on the steps. Surveying the throng Christina shouted, 'Come on guys, let's get this party started!'

They entered the building amidst whoops of excitement. The massive stone structure was decked in floating gold and black balloons and a faux fire feature in the main entrance. The lengthy hallway was filled with twinkling fairy lights to form an ethereal path inside. As various Bollywood inspired tunes poured forth from impressive giant surround speakers in the hallway and main auditorium, Eleanor was glad she had made the effort to attend. The cavernous room packed with revellers bolstered Eleanor's recognition of her human state. *She should never forget who she was.*

She didn't get a further chance to speak to Jack either. Whenever one of them found themselves to be free, the other would be whisked away by another friend or three. As the evening wore on, Eleanor did what she felt was right; smile, laugh and say the right thing at the right time. By pretending all was well, Eleanor became increasingly aware of an odd sense of displacement.

It had started out as a niggling feeling earlier that day which had now grown into a full-on objection as the evening wore on. She was an awkward resident of no-man's land, unsure of her place in the room and the world. As she surveyed the party from the middle of the dance-floor, the clinking glasses and loud punchy tunes failed to appease her.

She was suddenly hit by a crystal clear realisation. She didn't belong here. She didn't want to be here. And she was tired of pretending. Her immediate response was that of guilt. Her friends wanted her there because they wanted her to have a good time. She knew attending was the right thing to do, yet a part of her just wanted to leave the crowd behind. She felt as if she was standing inside a Tupperware box, engulfed by a misty grey gloom which afforded her a protected, stifling view of the world. In a room teeming with hundreds of joyful revellers, Eleanor felt disturbingly disorientated and incredibly alone.

Familiar black eyes flecked with grey hounded her subconscious. As the customary ache settled itself in her chest, she suddenly wanted to disappear and had an overwhelming urge to run down the long stone corridor and into the wide open space outside.

She glanced at her watch and nearly laughed at herself. She had lasted just three hours. She knew her friends wouldn't let her go without some degree of persuasion and she really wasn't in the mood to be cajoled.

She needed to get away. Slipping into the empty toilets on the first floor, she contemplated her next course of action. She could go back out and pretend everything was OK. The more favourable option was to go home, change out of her floor length dress and just be. She caught her reflection in the mirror. Despite the make-up and vibrant lipstick, the reflection staring back at her was a different Eleanor to the one that had started last year.

It was as if she was seeing herself for the first time in ages. The face staring back was unfamiliar and slightly jaundiced with tiredness. She suddenly understood why her friends were concerned about her and shaking her head, tried to think logically. Having a moment of self-realisation in the toilets at the end of year Ball was not ideal and splashing a little cold water on her flushed face, prepared to make her way home.

Through the pumping bass came the unmistakeable rumble of thunder. Great. She hadn't even packed an umbrella and hailing a taxi would be a nightmare in the rain. She hurried outside, poised at the top of the empty steps of the Town Hall as she wondered which route to take.

Waves of laughter and music floated through the air. Everyone was inside enjoying their last night together. Last year, she was part of that crowd. Yet today out of choice, she felt like an estranged outsider. She had erected barriers in the name of self-preservation and felt like she didn't belong anywhere. She took a few gulps of the cool evening air and glanced upwards. A gentle breeze played with her hair, getting rougher and more forceful by the second.

It had started to rain and she concluded that a downpour was imminent. Clutching the lower part of her dress to avoid tripping, she nimbly ran down the steps and looked around the empty roads for a taxi. She had no other choice but to call her local firm. As she opened her clutch-bag for her phone, someone called out behind her. She froze. She knew that voice anywhere.

'Eleanor.'

She stood still for a few seconds. At first she thought she had imagined it. She regularly replayed thoughts of Raphael and this had to be another one of those times. Yet the voice was so vivid that its reality rendered her momentarily unsteady. She slowly turned around. Raphael was standing ten yards away.

Her memory had served her well. He was exactly as she had remembered him. Piercing black eyes. Thick chocolate hair. That powerful six foot frame that she had imagined a million times over. He was a vision in black, wearing a coal cashmere jumper and black jeans with trademark nonchalance. Her heart did a sickening somersault, but she forced it to stay grounded. Like a tugging hot air balloon ready to soar into the sky, it was precariously tethered and held down against its will.

She was stunned into silence. As her brain kick-started into gear, she tried to keep her tone casual. She could feel her voice ready to crack. She had to focus on something, anything to stop her from thinking forbidden thoughts about the distracting figure in front of her.

Soft music from the Town Hall behind her floated through the air which was sufficient diversion. As her ears clung onto the melancholy notes of a retro pop song she found herself marginally calmer.

Raphael spoke in a level voice, 'How are you Eleanor? Hope you have been well?'

She paused for a second, uncertain how to go on. *What was he doing here?* Surely he didn't come to exchange niceties. Raising her chin with a defiant little tip she said, 'I'm great. You?'

A flicker of concern flashed across his face. 'I'm well.'

There was a pause as they both continued staring at each other. A million questions peppered her mind. She wanted to look away but couldn't. She dare not even blink. She didn't know how long she had left with him and this only heightened her anxiety. Breaking down was not an option.

She said casually, 'What brings you back to Earth? I mean, I thought you'd gone home.'

This time, the pause was noticeably longer. Eleanor held her breath, watching him whilst he in turn kept his eyes fixed on her.

He said in a tight voice, 'I shouldn't even be here. I know I had to rush back last time. I didn't have a chance to say goodbye properly.'

Pain, her steadfast friend of late, made a speedy return to stand in footsteps adjacent to hers. Her heart felt heavy, its unbearable burden at breaking point when she realised this was the final time she'd see Raphael. This was it. The end.

She bit her bottom lip and tried to gulp away the sudden deluge of emotions. She had already watched him leave once and her mind was close to descending into panic as she realised she would have to watch him leave again. She had to keep it brief. She waited a few seconds, buying time yet still unsure what to say. She just had to be focused. As her fingers curled around her clutch-bag, she pushed her mind to think of anything else but him. Forcing herself to think about the clutch-bag in her clammy hands as a diversion, she suddenly found herself wondering if the buttery soft suede was hard to fashion. Slightly distracted and mission half-accomplished she said lightly, 'So, when do you head back?'

'I'm not here long. I- I couldn't leave without saying goodbye properly.' He paused for a fraction of a second before he said in tight voice, 'I'll miss you.'

That was one of her questions answered. He wasn't sticking around. In less than a few minutes, he would have disappeared from her life for good. Her life would be free from Raphael. *Forever.*

She could no longer hear background music as her mind descended into numb distress. She felt as if she had been plunged headfirst in a vat of freezing water, submerged in icy depths where she couldn't think or breathe. Her voice sounded hollow in her head, as if someone else had taken her place. She wanted to shout that she loved him. She wanted to know why he had left so abruptly. She wanted to tell him how much she missed him. More than anything, she wanted him to tell her that he was going to stay.

Instead she said quietly, 'Ditto. I'll miss you too.'

To prolong their meeting would only make it more difficult. And she didn't want him to see her public meltdown. She wanted to hug him goodbye but knew that was dangerous territory. She knew that if she did, her weakened resolve would vanish and she would end up crying on his shoulder. He could never know that she loved him.

Exhaling she said adroitly, 'Listen, it's chilly and I have to get home. Bye Raphael.'

They were standing a mere three metres apart. She dug her fingernails into the palms of her hand. She imagined his scent and blinked away the dangerously prohibited thoughts. Turning on her heel, she started walking briskly in the opposite direction. She would hail a taxi from the main road. She would walk miles in her uncomfortably high six inch heels but she dare not stop here. Traitorous tears constrained till now broke ranks and flowed freely over her hot cheeks.

Her heart shrieked inside her chest. That silent scream had returned with a vengeance, deafening and loud enough to burst her eardrums. Sickening doubt crept in all over again. He had never cared about her. She had known all along but had refused to believe it.

She couldn't wait to get into a taxi. The confines of the cab would be a safe-haven, a place where she could sit down and cry her heart out. Those protective metallic car walls would be a makeshift fortress, absorbing her screams whilst not judging her. The cab driver would probably think she was some sort of loon, but at least Raphael wouldn't see her crying. She had taken three steps when she heard Raphael's voice behind her, clear and urgent.

'Eleanor? Do you love him?'

She froze in her tracks. *Was her mind playing cruel tricks on her?* She stood stock still. She had to have imagined Raphael's voice. She took another step forward when he said more insistently, 'Come on Eleanor! Do you love Michael?'

Confusion clouded her brain. Quickly wiping away her tears with her free hand, she slowly turned around. A low breeze stirred the trees on either side of the Town Hall entrance whilst the rain fell softly in a light drizzle.

She was now facing Raphael. They were only seven metres apart, which might as well have been seven hundred miles. Eleanor felt the gulf between them widen, a growing gorge filled with a perplexing amalgam of emotions. Pain. Anguish. Love. Heartbreak. Desire. But not a single modicum of hope. Through the pain, she was struggling to decipher why he was asking her about Michael.

What did Raphael know about Michael? Maybe, *just* maybe Raphael cared about her? She pushed that thought out of her head before it had time to treacherously germinate. The last thing she wanted was to entertain the notion that he might actually care about her. That would be too desperate. Pathetic. She dare not hope.

These past three months had seen hope dashed as it lay in a million pieces in the cavity where her heart beat erratically. Whenever the phone rang or a knock sounded at the door, she had answered pulse racing, nerves on fire, hoping with all her heart that it would be Raphael. The ensuing disappointment at Raphael's absence cut into her resolve like a battle wound doused in hot acid. She had abandoned hope and refused to even contemplate any situation that he may actually care for her.

Nearly a minute passed without either of them speaking. She was still unable to think straight. Under a veil of confusion and anguish, Eleanor contemplated telling the truth. How Raphael had broken her heart. How the past three months had been pure torture. How she had wanted to spend every minute of every day with him. But that would be a brainless move.

She struggled for clarity as the fog of mystification grew fuzzier. She wondered how long she would last before she physically broke down. A flash of lucid thought punctured the fog as she told herself that nothing good could come of her revelation. It would be easier to tell Raphael what he so obviously wanted to hear.

She replied in a boldly defiant voice, 'Michael's fine.'

Raphael shoved his hands in his pockets. His eyes bore into hers as he struggled to verbalise a sudden onslaught of frustration.

Tears pricked Eleanor's eyes and she was suddenly thankful for the light rainfall that camouflaged the tear tracks down her hot cheeks. She had to get away fast before it was obvious she was crying. With a renewed sense of purpose she said quickly, 'I've gotta go.'

She turned around and took a step away when she heard Raphael again, his voice strained and tense. 'Wait. Michael's wrong for you.'

For the second time, Eleanor turned around, heart pounding in her chest. Her resolve was wearing dangerously thin. In a last ditch attempt to walk away with her dignity intact, she ignored him and continued walking away. He had no right to keep her talking. He didn't care, she had finally accepted it.

She shouted over her shoulder vehemently, 'I'VE REALLY GOT TO GO!' As his words weighed on her mind, she suddenly spun round. 'Hang on... *What do you mean*? How is Michael wro-'

Raphael's eyes fixed on hers, scouring her face for tell-tale signs. He barked, 'You can do better. You deserve more. So much more.'

Eleanor was rooted to the spot. The grey fog of confusion increased in density. Raphael's questions made no sense. What did he mean to achieve by asking her random questions? Why did he speak about Michael with thinly disguised vitriol?

Suddenly, Eleanor's resolve shattered. Exasperated and bewildered she snapped, 'Now I REALLY don't know what the hell you're talking about! Why the sudden interest in Michael? I haven't seen him in months!'

Raphael's eyes clouded over as he said, 'But I thought-' He faltered, hastily changing tack in a bid to shed light and dissipate Eleanor's obvious anger and growing frustration. 'He said you were together when I saw him at your house..?'

Eleanor was unsure where the conversation was leading. Curiosity and mystification had temporarily stemmed the flow of tears down her cheeks. She said through gritted teeth, 'He *thought* we were going to get back together.' Now openly angry, she shouted, 'Didn't happen though! He's a mate, nothing more!'

Raphael's eyes flashed up at hers, relief flooding his face which bolstered Eleanor's confidence to voice feelings she had locked away since that fateful day in the park. It was now or never. She had nothing to lose and everything to gain. Shouting calmed her down. She was oddly serene.

Taking a deep breath she whispered, 'Nothing happened with Michael because I love someone else.'

Raphael immediately stiffened, tension creeping back onto his face. It took a few seconds for him to regain his composure. When he glanced up, Eleanor was staring at him.

Their eyes locked. The electric atmosphere was charged with an overwhelming surge of love from both transfixed parties. Confusion vanished, to be replaced by crystal clear clarity. Eleanor didn't know how, but in that magical split second she suddenly knew Raphael cared for her.

The very thought stunned her into silence as she swiftly became aware that he too knew she cared for him.

Raphael cleared the seven metres within seconds. Gathering her up in his arms, his mouth claimed hers in a crushing kiss. Circling her arms around his neck, she felt as if the world had ceased to spin on its axis. And she didn't care. After a few seconds, he lifted his head and gazed at her as if seeing her for the first time.

Butterflies danced in her stomach and floated across her chest. Her heart was light as air. When his hands fell to her waist to hold her in a gentle grasp, she was filled with delicious exhilarating charges where his hands rested on her. He couldn't take his eyes of her. Eleanor wanted to speak, yet a part of her feared she was dreaming. Fearing the return to harsh reality where Raphael was still absent, she remained quiet.

Her dilemma was fixed when Raphael said, 'I didn't think you cared for me like that.'

Eleanor shook her head as her hands rested on his chest. She said gently, 'I knew a few months ago. I was going to tell you in the park that day when you left. I just thought you didn't wanna know.'

He pulled her closer to say, 'I have been so stupid. I thought I was doing the right thing.'

It was Eleanor's turn to be speechless. Unable to stay angry with him she said in a gentle reproach, 'Why the hell didn't you say something sooner?'

She heard his voice above her head as he continued to hold her. He said in a pained whisper, 'I didn't know what I really wanted... till I met you.' He paused, continuing in a strangled voice, 'I should never have left you. It's all my fault. If I had known, we wouldn't have wasted these past few months. They were a horrific taster of what my life would be without you. I'm never leaving you. *Never.*'

He pulled her closer, wrapping his arms around her with an urgency that took her breath away. Eleanor felt as if she was floating thousands of miles into the sky. A thought brought her crashing back down to earth as she remembered Lucifer. She spoke hesitantly, unsure of what to say and even more apprehensive about his response. 'What about your father..?'

Raphael fell silent. He was deadly serious as he said, 'There is nothing he can do. I have been on Earth for what seems like a lifetime. I feel I have a purpose now. If it means going against him, then that's what I'll do.'

Eleanor whispered cautiously, 'You never know, he *may* come round? Boy am I glad you decided to visit.'

Smiling, she leaned forward to catch another overwhelming kiss, remaining in the protective circle of his arms all the while. It was still raining but she didn't care. She was with Raphael. The two lovers continued embracing, lost in the moment and oblivious to anything else.

A few miles away at Eleanor's house, a vigorous breeze whipped the curtains to and fro in the open window of Florence's old room. A sheet of material covering a rectangular object slid to the floor, revealing an easel. The painting was the work of an amateurish hand. It was signed by Florence. The subject of the painting was a distinguished young man, with familiar jet black eyes flecked with steely grey.

Back outside Shoreditch Town Hall, hundreds of miles above, the embracing lovers had a hidden audience. Lucifer watched, quietly incensed by the offensive scene he had just witnessed. He wasn't going to sit by and watch Raphael be with a human. It was time to actively get involved and show Raphael the right path.

Thousands of miles above Lucifer, Astrid watched the events unfold in Heaven with a growing smile. Her iridescent angel wings fluttered with excitement as she continued flying upwards. Giving the air a triumphant punch, she whispered in delight, 'Father will be proud.' She couldn't wait to relay the good news. Things were about to get very interesting.

# Not The End

# EXCERPT FROM SCREAMING SNOWFLAKES: THE SEQUEL

The darkened room immediately put Eleanor's nerves on edge. It was quiet. *Too quiet.* She gingerly took two steps forward. Bad move. She was immediately assaulted by fleeting moments of pure joy, then horrifying pain. *What the hell was wrong with her?* Focusing on her surroundings, she soon realised the room wasn't empty as she had originally thought. Milky candlelight flickered in the atrium, throwing slender grey fingers across the stone walls.

Edging nearer to the entrance she heard a low moan. Eleanor instantly froze. It was a cry that filled her with sick distress, like the strangled cry of a tortured animal breathing its last. Eleanor was momentarily torn; by wanting to help whoever was being hurt in the room a few yards away from her, and the dread in seeing the horrid spectacle that awaited her.

Shaking her still fuzzy head, she quickened her pace and entered the room. Hunched black shapes in parallel lines threw her off guard. Straight ahead she spied a pulpit. Trying to dismiss her disorientation, she realised the shadowy figures were mourners, their sorrowful eyes fixed on the coffin ahead.

Ice-cold fear coursed through her veins, firing a shot of adrenaline through her body. Edging further into the room, she noticed with a pang of horrifying panic that familiar faces lined the pews.

Now half-running to the front, the rustle of the collective movement of the mourners blanked out the pounding terror in her mind. She imagined the worst. One of her beloved friends or family lay dead in the mahogany casket up ahead.

She could turn around and scour the crowded pews, in a revolting process of elimination which would take a few minutes. Unable to wait a second longer, she took a deep ragged breath and stumbled nearer to see a large photo balanced on the closed coffin.

Eleanor blinked, trying to make sense of the scene. The picture looked familiar. Bright hazel eyes smiled back and she vaguely remembered where the picture was taken. For a split second, Eleanor thought she was looking in a mirror. And she knew she wasn't dreaming. In a wave of stultifying shock, Eleanor realised that the photograph was of her. She was standing at her own funeral.

# ABOUT THE AUTHOR

Amber is an award winning author, freelance writer and loquacious lifestyle blogger. A self confessed bibliophile with a penchant for fashion, film and PR, she is currently working hard on the Screaming Snowflakes Sequel, screenplay adaptation and nine novellas. She splits her time between cool Manchester and leafy Derbyshire and dreams of owning a Samoyed.